By day, **Maggie We**, she pens tales of sheets. She has a weakness for hot heroes and happy endings. She is the product of a charming rogue and a shameless flirt, and you only have to scratch the surface of this mild-mannered married lady to find a naughty streak a mile wide.

Beth Cornelison began working in public relations before pursuing her love of writing romance. She has won numerous honours for her work, including a nomination for the RWA *RITA*® Award for *The Christmas Stranger*. She enjoys featuring her cats (or friends' pets) in her stories and always has another book in the pipeline! She currently lives in Louisiana with her husband, one son and three spoiled cats. Contact her via her website, bethcornelison.com

OZARKS MISSING PERSON

MAGGIE WELLS

COLTON'S UNDERCOVER SEDUCTION

BETH CORNELISON

MILLS & BOON

First Published in Great Britain 2023
by Mills & Boon, an imprint of HarperCollins*Publishers* Ltd
1 London Bridge Street, London, SE1 9GF

www.harpercollins.co.uk

HarperCollins*Publishers*
Macken House, 39/40 Mayor Street Upper,
Dublin 1, D01 C9W8, Ireland

Ozarks Missing Person © 2023 Margaret Ethridge
Colton's Undercover Seduction © 2023 Harlequin Enterprises ULC

Special thanks and acknowledgement are given to Beth Cornelison for her contribution to *The Coltons of New York* series.

ISBN: 978-0-263-30722-1

0423

This book is produced from independently certified FSC™ paper to ensure responsible forest management.

For more information visit: www.harpercollins.co.uk/green

Printed and Bound in the UK using 100% Renewable Electricity at CPI Group (UK) Ltd, Croydon, CR0 4YY

OZARKS MISSING PERSON

MAGGIE WELLS

Thank you, Brinda, Kelli and Megan, as well as all my true crime addicts, for playing endless games of what-if with me. Sometimes truth really is stranger than fiction.

Prologue

Mallory Murray tipped her chin up and stared at the velvety black of the midnight sky. She would swear it was a shade darker on this tiny inlet of Table Rock Lake than anywhere else. The stars gleamed bright white against the backdrop. Thousands of them spread out like polka dots.

Beneath her feet, a powerful engine revved. The sleek boat knocked against the floating dock as Trey and another guy threw off the lines and hauled in the bumpers. Instinctively, she widened her stance to keep her balance. She was born on these lakes. Had been boating since she could walk. But her dad's ancient pontoon was nothing like the expensive ski boat she stood on now.

And she wasn't a carefree young girl excited to go swimming. She had a larger mission at hand. One she wasn't certain she could accomplish. The food she'd consumed since arriving at the Powerses' lake house threatened to come back up, but she closed her eyes and forced herself to breathe evenly. She had to focus.

Though she had grown up less than fifteen miles from the spot where Trey Powers's grandfather had built his eccentric but spectacular castle in the Ozark wilderness, it may as well have been a different galaxy. The locals and the wealthy families who established their weekend escapes on waterfront parcels didn't often mix. Their mutually beneficial relationship was cordial but nowhere near friendly. People like Mallory and sweet Mrs. Gibbons, the housekeeper Trey's family employed, were usually working in more of a service capacity. The lake people rarely mixed with locals socially.

Except for Mallory and Trey. She and Trey Powers had been *interacting* for nearly five years, off and on. Now, she was ready to flip the switch to on. Permanently.

"Everybody ready?" Trey called from his spot behind the wheel.

The night breeze blew her hair into her face as she turned, but Mallory didn't care. She aimed her brightest, widest smile on him, afraid if she tried to shout over the roar of the engine a quaver in her voice might give her away.

Trey grinned as a chorus of cheers rose from the four other passengers crammed onto the back of the boat. An answering roar came from the crowd on the pontoon in the next slip.

Mallory cast a wary glance at the revelers on the other boat. There were too many of them on board. There certainly weren't enough life jackets to go around. And nearly everyone had been drinking. Possibly for hours. But rules and regulations didn't apply to Trey Powers.

His family made them for others to follow.

With his hand wrapped around the throttle, Trey jerked his chin, signaling for her to come closer. She complied.

The kiss he planted on her was hard and sloppy. She could taste the lingering smokiness from the scotch he'd been drinking on his lips and did her best not to cringe. Trey was handsome. He was the heir to his family's law firm in Bentonville. Over the years, Mallory had often wondered which had come first, the Powers name or the actual power the people born under it had accumulated.

Her heart thrummed along with the engine as he eased the throttle up. The boat bumped the slip when he backed out, and she ducked away from the towing bar, where racks of wakeboards wavered perilously close.

She'd been relieved to see him today. Not because she'd missed him, but because almost eight weeks had passed since they were together, and she'd had no way to contact him. Trey liked to make a joke out of not giving her his phone number, telling her she'd see him when she saw him. And he always came around. But now... Now, she needed to see him and hadn't wanted to try to reach him through his family's firm.

Moving closer to where Trey stood at the wheel, she tried to shout over the blaring music coming from the boat's state-of-the-art sound system. "Maybe we shouldn't go out."

But Trey couldn't hear her. Or chose not to. He and his friends had already been partying when they stumbled into Stubby's, the roadside bar and grill on Highway 62 where she worked.

He'd told her they were on their way from Beaver Lake to the Powers place on Table Rock Lake for a crawfish boil. It was clear they'd been drinking most of the day, but Trey was his usual charming, friendly self. His face lit when he walked through the door and spotted her. The last she'd seen of him was the back of his mussed hair as he exited the storeroom behind the bar where they'd hooked up. Again.

But he must have been genuinely pleased to see her, because he left the pouty girl he'd walked in with to invite her to come along to his family's place on the lake for the party. He'd never invited her to go farther than the back room. Or the parking lot.

Mallory had untied her apron as fast at her eager fingers would allow. Steve, the guy who owned Stubby's, made his customary threats about firing her, but she'd ditched out on shifts before. She knew Steve's threats were empty ones. Good waitresses weren't easy to come by out in the Middle of Nowhere, Arkansas. When she showed up for her shift Saturday night, they'd both act like nothing had happened.

Trey revved the boat's powerful engine, jolting her into the present. She backed off a step. A midnight cruise with Trey Powers by her side was too tempting to pass up. They'd been playing this game of cat and mouse since she was eighteen, sleeping together every now and again for the better part of those years. But he'd been around less frequently this summer, and she could sense him slipping through her fingers. Yesterday it had looked like she was running out of options, but today it felt like fate was smiling on her.

She'd never been inside anywhere near as fancy the legendary lake house built by the first Tyrone Delray Powers. She'd done her best not to gawk when he led her into the place. On the outside, it looked like some kind of European castle, but on the inside it was all luxurious hunting lodge, complete with gleaming wood beams, real wood paneling and dozens of taxidermic trophies dotting the walls.

She could totally see herself throwing parties there once she and Trey made things official.

Trey gave the engines a bit more juice, and the boat began to move. Psyching herself up to play the wild-child role she knew he expected from her, she called out, "Let's do this!" with far more enthusiasm than she felt.

Trey threw his head back and laughed. Mallory smiled to herself, proud she'd pleased him. He'd once told her he liked her because she made him laugh. She was fairly sure the easy laughter they shared was what kept him coming back.

Trying to be unobtrusive, she grasped the safety bar as he swung the boat wide. One of the other women aboard fell forward against the back of Mallory's seat, giggling and crying out a slurry "Whoops!"

Even in the dim light, Mallory could see the petite girl's brown hair had been meticulously, and probably expensively, highlighted to a warm tawny gold. She dug her French-tipped nails into the pristine white leather upholstery as she attempted to regain her balance.

Of course, Trey chose that moment to take off at full speed.

The bow of the boat lifted, and the other girl tumbled back into one of Trey's friends. He stood out from the usual gaggle of young fellow hotshot lawyers who followed Trey around like ducklings. He was older. Stiffer. And Mallory would swear he looked vaguely familiar. Like she'd seen his face on the news or a billboard or something.

She tightened her grip on the safety bar. A startled laugh popped out of her as the front of the boat hit the water with a hard slap.

"Easy, cowboy," she called to Trey, but the wind ripped the words away.

Her hair streamed back from her face. Any minute now, Trey would turn against the night breeze and the loose strands would start whipping her mercilessly, but she didn't want to tie it back. She had to contain it every shift she worked at Stubby's. The wind sliding through it and lifting the weight of it from her shoulders felt glorious.

True to his reckless nature, Trey was driving too close to the shoreline for safety. As they zoomed past the shadowy figures of towering trees backlit by a sliver of moon, Mallory smirked. It was a good thing the Powers family and timber companies owned most of the adjoining acreage. There would be no neighbors to complain.

God, she loved this life. Deep down in her heart, she believed she was meant for it. She wanted it so badly she could taste it. And she was so close. All she had to do was convince Trey their future was written in the stars, and she'd have it all.

She wouldn't have to bust her hump working the way her

brother did, scraping together every bit of prestige he could. No, she would have everything she'd ever wanted tied up in one big package with a silky white bow.

Trey eased up on the speed long enough to shout something back to one of his pals. A chorus of voices protested, but Trey ignored them.

Trey rarely did anything except exactly what he wanted to do.

But Mallory had always been able to key into Trey's moods. Tonight he was restless and rowdy. The crowd he'd started with at Stubby's had tripled in size when the caterers had dumped the food onto butcher paper–covered trestle tables. After they feasted, the serious drinking began.

Shots were poured and tossed back with abandon. Dares and taunts flew back and forth across the massive fire pit built into the terraced patio. She knew when Trey said something about taking the boat out for a cruise, he would make it happen. She also knew when he was in one of these moods, the best thing anyone could do was go along.

Giving in, she yanked the elastic hair band from her wrist and bundled her hair up in a messy bun atop her head.

"You okay over there, beautiful?" Trey asked her.

Beautiful. He always called her beautiful. Like her looks were the sum total of who she was. And, to Trey, they probably were. Sometimes she wondered if he even remembered her name. But it didn't matter. Soon, he'd never forget it.

"Everything's perfect," she replied.

In that moment, she meant it.

Mallory gazed upward again and stared at the infinite blanket of stars above them. She fixated on one in particular. It burned so brightly she wondered if it was actually an airplane winging its way across the night sky. She stood engrossed, forgetting to take hold of the bar again or plant her feet to brace against the boat's sudden acceleration.

A sharp round of squawks and squeals erupted behind her. Trey swung the wheel wide to the left, playing chicken with the shoreline. Mallory righted herself enough to make a grab for the top of the windscreen, but her first attempt missed. She grabbed hold as the silhouettes of the looming trees moved closer at an alarming rate. Trey's laughter drifted to her on the wind.

"You're not scared, are you, beautiful?" he mocked.

She shook her head and released her hold, stubbornly refusing to give him the satisfaction. With her feet under her again and her knees flexed, she forced another smile and wagged her head. "Nope."

To prove her point, she shifted her gaze from the rapidly approaching shore to the sky yet again, looking upward, pretending she hadn't a care in the world. It was a beautiful sight. One of those clear summer nights when the heavens felt close enough to touch.

Another guy aboard gave a shout. Trey laughed and turned the wheel sharply. The boat pitched to starboard. Mallory continued to stare at the sky, pleased she wasn't the one to flinch, even if her stomach was heaving. Trey would be happy. If she made Trey happy, maybe he would make her happy in return. She hoped.

The boat slowed to a sedate cruise, and she exhaled long and shaky, grateful she hadn't lost her dinner over the side.

"You okay there?" he asked, his voice low and intimate.

She was still looking up, a smug smile curving her lips. She should have waited to tell him there, out on the water. It would have been much better than blurting it in the kitchen. She could have plastered a dopey, smitten smile on her face and let the wind carry the words *I'm pregnant* to him. Maybe he would have been more excited about it all.

Instead, he'd gone all lawyer on her. Asking all the questions she knew he would ask but hoped he wouldn't. It took all the restraint she could muster not to go off on him. She'd managed to nod and play it cool when he said they'd talk more about it in private.

She'd wait. See how he wanted to handle things. And if his answers weren't to her liking, maybe she'd see how his mama and daddy felt about having a grandbaby.

"I'm great," she answered, pressing her hand to her stomach as she leaned in to kiss his stubbled cheek. "Now get this sardine can moving."

"Yes, ma'am," he answered smartly and took up his position at the wheel once more.

There was a rev and a roar as the boat's turbocharged props kicked into gear. It was obnoxious, but she laughed out loud. The people behind them screeched, whooped and shouted. A cheer went up from the other boat as some of the guys lit Roman candles and fired them into the sky.

Trey slowed, allowing the others to turn and watch. A wakeboard someone hadn't secured to the rack slid across the decking as the boat rocked wildly in its own residual wake.

"Here, let me get this out from between us," Trey said, then he bent to scoop up the board. "Forgot to put it on the rack."

Out from between us. Soon there'd be nothing between them. Soon, he'd be all hers. She had to believe her dreams would come true.

Throwing her head back, she caught sight of a pink fireball in the sky. She traced its arc as she let the daydream take hold.

Trey Powers.

Mallory Powers.

Trey and Mallory Powers.

What would be a good nickname for sweet little Tyrone Delray Powers the Fourth? He had a cousin called Del. Maybe Chip?

She was tossing names around in her head when the deck shifted and Trey stepped closer. The change in momentum threw her. She heard the zip whistle of a bottle rocket zooming into the sky. The deck shifted again, and she reached up for the tow bar. A whisper of warm, whisky-scented breath tickled her cheek. She lowered her head to peer at Trey, but something hit her hard on the head. Distantly, she heard the *thunk* of it, but everything started to spin.

She was falling.

Fainting?

Someone shouted.

The chill of the water shocked her into stillness. Mallory caught one more glimpse of the twinkling stars.

Then everything went black.

Chapter One

Special Agent Grace Reed took a deep slug from the aluminum bottle she filled to the brim each morning. It made a loud clank as she placed it back on her desk, but she didn't tear her gaze from her computer. The screen was filled with the gap-toothed smile of five-year-old Treveon Robinson, a boy who disappeared while on a trip to the grocery store with his mom.

The case had kept her up all night. Missing children were automatically an instant cause of insomnia, but it wasn't only his disappearance bothering her. It was the knowledge there'd be no billboards or citywide awareness campaigns for Treveon.

Sure, there'd been a feature on the local news—a teary plea from his mama to send her baby home safely. They had issued an Amber alert, and phones all over Arkansas, Texas, Oklahoma and Missouri had buzzed. But the cold, hard truth of the matter was kids named Treveon didn't get the same attention from the media, and therefore the public, as kids named Cody or Tyler or Justin.

Could the worth of one boy be measured in a string of random letters used to form a name? A name Patricia Robinson said she'd chosen because her baby deserved a name as unique as he was.

The photograph had captured a mischievous gleam in the boy's dark eyes. He looked like an angel, but according to the stories his mother and grandmother had shared, he had a bit of the devil in him.

If she couldn't catch a break on his disappearance soon, she would have to turn his case over to McAvoy in the Crimes Against Children division. Staring into those eyes now, Grace swore to herself she would not forget Treveon.

Of course, she would continue the hunt for Treveon long after the news cycle dropped him into a bucket of sad statistics.

"Hey, Reed, I have another MP for you," the agent assigned to desk duty, Jim Thompson, called to her, waggling a phone receiver above his head.

And, of course, he was sending the missing person call to her. The guys always funneled them her way. Not because she was particularly good at solving the cases, but because they were too often addicts who'd gone on a bender, or spouses who'd decided to pack up and go. In short, the other agents couldn't be bothered.

There wasn't a lot of turnover in the Arkansas State Police Criminal Investigation Division. Particularly in Company D, based in her hometown of Fort Smith. Even after three years here, and five more in Little Rock, she was still one of the lower-ranking agents on the team.

Therefore, she drew the short straw when it came to catching cases and had unofficially become Miss Missing Persons to the rest of the guys. Not a job she'd ever aspired to hold. Like most ambitious detectives, Grace wanted to sink her teeth into some of the more high-profile cases.

But she was patient. The bigger cases would come. For now, she would keep searching for those most people forgot about the minute the news cycle moved on and the posters grew faded.

She glowered at the blinking red light indicating a call was holding for her and snatched up the receiver. "CID, Agent Reed speaking," she said briskly.

"Agent Reed? Brett Baines, Carroll County Sheriff's Department. I guess you're the go-to lady to talk to when it comes to girls who don't come home."

Grace recognized the deep male voice on the other end of the line. She and Baines had worked a previous case together. Closing her eyes, she sent up a silent prayer this case might end better than the last one had. "Deputy Baines,. How can I help you?"

"I got a call a while ago from a young lady named Kelli Simon. She tells me her roommate hasn't been home in days." He paused, letting the information sink in. "I get the impression from talking to her this isn't unusual behavior on the part of the roommate, but the electric bill is due, and the missing girl hasn't paid her part... Probably went up to Branson and blew it all on a purse or something."

He chuckled and Grace bristled. Bitingher lip to keep from biting his head off for that coming she plucked a pen from a coffee cup with the state police logo on it and pulled the notebook she kept on her desk closer. She scribbled, *electric bill due*, asking, "What was the name again?"

"Reported by Kelli Simon—"

"Kelly with a *Y*?" she asked.

"An *I*. Apparently, Kelli with an *I* called her roommate's place of employment to track her down and found out she hasn't been in to work, either."

"The missing woman's name?" Grace prompted.

"Murray. She's called Mallory Murray," Deputy Baines said, enunciating each syllable of the missing woman's name. "She's twenty-three years old, single, Caucasian, dark brown hair and blue eyes. Last seen at work on Friday evening."

Today was Tuesday. More than three days had passed, Grace noted as she added the details to her notes.

"And they're roommates?" she asked. "House? Apartment?"

"They rent a place here in Eureka. Apartment, I think," he said, seemingly looking back through his own notes.

Grace scribbled *Eureka Springs* at the top of the page. "Did she have any guesses as to a height or weight?"

"Miss Simon said maybe about five-six or-seven. She said she was a few inches taller than her and she's five-four. As for a weight, she only said skinny." He chuckled. "Not much help, I know. I have a daughter who's about that age, and *skinny* is a relative term to some young ladies."

Deputy Baines said the last with a hefty dose of good-old-boy bonhomie, but Grace was in no mood to play along. She could already envision the media coverage a pretty young white woman would garner, and while she knew every bit helped, she couldn't ignore the twinge of resentment she felt when her gaze strayed to Treveon's photo.

Dragging herself back, she forced herself to sit up straighter. Every citizen deserved her undivided attention. "Approximately five foot six or more and slim," she repeated, emphasizing the word *slim*.

"Yes, ma'am."

"I assume you're going to email me whatever information you have?" she asked.

"Yes, ma'am," the deputy repeated. He didn't sound sad to be handing this one off to the state police. "Ms. Simon said she was sending over some photos. I'll wait for those to come through and send it all to you at once."

Grace scowled at the notepad. How she wished she could clear these cases from her mind as easily as these guys moved them off their desks.

"I assume since you're passing this to me you gave the

roommate…uh, Ms. Simon, my contact info?" Grace asked. She drew a line from her period up to the top of the page, making an arrow out of it, and began to print the name *Kelli*.

"I told her you'd reach out to her," the deputy informed her. "I wasn't sure how snowed under you were, and I thought that might be better."

Grace tapped the end of her pen against the notebook. "Sure. Fine."

"Her cell number is…" He rattled it off. "Probably should try texting her. If she's anything like my kids, she won't answer a phone call from an unknown number."

Grace rolled her eyes at the man's derision but acknowledged him. "I will."

"I'll have her email address and other pertinent information in the report, and if I hear anything more from her before you can make contact, I'll refer her directly to you." He paused for a moment. "If it's okay with you, of course."

In no mood for his feigned deference, Grace sat up straighter and removed the receiver from where she held it pinched between her shoulder and ear. "Absolutely okay with me. Might as well eliminate the middleman, right?" She tossed her pen down. "Good speaking to you, Deputy. I'll be looking for your report."

Grace placed the receiver in its cradle and blew out a long breath. Leaning back in her chair, she tipped her chin to the ceiling and focused on the breathing exercises her bohemian sister, Faith, had insisted she learn.

Inhale, exhale. Inhale, hold, exhale.

She forced herself to repeat the exercise over and over. Whether it helped or not, she couldn't say, but it sure didn't hurt when it came to dealing with men like Baines. You'd think after spending her entire career letting their ingrained misogyny roll off her back, she'd be impervious to microaggressions.

But she wasn't.

While she waited for the deputy to pass along the information, Grace clicked through the pages of the file she'd accumulated on young Treveon. Her stomach roiled, and without thinking she opened the center drawer of her desk and pulled out a roll of antacids. She popped two tablets into her mouth and chomped down hard. There were days when she wondered why she'd chosen this path, and this was one of them.

But in all honesty, most days she couldn't imagine herself doing anything else. From the age of twelve, all she'd wanted was to be a detective. She knew in her soul her destiny was to be an instrument of justice. After all, someone had to make sense of her mother's senseless death. And the job was clearly up to her.

Sitting straighter in her chair, she reminded herself she couldn't win them all. But maybe, just maybe, she'd win one or two here and there and in her own way help make somebody else's life more bearable. Glancing at the open notebook, she spotted the phone number Baines had given her.

She sent a text first. Not because he'd suggested it, but because she wasn't a monster.

This is Sp Agt Grace Reed of the AR St Pol Crim Investigations Div. I heard UR looking for UR roommate May I call you?

Three dots appeared. At work but take my break in 5. Can I call U

Grace tapped out a quick Okay and set her phone aside. Sure enough, five minutes later, it rang.

"CID, Special Agent Reed speaking," she said, trying to inject a modicum of warmth into her voice.

"Um, hi," a tentative female voice replied.

Grace picked up her pen and poised it over her notebook.

She looked down at the notes she'd scrawled earlier and registered the missing girl's age. The caller came across as painfully young. She also sounded...genuinely worried.

"Yes? Hello, is this Kelli?"

"Yeah. Hi. I'm sorry to bother you," the caller began hesitantly. "She's probably flaking out on me—"

"It's no bother," Grace assured her, gently cutting her off. "Tell me what you know."

"Uh, well, my roommate hasn't come home in a few days, and when I called Stubby's, the place she works, they told me they haven't seen her since Friday night."

Grace frowned and jotted down the name of the missing person's employer, then circled *Friday* on the notes she'd taken from Baines as the day last seen. "And her name is Mallory?"

"Yes. Mallory Murray." The young woman hesitated for a moment. "To be honest, this isn't the first time she's taken off for a couple days, but usually she messages me something, you know?"

"And she hasn't been in touch?" Grace prompted, shifting to the edge of her seat.

"No. Nothing," the roommate said. "I tried texting her, because..." She trailed off. "Well, because she owes her half of the electric, and I have to pay the bill tomorrow," she finished in a rush. "She's tried to dodge bills in the past, but I'm not even getting read receipts."

"I understand," Grace said. And she did. "You've heard nothing from her since...?"

There was a pause on the other end. "I don't think I've actually spoken to her since Wednesday," she said. "We aren't really friends," she added easily. "I had a room to rent, and she answered the ad. She's only lived with me for three months."

And three months had been long enough for Kelli Simon

to determine her roommate was less than reliable. "And you say it's not unusual for her to take off for a few days?"

"Yeah, but I mean, I can usually track her down at work eventually. Besides, she wouldn't miss a Saturday shift at Stubby's. She says she gets her biggest tips on Saturdays."

"And Stubby's is...?"

She let the question hang out there, and Ms. Simon jumped on it. "Oh, it's a place out on Highway 62. Burgers, beers. Lots of lake people come in on weekends," she explained. "She's a waitress there. Occasionally bartender, depending on who's working."

"And she likes her job?"

There was a beat of silence. "I, uh, I have no idea," she admitted at last. "I guess. She brags about the cute guys who come in, and the tips and stuff."

"Do you know if she was seeing someone in particular?"

"No, not really. I mean, I'd hear her on the phone and stuff, and I know she went out a lot."

"Any names?"

"Maybe a Chad or something?" She paused. "And a Steve, but I think he was someone she worked with because she complained about him. I remember coming home early one day last week because my schedule opened up and she was on the phone with Steve asking if someone called Troy, or Trey, had come in."

"Troy or Trey," Grace murmured as she added the names to her notes. Curious, she asked, "And what do you do, Ms. Simon?"

"Me? I'm a nail tech. I work at a day spa here in town. The Lotus Flower?"

She spoke the name in an offhand sort of way indicating Grace should have heard of it. She hadn't. Each Criminal Investigation Division covered far more area than most people realized. Fort Smith was two hours away from the resort town of Eureka Springs. And even if she lived closer, Grace wasn't exactly the type to frequent spas, much to her sister's chagrin.

Grace read over her notes. "Has her family heard from her? Do you know?"

"As far as I know, she has a brother. She said her mom and dad died in a car wreck. I don't think she and her brother get along, though."

"No?"

"She says he's a jerk. Stuck-up. He's a hotshot attorney over in Bentonville."

"Do you know his name?"

Another silence followed. Finally, she said, "If she told me, I don't remember it. Maybe it started with an *M*, too? I remember thinking it was too much alliteration when she told me. Anyway, I don't think they were in touch often."

Grace got the distinct impression this well of information was tapped out, but still, she needed to follow up. Shouldn't be hard to find her brother if he actually was a lawyer.

Then again, maybe they'd all get lucky and Ms. Murray would find her way home on her own. "I see. Would tomorrow be a good day for us to talk in person?"

"In person?" the young woman questioned, like it hadn't occurred to her more than one conversation might be necessary.

"I'm based out of Fort Smith, but I could be in Eureka Springs by midmorning," Grace offered, not letting her off the hook.

"I have to work tomorrow," Kelli protested.

"Perhaps we can talk on your lunch hour." Grace wrote *Lotus Flower spa* on her pad and pushed on. "I'll text you in the morning and you can tell me when you'll be free. Please let me know if you hear from Ms. Murray."

After ending the call, she emailed her section chief to in-form him she'd be out of the office the next day. Then she sent up a silent prayer for the missing young woman and closed her notebook. The photo of sweet Treveon Robinson beamed out at her from her monitor.

Leaning in, she stared intently at the screen. "Hang in there. I'll find you, little guy. I promise."

With a heavy sigh, she minimized the photo and opened her web browser. How many attorneys named Murray could there be in the Bentonville area? Seconds later, a networking website called WhosIn gave her the answer.

There were two. The first listing she found was for a personal injury attorney named Allen Murray, but when she clicked the link to his firm's website, she found a photo of a balding man in his sixties.

The other lawyer was named Matthew. Clicking on a link for more info, she mentally chalked one up to Ms. Kelli Simon and her linguistic pet peeves. It appeared Matthew Murray was an assistant prosecuting attorney for Benton County.

There was no photo, but Grace knew in her gut this had to be the brother. And now that she'd located him, she picked up her phone and prepared herself to be the bearer of bad news.

Chapter Two

Matthew Murray was not having a good day. First, the barista at the coffee shop he'd been visiting every day for the past two years screwed up his order. Again. While he didn't mind starting his day with a hearty double shot of espresso, or even an Americano heavy with cream and sugar, he absolutely did not want the sickeningly sweet barely coffee-flavored drink he'd ended up with. If asked under oath, he'd swear at least a third of the cup was filled with foam.

The morning didn't get any better. He had an appearance with Judge Walton in the earliest time slot, and if there was ever someone who was less of a morning person than Matthew, it was Judge Anthony Walton. The judge wasn't one of Matthew's biggest fans.

On his first day working for the Benton County prosecuting attorney's office, Matthew had backed out of a tight parking space and bumped the car behind him. Not enough of an impact to cause any damage, but enough to make him wince as he pulled away.

Unfortunately, the car behind his belonged to the judge. And Judge Walton happened to be standing on the sidewalk watching the whole thing. A summons to His Honor's chambers was dispatched within the hour.

But whether Judge Walton liked him or not was immaterial. The case he'd been handed three weeks ago was a mess. The sheriff's deputies who'd pulled Harley Jenkins over had not followed protocol when they searched his pickup truck. Therefore, the seizure of the cranky old hippie's pot stash, while impressive, was not quite legal. Still, Jenkins had enough of a rap sheet for the PA to insist on prosecuting the case.

Or rather, on Matthew prosecuting the case.

Harley Jenkins called himself an activist, but in actuality he was simply an agitator, a man whose own belief system seemed to change with the prevailing winds. The only thing Jenkins truly shared with the other men living their hardscrabble lives in the hills north of Beaver Lake was disdain for the law. Local, state, federal—it didn't matter. They believed themselves to be above any form of regulation.

For the most part, they wanted to be left alone. Matthew wished the overzealous young sheriff's deputy who'd pulled old Harley over had obliged. The judge threw out the evidence collected during the botched search, dismissed the case, then proceeded to give Matthew a good old-fashioned dressing-down he expected to be passed along to his boss, Prosecuting Attorney Nathaniel Able.

Matthew poked his head around Nate's office door and found the PA sitting with his head bent over his laptop, fingers flying as he stared at the screen, engrossed by whatever he was composing.

"I have a message for you from the jurist voted least likely to enjoy having his time wasted," Matthew announced.

Nate jumped and jerked his hands from the keys. "Oh?" He sat back in his chair, dropping a mask of indifference over his initial surprise.

"Judge Walton dismissed the case against Harley Jenkins and said I was to tell you if we don't know any better than to push something like this onto his docket, he will personally lead the campaign opposing your reelection."

Nate's mouth twitched into a bemused half smile. "Excellent. If he raises a whole lot of money for my opponent, I won't have to do a bunch of rubber-chicken dinners to try to land this crap job again."

Matthew forced a slice of a smile and turned away. The two of them came from completely different worlds, and though he had political ambitions of his own, he wasn't sure he had it in him to go about it as determinedly as Nate.

His boss had once been northwest Arkansas's most highly recruited quarterback. He'd made the roster of a perennial favorite for the NCAA championship but never moved beyond the second string. In his junior year, he'd been savvy enough to start hunkering down and hitting the books. From there, he went straight from undergrad to law school, all funded by his proud parents and backed by hometown pride.

Matthew stopped by the coffee station to brew himself a cup of real coffee. His own upbringing had been about as jinxed as Nate's was charmed.

One of the ever-changing roster of law students who cycled through the office on internships hurried up to him as the machine gurgled to life. "Mr. Murray?" she asked, approaching him cautiously.

Matthew forced his smile into something more congenial. Tara? Tiffany? Trina? Her name started with a *T.* "Yeah? Hi, um…" He snapped his fingers twice, then gave up with a cringing smile. He hated being the guy who didn't learn people's names but believed it was worse to be the one who pretended he remembered. "I'm sorry, I forgot your name."

"Tia," she supplied.

"Yes! Tia!" He tapped his temple twice like he might hammer her name into a slot, but he knew she'd likely be gone from the office before it embedded. "Sorry. Hi, Tia."

He paused long enough to grab his now-full mug from under the spout. "And I'm Matthew. *Mr. Murray* makes me sound old." The second the words were out, he cringed on the inside. Now he sounded like a creeper. "I mean, I probably seem old to you, but I'm only twenty-nine."

"Oh, yeah. Um, right," she said quickly. "Twenty-nine is not old at all."

But her rushed delivery made her words sound insincere. To Tia, twenty-nine was ancient, he was sure. "Did you need me for something?" he asked, anxious to steer the conversation onto a more professional track.

"Oh! Yeah. You had a message from an investigator with the state police," she said, thrusting a sticky note at him. "She said she left you a voice mail but wanted to be sure you got back to her today, if possible."

Matthew frowned at the slip of paper. *Special Agent Grace Reed—ASP* was written in looping handwriting. Beneath it a phone number printed in deliberately neat blocks. He thought of his own message-taking skills and wondered if Tia had recopied the name and number from a more hastily scrawled version. Either way, he appreciated the effort.

"Thank you, Tia." He saluted her with his mug. "I'll give Special Agent, uh, Reed a call as soon as I can."

"You're welcome," the young intern called after him.

Once he reached his office, he set the mug on a stoneware razorback coaster and stuck the note to the center of his computer monitor. He docked his laptop, booted everything up and surveyed at the array of printed affidavits and files piled atop his desk. *Paperless office*, he thought and scoffed. The law would never be paperless.

To his left, the green light indicating he had a voice mail on his desk phone was flashing. He hit the speaker button and ran through the prompts to access his messages.

"Hello, Mr. Murray, this is Grace Reed with the Arkansas State Police Criminal Investigation Division out of Fort Smith. I'm wondering if you can tell me if you might be related to a young woman named Mallory Murray? If you are, would you please give me a call as soon as you receive this message? I would appreciate it. My number is…"

Mallory.

The state police were calling him about Mallory. They wanted to know if he knew Mallory. His troublesome baby sister was the subject of a phone call from the Criminal Investigation Division. Matthew sagged, allowing his shoulders to slump with the weight of his failure as he leaned forward and propped his forehead in the palm of his hand.

What had she done now? How much trouble was she in? And how much of it would blow back on him?

He knew the last question didn't exactly make him a candidate for brother of the year, but his relationship with his sister had long been rocky at best and downright combative in the low spots. When they'd last spoken, Mallory had told him to butt out of her life, and he'd been more than happy to do as she asked.

From the day she was born, they were oil and water. He'd been five—almost six—and couldn't understand why his parents were bringing this new baby into their perfect world. He knew his mother hadn't wanted another baby. He'd heard his parents talking about it, but like everyone else figured she'd come around to the idea. But from the moment they brought Mallory home, there was a new tension in the household.

Their upbringing had been what he'd call barely middle-class. His dad had a decent management job with a company that made truck parts, and his mom was an elementary school librarian. There'd never been a lot of money, but they'd scrimped and saved enough to send him to the University of Arkansas, with the help of a couple scholarships and a student loan. He figured the age gap between him and Mallory kept them from ever feeling truly close. Sadly, the gap grew into a gorge after their parents were killed in a car crash.

It happened two weeks prior to his undergrad graduation. Mallory had only been in eleventh grade. He'd already been accepted to law school but had deferred a year to help get his sister through her senior year. Not that she'd ever thanked him for putting his life on hold for her. Quite the opposite, in fact.

Mallory resented his role as guardian. She believed she was grown enough to be out on her own. On the day of her high school graduation, he'd handed over the keys to the house they'd grown up in, assuring her he had enough to cover the mortgage for at least a year. Feeling his job was done, he headed for Little Rock and law school with only the things he could fit in his car. She'd managed to hang onto the house for about a year before they were forced to sell.

Their attempts at togetherness usually took place around the holidays, when one or both of them was feeling lonely or nostalgic for the kind of Christmases they'd never had but saw on TV. More often than not, they ended with Mallory either begging him for money or blaming him for her bad choices. Or both. Inevitably, they also ended with one of them taking off, harsh words still hanging between them.

She'd always been reckless when it came to choosing the company she kept. He'd been able to help her out of a couple minor scrapes with the law, but they'd been nothing warranting more than a fine and an appearance in front of a judge.

But the state police criminal investigations people…they handled major crime. The kind of crime most rural sheriffs' departments were ill-equipped to tackle. If they were calling, Mallory had pushed her luck too far.

Picking up his phone, he carefully punched out the digits

on the sticky note. It rang twice before a no-nonsense female voice answered. "CID, Grace Reed speaking."

Matthew got the sense he was interrupting her. He could almost feel her annoyance emanating across the line. "Special Agent Reed, this is Matthew Murray. You left a message for me to call?"

"Oh." He heard a quiet exhalation. "Yes, sorry," she said, softening her tone. "Matthew Murray," she repeated, obviously switching gears. "Are you related to a young woman named Mallory Murray, by chance?"

"Yes, Mallory is my sister," he replied, keeping his pitch as even as possible. "Is there something I can help you with?"

"Well, uh, I hate giving this sort of news over the phone, but—"

Matthew tensed. When his parents had been killed, a police officer had been dispatched to the off-campus apartment he shared with two other guys. He was glad whatever bad news Special Agent Reed had to deliver could be transmitted via telephone.

"Go ahead," he prompted, snapping his mouth shut when he caught the creak in his voice.

"This morning I received a call from a young woman named Kelli Simon. She says she shares an apartment with your sister in Eureka Springs," she began. "She called the Carroll County Sheriff's Department this morning because your sister has not been seen since Friday."

Matthew was glad Special Agent Reed couldn't see him slump in relief at the news his sister was simply missing and not dead. He knew as well as anyone missing persons were often at risk, but it wasn't at all unusual for Mallory to disappear when it suited her. Exhaling long and slow, he forced himself to focus.

"Did she take anything with her? Did the roommate notice if she packed clothes or anything?"

"No," Agent Reed replied. "As far as Ms. Simon could tell, your sister left the apartment on Friday intending to go to work at a place called Stubby's on Highway 62, but she never came home. Her calls are going to voice mail, and she hasn't replied to any text messages."

Matthew sat back in his chair and pinched the bridge of his nose. At last, he raked his fingers through his hair. "Has she posted anything? Mallory loves to post pictures on social media." *Mainly pictures of herself,* he added silently. "Pictur-Spam is her favorite, I think, but there's always a new one."

Sitting up straight, he clicked on his web browser and typed in the address for the social media platform. He wasn't active on it himself, but he had an account, and he and his sister had followed one another there before the latest fall-out. Unless she'd blocked him, he should be able to see if she had made any recent posts.

"I've been able to access her public profile, but she may have some friends-only content I can't see," Special Agent Reed reported.

Matthew bit back the urge to tell her it was unlikely. Anything Mallory did, she wanted the whole world to see.

"The last post I could see was of the night sky, and it looked like the moon reflecting off the lake," the investigator continued. "It was posted Friday evening and geotagged near Table Rock Lake. Do you know if your sister has any friends in the area?"

Matthew found himself staring at the same image Grace Reed had described, but he was embarrassingly clueless as to whom Mallory kept company with. "No. I mean, I don't know," he said quickly. "We haven't been particularly close in recent years."

There was a pause on the other end of the line, and for a moment Matthew wondered if Grace Reed with all her superior detective skills had already deduced as much.

"Mr. Murray, unless your sister resurfaces in the next twelve hours, I'm planning to head to Eureka Springs tomorrow morning to meet with Ms. Simon and see their apartment. Perhaps there might be a clue left behind. Would you like to accompany me?"

Matthew swallowed hard. Would he like to? No. Should he? Probably. He hesitated, loath to admit to this stranger he was probably the last person who would be able to give any real insight into his sister's life, but it was true. They might have been siblings, but they weren't friends. Certainly not confidants.

Their lives had taken completely divergent paths, and Matthew could admit, if only to himself, he hadn't minded Mallory's absence. His sister was drama. His sister incited chaos.

His sister was missing.

Part of him wanted to bristle at the thought of chasing after her. There was nothing Mallory loved more than tension, and this was the sort of thing to rev her up. But what if… What if something had gone wrong? What if someone had abducted her, or worse?

Matthew shook his head, refusing to let himself go too far down the dark path yet. It was better for him to believe Mallory was off on one of her lost weekends. She had likely flaked out on the roommate and her job. His baby sister was an attention-seeking young woman with aspirations beyond her current circumstances. She'd always leap at a chance to graze greener pastures.

"Yes," he said after the pause had lasted a few seconds too long. "Uh, I would like to go with you, but I'm not sure I can get someone to cover my workload tomorrow morning." He hedged, tapping his pen against the pile of case notes and files.

He had another case in front of Judge Walton at nine, and the winding drive over the hills from Bentonville to the resort town of Eureka Springs would take an hour or more. Plus, he wasn't sure he was the right person to be meeting Mallory's roommate or pawing through her things. Heaven only knew what kind of fabrications she'd woven about their relationship.

"It's fine." Agent Reed dropped her voice into a confidential pitch. "Truthfully, I'm not sure the roommate wants to meet with me, and if we both show up, it might make her even less forthcoming." He heard the click of a computer mouse. "How about I come to Bentonville after I'm done speaking to Ms. Simon? I'd like to stop by this Stubby's place on my way. Perhaps by then I'll have more to tell you."

"Sounds good," Matthew replied, relieved to be exempted from the information gathering. "Are you thinking mid-to late afternoon?" he hazarded.

"Yes, most likely," she answered.

"Great. Come to the prosecuting attorney's offices when you get to town. I'll be here until at least seven or later."

"Perfect. See you tomorrow."

She ended the call without another word, and Matthew fell back in his seat. He stared at the ceiling, the phone still clutched in his hand. Mallory was missing. And he must be missing something, too, because the only emotion he could identify was irritation.

He truly must be an awful brother, he thought, shaking his head at himself.

Chapter Three

The Lotus Flower spa looked like the type of place Grace promised her sister they'd visit but never booked. She scanned the salon as she stood in the dimly lit reception area. She couldn't imagine checking in and telling the perky young woman wearing a headset she was there for some kind of Andean mud treatment or whatever new age services they offered. While she wasn't opposed to a massage after a hard workout, she couldn't picture herself booking an appointment at a place like this. It was too...perfect.

When she arrived, she'd simply flashed her credentials and asked to speak to Kelli Simon. The receptionist had been mildly freaked out the minute she'd introduced herself. She tried to reassure the young woman Kelli was not in any sort of trouble, but the panic on her face told Grace it didn't matter. Within minutes the entire staff would know someone from the state police had come to question one of their nail technicians.

"Agent Reed?" a petite red-haired woman said as she stepped through a door concealed in the wall.

Grace stifled the urge to jump and forced her mouth into a smile. "I didn't even see that door."

"I'm Kelli Simon," the young woman said, offering her hand. "Would you mind if we spoke outside?"

Grace gestured to the door. "Not at all. Lead the way."

Ms. Simon walked quickly past her and outside. Grace trailed. Kelli then hooked a right and headed for a coffee shop two doors down. Nodding to the entrance, she spared Grace a sheepish glance. "Do you mind if I run in and get a cappuccino? I'd be happy to order something for you."

"No, thank you." Grace gestured to one of the umbrella-shaded tables. "Why don't you grab your drink and I'll wait for you out here."

"Perfect," Kelli replied, ducking into the shop. "Be right back."

Grace wouldn't have minded a cold bottle of water, but she wanted to keep the meeting on more of a business footing than a social call. Grace was all too aware this meeting could be the start of an intense investigation. It was important to put Ms. Simon at ease, but she had to keep moving forward quickly.

She settled onto the hard metal chair and pulled a notebook and pen from her tote bag. She carried an electronic tablet with her, but found good old-fashioned note-taking seemed to make people more comfortable. People tended to stiffen up when they saw you typing information into a document in a way they didn't when they saw you make a quick note with a pen. She would transcribe the pertinent information into the electronic case file she'd share with her division and the county sheriff's office later.

Kelli Simon returned a few minutes later with an enormous paper cup in hand. She settled into the seat across from Grace and clasped the coffee between her fingers like she needed it to warm them despite temperatures already inching into the nineties.

Grace made note of the young woman's defensive posture and smiled as warmly as she could. "Thank you for seeing me today."

"You're welcome. I took my lunch early," she explained, glancing over her shoulder at the spa.

"There's nothing to be nervous about," Grace assured her, slanting a glance at the other woman's grip on the cup. "I'm only going to ask a few questions."

"Sorry." The apology seemed to be her usual opening gambit to any conversation, but she released her stranglehold on the cup. "They keep it freezing in the spa, and my hands are always wet. It can be hard to get them warm."

"Ah, I see." Grace nodded and offered another encouraging smile. "I totally understand. I'm often one of the only women in whatever office I'm working in, and the men tend to set the thermostat to meat-locker level. I keep a heater under my desk, and I've been known to run it all summer long."

Her confession seemed to help the younger woman relax. Lifting the cup, she took a quick sip, then placed it back on the filigreed metal table with exaggerated care.

"I still haven't heard anything from her," she said quietly.

"I'm sorry to hear that," Grace responded. She clicked open her pen and made a note on the pad. *Mallory Murray still missing as of Tuesday 11:24 a.m.* "No contact from anyone looking for her or asking about her?"

The other woman shook her head. "We didn't have friends in common. I'm not sure anyone she knows would have my number." She shrugged. "I did go through some of her things," she offered hesitantly. "In her room."

Intrigued, Grace leaned in. "Oh?"

She let the single syllable hang out there between them, knowing the other woman would feel compelled to fill the silence.

"Yeah. I didn't find a whole lot, but I can tell you her

brother's name is definitely Matthew. I found some paperwork that had both of their names on it."

Grace nodded but didn't offer up the fact she had already tracked down Matthew Murray. "What kind of paperwork?"

Kelli shrugged. "Legal-looking stuff? I think it had something to do with the sale of a house. Maybe their parents' house?" She opened her hands in a gesture to show she was guessing. "I don't know. I'm no expert."

"How long have you and Mallory been roommates?"

"About three months?" Again, she phrased her statement like a question. Grace wouldn't be able to refute any fact she put out there; she simply nodded and made note of it.

"And you guys met through…"

"A roommate service," Kelli answered, looking slightly abashed. "You know, online?"

Her pitch climbed again, and Grace wondered if the girl ever spoke in anything but interrogatories. "What kind of information did you exchange prior to deciding to sublet to her?"

"You know, the usual. Where she had a job, where she lived, if she had any problems with other roommates, if she smoked." She threw the last one out there as if this line of inquiry should be obvious to anyone.

"None of her answers raised any red flags? You said she'd been dodgy on paying some of the bills?"

Kelli nodded but shifted it into another shake of her head. "Not at first, but yeah. It was always something like she was in between paychecks or her tips weren't as good on a Saturday as she thought they would be. Usually, she would only need me to float her for a day or two," she explained. "But she always paid…eventually," she was quick to add.

Grace got the distinct impression Kelli Simon thought if she said anything too negative about her relationship with Mallory Murray, or showed any discord between them, it might make her a suspect. Hoping to build rapport, she set her pen down and nodded as she leaned in.

"I had a roommate like her in college," Grace informed her. "It's never their fault, but they can never get it together. That type of thing?" She let her voice rise on the last part, imitating Kelli's speech pattern in the hopes of ingratiating herself to the young woman.

"Exactly," Kelli responded immediately, sitting up straighter.

Grace smiled, pleased her ploy had worked. "I think we've all been there." She scribbled the words *late paying bills* on her notepad. "You said she might be seeing someone. When you looked through her stuff, did you find anything more about this guy she was seeing?"

Kelli bit her bottom lip, clearly wrestling with a decision. Sensing the other woman's desire to spill, Grace pressed gently.

"Anything at all."

"I cleaned the apartment the other night," the younger woman began. "I usually do on Sundays. I like to start the week fresh, you know?"

Grace thought of her own somewhat haphazard house-keeping. "Yeah, totally." When Kelli hesitated again, she pushed harder but focused her gaze on her notepad. She didn't want to scare the girl off. "Did you find something? Maybe something related to this mystery guy?"

"Well…" She drew on her poor abused lip again, then blurted, "I found a pregnancy test."

Grace's head popped up. "A pregnancy test? A used one?" This case might've been a whole lot more involved than what she had initially believed.

Kelli nodded but did not speak.

"And did it have a result?"

"Positive," the other woman whispered.

"Was it only the one test?" Grace asked, her gaze locked on the younger woman. "I believe some people take multiples to be sure."

"The box in the trash said there were two tests, but I only saw one of the stick things in it," Kelli asserted.

Grace let the information sink in. If the second test had come back positive as well, it was entirely possible Mallory had held on to it to show the father of her baby. And if the father of her baby was not the kind of man to be excited about such news, things may not have gone the way Mallory had planned.

"But you didn't find anything in her room? Nothing identifying the guy she was seeing by name? No cards or notes or anything?"

Kelli shook her head. "Nothing."

Grace made a note in her book. *Pregnant?* She underlined the word twice, drew arrows stemming from it. At the end of one she wrote the word *yes*, and at the end of the other she wrote the word *no*.

"Did she talk to you about this guy? Has she posted anything about him on social media? Given any indication as to whether he might be serious about her?" she hedged.

"No." Kelli wagged her head hard. "Like I said, we weren't friends at all. I sent her a request on PicturSpam not long after she moved in, but she never confirmed the follow. I got embarrassed and deleted the request."

Grace nodded. Social media was a minefield on multiple levels, but often in her line of work it turned out to be a gold mine.

"Okay. Well, I was able to locate her brother yesterday and reached out to him. He hasn't heard from her, either, but like you said, he told me they weren't close. I'm heading over to Bentonville when I leave here to talk to him, but

I'm wondering if you would mind if I took a quick peek at your apartment."

Kelli looked taken aback by the suggestion. "My apartment?"

Grace raised one eyebrow. "Yes." She closed her notebook. "I realize you're on your lunch hour, but I would appreciate it if I could at least see her room. Maybe you could show me the papers and box you found? I assume you kept them."

Kelli nodded. "Yes, I did. I didn't know… I wasn't sure if I should tell you. Heck, for all I know, it might not have even been Mallory's. She could have had a friend over or something."

Grace forced herself to smile and nod. Not a reasonable scenario, but she didn't want to slow her down. "Right, we don't know for certain."

Kelli inclined her head. "Okay, but I'll have to make it quick." She checked her phone. "I have an appointment booked in at one, and I need to get back to set up."

The metal feet of her chair scraped the sidewalk as Grace rose. "Do you live far from here? I can drive if you'd like," she offered.

Her search on the address Kelli had given showed they lived close to the spa. Still, she didn't want Kelli to feel like she was the one under investigation.

Kelli shook her head. "No need. It's only a few blocks. We could probably walk there faster."

Grace allowed Kelli to lead the way. "Must be nice to live this close to your work," she said as they turned onto a side street. Hoping to find a common thread with the now-skittish young woman, she offered some information of her own. "I have about a ten-minute drive every day, but some mornings it feels like thirty."

"We don't open until after ten, so most people are already at work," Kelli said. "But yeah, I like being able to walk to work. I used to go home for lunch just to get out for a while," she said with a shrug. She cast a shy glance at Grace. "Lately, I've been taking my lunch to work more often. It's kind of awkward to come home while she's there."

"Mallory didn't work during the day?"

"Her schedule changed a lot," Kelli replied. "Mostly evenings, but on weekends she'd pull a double because she liked the tips."

Grace matched her stride to Kelli's hurried pace. "And when you said it was awkward…?"

Again, the girl let one shoulder rise and fall. "She was there," she said, feigning nonchalance. "I, uh, I like to eat my lunch alone. I have to make conversation with clients all day long, and lunch is about the only hour I get to, you know, just be."

"I see."

Grace hummed. She did understand the younger woman's need to have space to breathe during the workday. She often felt the same herself. It wasn't easy being the only woman on her shift. There were days the conversations in the break room made her uncomfortable. Not because the guys said anything overt. They were all too well trained to go too far, but because she knew she didn't quite fit in. Even if she could talk baseball, football or basketball with most any man, she was always the token female in the conversation.

"Well, I appreciate you meeting with me today. And for caring enough to make the call to the police to start. It's not easy trying to piece together what you know about a person you barely know. I spend my days doing it, and it can be frustrating."

Kelli pointed to a brick duplex on the right. "This is me. Us, I mean," she corrected quickly. "And, yeah, it's kind of weird. I guess I thought maybe we'd become friends?"

Again she finished on a high note. Grace got the feeling she was asking if her expectations had been unrealistic.

"I get you."

"Anyway, early on, Mallory made it pretty clear she had her own thing going on and didn't want to get too friendly."

"What do you mean by her own thing?" Grace asked as the other woman unlocked the door to the duplex.

Kelli led the way into an apartment Grace would have said was decorated in early-twenty-something chic. The furniture was mainly comprised of castoffs or hand-me-downs, but dressed up with colorful paint or, in the case of the sofa, an artfully tucked slipcover.

"She preferred to hang out with the people she knew from work, I guess," Kelli said, sounding dejected. "Most of the people I work with are married or engaged. I'm not seeing anyone right now, and I thought she wasn't, so I figured we could hang out or go out together, but Mallory wasn't interested."

Grace bobbed her head in understanding. "Too bad. You seem pretty nice. I'm going to go out on a limb and say it was probably her loss."

Kelli clutched her coffee cup to her chest. "Yeah, her loss." She nodded to the narrow hallway off the living room. "Mallory's room is the one at the end of the hall, right across from the bathroom. There's not much in there, but I guess it won't hurt for you to take a look around."

"I did get her brother's permission, if that makes you feel better."

She stepped back and gestured for Grace to proceed. "I put the box with the test in the medicine cabinet. I figured if she showed up, I'd toss it in the trash and she'd never know I saw it."

Grace headed down the hall. "Thank you, but I'll want

to take it with me in case we can get any forensic information from it."

Behind her, Kelli gasped. "I didn't think about fingerprints. I didn't touch it, I swear. I mean, I touched the box, but not the test thingy. I used a tissue," she amended as she hurried after Grace. "I mean, she, uh, urinated on it, and I didn't want to touch anything, you know, kinda gross," she babbled.

"It's okay," Grace assured her as she stepped into the bathroom.

She opened the medicine cabinet and eyeballed the box. Sure enough, it claimed to include two tests. Rather than reaching for it, she turned to Kelli, who hovered in the doorway clutching her coffee cup.

"Do you have a plastic bag handy? Something with a zip top? Like a freezer bag?" She had a couple of evidence bags in her purse, but asking Kelli to find one would send the young woman to the kitchen and give her a moment alone in the space.

"Be right back," Kelli promised.

Grace leaned in and caught the open end of the box with her pen. Turning it in her direction, she could see Kelli hadn't been wrong. There was only one plastic stick in the box. She tipped the box over and peered down at the window on the wand. Plus sign.

A montage of different scenarios played in her head.

Mallory was unhappy about the pregnancy and had gone off to determine if she should go through with it?

The boyfriend was happy about the possibility of a baby and they'd hopped a plane to Vegas?

The boyfriend was unhappy and Mallory was now consigned to parts unknown?

The younger woman returned holding a gallon bag with a slider top, and Grace jerked herself out of her reverie.

"Perfect. Thank you," Grace said as she used the pen to lift the box from the cabinet and secure it in the bag. Then she dropped the whole thing into her tote and craned her neck to peer over Kelli's shoulder toward the room across the hall.

"Her room?"

"Oh." The young woman moved to let Grace pass. "Yes, this is hers. I kept the master because I pay more in rent, and—"

Not needing to hear more, Grace held up a hand as she passed. "I won't be long, I promise."

Kelli hadn't exaggerated. Mallory's room contained a mattress and box spring on the floor. The dresser and nightstand appeared to come from one of those kits you have to put together with a wrench that doesn't fit anything else in the world. The rest of the space was filled with clothes.

Tons of clothes.

Stepping over the mounds on the floor and ignoring the cascade of apparel spilling out of the closet, Grace immediately went to the nightstand and opened the drawer. There she found the usual detritus—hair elastics, bills, receipts, a couple of condoms in wrappers, a paperback romance novel and assorted lip balms. But beneath it all there appeared to be a folder embossed with the logo of a title company.

She pulled it from under the rest. "Was this the paperwork you found?" she asked, glancing over her shoulder at Kelli.

The younger woman blushed, obviously embarrassed to have been caught trying to cover up her snooping. "Yes."

Grace opened the folder and scanned the documents. They did indeed reference Mallory and Matthew Murray as the owners of a piece of property near Garfield, Arkansas.

"You're right. Looks like they sold some property they owned jointly."

Kelli nodded. "She told me she'd grown up over near Beaver Lake. I didn't put it together until I saw that folder."

"Put what together?" Grace asked, curious.

"You know, living here in Eureka but working at a place like Stubby's. She's into the whole lake life thing. Likes hanging out with the people who come up for the weekends."

"Like guys named Chad or Troy?"

Kelli wrinkled her nose. "Well, yeah. I mean, they sound like rich-person names, don't they?" Kelli gave a snort of derision. "All the guys I knew growing up were named Junior or Bubba or something like that."

Kelli had a point. Her mind flashed to Treveon, and she couldn't help marveling at how much weight something as seemingly innocuous as a name could have.

"You're right. Good thinking. I'll ask her brother if he has any ideas."

She did another circuit of the room, peering into the cluttered closet, then returning to the nightstand drawer and checking through it again. Convinced she had the most pertinent of clues stashed in a plastic bag, she smiled at Kelli Simon as she nodded her satisfaction with her search. "I'll get out of your hair and let you get back to work."

The younger woman exhaled, the tension in her stance visibly dissipating for a moment. She glanced at the fitness tracker strapped to her wrist and snapped to attention again. "Oh. Yeah, I'm sorry. I really do have to get back," she said, eyes widening.

Grace gave the apartment's common areas another once-over as they passed through. None of the chaos from Mallory's room spilled over. Either Kelli Simon had done an excellent job of her Sunday cleaning or her roommate rarely availed herself to the rest of the space.

As they exited the duplex and Kelli turned to lock the door, Grace gave the other woman a more deliberate inspection. Kelli was pretty in a girl-next-door sort of way. She possessed none of the languid beauty Mallory Murray projected in the photos emailed to her. The two seemed an odd pairing. Then again, Kelli herself had admitted they weren't actually friends.

"Thank you again," Grace said, extending a hand. "Please call me if you hear anything from Mallory. If I discover anything of note, I'll be sure to be in touch."

"I'd appreciate that," Kelli replied. She shifted her weight from one foot to the other. "I, uh—" she gestured down the hill toward the business district "—have to go."

"Go on ahead." Grace pointed in the opposite direction. "I couldn't find street parking, so I'm in a spot up here." Waving the younger woman on, she turned and headed for the other end of the block. Around the corner, she waited until she was certain Kelli was gone, then doubled back.

Moving at a more methodical pace, Grace took in everything she could about the street where Mallory Murray lived. She checked each gray car she passed to be sure it wasn't the five-year-old subcompact her brother said she drove. Not one of them had a window sticker that read, Sweet 'n' Sassy Southern Girl. Satisfied she'd ascertained all she could there, she climbed into her own car, programmed her navigation for Stubby's Bar and Grill, and headed west out of Eureka Springs.

Chapter Four

Matthew wasn't quite sure what he'd imagined Special Agent Grace Reed to look like when he'd spoken to her on the phone, but whatever image his brain had conjured, it came nowhere near the reality of her.

She was tall. Approaching six feet, he figured, by the way she nearly looked him straight in the eye as they shook hands. Her grip was firm and businesslike, but her dark brown hair fell loose past her shoulders in soft waves. Her gray slacks, silky T-shirt and neatly tailored blazer showed off a figure he'd call lean rather than thin.

For a moment, he lost himself in the notion of her taking him down. He'd bet money she could do it. To his own surprise, he found the thought of it intriguing rather than emasculating.

"Would you like to have a seat?" he asked, gesturing to one of the chairs positioned in front of his desk.

"Yes, thank you," she said, stepping past him to claim a chair.

Out of nervousness and habit, Matthew buttoned his suit jacket as he circled his desk to return to his chair, only to quickly unbutton it again to sit. "I've not had any news from Mallory," he said without preamble. "Has her roommate heard anything more from her?"

Agent Reed shook her head. "No, she's not heard from her, either. I spoke to Ms. Simon and visited your sister's apartment. She hasn't been home."

· The news stung more than Matthew thought it would. He sucked air in through his teeth but clamped his mouth shut. Years of law school had taught him listening usually garnered more answers than a barrage of questions. Agent Reed would get to what he needed to know.

"I stopped by Stubby's Bar and Grill on my way here, but Steve, the owner and person who was working the night Mallory disappeared, is out of town and won't be back until tomorrow. I'll go out there again and see if he can give any additional information."

Matthew nodded. He laced his fingers atop the blotter on his desk and found himself unable to meet Agent Reed's steady gaze. "I wish I had more information for you." He felt the color rise in his cheeks but didn't fight it.

He was Mallory's brother. He should be embarrassed he hadn't kept closer contact with his only sibling. "There's an age gap between me and Mallory. We've never been tight, but after our parents passed…" He let the rest of the thought drift away.

The detective nodded her understanding. "It happens."

"I've been racking my brain, trying to think back over the few conversations we have had in the past year or two." He sank back in his chair and pressed his fingertips to his forehead, smoothing his brows before letting his hands fall away. He looked up into her eyes and gave a helpless shrug.

"The fact of the matter is, we don't like each other much." One corner of his mouth lifted in a sardonic smile. "A horrible thing to say out loud, but it's true. She thinks I'm bossy and have a gigantic stick up my rear, and I think she's a… I don't know." He shifted his gaze, unable to maintain contact any longer. "A slacker, I guess."

She nodded, and he got the feeling she already knew all of this. It annoyed him. The notion that this stranger might have a better handle on his relationship with his only relative irked him enough to make him snap his mouth shut again.

But Agent Reed had other ideas.

"Tell me about her," she prompted, extracting her phone from her bag. "I'd like to record this, if you don't mind. I'll take notes, too, but once in a while people say things out loud they don't realize is important or gives us a clue," she explained.

Matthew stared at the phone for a moment, his gaze fixed on the red dot on the screen that would start recording their conversation. He knew anything he had to say could go on record if Agent Reed decided to turn her investigation in his direction, but he had nothing to hide.

"I agree. Please, start the recording."

Agent Reed set the phone on the desk and touched the button. She spoke her name, then noted the date and time of their conversation.

Before she could ask her first question, he jumped in. "I'd like to ask you whether you think I had anything to do with my sister's disappearance."

She looked up at him, her expression curious but unfazed. "*Should* I think you have something to do with your sister's disappearance?"

"No."

"I don't have any reason to believe you have been more connected to your sister than you claim," she concluded. "But I'm listening if you have a cause for concern."

Matthew gave his head a vigorous shake. "No. Nothing more than familial concern." He gave her a wry smile. "Call it lawyers' paranoia. We always get a bit nervous when there's going to be a record."

She returned his smile, and it made Matthew sit up in his

chair again. In its resting state, her face was sober. Stoic. An attractive sculpture of a serious woman. But her smile transformed her entirely. The warmth of it made him want to answer any questions she fired at him. He wondered if Special Agent Grace Reed was aware her smile was her superpower.

Catching himself, he waved a hand to the phone and nodded. "Ask away, Agent Reed."

Her smile burned brighter for a moment, then she dimmed it down as she studied him closely. "We play on the same side of the law, Mr. Murray. How about for the sake of this conversation you call me Grace and I'll call you Matthew?"

Matthew sat forward, his shoulders relaxing at the invitation to informality. "Okay, Grace."

"Is there anything you want to tell me about your sister, Mallory? Anything at all."

Matthew closed his eyes, and the image that had been haunting him since he'd first spoken to Grace flashed into his mind. It was a photograph his parents had kept on the mantel in the house where they grew up. In it, Mallory was probably about seven or eight. She'd performed in her first dance recital. She wore one of those fluffy ballerina dresses with sparkles and sequins sewn into the fabric, a rhinestone tiara, and a smile a mile wide.

It was the image that sprang to mind whenever he thought of his sister. In the photo, Mallory was the star she'd always wanted to be.

"Mal is a pretty girl. Always has been. Like the kind of pretty people would stop my parents to comment on. When she was younger, she liked to dance, sing…perform, basically anything onstage," he said, his brow furrowing as he tried to shape memories into words. "She likes attention. There were six years between us, but when we were younger, she stuck to me like glue. I didn't pay as much attention to her as she would have liked."

When he paused, Grace smiled. "Naturally. I'm sure the clinginess annoyed you."

"Yeah, it did," he admitted with a rueful huff of a laugh. "She loved—loves," he corrected, "anything sparkly or glittery, which holds zero interest for me…"

"Please continue."

"My parents doted on her. After me, they didn't think they'd have any more kids. She was a surprise."

"Tell me about your parents. They were killed in a car crash?" she said, her gaze boring into his.

"Yes. They were your average parents," he said with a shrug. "Our dad worked as a manager at a machine shop, and Mom worked at the school. They never had a lot of money. They helped as much as they could when I went off to college, but I got some scholarships and financial aid. They contributed what they could," he said slowly, "but it wasn't much in the grand scheme of things. It wasn't until last year I realized that Mallory had the impression Mom and Dad were footing the bill for me to go to college."

"Oh?"

"She blames me. I was the reason she couldn't have a car on her sixteenth birthday or the clothes she wished she had." He paused, tucked chin to his chest as he pushed down the bewilderment and frustration he'd felt when his sister had finally unleashed years of resentment on him.

"I didn't realize because I was pretty far removed from the home situation, but my parents were struggling financially. Not because I was in school, though. My dad drank too much. My mother tended to get her revenge on him through the home shopping channels." He chuckled, but there was no humor to it. "It was a pattern our whole lives. I think maybe Mallory saw too much of their dysfunctional dynamic and didn't have an example of how to work hard to get what you want."

Agent Reed leaned forward in her chair, bracing her elbows on her knees. Her expression stayed neutral. "What makes you say so?"

"Mallory has…let's call it an overinflated sense of entitlement." The corner of his mouth ticked up, and he lifted his hands in a futile gesture he hoped indicated his cluelessness. "I'm not sure where she got it. We never had money. We never wore the cool shoes or played the latest video games. Our parents were able to cover the essentials, but not a whole lot of the extras. For some reason, Mallory got it into her head she was owed those extras, and it was my fault she never had them."

"Why do you think she blames you?"

He looked directly at her. "Because she told me she does."

"Bluntly? I mean, she said as much out loud?"

"Yes, ma'am." He saw her cringe at the *ma'am*. "Sorry, reflex."

She waved him off. "No problem. When was it she told you she thought you were the reason she couldn't have nice things?"

"When our parents were killed in the crash, there was a bit of life insurance, but not quite enough to cover the costs of burying both of them. We put the house up for sale. When it finally did sell, I used what we earned from the proceeds to pay off what we owed the funeral home and split any remaining profit. Mallory was furious."

Her brow puckered. "Why?"

"Because I didn't use my own money to pay the bill," he explained. "She figured since Mom and Dad had contributed to my college education but not hers—she wasn't out of high school when they died—she was owed a larger portion of the estate."

"I see."

"She didn't care about the mountain of debt I had from

undergrad and the loans piling up from law school. It didn't matter how I explained things to her. She still ended up with a fairly decent lump sum after the dust settled, but nothing was ever enough for Mallory."

"And you feel this colored your relationship with your sister?"

"I know it did," he said succinctly. "We didn't get together often, but when we did, Mallory never failed to let me know she felt she was entitled to more."

"Did she ask you for money?"

He huffed a laugh. "Almost the minute I landed my first job. She wasn't interested in hearing about student loan payments."

"I assume whatever nest egg she had was gone?"

He nodded. "As far as I can tell, the only smart thing she did with the money was to buy a car. As for the rest, who knows where it went? She's come to me more than once asking to borrow money for security deposits on apartments. She rarely stays in one place for long."

"Do you give her money?"

He nodded. "I have in the past." He looked down at his clasped hands again and heaved a sigh. "I didn't when she called a few months ago. I told her she was old enough and should have her life more pulled together. I told her I was done with the handouts, and she told me she was done accepting scraps." He shook his head. "I can't help thinking about the picture."

"Picture?"

"My parents had a picture of her dressed up for a dance recital they kept on the mantel. You know, like the sparkly dress with the crown and everything?"

Grace nodded.

"I can't help wondering if maybe somehow my sister decided she was some kind of fairy-tale princess stuck in this life. Like Cinderella or Snow White. Like she was waiting for her prince to come along and rescue her. I mean, it's not unusual for kids who grow up around here to be envious of the kids who come up here to the lake houses. Some of them are massive."

Grace shifted in her seat, easing back against the chair again. She uncrossed and recrossed her legs, and because he still had blood coursing through his veins, Matthew couldn't help but marvel at how long those legs were.

"Can you expound?" she asked, jolting him from his thoughts. "I'm not from around here, but I'm sure the lakes are a big draw. What's the relationship between the locals and the people who own places up here on the lakes?"

Unlacing his fingers, he opened his hands again and let his shoulders rise and fall. "It's a classic case of the haves versus the have-nots," he said without rancor. "When the Army Corps of Engineers built the dams on the White River, they created a playground for the wealthy by flooding the homesteads of the poor." He raised his eyebrows. "You've lived in Arkansas how long, Agent Reed?"

"My whole life," she answered immediately.

"Then I don't have to tell you this is a state of extremes, do I? There's money up here in northwest Arkansas, and lots more in Little Rock, but not much between. You might find a pocket of it here and there, but most of the people around here fall into the have-not category."

"True."

"Up here it tends to be more evident than in some places. People from all over come to the Ozarks, to these lakes. They like the tranquility. They like how far removed this place is from the everyday hubbub of their lives. But most of them don't realize the people who live around these lakes every day are hustling to scrape out a life."

He gestured to the window behind him. "Sure, there are

some big businesses and some industry here in the towns along this stretch of interstate. But once you get away from town, there isn't much out there other than lakes and hills. If you don't have the credentials needed to land a job with one of the big corporations headquartered up here...there's not a lot of options."

She nodded.

"People up here are still eking out a living any way they can, like their forefathers." He thought about Harley Jenkins and how proud the man was of his granddad, the old moonshiner. "Some still farm. A few may run some cattle. Some rely on the tourism for their income."

"And working at a place like Stubby's, your sister is relying on the tourism for hers," Grace noted. "Her roommate told me Mallory makes some good tips on the weekends when the lake people are around."

Matthew nodded. "I'm sure she does. Like I said, Mallory's a pretty girl by about anybody's standards. But the tips aren't what she wants from the tourism industry," he said, his voice hardening even as the words came out.

"Oh?" Grace raised a single eyebrow. "What do you mean?"

"Mallory believes she is destined for a better life than the one she has," he explained. "It would be much easier to walk into the life she wants as opposed to earning it."

He paused. "Her main goal in life, it seems, is to meet and marry a wealthy man." He looked away from Grace's steady brown gaze. "I hate to put it so baldly," he admitted, fixating on the framed diploma hanging on his wall.

And he did hate to say so out loud. He'd worked hard to escape from the life laid out in front of him. Mallory had no idea how many late nights he'd ignored a rumbling stomach while studying, or the soul-crushing schmoozing he'd done to ingratiate himself with people who could influence his career.

He was a have-not trying to gain a toehold in the world where people had…something. But he was all too aware he'd never, no matter how hard he worked or how much money he had in his bank account, be counted as an equal to the people who had the real pull.

He knew he'd always be on the outside looking in unless someone magically handed him a golden ticket.

Mallory knew it, too.

The difference was, his sister wasn't about to work one ounce harder than she had to in order to get what she wanted. At least not the type of work that required anything more than a flirtatious smile and a willing nature.

"I don't mean to sound callous. And I'm not judging her." He gave another humorless laugh and turned back to meet Grace's eyes again. "Okay, maybe I am to a certain degree, but you have to understand, she told me all about her plans. This is the sum and total of Mallory Murray's life's ambition. She wants to marry a rich man. She wants to be taken care of. She wants everyone to envy her. She wants to be lifted out of the world she was born into."

He bit his lip and dipped his head as he drew a calming breath. At last, he forced a tired smile when he looked up again. "In a nutshell, that is the most basic thing I can tell you about my sister."

"Is it possible she's fulfilled her ambitions?" Grace asked, her gaze fixed intently on him.

Matthew fought the urge not to fidget. The detective was trying to get a read on him, but she wasn't going to find anything more than what she saw.

"It's entirely possible. Maybe she did meet the man of her dreams. Maybe they're in Las Vegas right now tying the knot. I wouldn't be surprised if she showed up with a pile of designer luggage and a rock the size of a baseball. I hope so," he added, feeling every minute of the previous night's sleeplessness. "I hope she has everything she's ever wanted. I want her to meet a guy who will treat her right, and for her to live the princess life she's always dreamed of."

"But you don't think that's the case," Grace interjected.

Matthew met her eyes again, and their gazes locked and held. "As you said earlier, we both work the same side of the law. You and I have seen how things usually pan out for young women like my sister. Tell me, how often have you seen the fairy tale come true?"

"I'm not sure I ever have," she answered with heart-stopping sincerity.

Matthew let himself slump back in his chair again and rubbed a tired hand across his forehead. "Neither have I, Grace. Neither have I."

The silence stretched between them. It seemed to go on for hours, but it was more likely seconds. At last, he heard the soft beep and lowered his hand to see she had switched off the recording. Grasping her phone, Grace leaned forward in her seat, her gaze steady on him.

"I'm going to do everything possible to find her."

He inclined his head in acknowledgment. "I'm willing to cooperate with this investigation however I can. We may not have been close, but I love my sister. I don't understand her, but I do love her."

Grace nodded, then dropped the phone into the bag at her feet. "I'm going to book a room here in town."

She extracted a business card from the outside pocket of the enormous bag she had with her and extended it to him clasped between her index and middle fingers. "My cell number is on there. Please feel free to call me if you think of anything that might be pertinent."

Matthew plucked one of his own business cards from the

holder on his desk and scrawled his mobile number on the back. "You already have the office number, but same here," he replied, passing the card to her. "What's our next step?"

She let one shoulder rise and fall. "I guess there's not much more I can do until I talk to Steve. The owner of Stubby's," she added.

"Sounds logical."

She nodded. "He was the one who was working with Mallory Friday night. I'll head over there tomorrow and see what information I can get from him about where she may have gone."

He rose as she did. "I'd appreciate an update on how it goes."

"Of course," she agreed, extending her hand.

He took it, but he couldn't help feeling she was sizing him up all over again as they shook.

She cocked her head to the side. "Would you like to come out to Stubby's with me?"

He blinked and forced himself to extract his hand from hers. "Do you think it would help?"

Grace gave him a wan smile. "Can't hurt. You're familiar with the area and the people. Maybe you'd pick up on something I would miss."

Matthew found himself nodding eagerly. "Yes. Absolutely."

"When should I pick you up?" she asked.

He blinked. It hadn't occurred to him she would be the one picking him up, but he quickly chided himself for the reflexive and antiquated response. This was her investigation. He was the one riding along.

"Would eleven o'clock be too late?" He gestured to the suit he wore. "I have something at eight, and I'd like a chance to run home and change into something less conspicuous if we plan to head into the hills."

She gave a brisk nod. "Yes. Good call. Ten o'clock it is." She hiked her bag onto her shoulder and raised a hand in a half wave. "See you then."

Matthew watched as she wound her way through the maze of desks in the open area and moved toward the exit. The second the door closed behind her, he dropped back into his chair, pulled open the center drawer of his desk and stared down at the photograph he'd found in a box the previous night.

He'd removed the snapshot from the frame when they'd packed up their parents' house, but Mallory's bright smile rivaled the tiara on her head, and her eyes sparkled like the glittery tutu she wore. He rubbed a hand over his mouth.

"Lord, Mal, what the heck have you gotten yourself into now?" he asked the girl in the photo.

Chapter Five

Stubby's Bar and Grill was located on Highway 62, where it held pride of place between Beaver Lake and the more well-known Table Rock Lake, which straddled the Arkansas-Missouri state line. Not a bad location for an area heavily dependent on tourism traffic for its economy. Grace drove her state-issued SUV confidently, handling the hills and turns of the rural highway with ease.

But the man in the passenger seat wasn't relaxed, despite the fact he'd traded his courtroom suit for some more casual clothes. His slate blue flat-front chinos and a polo shirt fit him well. So well Grace had to make a point of not staring when she first saw him.

As they drove, she glanced only at his feet for the first few miles. It was safer to focus on the deck shoes he wore without socks. Those she could mock in her mind. The rest? Well, he'd been handsome but professional in his suit. But now, he looked like one of those lake people everyone kept referencing. More approachable, but still miles out of her reach.

The silence in the car might have stretched into something awkward if his phone hadn't rung before they even left town. He cast her an apologetic glance and checked the screen. "Sorry, it's the office. We've had to do some reshuffling."

"Shuffle away," she said with a wave of her hand.

The call lasted the entire stretch of road skirting north Beaver Lake. Grace was thankful for the distraction. She had debated whether to mention Kelli's discovery of the pregnancy test but decided to keep the information to herself for a bit. It was not her news to share, and until there was actual confirmation from Mallory, it was pure speculation. As a lawyer, he would understand her reticence if it came to light.

Matthew apologized again as he ended his call, but she shook her head. "No worries."

He cast a wary glance at her, and she caught a huff of a laugh. "My assistant is snowed under, and I, uh..." He trailed off, propping his elbow on the door and rubbing a hand over his mouth without continuing the thought. "I never talk much about my family. I guess they were all a little shocked when I dropped the family-emergency excuse on them."

She regarded him briefly, then turned her attention back the road. She missed the safety of his sharp suit. "It's not an excuse. It's the situation at hand."

"Right. It's... I don't take a lot of vacation. I think they all assumed I didn't have, uh, anyone." He gave a rueful chuckle. "Which, let's face it, is pretty much the gist of it."

Grace took her eyes off the road long enough to pin him with a stare. "Lots of people aren't particularly close to their family, but it doesn't mean they don't care."

"Right," he repeated, but his voice fell flat.

He shifted in his seat, and she could feel his gaze on her but resisted the temptation to meet it. "How about you? What got you into police work?"

"My grandfather was with the Fort Smith PD. I guess it's in my blood. I did my undergrad at the U of A's Fort Smith campus and was recruited by the state police from there."

"No desire to stay local?"

She smirked. "Well, technically I did. I'm based out of Fort Smith, remember?"

"Right." He hummed as he digested the tidbit. "Family still there?"

She nodded. "My mom and my older sister, Faith."

"Faith and Grace," he murmured. "No Hope?"

She raised her brows and pinned him with a stare. "Nope. My dad was a firefighter and was killed on scene. They never got any further."

"I'm sorry."

"I was barely a toddler."

"Sorry all the same," he replied.

"Thank you."

"Well, police and fire. You had your choice of footsteps to follow," he prompted.

"But working with the state is a better fit. I wanted to specialize in major crimes investigation, and the CID plays a role in most cases at one point or another. Plus, better uniforms."

"You don't wear a uniform," he pointed out.

"But I have one, and I look badass in it."

He laughed out loud. "I don't doubt it."

Grace felt heat rise on her skin. Truthfully, the slight tingle signaling the rush of blood to her ears was oddly reassuring. She thought the ability to blush had been erased from her repertoire after many years on the force.

"Thank you," she replied crisply. "How about you? Have you always wanted to be a prosecutor?"

"I only knew I wanted to be something respectable," he said, letting the words come as the thoughts formed. "I always got good grades. My mom was big on me being a doctor. Unfortunately, I'm too squeamish for medicine."

"Hard to be squeamish when you're a prosecutor," Grace pointed out. "I'm sure you've seen some pretty gruesome things."

"Yes, but usually in crime scene photographs, not live and in person."

She nodded. "Good point. Big difference."

"Absolutely." He took a breath and drummed his fingers on the armrest of the door. "It seemed like every kid I met at Fayetteville had at least one parent who is a lawyer or doctor." He snickered, and she caught him shaking his head out of the corner of her eye. "Kind of a stupid way to choose a profession, but there you go. I went to school with all these kids who were being bankrolled by doctors and lawyers, and I figured if I wasn't going to be a doctor, I might as well try to be a lawyer."

"What made you choose to serve on the side of the good guys?"

"A lot of guys I went to high school with ended up on the wrong side of the law."

He thrummed his fingers again, and she looked over to see him peering out the side window, his jaw clenched.

"Of course, they always said they were innocent, but everybody knew they'd done whatever got them in trouble. I couldn't... I didn't think I could stomach defending somebody I knew was guilty."

"Understandable."

"Don't get me wrong—I have a lot of respect for defense attorneys. They have a tough job, and I do believe everybody deserves an advocate."

Grace couldn't stifle the derisive snort.

"Seriously. A competent defense is an absolute necessity. In order for our system of justice to work, it has to be a level playing field."

"But it's not a level playing field," she shot back, thinking of Treveon Robinson and his weeping mother. "The system is stacked against certain people—or rather, in favor of others."

"True. But I guess I thought I could do better at evening things out on the side of prosecution rather than defense."

"You're saying justice can't be served from the other side?" she challenged.

"I'm saying there's more money on the other side," he stated flatly. "And let's face it, money almost always wins. It's the American way."

They spent the rest of the drive talking about how various cases of local and regional interest had been handled, often nodding in agreement but occasionally engaging in heated debate.

Matthew pointed to a flashing roadside marquee on the left side of the highway. "Right up there."

She signaled and pulled into the cracked asphalt parking lot of Stubby's Bar and Grill. Slowing to a roll, Grace allowed herself a moment to take it all in.

The bar itself was a low cinder-block building. There didn't seem to be anything remarkable about it. The blocks had long ago been painted white but were now spattered with dirt and chipping in some spots. A portable sign with a flashing arrow had a message bragging they had the best burgers in the Ozarks, and advertised a happy hour special on bottled beer.

She crunched to a halt near the darkened double doors. The only other signage was the hand-painted lettering on the tinted glass. *Stubby's* was written in large, stylized script, and the words *Bar and Grill* were printed in a sans serif font below.

Beside her, Matthew exhaled long and loud. She turned to her passenger. Dark circles smudged his eyes. He was clean shaven, but his hair was tousled, the streaks of his fingers leaving tracks in the dark waves. His clothes were neatly pressed and stylish, but as he sat slumped in the passenger seat, she couldn't see any of the confidence he projected sitting behind his desk in the prosecuting attorney's office.

"You okay?" she asked.

He nodded. "Fine."

Grace repressed the urge to laugh at the terse response. It was clear the man was anything but fine, but she wasn't about to argue semantics with him. "I assume you've been here?"

He bobbed his head again. "Sure. Stubby's is sort of a landmark around here," he explained. "You'd be hard-pressed to find anyone who grew up in the vicinity who hadn't at least stopped in for a burger."

"Are they good?"

"Didn't you read the sign?" he asked, hooking a thumb toward the marquee. "Best burgers in the Ozarks."

"Are they?"

"I haven't done an exhaustive study, but I'd be willing to risk saying all of Carroll County."

"Is there a lot of competition for the title?"

He ducked his head, a smile curving his lips as he shook it. "Nope. At least not situated between the two lakes."

Grace had spent the previous evening studying maps of the area. The man-made lakes formed by the damming of the White River offered miles and miles of shoreline, much of it remarkably undeveloped.

"I bet those burgers and a cold beer taste good after a day out on the water."

"Nothing better," he said gruffly.

"Do you have a boat?"

He shook his head harder. "No. Maybe someday, but right now I don't have a lot of free time."

She nodded her understanding. Reaching for the door handle, she glanced over again to be sure. "You don't have to come in if you don't want to."

"No, it's good." He reached for his own door handle. "Let's go talk to Steve."

As they made their way to the plate-glass door, Grace frowned. "How familiar are you with this Steve guy?"

Matthew wobbled his hand. "Not personally. More in the way people in the area generally know other people. He's about ten years older than me. His dad was the original Stubby," he explained.

"The original Stubby, huh? There's been more than one?" she mused as he reached for the door handle.

"You'll understand the nickname when you see Steve." He paused and turned back to take in the parking area. "I don't see Mallory's car."

Grace nodded. "I didn't see one fitting the description you gave me when I came by yesterday, either."

"Interesting," he murmured as he pulled open the door.

Once inside, Grace took a moment to allow her eyes to adjust from the bright sunshine to the dim interior of the bar. There were few people in the place so early in the day. To their left, an older couple wearing golf clothes bent over baskets brimming with burgers and crinkle-cut fries. To their right, a man sagged on a stool, only his elbow keeping him upright.

Grace took a single step toward the bar, and the swinging doors she assumed led to the kitchen area pushed open. A short, squat man with a thick shock of wheat-colored hair backed through. He carried a heavy tray of what appeared to be freshly washed glasses to the bar and stowed them beneath, barely even stooping to make the task possible.

"Help you folks?" he asked without looking up.

"Yes, sir." Grace pulled her credentials from her bag and held them open for the man to inspect. "I'm Special Agent Grace Reed of the State Police Criminal Investigation Division. This is Matthew Murray from the Benton County prosecuting attorney's office."

The man's brow furrowed as he examined her identification. "Terence told me somebody came by yesterday looking for me," he said with a scowl. "What can I do for you?"

"I'm looking for information on one of your employees. Mallory Murray?"

Huffing, the short man turned away and snatched a towel from the back bar. "I told her not to bother me again. Whatever trouble she's gotten into, I'm not bailing her out. She is a good waitress, but good waitresses aren't too hard to find," he said dryly.

Grace took a step to the side, following him as he moved away from them. "We're hoping she's not in any trouble," she said earnestly. Casting a glance in Matthew's direction, she waited until he gave an almost imperceptible nod. "We wanted to ask you a few questions about Friday night."

Steve looked up from where he was wiping the bar. "Friday night?"

"Mallory Murray didn't return home Friday night and hasn't been seen since. Her roommate filed a missing-person report." She pivoted in Matthew's direction. "Mr. Murray is her brother."

The bartender looked up in surprise, his scowl deepening as he gave Matthew an unabashed once-over. "You're Mal's brother? The lawyer?"

Matthew nodded. "Yes."

Steve gave a snort. "She said you were some kind of big shot, but a person can't always pay much mind to what the girl says. Delusions of grandeur, my mama would have said," he muttered.

"We don't get to pick our siblings," Matthew retorted. "We only need to confirm she's alive and well."

"Beats me. I haven't seen your sister since she left here Friday night. If she found any trouble, it didn't happen here."

At the man's flat statement, Grace took another step toward Matthew, placing herself directly between the two men in their line of vision. "We appreciate your candor. Ms. Murray is Mr. Murray's only living family member, and I'm hoping to get some answers for him. She was scheduled to work Friday night, but we're not sure where she went from there. Do you have any idea?"

"She was scheduled, but she didn't stay long," the other man complained. "Ditched out for a party."

"Her car isn't in the parking lot," Matthew observed. "I guess she drove herself to wherever the party was?"

"I guess she did," Steve said, his expression stony.

"Any idea who might have been having this party?" Grace asked.

"The Powers kid," Steve said dismissively. "Cocky little jerk."

Grace wanted to laugh at the notion of a man she towered over by a head referring to anyone as "little," but beside her Matthew stiffened.

Pulling her notepad and pen from her bag, she flipped to a random page and scribbled the name. "Powers, you say?"

"Yeah. The young one, not his daddy," Steve clarified. "Never thought anyone would be more of a pain in the rear end than his daddy, but there you go. The rod was most definitely spared on the kid."

"Trey?" Matthew asked, his question barely more than a whisper. He cleared his throat. "You mean Trey Powers?"

Steve rolled his eyes. "Yeah, that's the one. Family has that crazy old castle over on Table Rock." His lips tightened and he shook his head. "He said something about havin' a crawfish boil that night, and she took off like a dog after a duck."

"A crawfish boil?"

"No doubt it was a catered affair," he added with a derisive snort. "Kid wouldn't know how to light his butt on fire if someone handed him a match."

The day drinker at the end of the bar barked a laugh, and

Grace turned her attention to him. "You know him? This Trey Powers?" She felt Matthew go rigid again when she spoke the name, but he didn't say anything.

"You talkin' to me?" the guy at the end of the bar asked.

"I might be," she countered. "Do you know Trey Powers?"

"Everyone around here does," he replied, gesturing to the entire bar with his beer bottle.

The couple who'd been eating abruptly scraped their chairs back, dropped a twenty onto the table and rose to leave. "Thank you! Great as always," the older man called, raising a hand in farewell as he ushered his wife to the door.

Grace split a puzzled glance between Steve, his departing customers and the lawyer who'd turned into a statue beside her. "I'm sorry, how does everyone know the, uh, Powers boy?"

"You're definitely not from around here," Steve replied.

"I'm acquainted with who they are," Matthew said quietly. "You're sure she was going with him?"

"That boy and your sister have been carrying on as long as Mallory's worked here. He comes around, and she goes chasin' right after him. And that's exactly what happened Friday night." Steve tossed his towel aside in disgust. "Well, I'm done with it. When she turns up again, she doesn't need to bother coming around here wanting her job back."

Grace opened her mouth to ask more questions but stopped when she felt a hand clamp around her elbow. Glancing over at Matthew in bewilderment, she saw only his furrowed brow and the firm, forbidding line of his mouth.

"Thanks for speaking with us," he said, preemptively bringing her interview to a close. "If I see Mallory before you do, I'll be sure to pass the message along."

Grace wanted to protest, but he gave her elbow another hard squeeze. She met his eyes and found him staring back at her with eyes wide with a plea for understanding. "Let's head out, shall we, Agent Reed?"

She got the hint. He obviously knew something he didn't want to say in front of the bar owner. Pulling out a card, she slid it across the bar. "I'd appreciate a call if you hear from her."

"Yeah, sure," Steve replied.

But Grace caught sight of him chucking the card beneath the bar as Matthew all but pulled her to the tinted glass doors.

The sunlight was blinding. They stood outside the door, blinking but not speaking. At last, Matthew started to move toward her car, and she gathered her wits again.

"What was that? Who are these Powers people? How can you be so sure Steve didn't have anything more to say? I had more questions," she said, lengthening her stride to match his.

Matthew stopped beside her SUV and drew a deep breath. "I'm giving us a chance to fall back and regroup. Trust me on this."

"Right, but—"

"Steve wasn't going to say anything helpful. The minute Mallory walked out his door, he was done with her."

"I guess we need to talk to this Trey Powers person, then," Grace persisted. "Where can we find him?"

Matthew's grim expression returned. "It's not as easy as you think." He nodded to the driver's side. "Let's go. I'll explain on the way back to town."

Grace frowned but acquiesced. She'd be a fool to discount his input. Still, the pieces weren't all fitting together for her. Opening her car door, she paused to look at Matthew.

"Should we head back to Bentonville now?" she asked across the roof of the vehicle. "Didn't Steve say they had a house on Table Rock Lake?" She hooked a thumb in the opposite direction.

"They do," Matthew confirmed. "But they don't actually live there," he added, a derisive smirk twisting his lips. "It's their lake house. The Powers family, and all that comes with them, you'll find in Bentonville."

Chapter Six

Matthew was quiet for the first few minutes of their ride back to Bentonville. Grace had to be champing at the bit to ask questions, but she remained silent as well. He appreciated her circumspection. If Mallory had taken off with Trey Powers, there would be a lot of knots to untangle.

At last, Grace cracked. "Who are these Powers people?"

"You had to have heard of some of them," Matthew insisted. "Senator William Powers?"

"This Trey guy is Senator Powers's son? I didn't think the senator had grown kids. Didn't he run on being the voice for the next generation of Arkansans? His kids are teenagers."

Matthew shook his head. "Not son, nephew." He turned to watch the passing scenery for a moment. "And yes, Senator Powers has a son from his first marriage, but he is the younger son. Tyrone Powers is the elder, and Trey's father. The family owns a law firm in Bentonville. Powers, Powers & Walton. Perhaps the other surname rings a bell?"

"Part of the Walton family?" she asked with raised eyebrows.

Matthew shrugged. "An offshoot. Close enough to be connected, but not close enough to be counting bags of money."

"You're saying these people have a lot of money and—"

She halted, seeming to struggle to find an alternative to the obvious word.

"Power," Matthew provided with a wry smile. "There's no better word for it. The last couple of generations have certainly lived up to their name."

"And Trey is how old?" she asked, glancing over at him.

He shrugged again. "A couple of years younger than me, maybe?" Matthew drummed his fingers on the armrest. "He's an attorney as well, but the Powers attorneys don't bother with schools like the U of A. I think he went to Harvard. Or Yale. One of the Ivy League schools."

"Fancy," she said dryly.

"Powers, Powers & Walton is what we would consider a white-shoe law firm in this area."

"What does that mean?"

"They don't like to get dirty. They make money by protecting other people with money. Most of their cases are business related. Lawsuits, contracts, mergers and acquisitions…but every once in a while, somebody's kid gets in trouble and PP&W is there to step in."

"As defense attorneys?"

He nodded.

"I assume they're good ones."

"The best money can buy." Matthew turned to look at her. "I haven't come up against any of them in court, but people in our office have."

"Doesn't sound like confronting this Trey guy is something you're looking forward to doing."

Matthew didn't detect any judgment in her observation. "Honestly, no. There's a lot of truth in the old adage about people having the best defense money can buy."

Her mouth thinned into a disapproving line, but she nodded. "You won't get any debate on the inequities of our justice system from me."

"You see firsthand how those who don't have money suffer at the hands of our system." He fell silent for a moment. "Firms like PP&W always find a way to stack the odds in their favor. I like taking on cases I have a chance to win."

"Don't you think taking only the cases you can win is a bit ignoble?"

Her disdain came through loud and clear. "I never claimed to be noble, Agent Reed. I'm an ambitious man. I have my eye on a political career. Not only do I need to build up my résumé as a prosecutor, but I also have to be careful about who I cross. So, no, I don't want to cross swords with the Powers family."

He looked away. He didn't want to watch her expression harden. But when she spoke, her words were gentle and understanding. "I get you. Everybody has ambitions. I've spent most of my career defending mine. I'd be a hypocrite to attack you for yours."

"I'm not a fan of knocking on Trey Powers's door. I will if I have to in order to help this investigation…and my sister," Matthew said, turning to look at her. "I'm only saying I might need to tread carefully. Hell, the judge I appeared in front of yesterday used to be the Walton in Powers, Powers & Walton. He is not my biggest fan."

"Oh?" She graced him with a smirky smile. "Contempt of court?"

"Dented his bumper," Matthew corrected.

She gasped. "Oh…my… God. I'd rather pay the contempt fine."

"I'm in judicial jail, I promise you," he said, returning her smile.

"Have you won anything in his courtroom since?"

"Of course I have," he said with a laugh. "The system is flawed, but it does work. At least, to a certain extent."

"Okay, well, don't worry, Counselor. I will handle talking to Trey Powers. No need for you to get involved."

"It won't be easy getting to him."

"I guess I'd better start my charm offensive now." He watched in a mix of amusement and horror as she initiated voice command on her phone and asked the automated assistant to call Powers, Powers & Walton in Bentonville, Arkansas.

He waited, eyebrows raised. Special Agent Grace Reed was proving to be as fearless as she was dogged. A quality that made an already attractive woman even more enticing.

A perky young receptionist answered the call. "Powers, Powers & Walton," she chirped.

"Yes, this is Special Agent Grace Reed of the Arkansas State Police Criminal Investigation Division. I need to speak to Trey Powers, please. Is he in?"

Matthew liked that she added the *please*, even though her statement wasn't remotely a request. She might be determined, but she wasn't a steamroller.

"I, uh," the young woman stammered. "Yes, ma'am." She paused, possibly realizing her tactical error. To her credit, attempted to raise the drawbridge again. "I can check. May I tell him what this is in reference to?"

"I'm afraid I can't say," Grace replied coolly.

There was another pause, then a curt, "One moment, please."

Matthew smirked. "Man, you're good," he murmured as the sound of classical piano trickled through the car's speakers.

"It's all in the delivery," she said, a smirk twitching her lips.

The two of them sat in tense silence while the piano concerto continued. Matthew would have bet money the next voice they heard was the receptionist returning to the line to tell them Trey was unavailable to take their call.

He would have lost.

Seconds later, a young male answered the phone with a mildly amused chuckle. "This is Trey Powers. May I help you?"

"Yes." Grace's grip on the steering wheel tightened, and she sat up straighter in the driver seat. "Mr. Powers, this is Special Agent Grace Reed from the Arkansas State Police Criminal Investigation Division."

"So I heard," Trey drawled, but Matthew caught the thread of annoyance that ran through each word. "What can I do for you, Miss Reed?"

Matthew swung his head to see Grace's eyes narrow, but she kept them fixed on the road ahead of them. "Agent Reed," she corrected evenly. "I'd like to set up an appointment to come in and speak to you in person, Mr. Powers."

"Concerning?"

"A young woman named Mallory Murray. I'm told the two of you are acquainted."

"Mallory Murray…" Powers repeated. "Oh, yes, Mallory. She works at Stubby's out on the highway, doesn't she?"

"Yes, sir," Grace said briskly. "Can you tell me when you last saw Ms. Murray?"

"Last saw her?" Powers asked, nonplussed. Matthew bristled at the stalling tactic. "It's been a while…"

"I'm told she left her shift at the bar to attend a party at your house last Friday evening."

"Was it last Friday? I guess so." He gave another one of those mirthless chuckles. "Sorry, it's been a long week already."

"And she was in good health when last you saw her?" Grace persisted.

There was no pause on the other end. "Absolutely. She was fine. Good health and good spirits. Beautiful as always."

"Did Miss Murray drive herself to the party at your house?" Grace asked.

"The party was not at my house here in town. It was at my family's lake house," Trey corrected, perceptibly haughtier than he'd been a few minutes ago. "And I assume she drove herself there."

"She didn't ride with you?" Grace pushed.

"Ride with me? No." The last word came out on a scoff. Matthew curled his fingers into loose fists. He wanted to introduce this cocky jerk to one of them. "No one rode with me."

"But you did invite her to come to the party at the lake house." It was a statement, not a question, but Grace's statement made it clear she expected a reply.

"I invited a number of people. It was a party. A crawfish boil. I was having it catered, so I knew there would be more than enough food," he said dismissively.

"Did you speak to Miss Murray at the party?" Grace carried on.

"Yes, we spoke," Trey answered, his words chosen with more care and spoken with deliberate measure.

Matthew sensed Grace was about to attempt to establish a more intimate connection. Trey must have felt the shift, too, because he covered the phone and spoke a few muffled words.

A second later, he said, "I'm sorry, I have a client waiting. I hope this has helped you with whatever you're investigating Mallory for, Agent Reed, but I'm afraid I have to go."

Grace didn't bother correcting his assumptions about why she was asking about Mallory, and Matthew had to admire her restraint. Agent Reed played her cards close. Nothing was given away for free. They'd confirmed a connection between his sister and Trey Powers. It would need to be enough for now.

"Thank you for speaking with me. Would it be okay if I call with any follow-up questions?" Grace asked politely.

"I'm always available to members of our law enforcement community," Trey replied, notably stiffer than he had been when the call started. "Goodbye. Good luck catching her."

A beep sounded through the speakers to signal the call had disconnected.

The hum of tires on hot tarmac filled the silence. Matthew bit his tongue, unwilling to be the one who broke peaceful contemplation. He wanted Grace's take on Trey, and for her opinions to be as untainted by his own as possible.

"Well, I guess I can say he was every bit as entitled as I expected," she commented mildly.

A snort escaped him. "Not more?"

"Well, he goes by the name Trey," she said, emphasizing the nickname by drawing the single syllable into multiples. "My expectations were pretty high."

"The Powers family is formidable," Matthew returned flatly. "You can try to talk to him again, but I'm fairly certain we just finished the last unguarded conversation you'll have with him."

Grace nodded. "I don't disagree with you."

"Where do we go from here?" Matthew asked.

"I might do some poking around online," Grace said offhandedly. "Try to get a bead on who some of the other guests were at this party. Maybe they'll have something more for us to go on. I'm not exactly sure if Mr. Powers is hedging or if he didn't pay much attention to your sister at the party."

Matthew shrugged. "Sounds like it could have gone either way. He didn't seem overly concerned about her or why anyone was asking about her."

Grace nodded. "He assumed she was in trouble. Usually

when I start asking questions about someone, the first thing people ask is if they're okay. Then they start to wonder what the person I'm asking about has done wrong."

Matthew turned to gaze out the window. A sign noting the mileage back to Bentonville flew past. "I'm starting to worry," he admitted grimly.

Out of the corner of his eye, he saw her glance over at him in surprise. "Only starting?"

He sighed. "I guess I was hoping she'd taken off with some guy. Finally landed the big fish she'd been hoping to catch."

"But you don't think she has?"

Matthew unfurled his fingers and rubbed his damp palms against his thighs. "There would have been no bigger fish at that party than Trey Powers. It was his party, and he strikes me as the type who likes to be the center of attention." He closed his eyes and allowed the droning hum of tires on pavement to fill his mind for a blessed minute. "No, Mallory would not have left the party with anyone but Trey."

"It's possible he invited some other rich friends," Grace said offhandedly.

Matthew wasn't biting. "No. A Friday night crawfish boil wouldn't have been enough of an event for him to fly in Ivy League pals."

She pursed her lips as she took in his supposition. "He'd have wanted to show off something swankier."

"Exactly. I'll try to poke around at the office. Maybe someone has a friend over at PP&W we can talk to in case we can't get to Trey again." He suspected he wouldn't have much luck, but he needed to do something.

"What makes you think I can't get to him again?" Grace asked, tapping the steering wheel in a staccato beat he could only assume was agitation.

"You won't be able to bluff and bully your way past the receptionist again," he said flatly.

"I didn't bluff or bully," she replied, indignant.

Her obvious offense brought a wry smile to his lips. "Okay, you won't be able to push your way in behind your badge."

"Says you," she muttered, casting a squinty-eyed stare his way.

"Ten bucks says they've already closed ranks," he said grimly.

"Sounds like a sucker bet," she responded on a sigh, eyes back on the road again. "Well, while you try to find an in with the suede-shoe crowd—"

"White shoe," he corrected.

"Whatever. I have a friend who specializes in tracing people online. I'll call in a favor if we can't find anything on our own, but officially, she's not supposed to look at cases unless she's assigned to them. We can take a crack at social media ourselves. After all, we're still not sure if she didn't up and take off to Vegas."

"I won't be much help to you, since I don't really use social media much, but I'll try to figure out who some of her old friends were. Maybe we can get some info from there."

"Sounds like we have our assignments," she said as they approached the Bentonville city limits. "Drop you back at the office? I assume your car is there."

Matthew checked his watch, saw it was still early afternoon, and sighed. "Yeah. I'd better go back in and see what I missed today."

Ten minutes later, Grace dropped him off in front of his office building with a promise to be in contact if she found anything of interest.

Matthew was two steps into the bustling office when Nate appeared in front of him. The prosecuting attorney gave him a slow, smirky once-over, then toasted Matthew. The paper tag attached to the tea bag in his ever-present mug fluttered with the movement. "Nice to see you again. Have we gone to casual Wednesdays now?"

Matthew shook his head, wondering how anyone could ever choose tea over coffee. "I left a message with Tracy," Matthew responded, trying not to sound defensive. "I had some business to attend to concerning my sister."

With the ease of a skilled politician, Nate assumed an expression of concerned sympathy. "I heard. Any luck?"

Matthew shook his head, not wanting to get into the nitty-gritty with his boss. Something about Nate made a person think he didn't care to be sullied with details. Matthew could never decide if this quality was ironic or not, considering Nate's job was to keep the more unsavory elements of society off the streets.

"No word yet, but Mallory has always been one to do her own thing. She could have taken off to go make jewelry in Taos."

Nate's brow beetled. "Does she make jewelry?"

Matthew shrugged. "Damned if I can tell you." He gestured toward his office. "Anyway, I figured I'd hole up in my office and spend the rest of the afternoon catching up on paperwork."

His boss dismissed him with a wave. "I was only busting your chops. Truth is, I wasn't even aware you had a sister. And I don't care if you need to sneak out and handle personal business once in a while. It's not like we've ever worked less than a ten-hour workday, right?"

Matthew had to fold his lips in and bite down to keep from refuting the statement. Nate was all about appearances. He liked to see everyone in the office—ready and raring to go.

"Right. Well, I'd better..." Matthew gestured in the direction of his office, anxious to move on.

He hated standing next to Nate in his casual clothes, even though they were perfectly acceptable office attire. As always, the prosecuting attorney was impeccably dressed. One of the inside jokes at the office was that he had each article of clothing labeled with the possibly perfect location to wear it. Striped polo shirt? Barbecue, kid's birthday party, shopping with the family. Blue blazer—informal business meetings. He didn't like casual Fridays but tolerated them because the rest of the world seemed to want them.

"Sure. Right. Back to work," Nate said with mock sternness.

Matthew tried to smile, but he never quite knew how to handle his boss. The man was a chameleon. Which was probably how he'd managed to become the youngest prosecuting attorney elected in the state. No doubt the skill had helped him make friends powerful enough to get him there.

The thought made him pause. "Hey, Nate?"

"Hmm?" The other man turned, and for a moment Matthew wondered if he'd ever seen him take a sip of tea from the mug he always held.

"Do you know Trey Powers?"

A flash of surprise crossed the other man's face, but he quickly covered it with a chuckle loaded with good humor. "Trey Powers? Of course I do. Well, I'm better acquainted with his father. Ty Powers manages a super PAC. They donated to my campaign. Why?"

Matthew made a mental note that the Powers family's political action committee was one of Nate's backers. "I guess my sister left work Friday to go to a party out at the Powers place on Table Rock Lake."

Nate nodded but looked placidly nonplussed by the information. "Ty likes to entertain out there. His father built an enormous house—looks like a European castle on the outside. All hunting lodge meets five-star ski chalet inside, of course."

Matthew couldn't contain his surprise. "You've been there?"

Nate nodded. "Most everyone who runs in political circles up here has. Since Ty's brother, Bill, decided to run for office, they got involved in all levels."

Nodding, Mathew held his ground while he digested the information. "But you've met Trey as well," he persisted.

"We've met." When he spoke, he raised and lowered one shoulder in a shrug so subtle a person who wasn't watching as intently as Matthew might have missed it. But a good prosecutor knew the value of body language, and nothing gave a person's insecurity away more quickly than a partial shrug. "He's younger. Runs with his own crowd."

"How about any of them?" he pressed. "Can you tell me who he runs around with?"

Nate frowned, but Matthew couldn't tell if it was in concentration or disapproval. "Mostly other young lawyers from PP&W. From what I hear, he didn't like being lost in a sea of other important people's kids when he went to school back East. Trey's all about being the big fish in the small pond."

"Ah."

"You're not thinking of asking Trey about your sister's whereabouts, are you?" Nate asked.

"He was the one who invited her to the party," Matthew countered. "We're hoping he can tell us where she went from there."

Nate raised his mug to his lips, blew on it, then lowered it again without taking a drink. Not meeting Matthew's gaze, he shook his head. "Listen, I understand she's your sister, and PP&W doesn't take on much criminal defense, but we don't want to get on their wrong side."

"The party was at their house."

"I understand. But Trey is the son of a man who runs a powerful firm belonging to a powerful and politically connected family. You have ambitions of your own, and I urge you to tread lightly."

"I'm not the one conducting the investigation. The state police have it."

Nate nodded. "Good. Let them do the poking and prodding."

He raised his mug in a farewell salute and turned to go back to his office. Matthew ground his molars as he made his way back to his own desk.

The thought of being told to hide behind Grace rankled, even though that had been his own instinct. But by the time he'd waved to his assistant and closed the door behind him, enough of his ire had abated for him to find humor in the vision of Special Agent Grace Reed repeatedly jabbing a bunch of Armani-clad attorneys with a single fingertip.

What Nate didn't get was the woman was more likely to employ a battering ram.

And Matthew wanted to be by her side when she used it to bust into the hallowed halls of Powers, Powers & Walton and demand to be told where his sister, Mallory, was hiding.

Chapter Seven

Grace's phone buzzed before she woke the next morning, which was never a good sign.

"Hello?" she answered, her voice husky with sleep.

"Agent Reed?" a man asked.

Grace recognized the voice instantly as her section chief, Ethan Scott. She sat up in bed. "Yes, good morning, Agent Scott," she replied, instantly more awake.

"I'm afraid it's not going to be a terribly good morning for you." He cleared his throat. "We fielded a call from some county guys this morning. A fisherman caught a body, and the general description fits one of your missing persons."

Grace closed her eyes again and braced herself. These calls were always awful, but they were particularly awful when they involved a child.

"Do they think it's Treveon Robinson?"

"No," Agent Scott answered succinctly. "I'm sorry, I should have been more specific. The call came from Carroll County. Table Rock Lake. The body fits the description of the young woman you are up there looking for...a Ms. Murray?"

Grace released a breath, but her heart rate kicked up. "Mallory Murray," she clarified.

"Yes. According to the guys on the scene, they think she's

been in the water for a while. The body is bloated but recognizable. You'll need to head out there to identify and investigate the scene, but the locals tell me they doubt the area where they found her is where she went into the lake. There are no houses or cabins anywhere around there."

Grace swallowed as she nodded. "I'll head out there now. I'll also take care of notifying next of kin," she informed him.

"Jim Thompson tells me you said Ms. Murray's brother is a prosecutor up there?"

"Yes, assistant prosecuting attorney for Benton County," she reported dutifully. "His name is Matthew Murray. He accompanied me to her place of employment to ask some questions yesterday afternoon."

"Did he?"

"I had hoped having somebody who grew up in the area would encourage the owner of the bar to be more forthcoming."

Agent Scott grunted in response. Grace was trying to determine if it was approval or disapproval when he spoke. "Good thinking," he said at last. "Some of the people up in those hills don't like to talk to strangers. Particularly strangers with badges." He sighed. "The coroner is on his way and will likely beat you out there. I'll send through the GPS coordinates the county guys passed on. Apparently, this fishing hole is accessible only by a gravel road."

Of course it is, she thought wryly. As a state dependent on its natural beauty to draw tourism, Arkansas wasn't keen to pave paradise.

To her boss, she said only, "Thank you."

"Okay. Well, I guess you have your marching orders for the day. Keep me posted," he instructed.

"Yes, sir," she replied.

Ending the call, Grace sat up even straighter and tried to get her bearings. Waking up in hotel rooms was always disconcerting. Waking up to bad news in a hotel room even more so.

A peek through the crack in the blinds told her the sun hadn't been up long. She wondered for a moment if she should ask Matthew Murray if he was willing to ride along to identify the body. He'd have to do it at some point, and taking him with her now would not only slice through some jurisdictional red tape, but also would save a lot of back-and-forth driving.

It might also help them gain precious time when it came to piecing together what could have happened to his sister.

She placed the phone back on the nightstand and swung her legs over the side of the bed. True to his word, her boss sent through the coordinates. She pulled up a map and squinted at her phone, wondering how far Mallory had to stray from the Powers house to end up in those particular backwoods.

She wouldn't have answers until she got going, so Grace sprang into action. Within fifteen minutes, she was showered and dressed in jeans and a T-shirt with the State Police logo on the front and *CID* across the back in block letters. After scraping her hair back into a low ponytail, she returned to the bed, where she sat down to put on her shoes. Like the ponytail, they were serviceable—scuffed black oxfords she wore more for comfort than style.

Once she was put together, she picked up her phone and cradled it in her hands, an internal war waging.

She knew nothing yet. It could have been an accident. Mallory could have gotten drunk and stumbled away from the party and into the lake. If there were enough guests, it was entirely possible no one noticed the waitress from the local burger joint wandering away.

A remote inlet with no houses nearby.

There were hundreds if not thousands of nooks and crannies in the lake's shoreline. Large parcels of undeveloped land. There would be wide swaths of area to search. There was nothing to say she'd been anywhere near the Powers family home when she ended up in the water. Heck, someone could have boosted the car, killed her and dumped her body in the lake.

Grace sighed and pulled up Matthew Murray's contact information, still not sure asking him to ride along was a good idea or not. There were too many scenarios, and she didn't have enough answers. But something told her she needed to give Matthew the option of seeing the scene.

She shook her head, refusing to overthink the day away. Her jaw set in agitation, she made the call. Matthew was a grown man. He could decide what was best for him.

Murray sounded far more awake than she expected when he answered with a brisk "Agent Reed?"

"Good morning," she greeted automatically. Then she closed her eyes on a wince. "Well, I'm sorry. It's not a good morning," she corrected herself.

"I take it you have some news on Mallory," he said flatly.

"A fisherman found a body in one of the inlets on Table Rock Lake. The county deputies on scene are fairly certain they have a match."

Matthew's sharp inhale of breath sounded tangled in his throat. And she felt her own constrict with sympathy.

"Where?"

"They found her in a pretty undeveloped area. No houses nearby." In answer to his unspoken question, she added, "I'm not sure exactly how far away it is from the Powers family lake house. All I have are GPS coordinates."

She heard another ragged rush of breath.

"I'm sorry," she added. "I haven't been out there to confirm as of yet. Right now, the county is handling things, but I'll need to canvass the scene and make an initial identification."

He didn't bother clearing the rasp from his throat. "I understand."

"I'm heading out there now. I can keep you informed as I—"

"I want to go with you," he interjected.

"I thought you might. Listen, you see a lot of things in your line of work—" she began.

"We both do," he interrupted again. "I'm aware of what to expect."

Or he thought he did. But he wouldn't be looking at photographs of a stranger. "If you come with me to identify, it would save us a step."

"Do you want me to meet you out there?"

Grace thought about it for a moment. It would be easier not to have the victim's brother in tow while she went over the scene, but the county guys probably knew best in this case. There likely wouldn't be much evidence to collect. Plus, the thought of asking him to drive those winding, hilly roads alone after receiving word that the last member of his family might be dead seemed cruel. He and his sister may not have been close, but she was all he had.

"I could pick you up if you'd like," she offered.

There was silence on the other end of the line. She assumed he was weighing the pros and cons as well.

At last, he said only, "I'll text you my address."

"On my way shortly."

Grace gathered the bag containing her evidence kit and her ASP windbreaker and headed for the door. She turned the radio off for the drive to Matthew Murray's place. She didn't have the patience for morning drive chatter.

To her surprise, Matthew didn't live in one of the thousands of new-construction condominiums littering the I-49 corridor, but rather in a bungalow on the south side of the old downtown Bentonville. She realized as she pulled up to the curb in front of the address that he was likely walking, or at least biking, distance from his office. Again, she suffered a bout of commute envy. She was about to text to let him know she was outside when the front door opened.

Matthew came out dressed in jeans and a University of Arkansas T-shirt. He wore hiking boots and carried a zippered hoodie in one hand. This was a man who was clearly accustomed to the terrain. Grace glanced down at her own shoes and hoped the sturdy soles would be up to the task.

Two aluminum travel cups were cradled in the crook of his arm. Matthew slid into the passenger seat, and the scent of freshly brewed coffee filled the air. Without asking, he offered her one of the cups. She gave him a wan smile. "I appreciate the thought, but I'm not a coffee drinker."

"Philistine," he said in a gruff whisper. "More for me."

"There's the upside," she said. Lifting her refillable water bottle from the cup holder, she took a swig. "I'm all about the hydration."

"Water is overrated." Matthew placed a travel mug in the other cup holder and took a deep swallow from the one he still held.

Grace slowed at a stop sign. Glancing over at him, she asked, "How are you holding up?"

"I'm trying not to dwell on it too much," he replied, turning to look out the passenger window. "Seems unreal."

"I understand."

And she did. Having lost her father at a young age, Grace understood what it was to mourn somebody even if you hadn't been particularly close. Thankfully, her relationship with her mother and her sister made up for the gap in her life. But Matthew wouldn't have anyone.

Hoping to keep her focus on the task at hand, she tapped the map displayed on the in-dash GPS. "Are you familiar at all with the area?"

"I'm familiar with most of it, but Table Rock has a lot of fingers. Tons of inlets and private roads."

"I'd like to get some information on where the Powers family's lake house is located. You have any sources who might be able to dig it up?" Matthew nodded, but she sensed hesitation in the movement. "Unless asking creates an uncomfortable situation for you."

He pulled a grimace. "My boss is pretty well acquainted with the family, but I don't want to ask him. He made it clear I should avoid poking the bear if I value my future."

Her eyebrows shot up. "Did he? He flat out told you not to talk to Trey Powers?"

Matthew chuckled. "We're attorneys. We don't flat out tell anyone anything." He drummed his fingers on his thigh. "But I got the message."

"I see."

"I could probably do some back-channel asking around, though," he said quietly. "Shouldn't be too hard to figure out. Property records are public."

"Yeah, but public records can be tricky. It might be held in a trust or something."

He nodded. "It gets complicated when a family has too much money." She glanced over at him. "I doubt it's held in only one person's name."

She frowned as she digested the information. "Right."

"Most have some kind of umbrella company with a name not obviously connected to them," he said distractedly. "Makes it easier to squeeze big chunks of property through the tax loopholes."

"No doubt."

"Any luck on the social media front?" he asked.

"I didn't get far in." She turned right onto the highway, as the navigation system directed. "I did go onto the law firm's website and took note of a few names of the younger associates. I figured they'd be more apt to post photos and other information on social media. There are headshots, too."

He nodded. "Good thinking."

"I haven't found much. A lot of people use only their first and middle names or nicknames as a way to keep employers from snooping around, but I did find a couple of people who posted pictures from a Christmas party the firm held last year. They tagged some of the other attorneys, but nothing pointed directly to this party at the lake."

"I'll see if my assistant, Tracy, can dig up some names of the paralegals or assistants over there," he told her, pulling his phone from his back pocket. "They may not be as paranoid as the attorneys themselves. It's not a big community. She may be able to poke around and possibly get some leads on people to talk to."

They rode in silence as he tapped out a couple of text messages.

Grace got the feeling he didn't want to talk much, which was a relief, because she was at a loss for what to say next. She reached for the car radio. "Music?"

"Please," he answered as he typed out another text.

After searching around a bit, she settled on a classic rock station but kept the volume low. They exchanged few words until the GPS directed them to turn off the two-lane road and onto a rutted lane of dirt and gravel.

The bumpy road jostled them around for a good minute.

"Sorry, I'm trying to go slow," she said, dividing a glance between him and the narrow lane. "This is pretty bad."

"Most of them are like this. Not enough money in the county to keep them up regularly. Plus, you get a lot of people on ATVs and dirt bikes out here tearing them up."

"Makes sense." She gave a soft "Oof" as they hit a particularly rough patch.

The road sloped sharply downhill. She checked the screen on the dash and determined they must be close to the shoreline, judging by the amount of blue water showing on the navigation. Sure enough, they came around another curve and spotted a handful of county vehicles clustered around an old two-tone pickup truck.

"This must be the place," he said grimly.

She pulled to a stop behind the van marked Coroner and turned to look at him. "You sure you're okay to do this here? I don't mind if you want to wait until they have her cleaned up a bit."

Matthew shook his head. "No. There's no sense in putting it off." He reached for the door handle. "I need to see for myself if it's her."

Grace nodded, killed the engine and reached for her jacket. Climbing out of the car, she said only, "Let's go."

The men gathered at the back of the coroner's van straightened as they approached.

"Deputy Carson?" Grace called out to the two uniformed men.

A tall, barrel-chested man with a stomach determined to test his shirt buttons stepped forward. "I'm Jeff Carson."

"Grace Reed, ASP CID," she said, extending her hand.

They shook, and he turned to the other men assembled. "This here is Deputy White," he said, indicating the other uniformed officer. "Mr. Nelson is the county coroner." He nodded to a man beside the other deputy, then he placed a hand on the shoulder an ashen-faced older man dressed in baggy cargo shorts and a well-worn T-shirt advertising a cigarette brand. "This is Willard Johnston. He's the one who found her."

Grace took each of their proffered hands in turn, then gestured to Matthew. "This is Matthew Murray. We believe the victim may be his sister. He's here to help us with identification," she said, directing the last to the coroner.

Nelson nodded. "We are fairly certain, judging from the photograph you have on file, but if you'll follow me."

She and Matthew trailed Nelson to the back of the van, where the double doors stood open. The other men did not follow. Grace could only assume they had seen enough for one day.

"I don't mind taking her in and, uh, making her more, uh, presentable," he said, casting a wary glance at Matthew.

"Mr. Murray is a prosecuting attorney for Benton County. He has seen bodies before."

Nelson hesitated, his hand on the zipper of the body bag. "All due respect, Mr. Murray, seeing a body pulled right out of the water and looking at a postmortem photo are totally different. It's rough, even when the victim is not kin."

"I understand," Matthew assured him, but his voice was hoarse. "It's okay."

The coroner nodded his understanding. "All right, then."

Nelson pulled his phone from his pocket, opened a voice-recording app and unzipped the bag about eighteen inches. He spoke the date, time and their approximate location into the phone, then parted the fabric.

"Mr. Murray, can you identify the body of this young woman?"

Matthew swallowed hard as he stared down at the water-bloated face, and empathy welled up inside Grace. No matter how often she had to witness the worst moments in a person's life, she'd never grown inured to them. She hoped she never would.

Grace put a steadying hand on his arm when he simply nodded. "We'll need you to give a verbal answer, if you can," she prompted gently.

"Yes," he croaked. "Yes, this is my sister." The last word caught on a sob.

"Her name?" she whispered, giving his arm a reassuring squeeze.

"Mallory," he managed to say in a strangled voice. "Mallory Murray."

With a heaving gasp, Matthew tore himself from her grasp and emptied the contents of his stomach into the trampled grass.

Chapter Eight

Grace climbed into the SUV and found Matthew grim-faced and firing off message after message on his phone. It chimed incessantly. His thumbs flew as she stowed her bag and slid into the driver's seat. Matthew didn't look up from the screen.

He didn't ask any questions—which she found particularly odd, considering his occupation and the personal connection—but she figured maybe he was embarrassed to have lost his coffee in the weeds. Three more messages had arrived before she hit the ignition. He answered them in quick succession.

Unnerved by the brittle air of hyperconcentration emanating from him, she felt compelled to break the silence.

"Nelson's first impression isn't drowning."

His head snapped back as if she'd punched him. She met his gaze directly, confident she now had his full attention. The phone in his lap dinged and dinged, but Matthew didn't look away.

"Based on what?" he asked.

It was a nonsensical question coming from a prosecutor, but Grace was glad she'd jolted him back into brother mode with the direct approach. She spoke quietly but with conviction.

"She sustained a blow to the head."

"Could have happened after she was in the water. Maybe she hit a submerged log and it knocked her unconscious."

The coroner had given her the usual spiel about not being certain until they were able to autopsy the body, but they were both professionals and had seen enough to draw some fairly strong initial conclusions.

"You're right. We have to wait for the postmortem," she conceded.

"But you think she was struck prior to going in the water."

"Pure conjecture," she admitted. The image of a positive pregnancy test flashed in her mind's eye.

They hadn't found anything in the pockets of the shorts Mallory had been wearing, but she might have left the other test in her car... Had she mentioned the pregnancy to Matthew? Should Grace say something now?

She decided to wait awhile longer. If their preliminary conclusions played out, an unwanted pregnancy could be a strong reason to give Trey Powers a good, long look. Assuming he was indeed the father.

Right now, all they had was a lot of supposition and not much evidence.

"The county deputies can't determine whether any of the items they've recovered from the scene might be evidence or if they're nothing more than trash washed up on the shore, but they bagged whatever they could find."

Grace instantly regretted the words she'd just spoken. This man's sister had washed up on the same shoreline, like someone's discarded goods. She wasn't working at her highest level at the moment. Determined to put things right, she cranked the wheel and began to make the tight back-and-forth turns to get them on the path headed out.

Matthew turned his head toward the lakeshore. "It could have happened anywhere out there."

"You're right. And I am sorry for your loss," Grace said quietly. "You two weren't close, but it doesn't make it any easier."

"Thank you," he answered gravely. He grunted as one wheel dropped into a hole in the sad excuse for a road. "While I was waiting, I was thinking...maybe we could swing back by Stubby's."

"Stubby's? Sure, but why?" she asked as she cranked the wheel and pointed the nose of the SUV in the direction of the highway.

"I was thinking we could show Steve some of the photos of the associates on the PP&W website. He might recognize some of them if they were with Trey Friday night."

A startled laugh popped out of her, and Grace turned to look at him instantly sheepish. "Sorry. I can't believe I didn't think of asking him myself."

"It may not give us anything, but I have to feel like I'm doing something."

"I understand." With cautious efficiency, she wove her way between the ruts and potholes, moving as quickly as she could without jarring them too much. "If what you say about PP&W is true, it may be easier to get to some of the other people who work there than Trey Powers himself."

"Exactly."

They bumped along in silence for a minute. "I made a few calls and, with Nelson's agreement, arranged for the coroner to transfer your sister to the Benton County coroner's facilities. They have a decent forensics lab there, and I figured you would prefer to have the initial postmortem handled locally. They will have to work with the state crime lab, though."

"Thank you, I appreciate the thought," he said with a slow nod. "Sorry again for..." He hooked a thumb over his shoulder but let the words trail away.

"No need to be sorry. I've seen twenty-year veterans lose

their lunch on scenes. It may or may not have happened to me as well," she added with a wry smile.

He looked over at her. "You can neither confirm nor deny?"

"Precisely."

"I understand."

When they finally hit the opening onto the paved county road, she slowed to a stop to be sure there was no oncoming traffic. No one. This was a weekday, and the county guys hadn't been wrong about the lack of development. The only reason Mr. Johnston had gone down there to fish was that it had been the spot where his own father had taken him as a boy.

She and Mathew exchanged a glance. In silent accord, she turned left, away from town and in the direction of Stubby's Bar and Grill.

"Any luck with your assistant?" she asked, nodding to the phone in his hands.

"No, not much," he said grimly. "Mostly, I've been going back and forth with Nate, lining out the cases I'm working on. Someone can step in for the next few days while I handle whatever arrangements need to be handled."

"Nate is the prosecuting attorney?"

Matthew nodded. "He's a nice guy. Mostly. Ambitious." He turned the word over in his head. "I guess it figures. He did his undergraduate at the U of A but went to Yale Law, so he has a foot in both worlds."

"I see."

"Anyway, we were trying to sort out what loose ends I might have."

"It'll be a few days until they can release her body."

He nodded. "Yeah, but I figure I'll need to get whatever she had at the apartment cleared out, get a handle on the state of her bills, bank accounts and other stuff."

Grace nodded, thinking of how sad it was that the remains of someone's life could be boiled down to the word *stuff*. She did not allow herself to give in to the pang of guilt when he mentioned going to the apartment in Eureka Springs. She wouldn't ask Mallory's roommate to keep the pregnancy test a secret, but she still wasn't sure she would tell Matthew about it. Yet.

She needed to put a few more puzzle pieces together first.

"OH, YEAH, SHE was definitely one," Steve said, jabbing a blunt finger at the screen of Grace's phone. "Looked even younger in person. I carded her."

"Did you?" Grace asked, mildly surprised to discover anyone was ever carded at Stubby's.

He squinted at the screen, nodding more emphatically. "She's wearin' makeup and a stuffy suit here, so she looks older, but the other day she was all freckled and had her hair in two braids like my nieces used to wear. Looked about twelve."

"You're certain Taylor Greene was in here the day Mallory took off to go to the party at the Powerses' place?" Matthew reiterated.

Steve shrugged. "If that's her name, yeah."

Grace waited as Matthew tapped out a note on his phone. A ballgame was showing on one of the bar's televisions, but the barfly who'd been there the previous day sat perched on the same stool watching what appeared to be a soap opera.

Dragging her attention away from the couple in a heated argument on the screen, she redoubled her efforts on getting information out of Steve. "And you think you possibly remember Joshua Potter," she pushed, thumbing through the headshots they'd swiped from the website until she landed on one of a man with a receding hairline and tortoiseshell glasses.

"Not as sure about him, but I remember a guy with glasses." Steve took a step back from the bar, twisting the towel he'd balled in one hand into a long rope. "Not as bad as the other guy. Obnoxious jerk. He actually snapped his fingers at me. Who does that in real life?" he asked, incredulous.

"Obnoxious jerks," Matthew murmured as he typed a note into his own phone.

"Exactly," Steve said, pointing at Matthew. "You think maybe Mal has taken off with one of these two? Or is it some kind of love-triangle thing?" Steve settled a hip against the cooler below the bar and crossed his short arms over his broad chest. "Gotta be honest, I never pegged Mallory for the type to get in the middle of something. The girl pretty much wanted what she wanted, and she wanted it all to herself, if you get what I'm saying."

Matthew looked up, clearly startled by the man's astute observation.

Grace stepped in. She didn't want either of them wandering too far down the path of extolling Mallory's myriad shortcomings. The woman may not have been anyone's idea of dependable, or even maybe trustworthy, while she was among them, but she didn't deserve to be dragged through the mud in death.

"No, we're no longer looking for Ms. Murray," she interjected smoothly.

Steve shook his head in confusion. He glanced at Matthew before letting his questioning gaze land on her again. "Not looking for her? What's this all about, then?"

"We're simply trying to determine who all may have been attending the party at the Powers house Friday night," she replied evenly.

"Yesterday you were in here asking questions about Mallory because you couldn't find her." He directed this at Matthew. "Now you tell me you're not looking for her anymore, but you still wanna come in here asking questions?"

The day drinker let out a derisive snort. "Some people need to mind their own damn business," he grumbled to no one in particular.

"It *is* my business," Matthew snapped. "She was my sister."

An uneasy silence filled the barroom as his use of the past tense in regard to Mallory settled over them like a shroud.

"Was?" Steve repeated blankly. He looked truly stricken, all the tough words he'd had for Mallory forgotten as the color drained from his florid face. "Mal's not… She's okay, isn't she? I mean, you're not looking for her anymore… You found her?"

Grace exhaled in a soft whoosh as Matthew dropped his gaze to the sticky floor. She spoke directly to Steve, low and confidential. "I'm afraid Ms. Murray's body was found this morning."

"Found?"

"A fisherman found her body," she said, keeping the details as sparse as she could while still conveying the gravity of the situation.

"A fisherman? Who? Where?"

"Table Rock," Matthew answered, dropping the words like wet sandbags between them with a thud.

Steve was quick on the uptake. His narrowing gaze flew to Matthew, then back to the phone in her hand. "And you're here askin' about all those lawyers because…" He snapped his jaw shut. "Holy Moses—"

He scraped a hand over his face, pulling on his jowls as he spun away from them. She could see his reflection in the mirror behind the bottles lining the back bar. He looked horrified.

And scared.

She saw his mouth move, but his voice was barely more than a whisper. "You think the Powers kid was involved."

"We have no evidence of foul play," Grace stated, enunciating each word with great care.

"No," Steve said as he turned back to her. "But you think he is."

"Since he was hosting the party, we are certainly interested in speaking with Mr. Powers. I would be interested in speaking to anybody who came in contact with Mallory after she left here last Friday evening. As I said, we have nothing concrete. We believe Ms. Murray perished between Friday evening, when she left here at about…" She trailed off, raising her eyebrows in a prompt.

Steve shrugged. "Around six thirty or seven, maybe? The dinner crowd had cleared out for the most part, but the lake people and the evening drinkers were starting to come in."

Grace nodded. "Right. Between seven o'clock Friday evening and five o'clock this morning, something happened to Mallory Murray. It's my job to piece together what those events may have been."

Steve shook his head. "I can't tell you anything more."

"And we appreciate your input," Grace said smoothly. "We wouldn't be bothering you again, except it occurred to us you might be able to help us identify who some of the other people in Mr. Powers's party might have been."

"I can't swear to any of it," Steve hastened to add. "Well… maybe the girl, but I didn't pay much attention to the group of them. I see a lot of people in a day. People from all walks of life. Unless you're a local, I don't pay much mind. No point in getting too into it with people who are breezing through, right?"

"Absolutely. No point in getting too involved."

Steve shifted his attention to Matthew, who'd switched off his phone and dropped it into his pocket. "I'm awful sorry about Mallory," the bartender said. "I was kind of a jerk about her yesterday, but I did like the girl. She was one of the best I'd ever had working here. God's honest truth."

"I appreciate you saying so," Matthew replied, offering Steve his hand to shake. "And trust me, I am well aware how frustrating Mallory could be. I don't blame you for getting teed off at her. She gets under my skin pretty regularly." He paused. "Got. She got under my skin pretty regularly," he repeated, his expression grim as he switched tenses.

Steve wrung the bar towel again. "I am sorry."

Grace pulled another of her business cards from her pocket and slid it across the bar as she had on her first visit. "If you think of anything else. Anything at all. Even if you think it isn't important, please feel free to call me. All my numbers are on the card."

Steve picked up her card and slid it into the back pocket of his jeans rather than tossing it under the bar. "I will. I promise."

Matthew nodded. "Appreciate your help."

They turned to go. As they reached the door, Steve called out to them again. "Will you keep me posted? About any arrangements?"

Matthew looked back at the other man, clearly startled by the request. "Arrangements?"

Steve gave them helpless shrug. "I'd send flowers or something."

Matthew bowed his head, but when he lifted it he said, "I appreciate the thought. Not sure what I'm going to do, but save the flower money. If you want do something, make a donation to a worthy cause. Anything you think Mallory would like," he suggested. "After all, you probably knew her better than I did."

Steve nodded and gave a mirthless chuckle. "I knew her

well enough to tell you there wasn't a cause she thought was more worthy than her own."

Matthew smiled at the comment, touching the end of his nose to indicate the accuracy of the other man's statement. "You hit the nail on the head there. Throw a party here for her one night. She'd have liked a party."

"Will do," Steve assured him. "I'll call if I think of anything else."

"Appreciate you." Grace raised a hand in farewell.

They stepped out of the dimly lit bar into the bright summer morning.

"I hope you don't mind that I told him," Grace said quickly. "I figured he was her employer and would have to be told eventually, and this way at least we could use the shock value to garner what information we could."

"No." He gave her a tired smile. "I don't mind."

He paused at the passenger door and looked back at the cinder-block building. "Well played, Agent Reed. What's our next move?"

She gave it a moment of thought. "Well, I think our next move is to head back to town. I'll need to call Kelli Simon and let her know Mallory has been found. You'll need to wait for the coroner's report to be complete before you can make arrangements, and I need figure out how to get in to see Trey Powers and friends."

"Easier said than done."

"Don't you worry, I have my ways," Grace answered with a confidence she didn't feel. But she'd make things happen; she always did. Clicking the key fob to unlock the doors, she said, "Saddle up, Counselor. I think this ride's about to get a whole lot more interesting."

Chapter Nine

Tom Petty hadn't lied when he said the waiting was the hardest part, but Matthew wasn't simply sitting around waiting for his phone to ring. Not when he knew deep in his gut a privileged coward like Trey Powers was involved in his sister's death. He didn't care if Powers's involvement was accidental or deliberate. At this point, intent didn't matter. If Trey had any inkling of Mallory falling into the water, he was at least an accessory after the fact.

Sitting in his sparsely furnished living room, he scrolled through Mallory's PicturSpam account. Again. But his sister hadn't posted any photos last Friday night. Nor were there any of her with Trey. The closest he'd come was a selfie she'd taken with another woman about her age. Her companion was a toothy blonde. They both had eyelashes too dark and thick to be natural and held tall hurricane glasses filled with a liquid so virulently green Matthew couldn't believe anyone would willingly ingest it.

He'd looked at the same picture at least a half dozen times in the days since Agent Reed told him Mallory had disappeared, and he hadn't noticed anything out of the ordinary. But now, after two trips to Stubby's and one truncated phone call with the cocksure princeling, he finally figured out why he kept coming back to it again and again.

A watch.

In the photo, a man's arm lay draped casually across his sister's shoulders. A man who apparently had breathtakingly expensive taste in wristwatches.

The oversize face of the watch was visible thanks to the casual drape of his arm. He'd had a roommate in law school who was obsessed with collecting watches, so Matthew knew they were as much of a status symbol for some men as diamonds or designer handbags were for some women. Matthew recognized the hallmark of a prestigious brand below the diamond at the top of the bright blue dial.

A few quick queries helped him pin it down. Whoever was staking his claim on Mallory had been wearing a Poseidon. Another search revealed the watch hadn't been available for sale at any jeweler in Arkansas. It was an exclusive model, and the nearest retailers with access were in Dallas, Kansas City or Baton Rouge.

There was a lot of money in the northwest corridor of Arkansas, but not many young people with the kind of money they could blow on spendy jewelry.

Most didn't bother. The area was rife with avid hikers or sportsmen. They'd go for a model with some sort of GPS rather than throw down for a blue sunburst face and a bunch of analog dials.

Matthew glanced at his own smart watch. He'd been leery of dropping a few hundred dollars on the latest model when it became available, but looking at the price tags attached to the man bling on the website, he felt far more secure in his frugal life choices.

"Pays to be oblivious," he muttered, tapping an icon on the display of the decidedly less prestigious watch he wore. "Call Grace Reed on mobile."

The automated assistant put the call through.

"Can't sleep?" Grace asked by way of greeting.

"I'm sorry," he grimaced, noticing the hour. It was after midnight. "Were you sleeping?"

"Nah. I'm a night owl," she assured him.

Since she sounded fully awake and alert, he took her at her word. "Hey, I came across something. Could be nothing, I'm not sure…"

"Hit me," she prompted.

"Can you pull up Mal's PicturSpam feed? I want you to look closer at one of the pictures."

He heard her tapping. "Okay. Which one am I looking for?"

"Fourth or fifth picture down, there's one of Mallory and another girl holding some nasty-looking green cocktails. See it?"

"Yup. Wouldn't drink one on a bet, though."

"Me, either." Matthew smiled, enjoying the moment of synchronicity in what was an otherwise surreal day. "A guy has his arm around Mal's shoulders. Can you zoom in on his watch?"

"His watch?" she repeated, not bothering to mask her puzzlement.

"Yeah."

A beat passed, and then she said, "Nice watch. Silver with a blue face, lots of dials."

"Do you see the brand symbol?"

"No," she said, drawing the words out. "Not really. Is it some kind of upside-down *T* or something?"

"An anchor."

"Oh. Yeah, okay, I see it now." She paused. "What about it?"

He tried to formulate how he might explain. "Okay, this is going to sound weird…probably because it *is* weird to many mere mortals, but some guys have a thing for watches."

"You didn't call me at midnight to confess some weird watch fetish, did you?"

"Not at all," he hastened to assure her. "But anyway, the guy I roomed with while I was in law school? He was one of those guys. Used to get jazzed about them. Like, he has a whole plan for which watches he would collect on his way to attaining his dream watch."

"O-kay," she drawled, clearly perplexed. "Are you trying to tell me you think your old roommate is in this picture?"

"No. He's in Los Angeles working his way up to a junior partnership at a firm specializing in entertainment law."

"And he wants this watch…"

"It's a Poseidon."

"And that's…good?"

"Well, I'm not sure where it ranks on my friend's sliding scale now, but this watch would come in at about one or two steps higher than his dream watch."

"Seriously?"

She sounded incredulous, and Matthew couldn't blame her. He felt pretty much the same.

"Yeah. Mike had his sights set on a stainless steel model, but judging by the dials and what I see on the website, I think this one might be white gold."

He sent her the link to the brand site. "Look under the Elite collection."

A minute later, Grace gave a low whistle. "Holy cow."

"No doubt," he said gravely.

"And you can get matching cuff links, if you feel like you need something extra after spending on a watch what most people would spend on a house," she said, her voice rising with her agitation.

"Rich people," he said in a flat, derisive voice.

GRACE LAUGHED. The sheer ridiculousness of spending tens of thousands of dollars on something that didn't provide food, shelter or any other basic necessity demanded she laugh.

Matthew laughed, too, and she instantly felt better. The man had seen his only family member zipped into a body bag hours ago, but he still could find humor in life's absurdities. She supposed it was something cops and prosecutors had in common.

As their chuckles quieted, she sighed. "Of course, I don't have to tell you this isn't evidence of any connection between your sister and Trey Powers."

"No, you don't," he said, resigned.

The silence hummed between them, but it felt oddly comfortable to Grace. A full minute must have passed before he spoke again.

"What do you do when you can't sleep?"

The chuckle that escaped her was mirthless. "Work."

"I can't concentrate," he confessed.

"Totally understandable. You've suffered a loss. You're grieving. It's not your job to concentrate right now—it's mine."

"I can't sit around waiting for something to happen."

While Grace understood the sentiment entirely, she needed to put him gently but firmly in his place. "I totally get you, but now your focus needs to be on Mallory. My focus will be on making sure anyone who may have been involved in her death is brought to justice."

"I thought we played on the same side." His reminder came out stiff and somewhat belligerent.

Grace could see how such stubbornness would serve him well as a prosecutor. "We are on the same side, but you're not the prosecutor, you're the brother." She waited a beat to let her admonishment sink in. But Matthew's response was not the escalation of agitation she anticipated.

"What if I can't be the brother she needs?" he asked at last. "I haven't been a good one up to this point, and it looks like I won't have any more chances."

"But you do," she reminded him, her voice gentle. "Mallory still needs you. Now more than ever. It might not be in the way either of you would have chosen, but the fact of the matter is you're all she has."

"And you," he said gruffly.

"Absolutely."

A pang of guilt twisted in her gut. She remembered the day she took the call from Mallory's roommate and how annoyed she'd been to be distracted from the case she'd deemed more worthy than the disappearance of a flighty party girl.

Grace knew all too well the chances of finding Treveon alive grew slimmer by the day, but whether her victims needed her in life or in death didn't matter. Like Treveon, Mallory would be counting on her to unravel the story.

"Usually when I can't sleep, I like to spend hours dwelling on the cases where I failed a victim and what I would have done differently," she confessed.

"And it helps you sleep?" he sounded incredulous.

"No. Never. But it fuels me. I am the one these people are counting on. It's what gives me the push I need to try harder, do better, be faster." She stopped there and swallowed hard. "I'm sorry I didn't get there fast enough for Mallory."

"You got there as fast as you could," he said gently. "You did. I have a gut feeling you're not going to allow Mallory's death to linger on your list of regrets."

"You and your gut don't know me at all, Counselor," she said, her voice husky with emotion.

"I've seen enough over the past couple of days," he reassured her. "I'm confident this will not be a case you'll lay awake replaying in your mind."

"I'm supposed to be comforting you," she reminded him.

Matthew chuckled. "Oddly enough, I do feel better."

"You start working on the things you need to do for Mallory. I'll call or text you as soon as I have any information from the coroner."

"And if it comes out it's more than an accident, you'll keep me up-to-date on any further investigation into any, uh, suspects?" he pushed.

"I don't believe this is going to fall under your jurisdiction," she reminded him.

"Please," he added. "The only way I can help her now is by helping you. Let me do whatever I can do."

Grace let silence stretch between them for a minute. "I'll be in touch, Mr. Murray. Try to get some sleep."

"You, too, Agent Reed. And thank you."

GRACE DID GET some sleep, but not a lot. After she ended the call with Matthew, she'd spent precious hours thinking about the stupid wristwatch he'd been worked up over. She couldn't imagine a world in which people paid insane money for a watch, but as Matthew pointed out, even among the wealthy there weren't many who could. Folks she would have considered well-off weren't in the same league as someone who could spend that kind of money on a piece of jewelry simply because they wanted it.

A morning spent researching the Powers family confirmed they had indeed reached an unfathomable level of wealthy. The original Tyrone Powers started accumulating the family fortune while working in the lumber industry. He was a logger in his teens, but he plowed every bit of his earnings into buying up land long before the area drew the attention of either conservationists or the US Department of the Interior.

According to an article she found, he'd decided to study the law in order to save on paying attorney's fees when negotiating contracts or fighting the growing conservation movement.

Her jaw dropped as she uncovered old Tyrone's involvement in one mind-bogglingly lucrative venture after another. He invested in Oklahoma oil wells, Texas cattle ranching, an investment firm based in Little Rock, and ended up being the personal attorney for a childhood pal who had a hankering to expand his local five-and-dime into a nationwide discount chain.

But, unlike his humble friend, Powers had no qualms about trampling anyone who got in the way of his ambitions.

Still stewing on all she'd read, and fueled with a healthy dose of righteous indignation, Grace prepared for her foray into the PP&W offices with steely-eyed determination.

Tyrone had made certain his sons had become attorneys as well, and he'd established Powers, Powers & Walton with his famous client's favorite cousin's kid.

His sons went on to help him amass even more power and prestige. He invested heavily in land development all along what would later become the industrial corridor of northwest Arkansas. After encountering a stubborn homesteader who refused to sell his acreage, Tyrone went through various legal and political back channels to essentially swindle the poor fellow out of the land.

A fact that made her even more keyed up to go toe to toe with them. Or rather, cop to lawyer.

Smoothing her hair flat against her scalp, she coiled the ends into a no-nonsense bun at her nape and thought about how Trey Powers's grandfather had funded the campaigns of local politicians and eventually gotten his son William elected to state office and later the Senate.

She stepped into the pants that went with the suit her sister referred to as her "extra-basic cop suit" and pulled a plain white blouse with a button-down collar from its hanger. Her sister despaired of this look, but Faith had no idea how basic

Grace was willing to be in order to convey the right message. Silks and high-heeled boots were for TV detectives.

The people at PP&W needed to understand she was the real deal.

Grace weighed her options as she surveyed her bag. She'd had the pants altered to make the belt loops large enough to accommodate an equipment belt if needed, but today it would be overkill. The boxy jacket hung loose enough to conceal the holster she wore at the small of her back when walking into a possibly tense situation, but if the meeting was seated, wearing a back holster would not only be extremely uncomfortable, but it would also make accessing her sidearm awkward.

The chances of needing her weapon in a roomful of attorneys were slim, but still, she wanted it on her body. Like the leather case holding her badge and credentials, it was part of the package. A person couldn't convincingly pull off full-on cop intimidation without carrying a sidearm.

So she opted for her ankle holster.

With the straps secured to her calf, she gave her socks one last tug. After the previous day's walk through the muck, she'd rinsed off her lug-soled oxfords and shined them up with one of the hotel washcloths. Glancing down at the scuffed toes, she gave a mental shrug. She'd done the best she could.

She reexamined her tote to be sure her cuffs, zip ties, notepad and tablet were in place, then pulled it from the seat of the sofa. Satisfied she had everything she needed, she checked her weapon, bent to insert it into the holster and secured it.

"Ready or not, here I come," she murmured as she walked out the hotel room door.

THE LARGE RECEPTION desk at Powers, Powers & Walton had the sort of sleek midcentury-modern design that looked both quintessential and cutting-edge. A young woman wearing a headset sat in the center of the command module answering phones and passing along messages with well-modulated, studiedly unruffled efficiency.

Grace waited until she finished putting a call through. She walked to the desk with her wallet open, flashing her badge and credentials. "Special Agent Grace Reed of the Arkansas State Police Criminal Investigation Division," she announced. "I'm here to see Trey Powers."

To her credit, the young woman didn't look at all fazed by either Grace's presence or pronouncement. Instead, she simply smiled and said, "One moment, please," in the same tone she used with the callers she dispatched with such alacrity.

She pressed a single fingertip to the earpiece of her headset. "Mrs. Branson? Special Agent Reed is here to see Mr. Powers." There was a pause, then the receptionist nodded. "Yes, ma'am. Right away."

Rising as smoothly as she spoke, she smiled at Grace. "If you'll follow me, Special Agent."

Grace pocketed her credentials and followed the young woman past a glass half wall separating the reception area from an open-plan office space. She eyeballed the series of doors that blocked off private offices at the other end of the space, assuming they'd head that way. Instead, the receptionist drew to a stop beside a set of oversize double doors.

"If you'll wait in here, please, Special Agent Reed," she said with a sweet smile. "Can I offer you coffee or tea?"

Grace spied a backlit mini fridge built into the coffee bar setup in the conference room, and a pitcher of water and an arrangement of glasses sat on the table. "No, thank you. Water is fine for me."

"Please help yourself."

The young woman disappeared, closing the door after her with a click. Grace gave a soft snort and strolled over to the large oval table dominating the room. A self-deprecating smile tugged at her lips. "So much for fear and intimidation."

She was about to pour a glass of water when the conference room door opened again.

"Special Agent Reed?" a man in his midfifties asked as he strode through the door. He was followed by another man who appeared to be ten years younger, six inches shorter and markedly rounder.

"I'm Harold Dennis, personal counsel to the Powers family," the older man announced. "This is my associate, Michelle Fraser."

Grace glanced back at the door as a woman closed it behind them. "Will Mr. Powers be joining us?"

Mr. Dennis shook his head. "I'm afraid Mr. Powers is in court this morning. His assistant asked we take the meeting with you. How can we be of help?"

He gestured for her to take a seat in one of the tall leather chairs. Grace set her bag down on the table with a heavy thud. "Were either of you in attendance at the crawfish boil Mr. Powers hosted last Friday evening?"

Ms. Fraser shook her head and glanced over at Mr. Dennis, as though he wondered if he'd missed an invitation. He, too, wagged his head, then answered. "No, ma'am."

"I'm not sure how you plan to be of help to me, then." Grace picked up her bag and hoisted it onto her shoulder again. "Can you tell me when I might be able to speak to Mr. Powers in person?"

"I don't handle his scheduling," Mr. Dennis replied, lifting a mocking brow.

"Fine," Grace said briskly. "If you'll point me in the direction of his assistant, I will make an appointment."

"Special Agent Reed, if you have questions for Mr. Powers, I'd be happy to convey them to him," Mr. Dennis offered.

"I'd prefer not to use an intermediary," she replied evenly.

"Perhaps if you were to submit the questions you have for Mr. Powers to me in writing," the older man continued, "we could clarify the timeline of Friday evening's festivities and hopefully fill in any blanks."

Grace offered him a cool smile. "I'll wait to speak to Mr. Powers in person."

"Your prerogative." Dennis inclined his head in a gesture she assumed was supposed to convey deference but somehow felt condescending.

"Ms. Fraser will introduce you to Serena, Mr. Powers's assistant, to coordinate a meeting when we are all available."

"Does Mr. Powers have reason to worry about speaking with police without counsel present?"

The older man shrugged and gave what was meant to appear as a helpless smile. "I don't have the vaguest idea what Mr. Powers worries about."

Tiring of the cat-and-mouse game, Grace nodded and turned to the other attorney. "If you would make the introduction, I would appreciate it."

Fifteen minutes later, she breezed past the sleek reception desk and out the doors, her temper simmering. Matthew had been right. It wasn't going to be easy to get near Trey Powers. But if the guard dogs at PP&W thought she would be put off by the runaround, they were sadly mistaken.

Chapter Ten

Grace Reed knew how to make an entrance, that was for sure. The minute she walked into the prosecuting attorney's offices, the air felt charged. The low murmur of voices paused for a few noticeable ticks of the clock. For the first time since he'd opened the folder containing a motion he intended to file in one of his cases, Matthew's concentration broke.

He had only planned to come into the office for a few hours to line things out for Nate, but it was already past noon and he was still up to his elbows in work. Without conscious thought, he rose from his chair as she approached his open door. Her expression might have looked neutral to anyone who hadn't spent the past two days studying her, but he knew at a glance whatever she had to tell him wasn't good.

Wordlessly, he gestured to the guest chair across from his desk once she closed the door. "What have you heard?" he asked, suddenly grateful for his own chair as his knees grew wobbly.

"I had a call from the Benton County coroner. The initial indication of blunt-force trauma was correct. Mallory struck or was struck by something."

"Before or after?"

"Hard to tell the exact timing, because she did aspirate

water, but the angle, size and shape of the injury don't line up with hitting her head on a log or something submerged in the water."

He fidgeted with the pen he'd left beside a pad of legal paper. "And the angle, size and shape were?"

"It appears to be something wide and flat. The injury was to the side of her skull, behind and above her ear." She gestured to the general vicinity on her own head. "Not generally consistent with someone hitting their head after they've fallen into a body of water."

"Someone hit her with something," he concluded.

She raised her hands in a staying motion. "It's early days."

He slumped into his chair. "When will they release her?"

"He said probably the end of next week."

Matthew nodded, his mind instantly shifting to funeral arrangements, because it was far preferable to thinking about his sister's murder.

"Have you been to her apartment yet?"

Grace's question jarred him from his thoughts. "What?"

"Have you gone to Eureka Springs to start sorting out Mallory's belongings?" she repeated, her diction careful.

He shook his head, gestured to his laptop and the pad filled with notes beside him. "No, I was going to call her roommate when I finished this and make sure it was okay to head over there, but I got…drawn in."

Grace pursed her lips. He knew that look well. Had worked with the police for too long. He wasn't getting the whole story.

"What? What am I missing?" he demanded.

She uncrossed her legs and sat forward in the chair, her elbows braced on her knees. "I want to be sure I'm clear. You have not been to the apartment Mallory shared with Kelli Simon, correct?"

He raised an eyebrow. The woman would have made a

fine prosecutor if she'd been inclined. "I have not," he stated, matching her concise delivery.

"Someone has," she said grimly as she pushed back in the chair again. "Ms. Simon called me when I was on my way here. She says she came home for lunch and discovered someone had been in her apartment."

"Burglary?"

She shook her head. "No electronics or items of value taken."

He frowned. "What makes her think someone was there?"

"The place had been tossed."

"Tossed?"

"Someone went through the apartment looking for something."

He blinked. "Looking for what?"

The thin line of her mouth told him the detective had her guesses but was reluctant to share them with him outright. He tried a different tactic.

"Okay, so far this morning you've been told my sister likely died by being struck in the head with something…" He broke off, waiting patiently for her to supply at least a tidbit of information.

"Something smooth and flat," she said at last.

Matthew swallowed the unexpected rush of emotion that rose when he tried to envision Mallory being struck. He drew a deep breath, then blew it out on a huff.

"Flat and smooth," he repeated. "I'm going to assume before her body went into the water."

"You can make that assumption, but we have no way of being certain."

"And you are also telling me her apartment has been… ransacked?"

"Correct."

"But what you aren't saying is you have your suspicions

about what they might be looking for, and you don't want to share them."

Grace startled. "It's more I'm debating how best to use the information."

"Against me?" he asked, incredulous.

"No. Against the person I suspect did this to her." He was still forming his next question when she raised a hand to stall him. "And no, I have no proof. No way of knowing my suspect had anything to do with an assault that may or may not have taken place, and no grounds to point any fingers."

Their gazes met and held, both of them all too acutely aware of the impotence of the moment.

"To make matters even more frustrating, I went to the PP&W office this morning."

His jaw dropped, but he quickly reeled in his surprise. "You did?"

She nodded. "Figured I'd storm the castle."

"How did it go?" he asked.

"I'll give you a guess for free," she said dismissively.

"He wasn't in."

Grace touched the end of her nose, pointed to him. "I did get to meet with a man named Harold Dennis, who is apparently the legal counsel to the Powers family, and another attorney named Fraser."

"Not surprising." He resisted the urge to remind her he'd told her so, but only because he knew she could hear the subtext.

"I suppose not, but it was worth a try."

"No way they were going to let that happen."

She opened her hands. "All I wanted was a simple sit-down with a man who by all accounts was with her the evening of her disappearance."

"There's no such thing as a 'simple sit-down,' and you

couldn't have been shocked to meet with his attorneys," Matthew insisted, not fooled for a minute.

The corner of her mouth twitched. "Okay, maybe I wasn't, but I was hoping I'd at least get him in the room with them."

"You'll have to come at him with something more than a desire for an informal chat."

"Right, but a girl can hope"

He frowned as he considered the possible reasons for the nonmeeting. "Fraser? I don't remember seeing anyone with that name among the associates. Fraser what?"

She shook her head. "Michelle Fraser."

Realization sent him back in his chair. "Whoa," he said quietly. "They must be worried."

Grace startled. "What makes you say so?"

"Michelle Fraser is the only attorney on the PP&W staff who specializes in criminal defense." He gave his head a bewildered shake. "You say her name three times out there," he said, pointing to the office beyond his door, "and people run for the holy water."

Grace nodded as the information sank in. "Interesting."

"Isn't it?" He eyed her narrowly. "I wonder what has them scared enough to bring her in this early in the game."

She hesitated only a moment. Then, leaning forward, she admitted, "I've been holding back on something I was thinking might get some traction with him."

"What's that?" he asked, perturbed to discover she hadn't been forthcoming with him, even though he knew it was standard for police to hold some evidence close until they knew it was most useful. "What do you have?"

"Your sister might have been pregnant."

The air whooshed from him. He had to blink until she came fully back into focus again. "What?"

"Mallory may have believed herself to be pregnant. I'm waiting for confirmation from the coroner's office, but Ms.

Simon found a positive at-home pregnancy test in the trash the weekend Mallory went missing," she explained. "When I went to her apartment, the box was there with only one positive test wand."

"Only one?" he asked, his head spinning with the import of this new information.

"It was a two-pack. Women often take multiple tests to be certain."

"Oh, God. Mal—"

"I'm sorry to put it bluntly, and I'm sorry not to have divulged this information sooner, but your reaction," she said, pointing to his face, "is the kind of visceral response I want to get from Mr. Powers."

"Pregnant," Matthew repeated.

"Yes. Possibly." She hesitated, her breath catching on the last. "I'm sorry. You have to be aware we hold some evidence back."

"Evidence?" Turning the word into a question gained him no ground, but he was struggling to wrap his mind around the bombshell she'd dropped. He needed a minute to fit all the pieces together.

She leaned in again, her eyes locking with his. "I need you to think as a prosecutor and not as a brother. Can you?"

"I haven't thought like a brother in years," he said hoarsely. "I suppose I can put it off for a few more minutes."

She inclined her head and looked him full in the face again. "I am not a lake person. I didn't grow up on water, but wouldn't the waves…the nature of water… I don't think she was killed on the shore."

She held up a hand to stave off any questions, but it was unnecessary. He couldn't have conjured a plausible query if his life depended on it.

"Pure speculation on my part," she admitted. "I haven't spoken to anybody about this yet, but it's my gut feeling."

"Based on?" he prompted.

"She wouldn't have ended up in a place so remote unless she was pushed there by currents. Would she?"

Matthew thought about it for a moment. "I'm no expert, either, but it seems logical. They weren't on a busy spot in the lake," he went on, allowing his train of thought to lead him down the path of probability. "It's actually the tail end. Most of the action takes place up in Missouri. Here in Arkansas, the more popular lakes are Beaver and Bull Shoals."

She nodded. "But there would still be enough movement on Table Rock to cause currents. I mean, it's a lake created by a dam. They have release water from locks, right? Plus, there's good old Mother Nature," she conceded. "I assume the wind and weather also play a part in moving the water around."

He smiled at her simple assumption. "Mother Nature would be insulted at being downgraded to a supporting role. Wind and weather are always the most dominant forces on any body of water."

She gave him a ghost of a smile. "My apologies to Mother Nature. I meant no insult."

"Your theory is Mallory was killed out in open water and her body washed ashore," he concluded.

"Unless you can see some reason for Mallory to have been in such an isolated spot without a vehicle?" she challenged.

He shook his head. "No, I'm with you."

"The vehicle is bothering me," she admitted. "I can't get into PP&W again until Monday, but—"

"You're going back Monday?"

She grinned primly. "I have an appointment."

"You are tenacious."

"You have no idea," she replied gravely. "I got an address, so I thought I'd drive out to the lake and see how close I can get to the Powerses' property without stepping over any lines."

He chuckled. "You think being in the vicinity won't cross a line?"

She smiled. "I'll stick to the public highways. I'm nothing more than a tourist who doesn't want to spend her afternoon staring at a brick wall."

"And taking a careful look around."

"Exactly."

"What do I do about the apartment?" he asked.

"I'll call the sheriff's office and see when they'll let you in. Listen, I know the coroner said he'd need most of next week, but you can go ahead and contact the funeral home and start making arrangements."

He chewed the inside of his cheek. Neither of those options sounded as appealing as spending an afternoon snooping around with Grace Reed. "Would you like some company on your drive?" he asked as she rose.

"I wouldn't mind," she answered honestly, "but I think it's more important for you to be here now taking care of the arrangements."

"If I don't want to?"

Her smile was tinged with sadness. "Understandable, but necessary. I'm going poking around, and poking around can get a person in trouble. I can take the heat, but it would be different for you."

He didn't want to get on the bad side of the Powers family.

"Hold tight for this afternoon. Let me see what I can sniff out on my own. I'll report back if there's anything of interest," she promised.

Matthew bobbed his head as he rose from his chair as well. "Maybe we can have dinner tonight when you get back." She looked at him with such surprise, he realized she'd been caught completely off guard by the invitation. "I mean, you can catch me up on anything you learn, and I can fill you in on where I'm at."

Her shoulders dropped, and Matthew felt a strong wave of disappointment as he braced for the rejection sure to come.

To his amazement, she nodded. "Okay, sounds good. Text me when and where."

"Will do."

She paused in the doorway, gripping the handle. "You want this open or closed when I go?"

Matthew stared at the door for a moment. He usually worked with it open, but he was feeling too raw to leave himself exposed to the prying eyes of his coworkers. "Closed would be great, thanks."

When she was gone, he stared at the blank panel of wood shutting out the rest of the world. In the silence, his mind started to whirl.

Mallory was dead.

Mallory might have been pregnant.

Mallory was most likely murdered.

And her big brother was going to help make sure the person who did it faced justice.

"So no big revelations," he concluded, reaching for a second slice of the Chicago-style pizza they'd ordered for dinner.

"No, couldn't even see the house from the road, but given what I saw on the map, I didn't truly expect to. I just wanted to get a feel for the area." Grace wiped her fingers on a paper napkin. "I can't believe you can eat two pieces of this."

He glanced down at his plate. "Some people can't eat when they're stressed. I can't stop," he confessed. "I'll probably only make it through half, but one wasn't enough."

"I get you." She smiled ruefully at the remaining pizza and sat back. "It was delicious. I've never had Chicago-style pizza."

"This area is full of transplants," he said, using the edge of his fork to cut off a hunk of pizza. "The owners used to work at one of the popular places in Chicago. When they decided to go into the restaurant business here, they stuck to their niche. People who used to live up north flock to it, and some of us natives have turned to the dark side."

"And the dark side is the side that puts the sauce on top?" she asked, sounding amused.

"Exactly."

"So, you were asking about how my day went. How about yours? Were you able to get arrangements sorted?"

Matthew set his fork down on the edge of his plate. "Yes." Their gazes met and held. "The coroner said he spoke to you. She was pregnant."

"Yes," Grace said softly. Then she added, "I'm sorry for your loss."

Her sincerity in delivering the trite expression nearly broke him. For most of the afternoon, he'd been able to think about nothing but the nieces and nephews he'd never imagined and now would never have. The sister he'd never truly understand. And the answers they might never get.

"Listen, Grace," he began, shifting forward on the springy seat of the booth.

"No good proposition ever starts with the word *listen*," she said dryly.

"It's not a proposition as much as a request," he amended.

"Go on."

"I'd like to come with you to PP&W Monday."

"I thought you wanted to avoid getting involved there?"

"As a prosecutor, it's not the wisest thing," he admitted, rubbing a hand over his mouth. "But in this case, I'm not the prosecutor. I'm her brother."

"You realize I don't usually bring members of a victim's family along on interviews, right?"

"I get that, but… I'm hip to all the lawyer tricks. I can tell you which questions they'll be trying to evade and how to translate the nonanswers—"

"And you don't think I have the same skill set?"

He could she was torn between being insulted and amused, so he rushed in for damage control.

"No, no. Not at all. I think…two sets of eyes and ears," he finished lamely.

"You feel like you need to do something."

"Yes." He stared down at the untouched slice of pizza on his plate and wondered how in the world he'd thought he could eat another bite.

Without asking, Grace caught the attention of their server and pantomimed their need for a to-go box.

"Tell you what. You go home and sleep on it, and I'll call you in the morning. If you still feel the same way, we'll discuss the possibility of playing good cop, bad lawyer with them."

"Sounds fair."

"I'm not entirely certain I'll get to meet with Powers. He might stonewall me again."

"Oh, he'll meet with you," Matthew said grimly. "His ego won't let him dodge twice."

Her eyebrows rose. "You think?"

Their server deftly boxed the remaining pizza—including his untouched slice—and slid the folder containing the check onto the table.

She reached for it, but he was faster.

"I have a per diem," she said stiffly.

"I coerced you into meeting the grieving brother for dinner. The least I can do is buy you a slice of pizza and half a glass of wine."

"Is that what this is?" she asked, pinning him with a stare.

"I—I probably didn't do as much for Mallory as I could have…when she was…" He trailed off.

"Most of us don't," she said quietly. He looked up, confused, and she gave him a rueful smile. "We don't tell the people we love how we feel about them often enough."

He winced. "I wasn't sure how I felt about Mallory, period. Our relationship was confusing and often frustrating."

"Family is family. We don't get to choose the one that fits best. We have to figure out how to make it work."

"I didn't do a good job of making things work."

She inclined her head. "It feels that way now, but maybe one day you'll cut yourself some slack. Relationships are two-sided." She took a sip of her mostly untouched wine, grabbed the pizza box and started to slide from the booth. "Come on. It's been a long day, and we both have a lot to think about."

He shoved a couple of bills into the folder and followed her lead. On the sidewalk outside the restaurant, she turned and shoved the box into his hands. "Go home. Don't drink any more alcohol, but maybe eat at least one more slice of pizza if you feel up to it. Sleep as well as you can. We'll talk in the morning."

Her concise delivery should have thrown him off, but it felt oddly good to be given a list of simple instructions to follow.

"Will do."

"Good night, Counselor."

To his surprise, she gave his arm a gentle squeeze of consolation as she moved past him in the direction of her car. He turned and watched as the lights flashed. She climbed into the driver's seat. A minute later, she pulled away without so much as another glance in his direction.

He stood there and waited until her taillights blended in

with traffic. Heaving a sigh, he headed for his own car. He'd
been given his orders, and Matthew figured it couldn't hurt
to follow them.

Chapter Eleven

When Grace walked into the conference room at PP&W again, she wasn't the least bit impressed by her surroundings. This made her feel slightly more in control. Plus, she wasn't alone. Matthew stood at her side, tall and somber in a gray suit and striped tie.

Neither of them was surprised to be met with a phalanx of attorneys when they were ushered into the room. She was scanning to see if their hotshot criminal defense attorney was among them when a man who could only be Trey Powers stepped away from the crowd. He looked exactly as she imagined him—young, handsome, tanned from his days on the lake, confident from the day he was born. He had brown hair with gold tips that looked like they hadn't been created by Mother Nature and blue eyes so light they were almost silver.

"Mr. Powers," she said, taking his proffered hand. "Thank you for meeting with me today."

"I'm sorry I wasn't in yesterday. When His Honor calls, we run."

He glanced past her shoulder, and the confusion that clouded his expression told her he'd spotted Matthew. He quickly wiped the slate clean. "I'm Trey Powers," he said, extending his hand like an eager car salesman. "It feels like we've met before somewhere," he continued with a vague shake of his head.

"Mr. Murray is Mallory Murray's brother," Grace informed him.

The information seemed to bring Powers up short. He froze for a moment, his hand still clasping Matthew's. "Brother?"

To his credit, Matthew didn't flinch. Nor did he respond to the puzzled inquiry. Grace was relieved he was sticking to his promise to let her do the talking. "Yes, Ms. Murray was Mr. Murray's younger sister."

"Was?" Powers divided a glance between her and Matthew, his expression one of unconvincing concern. Grace could only assume he'd been tipped off by the county coroner. Not a shocker. If the family was as tied in as Matthew said they were, they would have been tipped off about the recovery as soon as she requested the transfer to Benton County. Maybe sooner.

Trey glanced back at one of the immaculately clad attorneys who'd moved in behind him. Grace nodded a greeting to Harold Dennis, then gestured to the table. "If we could take a seat?"

"Of course," Mr. Dennis replied, speaking for the entire group.

At her direction, they quickly scattered to seats around the table, the PP&W attorneys flanking Trey and taking up almost all the seats on one side of the table.

Mr. Dennis rattled off a flurry of introductions, most of which were a jumble she'd have to sort out later, but she made sure to meet Ms. Fraser's eyes squarely. She wanted the criminal defense expert to know she'd been pointed out. The other woman stared back at her with cool blue eyes, her face impassive.

She also spotted Taylor Greene, the young brunette Steve

had identified from the headshots they'd showed him on their trip back to Stubby's, but she didn't see the young man with glasses he'd said was with them.

Matthew nodded to her as they took chairs at the center of the opposite side, facing them. The side eye he'd given Taylor told her he'd recognized Ms. Greene, too.

Grace took a moment to pull her notepad out of her tote and flip it open to her notes. She had her tablet, but since the others had chosen to go analog with pens and pads of paper arrayed in front of them, Grace was more than happy to let them set the tenor of the meeting. She was on a fishing expedition here. No sense in putting them on the defensive from the get-go.

"I'm afraid Ms. Murray's body was found early Friday morning," Grace announced, her eyes fixed on Trey Powers.

The attorneys murmured and muttered a mixture of surprise and condolences, but Grace kept her gaze locked on target.

"Her body?" Trey fell back in his chair and scraped a hand over his face, seeming to process the implication.

"Yes, sir," she responded, sliding a glance to the young woman at the end of the table.

Ms. Greene stared down at the legal pad and pen squared away in front of her, her face pale and her lips pressed into a thin line. Steve had been right to card her. Despite the severe black suit she wore, she looked considerably younger than the men around her.

Grace dragged her attention away from Taylor Greene and back to Powers. "Ms. Murray is dead."

Trey leaned in, concern knitting his brow as he laced his fingers together and propped them on the glossy table. "I'm sorry to hear. Mallory was a wonderful girl," he said, pointing the last comment directly to Matthew.

"Thank you," Matthew replied quietly.

"We understand Ms. Murray attended a party at your family's home on Table Rock Lake last Friday evening," she continued.

Trey didn't bother with any evasion. "Yes. We ran into her at Stubby's when we were on our way out there, and she was game to come along."

"Stubby's Bar and Grill on Highway 62?"

"Yes, ma'am," Powers replied.

Grace made a show of checking her notebook. "And she was working a shift at Stubby's that night?"

Trey's mouth twitched, but a sharp glance from Mr. Dennis had him smoothing his expression out again. "Yes. As I told you when we spoke on the phone, I invited her to join us."

"But she didn't ride with you or any of your other guests?"

"No, I don't believe so," he replied evenly. "Mallory liked to come and go as she pleased."

He turned to look at Mr. Dennis, but Grace saw his gaze slide to one of the other young lawyers. This one looked something like Powers's budget doppelgänger. He wore a suit in the same shade of bright blue. His hair was cut in a similar style but was noticeably thinner than Trey's. She couldn't quite ID the guy from the photos on the website.

She wouldn't get any further with this line of questioning until Mallory's vehicle was found, so Grace switched tactics.

"How long have you and Ms. Murray been acquainted?"

Powers blinked. The changeup worked. "Uh…" His focus again shifted to Mr. Dennis. When the attorney nodded his approval, Trey opened his hands and looked up at the ceiling, searching his memory. "Um, years. I think when we first met, she was still in high school." He paused for a second, then shook his head. "Or recently graduated."

Beside her, Matthew tensed.

"And how did you meet?" Grace asked.

"She was a waitress at Stubby's Bar and Grill. Has been forever," he said dismissively.

"And you frequented the establishment?"

He shrugged. "Everyone does."

Satisfied she had established the tenure of their acquaintance, she decided not to push on the more personal aspects. The last thing Grace wanted was for Trey Powers to twig to the notion she knew about a possible pregnancy.

"Mr. Powers, does your family keep a boat at your lake house?" she asked.

She saw Mr. Dennis stiffen, but before the older man could counsel his client, Trey chuckled and volunteered an answer. "We have four."

Grace did her best not to appear impressed by the number he tossed out with such brazen confidence, but it was hard not to be. Four boats seemed excessive for a lake in the middle of the Ozarks. "Four?"

Mr. Dennis tapped his pen on the legal pad in front of him, but Powers blustered on, his ego clearly in the driver's seat. "Yes, we have a pontoon boat, a johnboat, my father's bass boat and my boat."

Grace noted he didn't volunteer what type of boat his was precisely. "Your boat? What kind of boat do you have?"

"A ski boat," he said, tossing it off with a one-shouldered shrug.

His studied nonchalance told her it was most likely the top of the line as far as ski boats were concerned, but she could care less. She only wanted to confirm whether watercraft were available to take the partygoers out onto the lake the previous Friday night. "And were any of the boats in use during the party?"

"Almost all of them at one point or another," Trey responded, glancing at his friends with a chuckle. "We're all water rats."

"Well, not all of us," the young man beside Trey drawled with a snigger.

"Right." Trey let out a short laugh. "All except for Josh. He's not much of a boat guy. Can barely handle the jon-boat."

She made a note. She knew from growing up in a state where hunting was practically a religion that a joh-boat was a flat-bottomed boat equipped with an outboard motor. People used them for duck hunting or fishing along shorelines. "Josh?" she asked, glancing from one man to another.

"What do you expect from a guy from Missouri?" Powers's doppelgänger chimed in.

A couple of the other attorneys chuckled, but Grace's curiosity was piqued. The comment was clearly meant as an insult.

"Josh?" she asked, glancing from one man to another.

"Joshua Potter," Harold Dennis supplied. "Another one of our associates."

"Is he not here?"

"He's out of town on behalf of a client," Mr. Dennis explained.

"I see." Grace made a note, then turned to the attorney beside Trey Powers. "I'm sorry, I don't believe I caught your name."

The young man straightened in his seat. He clearly didn't appreciate being overlooked. "Chet Barrow. I'm an associate here at the firm."

"And you attended the crawfish boil?" she persisted.

"Yes, ma'am."

"And this Josh, did he have an accident with the boat?" she asked, eyebrows raised.

"No, not an accident," Trey answered, drawing all eyes back to him. "He took a girl out as the sun was setting and got the prop tangled up in the weeds. They needed to be towed away from shore."

The image of the muddy, grass-flattened bank where Mallory's body had been found sprang to mind.

"Near the house, or somewhere else on the lake?" she asked.

At this juncture, Mr. Dennis interceded. "I fail to see the relevance of this line of questioning, Agent Reed."

"Oh, I'm sorry," Grace said, insincerity dripping from every word. "Did I not make myself clear earlier? Mallory Murray's body was discovered by a fisherman. It had been washed ashore in one of the inlets on Table Rock Lake."

Before any of the younger attorneys could respond, Mr. Dennis jumped in to set the course of the conversation. "I'm terribly sorry to hear, but Agent Reed, I don't see how this young lady's unfortunate death can be tied directly to my client."

Grace gave her head a shake and opened her hands palm up. "I didn't mean to imply I was connecting your client directly to Ms. Murray's death. I was simply establishing where she might have spent her last hours and how she might have gotten out onto the lake."

"Do we have evidence she was out on the lake?" Mr. Dennis challenged. "Perhaps she fell into the water from the shore."

"I don't," Grace admitted, hoping by throwing this bone, they might be more inclined to be forthcoming about the events of the night.

"Was Ms. Murray's body found on or near the property owned by the Powers family?" Mr. Dennis pressed.

Grace shook her head again. "She was found on an inlet is located a few miles to the east of the Powerses' property."

"So you could say this entire meeting is a fishing expedition of sorts," Mr. Dennis said stiffly. He closed his leather portfolio and rose from his chair. The other attorneys scrambled to follow his lead.

Turning his attention to Matthew, Harold Dennis inclined his head a fraction of an inch. "I'm sure I speak for all of us when I say I'm terribly sorry to hear about your sister's death, Mr. Murray. I understand your desire to get answers as to what might have happened to her, but I don't believe you'll find them here."

Having spoken his piece, he focused on Grace.

"If you'll excuse us, Agent Reed," he said firmly. "I believe that's all the time we have today."

The entire Powers team collected their portfolios and murmured goodbyes.

"I wish you luck with your investigation," Mr. Dennis continued. "If you have any further questions for my client, I would appreciate it if you would direct them to me as his counsel."

Grace didn't bristle. She didn't try to play the heavy. There was no point at this juncture. She had nothing but conjecture and a secret in her back pocket. If she made this interaction into a confrontation, she'd only be closing off the possibility of further conversation.

She rose and extended her hand first to Trey Powers, then to his attorney, making direct eye contact with each of them. "Of course. I appreciate your help. And if you or any of your friends think of anything you think might be helpful, I would appreciate a call."

With that, she pulled a handful of business cards from her suit pocket and offered one to each attorney as they passed, making sure to press one into Taylor Greene's palm. The young woman hurried from the room, her head bowed.

Beside her, Matthew sat still as a statue. Grace reclaimed the seat next to him, her eyes fixed on the back of Trey Powers's head as he leaned in and whispered something to the attorney who was clearly emulating the heir apparent in style.

Their throaty chuckles carried back into the room before the heavy wooden door closed behind them.

Matthew turned on her, his eyes alight with righteous indignation. "You had him in a room and that's all you're going to ask? Of course they have boats. It's a lake house."

"Yes, but I wasn't sure how many or what kind," Grace said, unruffled by his ire. "Now I have specifics for a search warrant." She stared into his angry eyes, careful to keep her own expression calm and steady. She'd been confronted by too many frustrated and unhappy family members to take his displeasure personally. "Trust me, I have plenty to start with."

"If you think you're going to get a search warrant for their estate or any of those boats from a local judge, you're cracked," he said as she gathered her things.

She lowered her voice. "I'm not cracked. But this is not the place to discuss this."

She picked up her tote bag and rose from the chair again. Looking down at him, she heaved a heavy sigh. "I'm not sure what you expected to happen in this meeting, but I can tell you it went exactly as I anticipated. You're going to have to trust me. I am good at my job. And in case you've forgotten what that is, my job is to collect enough solid, irrefutable evidence for people like you to do *your* job."

Matthew blew out a breath, his shoulders sagging as he visibly deflated. "I'm sorry," he murmured.

Grace nudged his chair. "Come on. We can talk more in the car."

He pushed back his chair and followed her from the room.

Once they were seated in her state-issued SUV, he looked over at her. "What's your plan? Aside from the fact the circuit court judge for this area is the Walton in Powers, Powers & Walton, I promise you there isn't a judge in a five-county area whose robes weren't financed by the Powers family."

"I'll find a judge who isn't tied to the Powers purse strings," she said evenly. He scoffed, and she shook her head. "You forget, I'm not confined to county lines. This is a state investigation, and surely somewhere in the state of Arkansas I should be able to find one judge they don't own."

"Good luck," he said disparagingly.

"As a matter of fact, I already have a couple in mind." She started the car and put it into gear. "And I bet if you stop letting them get into your head, you can probably come up with other possibilities."

"They aren't in my head," he shot back, defensive.

"They are. You're as awed by them as Mallory was, but in a different way," she said, sliding him a glance as she pulled from the parking lot. "Don't let the flash and bluster blind you. That guy in there is scared. Scared enough to assemble his own dream team to take a simple meeting with a lowly detective from the state police."

"I doubt he goes anywhere without an entourage," Matthew responded dully.

Grace spared him another glance but found rather than sulking, he appeared thoughtful. She smiled. She could almost see the gears turning in his head.

"Right," she said encouragingly. "And when there's a crowd, there's bound to be a witness. It's only a matter of watching and waiting."

He inspected her as she pulled out onto the street. "You already have a mark," he concluded.

She nodded. "Yep."

"The one at the end…the woman Steve ID'd," he said slowly.

Grace nodded as he slotted the puzzle pieces into place. "Taylor Greene. The one he carded when they came into Stubby's."

She could feel his gaze on her, warm and appraising. "You think she'll roll?"

"I think she's the weakest link."

"What makes you say so?" he asked, sounding genuinely curious.

Grace smiled. "Because she's either hopelessly in love with Trey Powers or she loathes him," she answered. "I only have to figure out which buttons to push." She let her statement hang there for a moment, then she glanced over at him as she switched tacks. "Do me a favor?"

"Sure, what can I do?"

"Petition your friend Judge Walton for those search warrants?"

He scoffed. "Why? I told you he'll never issue them."

"I want the Powers team to think they have me stymied. The cockier they get, the more likely they are to slip up."

"I'm not sure," he began.

She understood his hesitance but wasn't about to let him off the hook. If they were going to unravel the sequence of events surrounding Mallory's death, they would have to start picking at the knot. If she went to another judge without trying to act locally, it might arouse suspicion with the Powers team. If they were thwarted by the local judge and went elsewhere to get the warrants, it was possible the folks at PP&W would consider them little more than an annoyance.

"It could prove to be tricky for me," Matthew said quietly.

"I understand. I'll ask someone in my office to file the paperwork," she offered, turning to watch his reaction as she stopped at a light.

His rejection was almost instantaneous. "I need to do something…"

"You are even if you aren't pushing the paperwork," she assured him. "Think of it this way—if getting to Trey Powers is the goal, I'm going to need to get around his defenders. I need you to be my point man. Set a pick or two, to speak."

He looked over at her in surprise. "You speak basketball?"

She chortled and pressed the accelerator. "I hit five-ten in the sixth grade. What do you think?"

"I think I'm even more impressed than I was before," he said, sounding truly admiring.

Grace smiled but kept her eyes on the road. "Yeah, well, wait until you see me dunk."

Chapter Twelve

"Good morning."

Matthew looked up to find his boss hovering in his doorway. "Morning."

"I thought you were taking some days off," Nate commented, confusion puckering his forehead. He stepped inside and closed the door behind him.

"I'm still waiting for the coroner to release Mallory's body," he explained, instinctively hitting the save icon and lowering the screen of his laptop until it was mostly closed. He'd been reviewing the timeline they'd pieced together from Friday night through the meeting at PP&W, and he didn't want Nate to know he'd been anywhere near the firm if he didn't have to. "I'm going to Eureka Springs this evening to gather Mallory's things."

"Ah, I see," Nate replied quietly. "I still can't believe I didn't know you had a sister."

Matthew eyed him curiously. They'd always been friendly, but they weren't exactly friends. "I don't know if *you* have siblings," he pointed out. "I mean, I know you're married and have kids. I guess people tend to talk about more about their kids at work."

Nate raised both eyebrows. "I suppose." Jerking his chin up, his gaze fixed on Matthew's laptop. "Are you working on anything we can help you with? I can reassign cases if you need me to."

Matthew shook his head. "Nah. Catching up on some paperwork while I play the waiting game."

His boss gave another slow nod. "I hear you and the investigating officer looking into your sister's death visited PP&W."

Matthew didn't flinch. Years of working with Nate had prepared him for this roundabout conversation.

"Yeah, we did." He offered no more explanation. If Nate wanted to know something specific, he'd have to ask an actual question.

"Unusual," the prosecuting attorney said, propping his shoulder against the door frame in a studiously casual pose. Matthew felt an urge to jump up and push him off balance.

"Is it?" he returned evenly.

Nate snorted. They were both aware the police didn't take grieving family members along on witness interviews. "Be careful, Matt."

Matthew stiffened, both at the warning and the nickname he never used. Nate knew he hated it.

"Be careful? I never opened my mouth."

It was close enough to the truth. He hadn't asked any of the questions or done more than murmur thanks for the condolences offered by people in the room.

"You know what I mean," Nate said, pushing away from the door frame and drawing himself up to his full height. "You have plans for the future. Because of those plans, you've purposefully avoided going head to head with PP&W. Don't turn yourself into an adversary now."

"I didn't realize my presence would be seen as adversarial," Matthew replied disingenuously.

Nate's usually smiling mouth thinned into a line. "You're

acting foolish and reckless," he observed. "I never pegged you for either of those things."

Matthew was saved from answering by the blare of his phone. The sound sliced through the tension in the room and bounced off the walls, disarmingly jubilant against the backdrop of the conversation.

Normally he would have silenced it without a glance when talking with Nate, but he seized it as a ticket out of their conversation. A peek at the screen showed the caller to be Grace. He accepted the call but said only, "Hey, can you give me a moment?"

"Sure," she replied.

Muting the phone, Matthew looked back at the man hovering in his doorway. "Don't worry. I have no intention of being foolish or reckless," he stated, holding Nate's gaze.

The other man nodded once and took a step back. "Good. I'll let you get to your call." He rapped two knuckles against the door frame. "Take it easy on yourself. We'll all be here, and all of this will be waiting for you." He opened the office door, then gestured grandiosely to the open-plan office humming with activity.

"Yeah." Matthew nodded and forced himself to return the smile. "The bad guys never take a day off."

"Truth," Nate called over his shoulder as he walked away.

Matthew waited until he was certain the other man was gone, then he unmuted the call. "Grace?"

"Yes, is this a bad time?"

"No, I had to finish a conversation."

He rocked back in his chair and peered out his open office door to be sure no one was lurking nearby. "You know what? I think I'm going to get out of here."

"Oh?"

He lowered his voice as he sandwiched the phone between his ear and shoulder. "Somehow, Nate knew I was at PP&W

this morning. He also made it clear he didn't approve of my being there."

"Does it matter if he approves or not?" Grace asked.

"To a certain extent. The man is my boss."

"You shouldn't be in the office anyway."

"It's here or an empty apartment," he said grimly. "I thought it might be better to be around people, but now I don't know."

"How about one person?" she asked.

"Excuse me?"

"How about being around one person?" She paused, and Matthew found himself holding his breath until she spoke again. "I'm at the StayOn extended stay over on Washington Street. I've got a whole office set up here, complete with a whiteboard and markers."

"You're inviting me to come there to work?"

"I'm inviting you to come here and work on your sister's case," she said, spelling it out for him. "I'm afraid I have some not-great news."

"Well, that seems to be the theme this week."

"I know."

"Might as well hit me with it."

"Maybe your paranoia is rubbing off on me, but I don't want to get into details over the phone," she said, overenunciating the last few words to make her point. "Can you meet me here?"

Instantly on guard, he demanded, "Give me a rough idea."

"They found Mallory's car."

Something about her lack of inflection set his antennae twitching. "And?"

"It was in a lake."

"Wow. I wish I could say I was shocked," Matthew said stiffly.

"Yeah. Unfortunately, it's not going to make our quest to

get access to the Powers property any easier," she said in a voice tinged with genuine regret.

"No? Why not?" he asked, closing the lid of his laptop and reaching for his messenger bag in one practiced movement. He had the computer jammed halfway in the pouch when she finally broke the news.

"Wrong lake."

"WHERE WAS IT?" he pressed when she opened the door to room 152.

"Hello to you, too." She stepped back and waved him into the room. The minute the door slammed shut behind him, she pointed to a whiteboard propped on the sofa. "Beaver Lake. Not far off Highway 62."

"Beaver Lake?" he repeated, unable to process the incongruity.

"Yeah. On the west side. I'm guessing about fifteen miles from the Powers place as the crow flies, but it would take longer to get there on the highway."

He dropped his bag at the base of the breakfast bar. Moving into the suite's living area, he propped his hands on his hips. "No more than five minutes from Stubby's," he murmured. "We've been driving back and forth past it all week."

"We wouldn't have seen anything. We didn't go down to Beaver Lake," she reminded him. "A guy training to re-up his scuba certification caught sight of the license plate and noticed the tag was current."

Matthew dropped down onto one of the barely padded stools and gazed at her. "She paid her registration. For once, Mallory didn't flake on something."

He scrubbed his face. A morass of incredulity and self-recrimination for continuing to think poorly of his sister, even in death, threatened to smother him.

Grace blew out a breath. "I know you said you'd do it, but

I asked one of my colleagues to request the search warrants for the Powerses' house and boats from Judge Walton this morning," she informed him. "Thankfully, this information had not yet come to light. Maybe there's a chance."

"A snowball's chance," Matthew said grudgingly. "Where is the car now?"

"It's being hauled to impound on a flatbed. We had a forensic diver go in and recover anything they could find in the glove box and console. They'll also work on the car to see if they can recover any prints, hair, other DNA."

Matthew felt a flicker of hope sputter to life in his chest. "Depending on how well contained the cabin was, they may be able to get some fingerprint residue," he said, giving voice to the flutter of optimism.

"The windows were rolled down," she informed him, her expression somber. "The team tells me there are some other things they can do, but I'm betting we won't find any evidence of anyone other than Mallory in her car. Plus, I doubt Trey Powers was the kind to go riding around town in his gal pal's subcompact."

"Definitely not," he agreed. "The guy drives a Porsche."

"The team tells me whoever sank this car knew what they were doing."

"Professionals?" He was tempted to scoff at the idea but was unable to rule out the possibility of Powers hiring someone to ditch the vehicle.

"I can't say professionals, but we can be pretty sure Mallory didn't roll all her windows down, drive into Beaver Lake, swim to shore, hitch a ride over to Table Rock and bash herself in the back of the head with something smooth and flat until she fell into the water," she said, brusque with impatience.

"Right. It doesn't make sense."

"I'm figuring they didn't want that car found anywhere

near the Powers place. Either way, something stinks like old fish. I've called in a favor with some IT people I know. They may be able to go deeper with Mallory's social media and try to dig some things out."

"Cool."

"Let's compare notes and impressions. We can order some food and wait for either forensics or the judge to give us something more to go on. Have you eaten today?"

Matthew's stomach flipped at the mention of food. He couldn't focus on food. Bigger questions preyed on his mind.

"And if forensics comes up empty?" he couldn't resist asking. "What if there's no evidence pointing to Trey Powers?"

"We'll get something."

"Even with the pregnancy, I'm not sure we can prove the child was his," he argued.

"You don't seem to have much faith in science," she said tartly.

"I believe in science, but we don't know how pregnant she was. My gut tells me we're not going to get lucky enough to connect one shred of Trey Powers's DNA to my sister."

"You give him far more credit than he's due, Matthew. This guy is only human. His friends and colleagues are, too. They aren't supervillains from a comic book. They're people. And if there's one fact we know for certain about people, it's that somewhere along the line, they all screw up."

Matthew swallowed hard, slid off the stool and stalked over to the whiteboard she had propped on what appeared to be a rock-hard sofa. Looking at the dry-erase board covered in messy scrawl and squiggling lines connecting one fact to another was oddly calming. Forcing himself to inhale and exhale, he nodded.

"Yeah, they do."

She stepped up beside him, her shoulder grazing his as

they both stared at the board. "How many impossible cases have you seen break open because one thing got overlooked?"

"Too many."

"And how many have you seen break wide-open because somebody refused to blink when it came down to playing chicken? There's no hiding the truth entirely. Somebody knows what happened to Mallory, and they are nothing more or less than a human being."

He gave her a half smile to go with his sidelong glance. "You make a good case, Agent Reed. Are you sure you didn't miss your calling? The ability to spin a logic-defying situation makes a good lawyer."

She leaned forward to adjust the positioning of a magnet she'd used to tack down the edge of an Arkansas highway map. "The problem is, I have a moral compass." She spoke over her shoulder at him, smirking.

"Yeah, they can be pesky," he agreed with a shrug.

"I think I need a sandwich." She pulled her phone from her pocket and wandered back to the kitchenette. "Sandwiches work for you?"

To his surprise, his stomach answered with a gurgle. Pursing his lips, he stared at the map, his gaze tracking the distance between the western shore of Beaver Lake and the trailing inlets of Table Rock. The end of the lake stretched across state lines from Missouri like grasping fingers.

"Works for me," he agreed distractedly. "You know, it doesn't take long to get from one lake to the other if you know the back roads."

"Oh, yeah?" Her brows lifted as she looked up from her phone. "Maybe we start by looking at any of Trey's buddies who grew up around here." She returned her attention to the screen. "I'm ordering Italian subs."

"Perfect." Turning on his heel, Matthew moved back to the bar, where he pulled his laptop from his bag and opened it. "I'm pretty sure the guy who was in there this morning—whatever his name was Barrow?—I think I read on the website he's an East Coaster. Probably a prep school pal or something."

She snorted softly but continued to process their order. "Funny, I always imagined those guys as being ultraconfident, but he came across as…"

"Needy?" Matthew asked as he clicked through to the PP&W staff photos.

"I was thinking sad, but needy works, too," she murmured. "Definitely a hanger-on." Her phone chimed, and she looked up with a smile. "There. Sustenance is on the way."

She moved back to her board. "Okay, now we have Taylor Greene at the bar, the party and in the meeting. What's her story?"

Matthew clicked over to the photo of the wholesome-looking brunette. "Looks like the girl-next-door type."

"For some reason, I'm always more suspicious of the girl-next-door types," Grace murmured as she squinted at the board.

He chuckled. "Why am I not surprised?"

She looked over her shoulder at him. "You think you have me pegged, Counselor?"

For a moment he was dumbstruck again by how attractive he found her. Confidence and competence—they were as much a part of her as her strikingly dark brown eyes or the smattering of freckles across her nose. And the whole package was a potent one.

"Not at all. I'm simply assuming you're suspicious by nature. Occupational hazard."

She seemed to give thought consideration. "Yeah, okay. I can admit I am." She moved a note she'd made about the car and photo of Mallory printed from her PicturSpam ac-

count aside, then picked up one of the markers scattered on
the coffee table.

"The Powers place is here." She pointed to the spot marked
with a red dot on the map. "Her body was found here," she
said, jabbing a finger at a second dot to the north and east of
the spit of land where the first Tyrone Powers had built his
family fortress. She trailed the same fingertip along Highway
62, past the junction where Highway 37 took people up into
Missouri and back down toward the town of Garfield. "You
and Mallory grew up around here?" She tapped the map.

"Yes, but not in town. Out off the highway on the Beaver
Lake side," he clarified.

"Her car was found here."

She marked the spot on the western shore with a black X.
"Would have been closer to dump it on the east side."

"Definitely more accessible." Matthew squinted at the
spot she'd marked. "There's more development on the dam
side. Campgrounds, resorts—"

"But there would also be people who might notice someone pushing a car off into the water," she concluded.

"Been a while since I've been over there, but the car was
found on the west side. North end." He tapped his lips with
his forefinger. "There used to be only one road in up there.
May still be if it's still timber company land." He peered at
the map. "You're right. We need to take a closer look at anyone connected to Trey or PP&W who grew up in the area."

"Or at least vacationed here regularly."

"Right." Matthew went back to the bar to reclaim his laptop. "Lake people, at least the regulars, would know the area
as well as the locals."

"Now we have something to dig into while we wait for
our food," she said, picking up the board and moving it to
lean against the wall. "Have a seat. I'll grab my notes and a
couple bottles of water."

Matthew watched her move about the room, collecting everything she might need in order to keep up her pursuit. She'd been correct to coerce him into coming here to work. This was neutral territory, safe from the office and local politics. And two heads were far better than one. Particularly when his hadn't been entirely in the game. Until now.

He'd been laboring under the delusion he could play both sides—save his sister and avoid crossing swords with the Powers family for the sake of his career ambitions. But it was never going to be possible.

Grace and her unerring moral compass were pointing him toward a different future than he'd envisioned, and he wasn't certain he was grateful for it. But he was grateful Mallory had Grace to stand up for her.

"Hey, Grace?"

"Hmm?" she said as she pulled a tablet and a power cord from her bag.

"Thanks for this," he said, his voice catching on the last. He cleared his throat. "For everything, but mostly for getting me out of the office and over here. I didn't realize how much I needed a change of scenery."

She smiled, and her dark eyes lit with amusement. "If this is a change of scenery for you, you need to get out more, Mr. Murray."

Her phone rang, and she pulled it from her pocket. She shot him a glance and made a face when she saw who was calling. "Let's see if we got our warrants, shall we?" She accepted the call and tapped for the icon to send it to speaker. "Any luck, Jim?"

"It's a no-go with Judge Walton, Grace," a man said without preamble.

"Had to go there first. Would you submit to Judge Cellini for me, please?"

"Already have," the man she called Jim responded. "I'll let you know when she signs off."

"Appreciate your help," Grace said shortly. She seemed to hesitate for a moment, then asked briskly, "Any movement on the Robinson case?"

"No. I had a call from McAvoy in Crimes Against Children. He wanted to know if he should take over since this turned into a possible homicide, but I put him off."

She sighed. "I should let him have it," she said, her shoulder slumping. "Lord knows I'm not getting anything on my end."

"You want me to give him a shout?" the other agent asked.

Grace shook her head. "Nah. I'm going to make a couple more calls and some more notes. If I don't shake anything loose in the next day, I'll call him myself."

"I'll get back to you as soon as we have the warrants. You have forensics people on standby?" the man on the other end asked.

"Ready and raring," she assured him. "Thanks again, Jim. I owe you."

Grace ended the call, dropped down onto the opposite end of the sofa and leaned over to jam the charger into a wall socket.

"He sounds pretty sure this other judge will issue the warrants," Matthew commented.

Grace's mouth pulled into a thin line. "Judge Cellini does a lot of work with victim advocacy groups in the Fort Smith area. Particularly female victims of abuse and violent crime. She'll issue the warrants."

"Good."

She plugged the other end of the cord into her tablet. "I'll pull the names from the firm's website, and you search for them on WhosIn. If someone has notifications set to show who's looking at their profile, they'll see another attorney and not the state police."

"Good call. This is why they gave you the shiny badge," he said, pointing at her. "Let's start headhunting."

Chapter Thirteen

The following morning, Grace dispatched the forensics teams she'd had standing by with warrants in hand. She'd set her sights on the target she and Matthew had agreed was the weakest link in the PP&W wall of silence.

Parking her SUV across the street from the law firm's front entrance, she scanned each car turning into the lot adjacent to the building. Her target sat too close to the steering wheel of a shiny eco-friendly hybrid. Taylor Greene appeared to be as uncertain about driving as she'd been about attending the previous day's meeting.

Grace switched off the ignition and climbed from the car. She crossed the street and the parking lot at a brisk pace, her head down so her hair provided some camouflage for her sneak attack.

Taylor hadn't even turned off her car. She rummaged around, gathering her belongings while she sang along with the music blaring inside the car. Grace cocked her head and hummed along until she picked up the thread of melody. Ms. Greene liked anthems of strength for young female empowerment disguised as pop songs. Duly noted.

She tapped on the driver's window with two knuckles. The young woman startled but turned instantly wary when she saw Grace.

Grace's eyebrows rose as Taylor turned down the volume and pushed the button to lower her window a scant few inches. "Sorry, I didn't mean to scare you." Grace tried to make her smile as friendly and unthreatening as possible. "One of my favorite songs."

Taylor Greene wasn't buying. She looked terrified, but Grace had to give her props for turning up the bravado when she asked, "May I help you?"

Grace flipped open her credentials as a courtesy. Okay, maybe it wasn't simply a courtesy. The badge and ID packed a wallop in certain situations. Still, she needed this woman's help, not a confrontation, so she kept her smile firmly in place, casual and friendly.

"I'm Grace Reed from the state police. We met yesterday?"

"Yes, I remember you."

Grace pocketed her badge. "I was hoping we could speak. You and I. Privately."

"I don't think that's a good idea—"

Grace saw her fumble for the button to raise the window and curled her fingers over the top of the glass to stop her. "Please. I know you were at the party Trey Powers hosted last Friday night. I need to talk to you some more about it, and I think we'd both prefer not to make a production out of it."

"How do you know if I was at the party?" the young woman asked, looking truly cornered.

Taylor wasn't as adroit as she should have been. "You were in pictures on social media."

The woman stared at her, aghast, as realization dawned. "You've been stalking me on social media?" she demanded. "You had no right—"

"No, ma'am," she quickly assured her, but she made a mental note to pay closer attention to Ms. Greene's accounts if they could gain access. "The photo was posted on Mallory Murray's PicturSpam account. I recognized you at the meeting yesterday, but I didn't want to say anything when there were so many—" she paused for a moment and leaned in "—guys around."

"I can't speak to you right now. I'm going to be late for work," Taylor said stiffly. "If you'll excuse me."

"I won't keep you long," Grace promised, stepping back slightly to make it clear she had no intention of boxing her in. "But a woman close to your age has died under what I think we can all agree are suspicious circumstances, and you were at the place where she was last seen alive."

Taylor Greene's already-fair complexion paled a shade.

"I was hoping you and I could talk privately. Of course, it's up to you if we speak in an official capacity. If you and your attorneys would like to meet me in, say—" she made a show of checking her watch "—an hour, I'm sure I can arrange a meeting room at the Benton County Sheriff's Department."

Taylor's gaze darted to the building. She shook her head quickly. "Listen, I went to a party, but I wasn't even invited personally. I sort of…ended up there."

"It shouldn't be a long conversation." Grace pulled yet another business card out of her pocket and passed it through the window. "I'm going to head to the coffee shop a couple blocks over. The Bean & Leaf? I need to pick up something to eat since I skipped breakfast." She smiled again and patted her stomach. "I wanted to catch you early if I could."

Grace hoped she came across as open and nonthreatening, but it was hard when you stood almost six feet tall. She needed a break, and if she could convince Taylor to talk to her, maybe they could turn the fissure in the PP&W facade into a crack. "If you haven't already had your morning coffee, maybe you'll stop by?"

Taylor took the card, but her hand fell to her lap, as did her gaze. "I can't make any promises."

"I won't ask you for any," Grace assured her. "I'm only looking for any information I can get to help me piece together what might have happened to Ms. Murray."

"I didn't know her," Taylor responded too hastily.

"Neither did I," Grace replied as she backed away another step. "But that doesn't mean she doesn't deserve justice, does it?"

Having delivered her message, Grace turned on her heel and walked back to her vehicle. When she slid in the driver's seat, she noted Taylor Greene still sitting in her car. She didn't appear to be talking to anyone or frantically texting. Choosing to read her lack of action as a good sign, Grace started the engine. If she hadn't run for the shelter of the PP&W offices by now, there was a chance she'd managed to snag her.

Wheeling her SUV out of the lot, she headed directly to the coffee shop. Her stomach gurgled. The part about skipping breakfast hadn't been a lie. Either way she'd get something out of this excursion.

She planned to text Matthew when she arrived at the coffee shop. When he'd left her hotel command center the previous night, he'd seemed bolstered by both the sandwich and their plan of action. She wanted to keep him in the loop as much as possible. His prosecutor's perspective was proving invaluable to her, and at this point, she needed every advantage she could get.

She took it as another good sign when a spot opened near the popular morning stop. Grabbing her bag, she headed inside the coffee shop. Like many of the businesses in the area, the interior was crammed full of rustic farmhouse decor. The thick soles of her shoes made no sound on the wide plank floor, but the place was buzzing.

A bottle of overpriced water and a cinnamon roll in hand, Grace made her way to the only open table—a tiny two-top crammed up against what appeared to be an old-fashioned pie safe. As she wound her way closer, she saw the owners had repurposed the cabinet to display packages of coffees and teas, mugs, and other kitschy detritus for caffeine junkies to purchase.

She tapped out a quick message to Matthew letting him know the team had been dispatched to the Powerses' lake house. Not wanting any distraction, she turned her phone facedown on the tabletop. She'd update Matthew on meeting with Taylor later. Hopefully, she'd have more to tell than a tale of accosting a young woman in a parking lot.

Stabbing the cinnamon roll with her fork, she glanced up surreptitiously whenever the bell above the door rang. She was only three bites into the gooey pastry when Taylor Greene walked in. But instead of going to the counter and placing an order, the younger woman made a beeline toward her.

She didn't take the open chair, though. Hovering near Grace's shoulder, she studied the rack of retail items. "This isn't a good place for me to talk," Taylor confided. "Tons of people from PP&W come here every day."

Grace nodded and turned to the window, paying no attention to the young woman standing next to her table.

"Name another spot," Grace answered, gathering up another forkful of the roll.

To her credit, Taylor hesitated only for a moment. "There's a place a few miles up the road in Springdale. It's called the Daybreak Diner. I've told the office I have to meet with a client this morning. I can meet you there in an hour."

Grace swallowed hard and gave a brief nod. "I'll be there."

Taylor looked nervous, and Grace felt for her. She was stuck between a rock and a hard place. Wanting to build rapport with this skittish witness, she cocked her to study the selection as well.

"I hear the sleepy-time blend is delicious," she said conversationally. If there was anyone from PP&W in there, she could make this meeting seem purely coincidental.

Taylor was quick to catch on. She wrinkled her nose and backed away, shaking her head. "I'm not much of a tea drinker, but I know somebody who is." She aimed a forced-looking smile at Grace. "Except the last thing I want him to be is sleepy."

Grace chuckled. "Totally understand. I can't begin to tell you which one would have the most caffeine." She added a laugh so fake she wanted to take it back. Thankfully, Taylor rushed in to cover.

She waved a dismissive hand at the display. "He's more of the boil-a-bag type anyway. I probably shouldn't bother."

"If he's easily pleased, no sense in messing with a good thing," Grace concluded, then returned to the breakfast she no longer wanted.

Excitement made her stomach jittery. Without another word, Taylor turned to go, but something in Grace's gut told her Ms. Greene might be the wedge she needed to break this case wide-open.

THE DAYBREAK DINER was the polar opposite of the Bean & Leaf. Instead of trendy reclaimed wood and metal signs meant to appear antique, the restaurant's interior was a genuine throwback to the 1980s. True to her word, Taylor sat in one of the brown vinyl booths spinning a heavy mug filled with coffee on the paper mat someone had placed beneath it to protect the table's Formica surface.

"Hey," Grace said, tossing her bag onto the bench opposite the younger woman. "Thanks for meeting me."

"I don't have long," Taylor returned, her voice snappish and her body language closed off.

"I'll get straight to it." Graced pulled her notepad and

pen from her tote. "You said you weren't invited to the party yourself?"

"Coffee?" a waiter wearing a bored expression asked, already reaching for the mug he carried on a tray holding a half-filled carafe of black sludge.

Grace kept her gaze fixed on Taylor. "Water for me, please."

He turned away with a huff. Grace studied the other woman for any nonverbal cues. "Not invited…?"

"Well, no," Taylor conceded. "I was at Beaver Lake on a boat with someone else. We pulled into a slip alongside another boat, and the guys were talking back and forth. Trey said he was having a party at his family's place on Table Rock and pretty much invited everyone who was there."

"Who was there?" Grace asked as their waiter plopped a paper mat and glass of water down in front of her.

"Menus?" he asked, sounding even more uninterested than he had before.

"No, thank you," Taylor answered briskly. When he left again, she refocused on Grace. "I'd rather not give names."

Grace raised an eyebrow at the refusal. "Because you fear repercussions from PP&W?"

"Because the person I was with has nothing to do with who was at Trey's party," she parried.

"I bed to differ."

"He doesn't even work for PP&W."

Grace noted the pronoun slip. Taylor had said the "guys" were talking back and forth. A man. But whoever she was with was not one of the attorneys Steve had identified from the PP&W website.

"Why not share his name?" she asked, phrasing the question as neutrally as possible.

"Because I can tell you he had nothing to do with anything involving Mallory Murray."

"How do you know?"

"I know because he was with me."

"And you can't share his name because…?" When Taylor didn't answer, Grace was left to speculate. "He's clearly friendly with Trey Powers, but he doesn't work for PP&W. And you don't want to share his name because he's…involved with someone else?"

Taylor's head jerked back, but she raised her chin in stubborn defiance.

"Maybe married?" Grace pressed.

"I have to leave." Taylor moved to gather her purse.

"No, wait," Grace started to reach across the table, but paused prior to making contact. "I'll leave it. For now," she added under her breath. "What happened then? How did you get from Beaver Lake to the Powerses' place?"

"We got everything secured at the marina, then I rode with my friend."

"Is it normal to hop from lake to lake like that?"

Taylor shrugged. "I wouldn't say it's normal, but some people do it. I guess they get bored with what they have."

Grace picked up on the other woman's mild disapproval but didn't push. "And how did you end up at Stubby's Bar & Grill?"

Taylor's eyes widened for a moment, but she quickly masked her surprise. "Oh, Stubby's?" she said, sounding forced. "We were hungry. Everyone stops there after a day at the lake."

"You weren't worried about running into anyone who might know your, uh, friend there?" she asked, emphasizing the word.

Again, her pointed chin popped up. "He wasn't worried about it, so neither was I."

"Fair enough," Grace conceded. "I'm assuming y'all were

playing follow the leader, since there were a few other people from PP&W."

"How do you know?" Taylor asked, not bothering to hide her surprise.

"Witness identification," Grace answered, noncommittal. "You and your new group of friends followed Mr. Powers to Stubby's Bar & Grill, where he started flirting with Ms. Murray," she ventured.

"I wouldn't say they were flirting."

"What would you say?" Grace asked, hoping to glean further insight from the lawyer's almost compulsive need to correct the facts as she knew them.

She shrugged. "Well, they clearly knew each other well. At first, I thought they might be a couple, but it's hard to imagine Trey dating someone like her."

"Someone like her?"

Taylor rolled her eyes and huffed a sigh. "Come on. She was pretty and all, but she was a waitress in a dive bar."

"You didn't think she was Mr. Powers's type," Grace determined.

"Not for something, you know, long-term. Frankly, I was surprised when he asked her if she wanted to come. The guys he was with weren't exactly polite to her."

"I see." She pivoted. "How long have you been with the firm?"

The change of tactic seemed to throw her. "Me? Three months. Why?"

"Only curious." She was fairly new. She might feel her position with the firm to be vulnerable. "I assume you know Joshua Potter? He was with Mr. Powers that night, but I noticed he wasn't in the meeting yesterday. Why is that?"

She hesitated only for a moment but must have decided there was no use in trying to deny information Grace already had. "He's down in Little Rock , working on a case."

"Do y'all get called to Little Rock often?" she asked as she made a note on her pad.

"Actually, yes."

Taylor sat up a little straighter and tossed her dark hair over her shoulder. She clearly thought making a trek to the state capital inferred a level of prestige. The temptation to tell this innocent young woman exactly how often Grace made the trip herself was strong, but she resisted. Seeing a chance to pander to her ego, Grace ran with it.

"Must be a big case."

"We have a lot of important clients," Taylor replied.

"I bet."

"Senator Powers is Trey's uncle," she offered without segue.

Intrigued by the turn the conversation had taken, Grace looked up, happy to go along for the ride. "I think I heard that somewhere," she said mildly. "Does the firm do legal work for the senator?"

Taylor blinked as if the answer to the question was blatantly obvious. "Well, yeah."

Grace pounced. "And was Senator Powers at this party his nephew was hosting?"

"What? No," Taylor answered, shaking her head and wrinkling her nose at the thought. "No, he's, uh, old. He wouldn't be at a party like this."

"A party like what?" Grace prompted.

"You know…a party. A party where people were partying… Young people." She finally ground to a halt there. "You know what? I do have to go now," she said, snatching up her purse and sliding from the booth in one fluid motion.

Grace followed suit, ignoring their server's shouts about their unpaid check as she followed Taylor into the parking lot.

"Hey, someone needs to pay," the waiter yelled from the open doorway.

Grace held up her badge and signaled for him to wait with one finger. She caught up to Taylor as she was opening her car door. Catching it in one hand, Grace held it open, allowing her guest to take a seat but preventing her from driving away. "Why didn't they send you to Little Rock, Taylor?" she asked. "Did they think you didn't know anything, or do they have something on you they know will keep you quiet?

"Your boyfriend is married, isn't he?" Grace tried the angle again, hoping to get a confession.

"Leave me alone. I have nothing left to say to you," Taylor said, trying to pull the door closed.

But Grace held firm. "Did they threaten you? Him?" Grace persisted. "Are you protecting him?"

"You don't understand," Taylor said, her voice breaking.

"But I do," Grace insisted, keeping her tone businesslike. "I understand a young woman is dead, and I believe you might know how it all happened."

Taylor began to cry in earnest but dashed the tears from her cheeks as fast as they spilled over. "I don't know, and you don't, either. You don't have any proof."

"I'll get the proof," Grace answered with a certainty she felt down to the soles of her shoes.

"It won't matter if you do. You know who they are. You know how connected the family is," Taylor said angrily. Gripping the steering wheel, she stared straight ahead as she whispered, "They'll ruin you."

"I don't care," Grace replied evenly. "I'll take them down with me."

"No, you won't."

"Did they tell you they'd trash your career if you told anyone what happened to Mallory Murray?"

"You don't know anything," she shot back, biting off each word. "Let me go. This conversation is over."

Seeing no advantage to turning a possible witness who

might be wavering in her convictions into an adversary, Grace stepped back. "Thank you for meeting with me," she said as she released her hold on the car door.

Taylor slammed it shut without reply. Grace stood her ground as the other woman backed up without looking. She tore from the parking lot, crumbling asphalt flying from under her tires.

Grace drew a long breath and let it go slowly, taking a moment to let her brain catalog the bits and pieces she'd extracted from the encounter.

"You might be a cop, but someone still has to pay," their sullen waiter insisted, holding the diner door open wide.

Grace extracted a five-dollar bill from her bag and shoved it at the young man, who automatically grabbed hold of it. Turning on her heel, she jerked the strap of her tote onto her shoulder as she made for her car.

"Don't worry. I always make sure someone pays," she said, voicing her promise for all the universe to hear.

Chapter Fourteen

Matthew sat at his desk scrolling through his sister's PicturSpam account. Again. Looking at these photos had become some kind of obsession. Unable to sleep, he'd come
in early and barricaded himself inside his office. So far, not
one person had come tapping on his closed door, and he was
grateful. It was enough to hear the bustle happening on the
other side. He didn't want to be alone, but he didn't want to
be a part of it.

He was only waiting for Grace to call and tell him he
could come hide out in her war room again.

He scrolled through the images once more. He wasn't a
social media guy, but he knew enough about the various plat-
forms to understand he was only seeing a fraction of what
Mallory had put out into the world. His sister loved to talk
about herself too much to have posted fewer than a hundred
photos on the world's most accessed platform.

His phone rang, and he glanced at the screen hoping to
see Grace's name. Unfortunately, the call appeared to be
coming from the coroner's office. Drawing a deep breath,
he snatched it from the desk.

"Matthew Murray."

"Mr. Murray, this is Stu Mardle."

Matthew let the breath go slowly. He'd interacted with Stu

on several occasions over the years. The prosecuting attorney often leaned on the county coroner to provide expert advice on cases beyond the results of routine autopsies. Matthew was fairly sure the medical examiner had never referred to him by his surname.

"Yes. Hello, Stu. I take it you have results?" he responded, hoping to make it clear he didn't expect the man to stand on ceremony just because Matthew was the victim's next of kin.

"I've forwarded my report to Special Agent Reed." Stu sighed. "Damn, Matthew, I couldn't *not* call you. I'm sorry for your loss."

"I appreciate you," he replied, his voice growing hoarse. "I don't suppose you have anything you can tell me?"

"You know how hard it is when a body is pulled from water. We're assuming she was there a few days or more."

"Which can slow any decomposition," Matthew interjected.

"And the clock sped up the minute she was on dry land again," the pathologist reminded him. "One thing we do know for certain is there was a blow to her head."

"With a flat object," Matthew said dully.

"Flat, smooth, but with some kind of divot or channel. A depression in the surface of some kind. Definitely not a log or anything rough. Some kind of finished surface." He paused. "I shouldn't say more than that until the agent from CID wants to release the information."

Matthew nodded his understanding, belatedly remembering the man on the other end couldn't see him. "Yes. Of course," he said quickly. "I understand. I'm expecting to hear from Agent Reed soon."

"I'm sorry, Matthew. Helluva thing."

"Thanks, Stu. I appreciate the call."

After hitting the end button, he rocked back in his chair, the phone clasped in his hand. A smooth, flat object with a divot or channel. He swished his chair back and forth as he tried to stir his sluggish brain to life and come up with some ideas, but a thick, oppressive fog had descended on him.

The only thing he wanted to do was call Grace, but he couldn't. She had texted to say she had a meeting set up with Taylor Greene, and he didn't want to disturb her. But a text—he could send a text asking her to call as soon as she was available. He was trying to rouse himself enough to do just that when his office door flew open and Nate stormed in.

"Who the hell do you think you are?" he demanded without preamble.

Instinctively, Matthew curled the hand holding his phone into his chest. His boss stood in the now open doorway.

"She has no clue who she's messing with—"

He gaped at Nate's disheveled hair, mug-free hand and scowling expression. He'd never seen the man ruffled. Nor had he heard him angry. And he was upset about… Grace? The shroud of lethargy instantly lifted. He surged to his feet, unwilling to cede the position of dominance in his own office.

"Who does *who* think they're messing with?" he deflected.

"They have search warrants for the house and all the watercraft," Nate exclaimed.

Matthew stared at him, astounded by the consummate politician's sudden lack of self-control. Apparently he wasn't the only one. Nearly every lawyer and assistant in the open-concept office was practically falling out of their chair to get a better view of the floor show.

"Hey, take it down a notch," Matthew cautioned, making a tamping motion with his hand.

"I will not take it down a notch," the PA retorted, his voice rising to a shout. "I had Harold Dennis climbing straight up my backside, and I can tell you your name was mentioned more than once."

Matthew stepped forward, grasped Nate's arm and jerked him aside enough to swing the office door closed. The moment they were alone, he locked eyes with his boss.

"I don't care if Harold Dennis was using every letter of my name to spell out the numerous ways you're up *his* backside," Matthew hissed. "You're a damn prosecuting attorney. A crime has been committed. I don't know if you've forgotten, but you're supposed to be on the side of the law."

"Who says there's been a crime? You? The grieving *brother*?"

He said the last with heavy sarcasm, and it cut Matthew to the quick. Nate had hit the nail on the head. The brain fog? It was grief. Partnered with a few bonuses…like shock.

Disbelief.

Disillusionment.

He almost laughed when the last word popped into his head. He'd thought he couldn't get any more jaded, but he was wrong.

"Mallory was struck from behind. The coroner's report has been sent to CID." He paused to take a shaky breath. "My sister was killed. She either fell or was dropped into Table Rock Lake. Someone left her there. Either way, a crime was committed."

"You have no proof Trey Powers is involved in any way," Nate persisted.

"We have proof the last place she was seen alive was at the Powerses' lake house. A judge seemed to think we had enough cause to search the place."

"I'd like to know which judge issued those warrants—" Nate began.

"I'm sure Harold Dennis can tell you. They do have to be signed, after all."

"No judge in three counties would dare—"

"Don't finish that sentence," Matthew ordered, holding up a hand.

To his credit, Nate stopped speaking. Matthew held his former mentor's gaze.

"I *am* a grieving brother," he said quietly. "I'm also a citizen. One who not only voted for you but also worked on your campaign. I'm not going to pretend I don't know who butters the bread around here. Please listen to me when I tell you I will not hesitate to report you to the bar if you do anything other than help the police convict whoever did this to Mallory. No matter who was involved."

He waited a beat, lifted a hand to Nate's shoulder and gave it a meaningful squeeze. "Are we clear?"

"Matthew, you don't understand—" Nate began, suddenly cajoling. Almost pleading.

"I do understand," Matthew shot back, letting his hand fall away. He spun around and scooped his laptop from his desk. Next, he snatched the messenger bag from the floor by its strap. "I understand better than you want me to," he said as he stuffed the computer into the bag.

Nate started to speak, but Matthew shook his head, emphatically insisting the other man remain silent. When Nate snapped his jaw shut, Matt would swear he heard the man's teeth clack.

"I'm going to take my bereavement leave starting now," he said quietly. Stepping past Nate, he opened the door. "I'm sure we'll be talking soon."

"CAN YOU BELIEVE HIM?" Matthew cried, pacing the breadth of Grace's hotel room.

"Sadly, yes, I can," she murmured from her perch at the breakfast bar, her eyes glued to the screen of her tablet.

"Yeah, well, you don't know the half of what it's like to work with him day in and day out," he continued, refusing to let his rant be derailed by her inattention. "He wears shorts with the embroidered whales and anchors on them. What guy under seventy wears those?"

"Apparently one guy does."

At least she was replying on cue. Undeterred, Matthew paced the living area of the suite and unloaded all of it. "He has his teeth professionally whitened and likes to brag about the 'push presents' he gave his wife for each of their kids."

"Better have been diamonds," she said as she continued scrolling.

"For Hayden yes, but for Natalie she got a BMW. I guess she needed an SUV once they acquired the second kid and a Labrador."

"Nice."

Starting to get peeved by her lack of annoyance, he dug deep for something to set her off so they could hate on Nate together. "He only drinks tea."

"People say it's the house wine of the South."

"Not sweet tea, hot tea." He wrinkled his nose. "And not even real tea like the British, but the nasty 'stick a bag in the mug and drink some hot water that tastes like yesterday's socks' kind of tea."

"Ugh. Sounds awful," she mumbled.

Frustrated beyond words, he literally threw his hands in the air. "Okay, I give up. What the hell are you working on over there?"

At last, she looked up. "I'm going through the pathology report."

Matthew ran his hand over his face. "I told you what Stu said, right?"

"I think it was in there somewhere, but reading the report itself is much easier than trying to read between the lines of whatever you're going on and on about."

"I was trying to tell you my boss, the duly elected prosecuting attorney for this county, came into my office irate because I wasn't stopping you from investigating the death of a young woman who happens to be my sister."

"Yeah, but there was a lot of stuff about whales, tea parties and push presents. I stopped trying to sort it all out." She gave him a wan smile and tapped the screen of her tablet. "Your friend Stu is thorough but quite concise."

"Yeah, he is."

His sullenness must have seeped through to her, because she finally met his gaze.

"I'm sorry your boss is upset. But he's not my boss and I'm not afraid of these Powers people. The team is picking up fingerprints all over the boats, and I have a gut feeling we're on the right track." She paused and took a deep breath. "But I totally understand if you want to step back and stay out of the line of fire. You have your future to think about. I will see this through, I promise you."

"I don't want to step back," he said, markedly calmer. "I need to be a part of the solution."

"You need to let his anger roll off your back," she said, her eyes darting to her phone. "Ooh. Here's something to distract us."

"What is it?" he asked, craning his neck to peer at the message on the screen.

"I believe it may be the password for Taylor Greene's PicturSpam account."

"You know using illegally obtained information isn't going to hold up in court," Matthew warned.

"I'm not looking for evidence, Counselor. I'm looking for an angle. This girl feels like she is on the outside looking in at PP&W. I need to find a way to push those buttons."

She tapped away at her tablet until the screen filled with images posted with the handle @TGTigress95. She had started to scroll through them when another notification appeared. "Looks like she got into Mallory's as well. Do you want me to go through hers while you do Taylor's? There may be stuff on there a brother shouldn't see," she said, wrinkling her nose.

Matthew seemed to weigh his options. "Let's make a go at Taylor's first. We can deep dive on Mallory's if we see something to take us there. If you don't mind," he added, almost as an afterthought.

Grace shook her head. "Not at all." She nudged the tablet in his direction so they could both see the screen. "Bring the site up on your laptop and log in so we can compare one to the other if we need to."

"Sure." Matthew opened his sister's public profile. Grace leaned in and tapped in the username and password. Sure enough, hundreds more images loaded the moment she hit Enter.

"Jackpot," she murmured under her breath.

"HO-LY," MATTHEW SAID in a shocked whisper.

Grace made a face as she cast him a sidelong glance. "What?"

"Nate," he replied, his face a picture of stunned disbelief.

She rolled her eyes, but her gaze tracked back to a beaming selfie Mallory had posted the night she disappeared. "Are you still babbling on about your boss?"

"No, I'm telling you this is Nate," he said, jabbing a finger her tablet.

Intrigued by the urgency in his voice, Grace followed his finger to a picture of a blond all-American-looking type with his arm slung around Taylor Greene's shoulder.

She squinted at the photo. "Didn't you tell me he was married?"

"He *is* married," Matthew confirmed.

"Definitely not separated or divorced?" she prompted.

Matthew shook his head adamantly. "He's a politician. He's as married as married can be. Two kids and a Labrador, remember? Push presents, a McMansion over in Hickory Hills and a gated subdivision near Beaver Lake."

Grace leaned over far enough to scroll through more of Taylor's photos. "Well, I'd say they appear to be more than friends." She frowned at another one of the photos. "How old is he?"

"Older than me. Thirty-eight? Thirty-nine?" Matthew reported.

"She's fresh out of school. Can't be more than twenty-six, though she looks much younger. How old are people when they finish law school?"

He shrugged. "Depends on if they go right into it. Direct from undergrad straight through to passing the bar, probably twenty-five unless they're some kind of prodigy."

"She's smart, but I don't think she's the skipping-multiple-grades kind of smart," Grace surmised. "She is naive, though. And I get the feeling she also has one of those pesky moral compasses most of you lawyer types lack."

"More of us have one than you think," he insisted.

"If you can introduce me to more than a handful, I'll buy the next pizza," she said as she continued flipping from photo to photo.

"Nate and this girl…"

"Wait." She stared hard at the photos, mentally replaying everything Taylor had told her about the friend she'd been out with that Friday night. "Does this Nate guy have a boat?"

"Of course he does." Matthew nodded. "Tons of people around here do, and not only people with money."

"I believe Ms. Greene was out on the boat with Mr.…." She paused long enough for him to pick up the cue.

"Able," he supplied. "Nathaniel Able."

"Mr. Able and Ms. Greene were out on his boat last Friday evening when they ran into Trey Powers and his friends, and Trey invited them to his crawfish boil."

"Friday," Matthew repeated. "I remember Nate saying something about his wife and the kids being at her family's beach house in Florida week before last. He took off early on Friday. Said he was going fishing."

"He caught something."

Grace sifted through photo after photo, scanning the background of each one for clues. She stared at the photo of the two people together as she rewound the conversation she and Taylor had in the first coffee shop. "Did you call him a tea drinker?"

"What?"

"When you were rambling on earlier, didn't you say something about Nate drinking tea?"

"You were listening?"

"I pick up all sorts of information from ambient noise."

"Yes, Nate drinks hot tea instead of coffee."

"Fancy tea or plain old bags?"

"The bag kind, why?"

"Confirming. I can tell you without a doubt Taylor Greene and your boss were involved in something more than a fling. At least, it's more on her side."

"Huh. Wow. I always thought Nate was a straight arrow." Matthew frowned. "He's a stickler for having things a certain way—making sure everyone dresses appropriately, keeping up appearances."

"Well, I doubt he was showing her off at fund-raising dinners," Grace said as she leaned closer to him to inspect the photos on the tablet she'd handed over.

"Do you want this back?" he asked, scooting it closer to where his laptop sat ignored.

"Hang on," she murmured. When she stopped scrolling, she tapped the screen. "There," she said, pointing to one of the last photos posted. It was of a group of people seated around an outdoor fire pit.

In the background, a well-lit dock provided access to four boats and a couple of personal watercraft. One of those boats was a sleek red ski boat with multiple wakeboards attached to the towing bar.

Inspired, Grace picked up her phone, opened her messaging app and tapped out a quick directive to the head of the forensics team asking how many wakeboards they'd found attached to the rack when they were on-site. A few minutes later, a message bubble appeared with the number four.

Grace snatched up the tablet, ignoring Matthew's grunt of protest as she opened the photo to full screen. She used her fingers to expand and refocus, homing in on the red boat. When she was finally able to zoom in on a clear shot of the ski boat, she blew out a low whistle.

"Three. There are only three wakeboards attached to the rack. Two on the driver's side, one over by where Mallory might have been standing."

"Conjecture, but I'll allow it," he said brusquely. "Where are you going with this?"

"Forensics found four attached to the rack when they reached the boat today. Two on each side."

"And the wakeboards are important because?" Matthew asked, trying to keep up. His frown morphed into a triumphant smile when at last he caught on. "They're objects with smooth, flat surfaces," he concluded.

"Do you know anything about wakeboards?"

"Yeah." He nodded slowly. "I've ridden them."

"Are they completely flat on the bottom, or do they have fins and—"

"Channels," he supplied in a whisper.

Grace snatched up her phone again, but she didn't bother typing out a message. She pressed the button to make a call.

"Hey, it's Grace Reed," she said when the person on the other end picked up. "I need you to pay special attention to the wakeboards. Particularly—" she leaned in and squinted at the photo, trying to make out the colors "—any board not painted black, blue or tie-dye-looking rainbow."

She let her gaze travel over all the details of the ski boat. If Trey were driving, Mallory would have stuck close to him. If he'd been driving after having a few drinks, she was likely hanging onto something. Had she been drinking? Maybe not if she knew she was pregnant. Had she leaned over the edge to vomit and lost her balance? Possibly, but that wouldn't explain the blow to the back of the head. But an unwanted pregnancy would.

"Closely examine the tow bar, the grab handle on the passenger side and maybe the dashboard. Anything somebody might have grabbed hold of for balance. Even the backs of the seats."

She listened in for a moment, then nodded. "Yes, let's concentrate on the ski boat first. I'm pretty sure she was on it."

She ended the call and placed her phone back on the bar. When she looked up, she found Matthew staring at her, horror etched into his handsome features.

"Someone hit her with a wakeboard," Matthew said, his voice hoarse.

"It's possible. Or she stumbled and hit her head against one mounted on the rack. Either way, I'm willing to bet she never made it back to the dock on Trey Powers's ski boat."

Chapter Fifteen

Matthew had thought the waiting was bad on the legal end of the system. Now, he realized he'd had no idea. Sure, juries deliberated for hours on end, and in one instance for days, but in those cases he hadn't had a personal stake in the outcome. He hadn't had to wait for a case to come together. When he got involved in a case, the police usually had things packaged up all neat and tidy.

It was eye-opening to discover how much Mallory's death was affecting him. In life she'd been an annoyance. He knew his sister had no ambitions beyond marrying well, but he supposed a part of him had hoped she'd find fulfillment in her role as a wealthy wife and mother. The possibility of the two of them finding some common ground was always out there.

It blew his mind to realize it would never happen.

In barely more than a week, everything had changed. Mallory had been alive and well and possibly scheming. And he'd been alive and well and wanting nothing do with her. What horrible, unthinking creatures people could be, he thought, rubbing a hand over his face. He'd been as selfish as she was in his own way. At best, self-absorbed.

He lay on the sofa in the sitting room of Grace's suite. For some reason, he couldn't force himself to go home. Eventually, she must have realized he was camped out, because she'd pulled a spare pillow and blanket off the shelf in the closet and handed them to him before heading into the bedroom.

Neither of them had made any mention of him going home. Nor had they made a plan for how to proceed once they knew for certain forensic evidence was available.

What was the deal with the car? His gaze traced nonexistent patterns on the ceiling. How had Mallory's car ended up in an entirely different lake?

If forensics came back with any kind of evidence placing Mallory on Trey Powers's boat, there was no way her vehicle had made it to Beaver Lake with Mallory behind the wheel.

Whoever had ditched it had been smart to lower the windows to be sure the vehicle was fully submerged. Most everything in it had either been ruined by water or washed away entirely. Whoever had done it had known how to compromise evidence.

Matthew sighed and swung his feet down from the sofa. His back popped as he leveraged himself into a standing position. It was going to be a long night, and he was parched. In the kitchenette, he refilled his empty water bottle from the tap. Water dripped onto his foot as he tipped it to his lips.

"Can't sleep?"

He jumped. The water missed his mouth and dribbled down his chin. He quickly swept it away with the back of his hand, whirling to find Grace standing behind him clad only in a set of striped cotton pajamas with drawstring pants an inch too short for her long legs.

Matthew stared at her bare feet, arrested by the pink polish he spotted on her toes when she covered one bare foot with the other.

He swallowed hard. "Huh? I mean, no." He winced. "Sorry if I woke you. I just wanted to get some water."

"I wasn't sleeping," she said, moving past him to pull a

chilled bottle from the mini refrigerator. "And you don't have to drink from the tap if you don't want to. I have plenty in here." She pointed to the fridge with her unopened bottle.

"Tap works for me," he answered with a smile. "Never let it be said I'm a water snob."

"I won't," she replied somberly. "Aside from the obvious, anything running around in your head you want to offload?"

"Mallory's car—" he began, but she cut him off with an enthusiastic nod.

"Yeah, me, too. Someone else drove it to Beaver Lake."

He exhaled, relieved to know they were on the same page. "The spot where they dumped it isn't an obvious choice."

Grace walked over to the breakfast bar and looked at the list of names they'd been able to attach to faces on Taylor's and Mallory's photo feeds. "We can eliminate two of the guys we have on this list. The only one left would be Nate Able."

"And Taylor Greene." Matthew shook his head. "I still can't wrap my head around those two being a couple."

"It's possible they took the car together," she reasoned.

"And that would mean they were both witnesses to whatever happened to Mallory. I guess it sort of makes sense, aside from the fact it goes against everything they both swore to uphold," he mused.

"They both had a stake in keeping whatever happened quiet. Particularly Nate." Grace jabbed a finger at the photo of Taylor and Nate wrapped around one another. "He had everything to lose if their relationship came to light, and she had a lot to lose if she didn't keep whatever happened out on the lake quiet."

"I can't imagine believing a job is important enough to cover up a crime," he said, still trying to frame the theory in his head.

"I think we may have struck on why she's struggling. Pesky moral compass and all."

"That sounded sort of like a compliment," he teased.

She smiled but didn't take the bait. "I need to press Taylor harder," she thought out loud. "Question her like her presence was already a foregone conclusion. After all, they can't know for sure what forensics has or hasn't found. They may not even know the vehicle was pulled from the lake."

Matthew snorted. "Nate knows by now, I'm sure. And I'm willing to bet if he knows, Taylor knows. And let's face it, the people at PP&W will, too."

"There you go thinking they're omniscient again."

"Not omniscient, only highly connected," he corrected. "I agree, though. Taylor is the one to press."

Grace tapped the lid of her bottled water with a fingernail. "I'm going to check on the car first thing in the morning. See if there's any evidence of anyone other than Mallory in there."

"Good plan," he said, taking a fastidious sip from his own bottle.

"It's possible they'll find something."

Matthew appreciated her attempt at reassurance. He gave her a crooked smile. "Possible, but not probable. Either way, we can and will work with what we have."

She nodded. "Yes, we will."

"Thanks again for letting me hang out here. If I go home, I'm afraid my imagination will run even further afield. You're good at keeping me grounded."

Grace smiled and it lit a spark in her eyes. "Good night, Counselor," she said quietly.

"Good night, Grace."

She backed toward the bedroom door again. "I'll let you know if I get any information overnight. Otherwise, try to get some rest."

A second later she was gone, and the door clicked loudly in the silent room.

GRACE STOOD BESIDE the sofa in the suite's sitting room, torn. He looked so peaceful. Relaxed. She hated to wake him. Particularly when the news she had to give was of a grisly nature. But she wasn't here to watch this handsome man sleep, she was here to catch his sister's killer.

She tried to wake him a gentle shake. "Hey."

Matthew tried to roll away, but he had nowhere to go. His nose ended up pressed to the back of the sofa. His grunt and groans of displeasure mirrored her own visceral reaction to having him turn away from her. Annoyed by the pang of wistful regret twisting in her belly, she gripped his shoulder and squeezed. Hard.

"Hey, wake up," she ordered, shaking him roughly.

"Ah, sheesh," he grumbled, batting her hand away. "Police brutality."

"We have a partial fingerprint."

His eyes flew open, and he sat bolt upright. "Mallory's?"

"No, the pope's," she returned, spinning away from him. "Yes, Mallory's. On one of the grab bars on Trey Powers's boat," she called over her shoulder. "Give me a minute to finish getting dressed. We're heading down to the sheriff's department. I asked them to hold a room for me. We'll meet with the head of the evidence-receiving team there."

"I need coffee," he called after her. "And we'll have to swing by my place. I need to shower and change."

Grace snorted. "You'd better get moving, because I can be out of here in less than two minutes."

After a drive-through coffee run, they made a quick pit stop at his apartment for Matthew to freshen up. The drive to the county sheriff's offices took fifteen long, tense minutes.

"I'm glad they built this out here and not by the courthouse," Matthew said as they turned into the sprawling complex on the west side of town.

"Convenient to have the offices attached to the detention

center," she said, eyeballing the razor wire–topped fence enclosing the back of the property.

"With the way things are growing up here, they couldn't keep everything downtown."

"Makes sense."

They parked and walked into the building, Matthew clutching an enormous to-go cup.

Mark Atkins, the receiving officer from the Department of Public Health's State Crime Laboratory greeted them in a windowless meeting room off the main hallway.

After handshakes were exchanged and introductions made, Grace leaned in. "I know it's unusual to have a member of the victim's family on hand at this stage, but Mr. Murray is the assistant prosecuting attorney for Benton County and grew up in the area. His expertise has been instrumental smoothing the way for this investigation."

Atkins's bushy eyebrows rose. "Judging by the house, the boats and the number of lawyers who showed up to oversee the search, it looks like you've had to do a lot of smoothing. We don't usually have such an, uh, attentive audience when we do our thing."

"Yes, well, I'm pretty sure I'm never going to make it onto the Powers family's Christmas card list," Matthew said dryly.

Grace dropped into one of the molded plastic chairs. "What have you got for me?"

"Two things at this point," Atkins reported. "Of course, these are preliminary findings, and everything we've found—both on the scene and in the vehicle—has been sent to the lab in Little Rock for further confirmation."

"Of course," Grace confirmed.

"We picked up a clear partial print from one of the grab bars. Comparison in the mobile lab shows it to be a match for your, uh…" He broke off, glancing at Matthew with uncertainty.

"Victim," Matthew supplied gruffly.

"Yes, victim," Atkins continued.

He showed them a screen capture of fingerprint whorls on his tablet. Matthew peered over her shoulder when he passed the tablet to Grace. She was no expert, but it looked like a match to her. Still, evidence of Mallory's presence on the boat didn't give them anything concrete. She might have gone for rides on the lake with Powers every weekend, for all they knew.

After Grace and Matthew had both examined the image, she placed the tablet in the center of the table. "Any hair?"

"Yes, quite a bit. Too much to differentiate at the scene," Atkins answered with an apologetic grimace.

She was about to ask the big question when he stopped her with a brisk nod.

"There were strands of hair collected from one of the boards attached to the rack, though." Again he sent an apologetic glance at Matthew. "We bagged the whole board, but I'd estimate the strands to be between sixteen and eighteen inches long."

"And what color was the board?" Grace asked.

Atkins's expression was a bizarre mixture of triumph and distaste. He was exultant to have found something, but also disgusted by what the evidence might mean.

"This board was red and black. Glossy finish, not as long as the others."

He slid a finger across the tablet, and a photo of a red wakeboard in a large evidence bag filled the screen. "It measures less than seventeen inches wide."

They were looking at the top of the board, where a rider would attach to bindings. "Do you have other angles?"

"Yes." He swiped again, and slightly curved edges of the board were shown. The next was a photo of the bottom of the board. Small tail fins anchored one end, and two shallow channels ran the length of the board.

The next photo showed the board attached to the tow bar. It was large bar that formed an arch behind the driver and passenger seats, almost sectioning off the open seating and the deck at rear of the boat.

"Mallory wasn't short," Grace mused as she flipped through the photos again. "It's possible she could have fallen backward and hit her head on one of the wakeboards."

Matthew and Atkins nodded along, but Matthew interjected. "But the red board would not have been mounted on the rack. The photos from that night only showed the other three boards."

Grace nodded. "True."

She puzzled over the forensic photos again, fumbling to pull her own tablet from her bag. The picture posted on Taylor Greene's PicturSpam feed popped up the moment she opened the app. She used her fingers to zoom in again, needing to be sure she hadn't imagined there were only three boards attached to the rack.

"No. There were only three that night, and only one on the side of the boat where Mallory might have been standing." She passed Atkins his tablet back.

"All of this needs to be verified at the lab. I'll be sure to be in contact with you as soon as I get anything," the forensics expert assured her.

"I appreciate you staying behind to talk to us for a few minutes." She nodded to his tablet. "Would you mind sending those to me?"

The other man hesitated for a moment. "I shouldn't. Once we have confirmation about the prints and can identify the hair found on the board, I can send you official photos, but I shouldn't give you anything until then."

Grace gave a hum of disappointment but offered a know-ing smile. "I understand."

They'd moved to gather their belongings when Atkins leaned over and tapped at the bottom of his screen. A sec-ond later, a request to receive files via Bluetooth connection appeared on Grace's tablet. She accepted without saying a word.

"I appreciate you staying to give us what information you could." Grace held his gaze as they shook hands.

"It's my pleasure, Agent Reed." He turned to Matthew. "My condolences on your loss, Mr. Murray." With a nod, Mark stepped past them and left the windowless meeting room.

Matthew dropped back down into the plastic chair with a heavy thud. "She didn't stumble back into those boards."

"As you pointed out, this particular board wasn't there to stumble into."

Grace took her seat again, and together they went through the photos Atkins had shared with her. "Even if it comes back as a match for Mallory's hair, it's going to be hard to prove intent."

"Yes, it will."

"But hope is not lost," Grace murmured as she double-checked to be sure the pictures were saved to her photo roll.

Turning to the man beside her, she cocked an eyebrow. "It may not be easy, but it's not impossible. We know there were witnesses. We know who those witnesses were. All we need is to get one crack and the rest will fall into place."

"Do you think she'll crack?" Matthew asked.

Grace didn't need a name to know which she she meant. "I think she's our best bet."

"They're not going to let you near her unguarded again."

"You think I'm scared of a bunch of suits?" The Powers team were not the kind of attorneys who hustled up work by advertising on billboards. They drew the cream of the crop. They had every weapon at their disposal.

Money.

Power.

Influence.

And, most important, leverage.

But they wouldn't be toting actual weapons into the conference room. At least, she hoped not.

"You know they're going to drag your boss down with them," she said, watching his face to see exactly how the statement landed.

"I know."

"There will be some who will say you're pursuing this to create a vacuum in the prosecuting attorney's office."

Matthew gave an incredulous bark of laughter and stared at her in bemused amazement. "Are you serious?"

She gave a helpless shrug.

"You think people will believe I had my sister killed by the son of one of the area's most influential families in order to bring down my boss so I can slide into this job?"

Grace chuckled at his assessment. "I'm not saying its believable, but there will be people who will twist this story every which way but loose. You need to be prepared for fallout."

"I wasn't prepared to have my sister disappear only to find her body in a lake days later, yet here I am, still functioning."

"True."

"They can come at me if they want. You're the one who keeps telling me I've got this damn moral compass," he added, pinning her with a glare.

Grace nodded and began to pack her things into her tote bag. "Come on. Let's give them their room back. We'll head to the suite, where we can talk in private. I need to figure out the best way to finagle an appointment to see Taylor Greene."

As they were leaving the Benton County detention center, Grace's phone rang. She pulled it from her bag and scowled when she saw Ethan Scott's name on the screen. She immediately accepted the call.

"Hey, Chief, what's up?" she asked, trying to tamp down the tension rising inside her.

"I need to talk to you about Treveon Robinson," her boss said without a greeting, and her stomach dropped to her feet.

She hadn't thought about Treveon for one minute since she told Jim Thompson not to hand over his case, and now Chief Scott was calling her. Grace realized with a jolt she was no better than anyone else—she'd put the boy's disappearance out of her mind while she pursued a bigger, juicier case.

Chapter Sixteen

Grace halted in her tracks. She'd failed him. She'd failed Mallory. Why hadn't she done more to find him sooner? She must have looked as thrown as she felt, because Matthew's eyes widened in concern.

"Where?" she asked, needing to hear the answer she dreaded, no matter how much it would hurt.

"He was spotted in a Texarkana shopping center. Someone took down the information on the car. When police got there, he was with a man who claimed to be his father," he reported.

Treveon was alive.

She couldn't speak. Relief and fury warred inside her. Treveon's mother had sworn up and down the boy's father wasn't involved in his life, though they had been married. It was possible no crime had been committed at all.

"The local child services department has him in their custody now. I'm turning this case over to Crimes Against Children. They'll sort out the custody question, and they can get the Bureau involved if indeed it turns out to be kidnapping."

"Oh… Okay. Thank you for letting me know, sir."

"Well, you were hot on this one when you caught the Murray case, but now you are free to focus your energies entirely on what you have going there."

"I appreciate the call. Thank you."

The news Treveon was safe and well should have elated her, and it did. Sort of. But cop emotions were often the opposite of what her sister termed "real people" emotions. She'd put Treveon on the back burner, and now someone else was going to be the one to deliver him back to his mother. And she was disappointed about it. How messed up was she?

"Anything happening with your investigation there?" her boss asked.

Grace turned in a slow circle, taking in her surroundings. "I'll call you from a more private location with an update," she promised him, careful to keeping her voice neutral and businesslike. "The quick and dirty is, I'm waiting on more concrete information from the crime lab."

He replied he'd be expecting her status report, and she ended the call.

"What is it? What happened? You went white as a sheet," Matthew persisted, barely giving her a second to breathe. "Is it Powers? Did they try to shut things down?"

"Not everything is about this case," Grace snapped. He blinked in shock, and she gritted her teeth. "Sorry. Another case."

"I gather." He gestured for her to start walking again.

"Something I was working on when—"

"No need to explain," he said, cutting her off. "Let's go."

"I—"

He stopped and stared straight into her eyes. "I understand."

The funny thing was, she knew in her gut he truly did. They were alike, she and Matthew. Both driven to do their best by the people counting on them. She wasn't about to let off the gas now.

"I'm going to meet with Taylor Greene," she announced as she set her sights on the parking lot. "It's time to apply pressure."

GRACE AND MATTHEW sat in the same plush leather executive chairs they'd occupied on their last visit to PP&W. The difference was, they'd been left alone in the room and had been for at least fifteen minutes.

"You think they're messing with us?" she asked, checking her watch again.

"Undoubtedly. Plus, I assume they're doing some strategizing."

They'd arrived at the PP&W office unannounced. Grace had flashed her badge and informed the receptionist she needed to see Mr. Trey Powers, Ms. Taylor Greene and Mr. Joshua Potter as soon as possible. Without asking permission, she marched into the conference room with a full head of steam.

"I wonder if Joshua Potter will magically be teleported back from Little Rock," she mused.

"I doubt he ever left town."

Tipping her head back, she stared up at the ceiling. "If you were Mallory, where would you have stashed the stick?" she mused aloud.

"The what?"

"Never mind. I was thinking about the other test, but not now," she said, pitching her voice low but not bothering to mask her impatience.

"Oh. I was hoping it would turn up in her car, but no luck there."

Grace heaved a sigh. They'd received a call on their way across town. Mallory's purse had been found locked in the trunk, but the compartment had flooded. Her wallet survived, but her driver's license was not in it. And, sadly, there'd been no sign of the second pregnancy test.

Matthew suspected she'd had her license and the test in the console of the car or on her person, but Grace wasn't sure. If she had something she thought might turn out to be her golden ticket, the first thing she would do would be to lock it up somewhere no one else could access. Like a bank box or a safe.

"What are the odds she had a safety-deposit box?" she asked.

Matthew snorted a laugh. "I'd say slim. She had at least two banks shut down her checking accounts for excessive overdrafts."

"Hmm." Grace tapped her pen against the pad of paper in front of her. "She would have put it someplace safe. Someplace no one would think to look." She twisted her chair back and forth as she thought. "Not at the apartment, not in her car—"

"We hope," Matthew interjected.

"Not on her person," she continued, letting her mind wander to all the places a woman might stash something valuable only to her. Her thoughts instantly traveled to the center drawer of her desk at the Fort Smith office, where she kept her father's old badge as both a talisman and a reminder. "Could she have hidden it at Stubby's?"

"Stubby's?" Matthew asked, surprised by the notion. "Why?"

She shrugged. "Maybe she wanted to see how Trey responded to the news first. For all we know, he's been violent or threatened her in the past. Your sister seemed to be cautious with people. She kept her roommate at arm's length, and there was barely anything personal at her place. Maybe she had reason not to trust Trey completely?"

"But she'd trust Steve," he said, almost to himself. "If not him personally, she might be willing to risk leaving something on the premises. She'd worked there for years."

Grace murmured to herself as she made a note on her pad. "Check Stubby's."

As she was drawing and redrawing a box around the word, Matthew's phone buzzed, dancing across the polished mahogany surface of the conference table. Grace opened her mouth to give him some grief for leaving it on when she felt her own vibrate in her suit pocket. Exchanging sheepish smiles, they both reached for their devices.

"This will be when they come in," she mumbled as she unlocked the screen.

"Huh," Matthew huffed, reading his message. "Apparently, I'm committing career suicide today."

He turned the phone to show her the message from Nate Able.

"Already alerted to our presence," she said, affecting an impressed nod. "Bets on whether it was Taylor or someone higher up tipping him off?"

He waved the offer away. "Either way I lose, right?"

"Right."

Grace's mood turned grim. Matthew did have more to lose by being here, but when she'd suggested he stay behind, he'd told her she'd have to cuff him to the car. She'd actually considered it for a moment. It was one thing for her to beat the hornets' nest, but she didn't have to deal with these people once she sewed up this case. Matthew had plans for a life here.

Looking down at her own phone, Grace let out a bark of laughter when she saw the message. Sure enough, the chief had sent a warning she'd ticked off the head honcho. He instructed her not to leave without the goods.

Right on cue, the conference room door swung open and

an imposing man with Trey's handsome features and silver streaks in his perfectly barbered hair strode in.

She and Matthew stood. He had the sort of presence that commanded it. Trey followed a pace behind the man, and trailing him were a good dozen or more suits, each clutching their own pens, pads or portfolios.

"Tyrone Powers," the older man said, extending a hand to Grace. "And you are Special Agent Grace Reed."

"Yes, sir," she replied respectfully.

"I've heard you're quite tenacious, Agent Reed," he said, giving her hand another squeeze.

She was about to respond, but the man had already turned his spotlight on Matthew. "Mr. Murray. I am sorry about your loss," he said as they clasped hands. "Too young. Such a shame."

Following directly behind his father, Trey gave them a perfunctory hello and handshake. Grace noted he appeared considerably less cocky than he had in their previous meeting.

She watched as the other lawyers filled in around the table, leaving the two chairs opposite Grace and Matthew open. Sure enough, the father and son laid claim to them. A tall, thin man with floppy dark hair who matched the headshot they'd identified as Joshua Potter sat on Grace's far right. Taylor Greene sat at the opposite end of the conference table. For a moment, she wondered if the seating arrangement was purposeful.

"Thank you for meeting with me," she began, addressing the room in general. "I admit I wasn't expecting to have such a large audience."

"While we appreciate the gravity of what happened to Ms. Murray, the associates at Powers, Powers & Walton do not have unlimited time to answer questions about somebody they'd met at a single social occasion," Harold Dennis began stiffly.

Tyrone Powers reached over and pressed a staying hand to his attorney's forearm. "Hal, a young lady is dead," he said in a drawl as soft and genteelly Southern as a character in a Tennessee Williams play. "I know Special Agent Reed would not be here if she didn't feel it was necessary."

Grace and Matthew exchanged a glance. It was clear the elder Powers and his counsel had decided who was going to play good cop in this scenario. But Grace was the only real cop in the room and could play the game better than either of them.

"Absolutely not, sir," she agreed briskly. "It's come to our attention that Ms. Murray may have been involved in a relationship with someone at the party. This relationship," she continued, choosing her words with extreme care, "might have been one some people would consider a sensitive subject."

"Sensitive how?" Harold Dennis asked.

"A secret relationship, sir," Grace said, politely pouring on her own brand of Southern charm.

"A secret relationship," Tyrone Powers repeated, sounding mildly amused. "Definitely intriguing. Do go on, Agent Reed. Who do you believe was involved in this 'secret' relationship?"

Beside him, Trey cringed as his father crooked his fingers to simulate air quotes.

Grace made a point of glancing at the array of attorneys situated around the table. "Once again, I think it might be better for everybody involved if we were to have this conversation with only the individuals who attended the party."

"Not going to happen," Harold Dennis replied tartly. "Ask your questions, Agent Reed. These people are busy, and you can't afford our hourly rate."

"True," Grace said with a smile. "Certainly not on a state government salary."

She glanced over at Matthew, who gave an almost imperceptible nod. They'd practiced the move in the car. Multiple times. She'd wanted it to appear he was giving his blessing to asking the uncomfortable questions, but not without some reservation.

"I believe Mallory Murray was attending the party as the guest of Nathaniel Able."

Grace heard Taylor's sharp intake of breath but forced herself not to turn in the young woman's direction. She wanted Taylor to see exactly how quickly the men around this table would throw her lover under the bus if it meant saving one of their own.

"Nathaniel Able?" Tyrone Powers asked, his tone indicating he was truly shocked. "Nate?" He shifted his gaze to Matthew. "Nate Able, the prosecuting attorney for Benton County? Your boss?"

Matthew did nothing more than open his hands in a gesture of futility. "My sister is dead, Mr. Powers. I want answers."

Harold Dennis spoke up, picking each word he uttered carefully. "Do you have evidence of such a relationship?"

"We have evidence of a relationship. Mr. Able has not been particularly circumspect with regard to honoring his wedding vows," Grace said, choosing her words with equal care.

"Oh, well—" Tyrone Powers let the thought hang there as he glanced over at his son. "Did you know Nate Able was having an affair?"

Grace had to admire the older man's acumen. He'd asked his son a direct question, but not one specific enough Trey would have to lie in order to answer it.

"Yes, sir."

Tyrone nodded and swallowed. His grimace told her he found this particular admission distasteful. "I see. And you allowed this…affair to carry on at our family home on the lake?"

Grace wanted to sit back and watch this farce play out, but she had to keep pushing. She needed to see exactly how much it would take for the Powers men to pin Mallory's death on Nate Able. She wasn't certain how far she would have to go to make Taylor Greene break ranks.

"To be honest, sir," Trey began, addressing his father respectfully, "I invited Nate to the party, but I didn't realize he'd be bringing a date along."

Grace did her best to keep her features neutral. She could almost feel the panic bubbling up inside Taylor. A surge of raw energy emanated from her side of the room like a wave of sound carrying across water. The others must have felt it, too, because she caught more than a few confused glances exchanged between the assembled attorneys.

"Agent Reed, I hope you understand neither my wife nor I condone such behavior," Tyrone Powers said smoothly. He shot his son a sidelong glance she assumed was meant to be censorious. "And I certainly don't approve of my son providing a forum for such behavior."

"I'm not here to pass judgment on your family, Mr. Powers," she said stonily. "I'm only here to get to the bottom of what might have happened to Ms. Murray. We don't believe her death was an accident."

"Has the coroner given a probable cause of death?" Harold Dennis cut in.

She nodded, though she was fairly certain the Powers team already had access to the coroner's report. "Ms. Murray sustained a blow to the back of her head. It appears someone struck her from behind. She either fell or was pushed into the water."

The people sitting opposite them absorbed this information with a disturbing lack of reaction, but Harold Dennis did cut a glance in the direction of Taylor Greene, and even Grace could read the warning in the older man's icy stare.

"There are at least three people in this room, maybe more, who we can confirm were there Friday night. We're hoping as officers of the court, you will come forward to bear witness to what actually took place," she said, staring directly at Joshua Potter.

The young man wagged his head in vehement denial. "I was there that night but spent most of the evening hanging out by the fire pit. I was talking to a girl I knew from school and, you know..." he trailed off with a shrug. "I don't like boats."

"He was hitting on Ainsley Markham again," Trey chimed in.

"And getting shot down again," Chet Barrow, Trey's budget doppelgänger, added, not bothering to mask his mockery.

"I see." Grace scribbled the words *no Josh* on the pad in front of her. She looked at the young man who clearly wished he were the heir to the Powers fiefdom. Knowing it would likely provoke him, she asked, "I'm sorry, I know we were introduced, but what was your name again?"

The young lawyer sat up straighter, noticeably offended by not being remembered. "Barrow. Chet Barrow."

Grace flashed him her sweetest smile. "Yes, I remember now." She zeroed in on him, her eyes narrowing as she used the cocky young man to push poor Taylor Greene closer to the edge. "You seem to be an observant man, Mr. Barrow. I think we can all agree Ms. Murray was an attractive young woman. Surely you saw her at the party with Mr. Able, didn't you?"

"I, uh..." He glanced at Trey, then at Tyrone Powers, who gave an encouraging nod. "I saw them there."

"You saw them there together," Grace pushed for clarification.

His gaze returned to Trey, who sat staring back at Grace,

his expression impassive. Finally, Barrow nodded enthusi-astically. "Yes. She and Able seemed to be pretty hot and heavy. I assumed Trey was doing them a favor by making such a show out of inviting her to the party. I mean, she's a waitress in a bar, right?"

"Right," she replied mildly.

His misogyny and plain old-fashioned snobbery had Grace seething inside, but she knew in her gut it wouldn't take much more to make Taylor Greene erupt. She was winding up another shot at Nate when Barrow piped in again.

Clearly warming to the spotlight, he forged ahead with the lie. "And everyone knows old Nate is kind of a dog when it comes to women. Not picky, if you know—"

"He is, too!" Taylor Greene burst forth.

All heads swiveled in her direction. At last, Grace turned to find the diminutive brunette had shot to her feet. Her fists were clenched, and her eyes blazed.

"Excuse me?" Harold Dennis asked coolly, his jaw set hard.

But Taylor was beyond caring. "He is not a dog. He has impeccable taste!"

Grace chanced a quick glance at Matthew. "What makes you say so, Ms. Greene?" Grace asked, sounding no more curious than someone asking how her day was going.

"Because *I* am the one who is having an affair with Nate Able. *I* am the woman he brought to the party." Her voice trembled when she spoke, but Grace instantly recognized it shook from rage, not fear. "They're lying." She spat the word. "They have to lie because everyone knows he did it. Everyone knows he's the reason she's dead."

Both Tyrone and Trey Powers began to speak at once, Tyrone in a placating voice, while his son's was decidedly more disdainful. But it was Harold Dennis who barked the order for the insubordinate junior associate to take her seat and stop speaking.

To her credit, Taylor did neither.

"Everyone knows *who* did it? *Who* is the reason?" Grace prompted, her gaze fixed on Taylor.

"I told you," she said, turning on Grace. "I told you about me and Nate. You know they're lying."

"I need you to tell me what happened to Mallory," Grace replied, calm and even. "Who did what?"

"Ms. Greene," Tyrone Powers said sternly as he rose from his chair.

She blinked, then looked at Trey's father imploringly. When she spoke, her voice was barely more than a stunned whisper. "He left her there. *He*…left her there. Like she was nothing more than a piece of trash."

Chapter Seventeen

Vitriol. Matthew had heard a lot of nasty things said about victims in the past, but seldom did he hear such vehement denials and denunciations of both Mallory and Taylor as he did in the sixty seconds after Taylor Greene's whispered accusation.

He let the words roll over him for a minute more, absorbing some of their impact as his due. After all, he'd said similar things about Mallory.

"Scheming—"

"Liar, you didn't see anything—"

"Why he would bother with anyone like you—"

"Your career is over, young lady. I will personally see to it no firm in this state—"

And so it went. Matthew didn't even bother trying to track who was saying what. He was too focused on watching Trey Powers.

The other man sat silent and still, his mouth clamped shut tight. A muscle ticked in his jaw, but he didn't speak another word.

Beside him, his previously serene father had turned into a whirlwind of bluff and bluster. Chaos reigned in the room, and only he, Grace and Trey seemed to stay above the fray.

Or rather, below it, because everyone else had leaped from their chairs to start shouting over one another.

"My son was not involved with that woman," Tyrone Powers bellowed.

Everyone fell quiet then, and Matthew dragged his attention from the son to the father. The elder Powers looked flustered—his neck and face florid above the collar of his white-on-white-striped collar and his hair falling onto his forehead.

"He was," Taylor Greene shouted back, heedless of the sudden silence enveloping the room. "They were together. And it wasn't a new thing. I saw the way they looked at each other. I saw the way they were talking at the party, all close and intense. Something was going on between them."

"You're fired," the older man said bluntly. "Get the hell out of my office."

"Now, Ty—" It was Harold Dennis's turn to try to smooth the waters.

But Taylor Greene was done. "You know what? Fine." She snatched her portfolio from the table and took a stumbling step back. "I'm done with the lies. I'm done with all of it."

"Ms. Greene, I'm afraid the terms of your employment agreement—" Dennis began.

The young woman snorted. "My employment agreement?" she asked derisively. "Where is the part about covering up murder written into my agreement?"

Grace rose to meet the young woman face-to-face. "Did you witness the assault on Ms. Murray?"

Matthew tried to get up, too, but couldn't get his feet under him.

"There's no proof. My client—" Mr. Dennis tried again.

Matthew watched as Grace crossed to Taylor Greene and looked the young woman in the eye, but she kept her voice pitched too low for him to hear what she said.

"You knew!" the younger woman cried. "Why should I tell you anything? You used what I told you for leverage. You pushed and pushed until...oh my God." Her gaze flew to Tyrone Powers once more. "I didn't mean to. I... I needed to protect Nate. What she was saying about Nate and that Mallory woman was not true."

"Did you witness Mr. Powers harming Ms. Murray?" Grace asked again, the pointed question cutting through various conversations.

Matt turned his attention back to Powers, interested to see how the question played out on the man who had clearly believed himself to be untouchable up until this moment. But Trey, with his father's hand planted firmly on his shoulder, remained mute.

"What cause would my client have to do such a thing?" Harold Dennis blundered on.

"You have no proof Ms. Murray was harmed while in Mr. Powers's company," Michelle Fraser interjected coolly. "You have no motivation."

Matthew felt compelled to speak. "I can tell you without a qualm we have enough evidence to arrest at least four people in this room today." He spoke quietly enough that the raised voices around him fell away.

Heads swiveled to Harold Dennis, and the other man stilled. "On what charges?"

"Operating watercraft under the influence?" He tossed it out like a fishing hook into chum-baited waters. The other man, nonplussed, couldn't respond. "Or leaving the scene of an accident?" He raised a hand and pointed in Taylor Greene's general direction, his eyes still locked on Trey. "She said you did."

"One unfounded accusation doesn't mean—" Michelle Fraser began.

"Assault? Aggravated assault? Reckless endangerment?

Those are all possibilities, and we haven't even gotten to intent. Intent opens up a lot of other possibilities." He shifted his gaze to one after the other. "And I'm sure as officers of the court, all your friends know there's a whole menu of possible charges waiting for them, too. Failure to report an accident, obstruction of justice, possibly even tampering with evidence? Any of those sound like a good fit?" he asked, glancing over at Grace.

"Sky's the limit," she replied coolly.

"Literally," Matthew said, the word dry as dust. "Don't forget, Table Rock Lake is considered a federal waterway. There could be a whole slew of federal charges facing whoever was involved."

"True," Grace confirmed.

He turned his attention back to Trey. No one moved. No one spoke. An unnatural silence filled the room.

"Frankly, I'm leaning more toward murder, but I may be biased," he said, holding the other man's gaze. "Premeditation is the big question."

Mr. Dennis recovered first, but when he spoke, the words came out hollow. "You have no reason to believe—"

Matthew ignored him, his eyes narrowing on Trey. At last, the other man broke, shifting his attention to Tyrone Powers. He clearly expected his daddy could save him.

"When did Mallory tell you she was pregnant, Trey?" Matthew asked, his voice lethally quiet.

The elder Powers flinched, but the younger went stock-still, like an animal who knew he was caught in the hunter's sight line.

"Do not answer any questions," Ms. Fraser interjected.

"Did you know she was pregnant when you came to Stubby's? When you took her out on your boat?" Matthew persisted.

"Pregnant?" Ty Powers asked, turning a befuddled gaze at his son.

Ignoring counsel's advice to keep his mouth shut, Trey turned to his father. "If she was, it's not mine," he said imploringly. "I hadn't seen her in almost two months."

"But you don't deny having intercourse with her," Grace said, moving back to her spot and planting her hands firmly on the conference table. "You and Ms. Murray have had sexual relations."

"Yeah, but—"

Trey's protests were cut off by Michelle Fraser's shout. "Shut up. Now!"

In the residual silence, Grace picked up her cell phone.

"Everybody back to their offices immediately," Harold Dennis barked.

"No," Grace retorted. Holding her phone in her left hand, she stepped in front of the conference room doors. Matthew gawked at mulish set of her chin as she raised the phone to her mouth. "I'm going to need you all to stay here, please."

"You can't—"

But Grace wasn't listening to anything more Harold had to say. Instead, she switched her phone to speaker mode. "Sheriff Stenton?" she asked when a gravelly voiced man answered.

"Yes, ma'am."

"This is Special Agent Grace Reed of the Arkansas State Police," she said, her gaze locking first with Harold Dennis, then skimming over Tyrone Powers and landing on his son. "Is the backup and transport I requested earlier ready?"

"Yes, ma'am. We're right outside."

Grace nodded. "Please, come in. I'll have at least four detainees, and I imagine each of them is going to want to lawyer up separately."

She ended the call, then asked the room in general, "Is

there anyone here who needs me to remind them of their Miranda rights?"

Matthew rose and went to stand next to her. "How can I help?" he asked.

She leaned over and whispered, "You might want to give the people in your office a heads-up. I have a team heading in there now, too."

Grace stepped aside at a tap on the door. Over Harold Dennis's increasingly voluble protests, she twisted the handle and allowed a group of sheriff's deputies to enter the room.

Matthew watched them pass without moving. "I'll call, but I'm not stepping out."

He called his assistant, Tracy.

"Matthew? What's happening? Nate's in a hell of a mood."

"Hey, listen, I can't talk long," he said to his assistant. "Some stuff is about to go down with Nate. I can't get into it now. I need you to stay calm and make sure everyone else does, too. I'll be there as soon as I can."

He ended the call to preempt the barrage of questions he knew would be forthcoming. As Grace directed the deputies to each of the persons they'd identified as party guests, he speed-dialed his boss.

"What the hell is going on?" Nate snapped. "Where are you?"

"I'm at the offices of Powers, Powers & Walton," he replied calmly.

"Why? We've talked about this. Nothing good can come of—"

"I'm watching your friend Trey Powers get cuffed as we speak," Matthew said, cutting him off. "They're also taking guys named Joshua Potter and Chet Barrow, as well as a Ms. Taylor Greene into custody for questioning."

"On what grounds?" Nate demanded. Matthew heard the echo of a hard rap on a door and held his breath.

Nate place a finger over the microphone to muffle the sound, but his voice still came through clear enough when he called out, "Come back later. I'm busy."

"I don't think they'll come back later, Nate," Matthew said quietly.

Through the phone he could hear a louder knock and an officious voice call out, "Nathaniel Able?"

Nate came back on the line. "What the hell is this, Murray? What's happening here?"

"I'm afraid Taylor Greene has placed you at the same party she was attending the evening Mallory went missing," he explained. "The party at the Powerses' lake house."

"She's lying," Nate responded without hesitation.

"Unfortunately for you, she's not. I've seen photographs of the two of you together. Come on, Nate, you know the internet is forever. How could you have been so foolish?"

The minute the question escaped him, Matthew wondered if he was asking his boss how he'd been foolish enough to get caught, or foolish enough to put himself in the situation to start. Either way, it didn't matter. Nate's career as a prosecutor and his dreams of political glory were likely over.

Or not. It seemed politicians were able to get away with far more these days. Perhaps the cover-up of Mallory's death would end up being something Nate would have to spin, but it was possible the scandal wouldn't keep him from winning future elections. Particularly not if his wife stayed by his side.

And if he stayed on the right side of Tyrone Powers.

"Go with them quietly. Answer what questions you can and be sure to give Susan some warning."

"I swear, if you've done anything to jeopardize my—"

"I haven't done anything other than try to find out what happened to my sister. You remember my sister now, don't you, Nate? She's the one you and your buddies left floating alone in the dark on Table Rock Lake."

"I have no idea what you're talking about," Nate said stiffly.

Matthew swallowed hard. All around him, deputies were snapping handcuffs and running through the litany of arrest. From the head of the table, Harold Dennis barked out the names of other attorneys in the room, assigning one to each of the detainees.

He heard the deputy on the other end of the line say to Nate, "I'm going to need you to end your call and come with me, sir."

Three short beeps marked the disconnection. Matthew lowered the phone and stepped to the side, allowing one of the deputies to lead a bewildered-looking Joshua Potter from the room. He watched as the deputy leading Barrow followed, the younger man grumbling under his breath about how they were all making a big, big mistake. Grace stepped in beside him while Taylor Greene was led out the door; her eyes were downcast, but her frustrated sobs had dried to hiccups.

"You okay?" she asked in a low voice as two more attorneys scurried out of the room.

"Yeah."

Matthew's focus shifted to Trey Powers, who stood conferring with his father and lawyers. The deputy had cuffed his hands in front of him but kept a loose hold on the crook of his arm. Matthew noticed how he'd subtly turned away from their hissed whispers. Even under arrest, the Powers men received special treatment.

"You'd better head to your office while I deal with all this. It's going to be a circus over there."

Matthew nodded. "You're probably right."

"I'm going to have to get the Carroll County prosecutor filled in, but I'll touch base with you as soon as I get a minute."

"I doubt any of them talk from here on out."

Grace gave him a half smile. "I think Taylor will. I believe the young woman may actually have one of those…what do you call it? A moral compass?"

"I wouldn't know," Matthew replied, deadpan.

"Oh, right, you're one of them, too."

"I am not one of them," he shot back immediately.

Grace gave his arm a reassuring pat. "No. No, you're not."

Stepping forward, she turned her attention to the group on the other side of the room. Tyrone and Trey seemed to be stalling while Harold Dennis conferred with Michelle Fraser.

"Mr. Powers?" Grace prompted. When they deigned to turn her way, she raised both eyebrows and smirked at the powerful trio. "I promise y'all will have hours to play catch-up, but you're holding me and Deputy, uh…" She tilted her head, trying to read the name pinned to the officer's uniform.

"Smith," he supplied for her.

"You're keeping Deputy Smith from his other duties, and I'm tired of waiting for you. Let's move it out."

With the brusque order, Grace unleashed a smile so triumphant, Matthew felt his chest tighten even as Tyrone Powers flushed nearly violet.

At last, Trey started to move to the door with Michelle Fraser close on his heels, but Tyrone Powers halted them with an abrupt "Stop!" With a fiery glare at Grace, he unbuttoned the jacket of his exquisitely tailored suit. "Hold out your arms," he instructed his son.

Trey did as he was told, but in doing so, the sleeves of his own suit jacket rode up.

Recognition shot through Matthew like a lightning bolt when he spotted the expensive watch on the man's wrist. Grace must have seen it, too, because she straightened to her full height as the older man draped his folded jacket over his son's wrists to conceal the cuffs.

Grace gave Matthew a speaking glance before she fell

into step behind Trey and the deputy. "I like your cuff links," she said in a voice loud enough to carry back to him. "And they match your watch. Such a pretty blue. Are they white gold or platinum?"

Matthew had to stifle a chuckle as he followed the two older lawyers out of the conference room and toward the exterior doors. Harold Dennis held one of the glass panel doors open for them to pass through, but Tyrone hung back.

Matthew could only assume it was because he wanted to put distance between Grace and themselves as he whispered, "This was not your brightest hour, Murray. When we're through with you, no one will elect you dogcatcher."

Meeting the other man's steely gaze, Matthew simply shrugged. "I guess it's a good thing I'm not running for dogcatcher."

While Grace and the others headed for the parking area, Matthew took off at a brisk pace in the opposite direction. His gaze fixed straight ahead, he power walked down Central toward the courthouse and the county offices. Cutting through to one of the back entrances, he passed the spot where he'd backed into Judge Walton's car a lifetime ago.

He nodded to the sheriff's deputy on security duty, showed his ID and emptied his pockets into a tray to be clear for the metal detector. Once he'd collected his belongings, he turned down the main corridor and started off in a trot. He reached the prosecuting attorney's offices just as Nate was being escorted into the hall wearing a set of cuffs.

Stripping off his own jacket, Matthew threw it over the shiny silver bracelets his boss wore.

"Yeah, thanks a lot," Nate said derisively. .

"We're not even going to get into who did what to whom," Matthew said in a low voice. "My advice to you is to cooperate. Help them build this case. You know what Powers did was wrong. You know you're all accessories after the fact regardless. Cut whatever deal you need to cut and save what's left of your life. Otherwise, I will do everything I can to make sure your career is buried along with my sister. You got me?"

Nate sneered as he reared back. "Thanks for your unsolicited advice, Counselor."

"Take it or leave it," Matthew called after him as the deputies led him away. "Free of charge and everything. Bet you Powers won't say the same thing."

When he turned back to the open door, he found every pair of eyes in the office trained on him. Sparing one last glance at Nate's back, Matthew stepped into the office and did his best to make order out of chaos.

Chapter Eighteen

Though she expected the knock at her door, Grace still jumped when it came. The weeks following the arrests of the people involved with Mallory Murray's disappearance and death had been maddening. As Matthew predicted, most of the Powers team clammed up. They could barely get single-word answers out of any of them without another attorney vetting the question and approving their answer or nonanswer.

Thankfully, Nate Able had decided to give the press a couple of sound bites on the courthouse steps upon his release on bond. He'd stated he had not witnessed any part of Ms. Murray's misadventure, claimed he'd never believed there was anything to cover up because he didn't know anything had happened, but worst of all, he'd categorically denied the affair he was accused of having with one of the attorneys at PP&W.

The problems for Nate compounded when his wife, Susan, refused to return from Florida and take her place by his side. Instead, she told the press she had been aware of her husband's infidelity and had hired an investigator to follow him to gather proof in the week she was gone. Her investigator was able to produce photos taken the morning after the party. The incriminating photographs showed the Benton County prosecuting attorney behind the wheel of a gray compact car matching the description of the deceased's vehicle.

Within minutes of his second arrest, the county board called for Nate's resignation. Matthew had been appointed acting prosecuting attorney within the day. It was all such a whirlwind he and Grace had barely had a minute to exchange text messages and voice mails updating one another on what was happening on their end.

After a week of spending a good chunk of their waking hours together, Grace found herself missing him. Not only his insights and the company, but his presence. Now he stood outside the open door to her hotel room waiting to be invited in. Her heart started to beat faster as she drank in the sight of him. He was dressed in chinos and a short-sleeved button-down. Even his casual clothes fit his long, lean body like a glove.

"Hey," she said, stepping back to allow him entry. "What a crazy couple of weeks, huh?"

"An understatement." He looked her up and down, a smile tugging at his lips. "You look, uh—" he paused for a beat "—nice."

Color raced to her cheeks. At first, she wasn't sure if he was holding back or simply being polite, but his smile was warm and appreciative.

"You didn't have to dress up," he said, but everything about his demeanor told her he was glad she had.

When he'd asked her to come with him to the cemetery where Mallory's ashes would be placed beside their parents', she'd realized she didn't have anything appropriate to wear. Everything she owned was cop wear, and in this instance, she wanted him to see her as more than a detective. So she'd made a quick trip to the mall, where she bought a casual but pretty dress and sandals her sister approved via video chat.

"Thanks for your help with the jurisdictional mess," he said sincerely.

"It was the least I could do," she replied, trying to sound offhand but unable to control her skittering heartbeat.

With the backing of the state police, Grace was able to get the junior Benton County attorney Matthew had assigned to the case, the Carroll County PA and officials from the federal government to agree on referring the case to one of the circuit courts in central Arkansas. Hopefully, the move would be enough to mitigate some of the family's influence on the court system.

His gaze traveled around the sitting area. She'd packed up most of her gear already. By evening, she'd be back in her apartment in Fort Smith, and the following week she'd be at her desk again, catching the missing-persons cases no one else wanted to handle.

"Looks like you're about ready to clear out."

"I got most of it gathered last night," she answered, trying to sound indifferent.

He gave a sigh and a tired smile. "I guess we should go do this."

Grace nodded, then grabbed her purse and keys from the breakfast bar.

Matthew pulled his own key ring from his pocket and jangled it. "I'm driving this time."

"I don't know... Is it safe to ride with the mysterious bumper smasher?" she teased, pulling the door shut behind her.

"Yeah, now you're making me wish it was some kind of jacked-up 4x4," he complained good-naturedly.

He held the car door for her as she slid into the sporty SUV parked beside her decidedly more clunky-looking state vehicle.

Neither of them spoke as they left the parking area and headed northeast on Highway 62. The moment they were outside the city limits, he glanced over at her. "It means a lot to me, you coming along today. I didn't want to do a whole service and everything."

"I understand."

"They threw a party in Mallory's honor at Stubby's last weekend."

"Did you go?"

He shook his head. "Nah. Never was my scene, and I figured me being there would make people feel like they had to behave in front of the bereaved brother."

She nodded. "Kelli Simon told me you cleared Mallory's things out of the apartment."

He nodded. "There wasn't much to keep. I donated most of her clothes and stuff."

"Nice," she said approvingly.

The miles flew by, and they slipped into the same easy silence they'd had since the start. As they passed Stubby's Bar & Grill, the back of her neck prickled, but Grace chalked the sensation up to residual excitement at closing the case.

The scene at the modest cemetery east of Garfield might have looked sad to anyone passing by, but somehow it seemed right for Matthew and Mallory. Grace hung back, standing close to the man who'd opened the small grave while Matthew knelt beside a headstone carved with only the family name.

She bowed her head as he spoke.

"I'm sorry, Mal. Sorry we weren't closer. Sorry I wasn't a better brother. Sorry this happened to you." He paused to take a shuddering breath. "I know this guy is slippery, but I promise you, we will go after him with everything we have. Trey Powers will pay for what he did to you."

Grace sighed. At the moment, the biggest charge they could nail Powers with was leaving the scene, but she knew deep in her bones Matthew was right. They would find the key. Trey Powers would not get off on a technicality or buy his way out of this mess with his family's money.

After Matthew had spoken his piece and his sister was laid to rest, he and Grace returned to the car. The moment they were back on the highway, he shot her an uneasy glance. "I don't know if I could possibly come up with a more inappropriate time and place to say what I want to say to you, but if I've learned anything from Mallory's death, it's that I have to say it anyway."

"Okay," she replied, curiosity piqued.

"I like you, Grace. Despite the circumstances, I liked being with you. And I would like to see more of you." He cast another sidelong glance in her direction. "Not in a professional capacity."

Once again, her heart began to pound. "I, uh, yeah. I feel the same way, but I didn't want to say something because—" she circled a hand, hoping to encompass all the circumstances under which they met "—everything."

"Fort Smith isn't far," he ventured.

"Nope. It's an easy drive up 49."

He let off the gas as soon as they hit a straight stretch and turned to her. "Would you have dinner with me one night? We can meet in the middle if you want."

She smirked as she envisioned the rural stretch of highway between the cities of Fort Smith and Fayetteville. "I think they do two-for-one corn dogs at the gas station in West Fork."

The suggestion earned her a grin. "Okay, I'll come to you."

"Either way," she said agreeably.

They drove in contented quiet for a minute. When Matthew reached over and touched the back of her hand, she turned it palm up. He laced his fingers through hers.

"You're not going to give me a ticket for not having both hands on the wheel, are you?"

"I can be bribed."

"Oh, yeah?" He gave her fingers a squeeze. "With what?"

She jerked her chin toward the squat cinder-block building they approached. "Buy me a Stubby's burger? I hear they're the best around."

Without releasing her hand, he signaled his intention to turn into the crumbling asphalt lot.

Inside the dimly lit bar, they waved hello to Steve.

"You're late for the party," he informed them.

"How was it?" Grace asked as Matthew pointed to a table.

"It was a doozy," their resident day drinker called from his seat at the end of the bar.

"Can we get two burgers?" Matthew asked, holding up two fingers.

"Coming up," Steve replied.

"Water?" he asked Grace.

"Please." She hooked a thumb over her shoulder. "I'm going to the ladies'."

Matthew nodded, and she walked away. A part of her wanted to do a giddy dance. He wanted to see her again.

Slipping into the dank ladies' room, she locked the door behind her and pulled her phone from her bag. Thumbs flying, she texted her sister.

He asked me out!

While she waited to see if the dots indicating an incoming message appeared, she glanced up and caught sight of an ancient metal vending machine attached to the wall. One side purported to sell feminine products and the other condoms.

She focused on her phone again. No message from her sister came through, but the creeping sensation along the back of her neck had returned. She spun in a slow circle. Out of the corner of her eye, she noticed that the door to the vending machine wasn't properly secured.

There were no scratches to indicate someone had tried to pry it open, but a shiver traveled down her spine. Dropping her phone back into her bag, Grace reached for the corner of the cabinet and pulled.

A shower of paper-wrapped tampons and condom squares spilled out at her feet. As did a zip-top bag holding a white wand with a blue cap and a plastic card.

Grace squatted to make a closer inspection. Using the hem of her dress, she picked up one corner of the bag. The white stick showed a clear plus sign in the window. Mallory Murray beamed back at her from an Arkansas driver's license.

"There you are," Grace whispered as she inspected the bag's contents to be certain she wasn't imagining her good fortune.

She wasn't.

It wasn't quite the gotcha she needed to nail Trey Powers for murder, but the fact Mallory had hidden these items might help prove she was concerned about his reaction to the news of his impending fatherhood.

Releasing the bag, she reached for her phone again. Ignoring the rapid-fire texts from her sister about what she'd wear and where they'd go, Grace shot several photos of the bag, its contents, the wrapped tampons and condoms, and finally the machine itself.

Covering the bag in a paper towel to protect it, she stepped out into the barroom and walked up to Steve at the bar. "I'm sorry," she murmured, "I'm going to need to cordon off your ladies' room. Would you please call the county sheriff to come out?"

"What is it?" Matthew asked, rising from the nearby table where he sat with their sweating drinks.

"I found test number two and Mallory's driver's license," she informed him. "This isn't over."

She held up her phone to show him the photos she'd snapped. He swallowed hard, still looking at the screen as another message from Faith came through.

Take a picture of him. I need a visual. Oh, and whatever you do, don't let Hottie McMurray see you in your cop suit.

"Too late," he whispered, looking down at her with such blatant admiration her breath tangled in her throat. "Tell her I've seen you in your cop suit, Grace, and it was a beautiful sight to behold."

"We'll get him, Matthew. Somehow, someway, we'll make sure this sticks."

Looking straight into her eyes, he lowered his head until his lips were mere millimeters from hers. "Yes. We will."

His kiss was soft. Lingering. Filled with promise.

"Have I told you how glad I am we're on the same side?"

"No, but I am, too," she whispered. "I'd hate to have to take you down."

* * * * *

COLTON'S UNDERCOVER SEDUCTION

BETH CORNELISON

Chapter One

Humphrey Kelly, covered in blood and gasping for breath, glared at her and pointed an accusing finger. "Do something, rookie! You wanted to be a cop, now prove yourself! Find me! Save me!"

Panic filled Eva Colton's chest. She tried to back away from the accusing finger but couldn't. She found it hard to draw a breath. "I'm trying!"

Humphrey, the man who'd done so much for her family and was like a second father to the Colton siblings, reached a bony finger toward her and poked her face. Once. Twice. Three times. "Find me!"

Poke, poke.

Eva woke with a shallow gasp, her pulse thumping wildly. Carnegie, her overweight ginger cat, sat on her chest, patting her cheek with a paw. *"Mrow."* Poke, poke.

Grunting, she scratched Rocky's head and closed her eyes with a dramatic sigh. "Bad dream." Except Humphrey Kelly's disappearance wasn't imagined. Her heart ached knowing he was still missing some three-plus months after mysteriously vanishing while at the courthouse downtown.

"Mrow?" Carnegie asked. Yes, asked. Because the rise in pitch and tilt of his head told Eva it was definitely a question. As in, *Can I get some breakfast, please?*

"Yeah, of course, buddy. I'm coming." She angled her head to check the time on her bedside clock and groaned. She had fifty-eight minutes to get showered and get from her East Village apartment to the Ninety-Eighth Precinct in Brooklyn to avoid being late. And she would not be late. Not only was that anathema to her type A rule-following leanings, but it would lead to a dressing-down from her partner, hard-ass Mitch Mallard. Not the way she wanted to start a new workweek.

Because she was a rookie, only nine months on the job at the Ninety-Eighth, her partner thought she didn't know what was what, and he prided himself in lording his twenty years' experience over her. If he didn't outrank her, she might challenge the condescending jerk to a contest. She could recite New York statutes and police procedure, chapter and verse. What she lacked in time on the job, she made up for in procedural knowledge…and maybe a bit of osmosis. After all, her oldest brother, Sean, was an experienced cop at the Ninety-Eighth Precinct. Their father had been an accomplished private investigator, as her middle brother, Cormac, was now, often working in concert with the Ninety-Eighth. Her brother Liam? Well, Liam knew more about the ins and outs of law enforcement and criminal activity than most people, despite the fact that he'd spent some time on the wrong side of the law…or maybe because of it.

Rookie or not, Eva *knew* police work. She just needed more hands-on experience, and she was confident she would race up the ranks—if Mitch wouldn't ruin things for her. The jerk. She gritted her teeth in frustration, nudged Carnegie aside and tossed back the covers. "So get a move on, Colton. No point giving the blowhard more fuel for his hot air machine."

She hustled to the kitchenette of her apartment—where she found a sticky note from her roommate, Kara, saying she'd be late that night—filled Carnie's food bowl and then hurried to the shower. Ten minutes later, she was dressed, her wet auburn hair slicked back into a ponytail, and was speeding down the stairs. The yeasty scent of fresh pizza dough being prepared for the day in the restaurant on the ground floor of her building filled the stairwell. Eva's stomach growled. She'd not taken time for breakfast and prayed there were bagels or muffins or something at the precinct.

Maria DeLuca, wife of the pizza joint's owner, was sweeping the sidewalk in front of the restaurant door as Eva jogged outside and headed for the subway.

"Good morning, Eva! Beautiful day, no?"

She smiled at the short older woman, whose back had begun to stoop with age and a lifetime of hard work. "Good morning, Maria. Yes, lovely day. Have a good one. Gotta run!"

"Take time to eat! You're too skinny!" Mrs. DeLuca called after her, a common refrain from the woman who clearly equated feeding people with a love language.

Eva raised a hand in acknowledgment as she hurried down the block, dodging other morning commuters rushing toward Union Square. She lifted her eyes to find the spot where the sun was just illuminating the towering Manhattan skyline. The sky was a startling April blue, and spring hummed in the air. God, she loved her city. Especially this time of year, when flowers bloomed in the parks and pots outside doorways, and trees budded with tiny leaves in every shade of green.

The subway ride was uneventful this morning, thank God,—and she darted into the squad room with a full two minutes to spare. Ha! She'd even beat the high-and-mighty Mitch this morning.

She'd just dropped into her desk chair and Reevesed on her laptop when her brother Sean strolled by with a mug of coffee in his hand and a worried look creasing his brow. His frown didn't bode well. "Eva, can I see you in my office?"

"What's up?"

In answer, he hitched his head toward his tiny Spartan office and walked away. Eva cast a longing glance toward the breakroom, her stomach rumbling, but dutifully followed Sean into his closet of an office. Brother or not, he outranked her, and she would not give anyone in the precinct a reason to question her abilities or loyalty to the job.

"Am I in trouble?" she said in a teasing manner as she stopped in the threshold. She flashed Sean a lopsided grin, but her gut was tense. Since becoming engaged to body-guard-for-hire Orla Roberts in January, Sean was usually smiling, at least in his eyes. But the happy glow he'd been sporting lately was dimmed today, and Eva frowned. "Is everything all right? Is it Orla? Did something happen?"

Sean jerked his head up from the file he was studying at the mention of Orla's name. "Huh? What? No, this has nothing to do with Orla." Ah, there was the twinkle in his eye again...

"Okay. So...?"

Sean cleared his throat. "You're temporarily getting a new partner."

She straightened. "I am? Why?"

"Mallard's wife called this morning. He has a severe case of mono. Can't talk, throat's a mess, and because of Mitch's past heart issues, his doctor has ordered him to stay in bed and rest for at least two weeks. Apparently, a case as bad as what Mitch has can screw up your organs..." Sean shrugged.

Eva's spirits lifted, and she worked hard to suppress the grin that burgeoned on her lips. Even though Sean was aware of her resentment for Mitch's borderline bullying, openly reveling in his absence from the precinct and her vacation from his condescension was not good form. She bit the inside of her cheek and nodded.

Sean waved toward a chair, inviting her in, and she stepped farther into her brother's office and took a seat. "Okay. So who am I working with?"

Just about anyone in the 98th Precinct was better than Mitch. The other officers might kid her the way they teased all the rookies, but at least they recognized her abilities. And kept their distance. Everyone knew she was Sean's little sister and had no intention of crossing her protective brother. She ran through a quick mental checklist of potential partners. Who worked alone? Whose partner was on vacation?

Henshaw would be easy to work with. Chuck Grayson had recently retired, and Nelson hadn't been reassigned yet. She could see herself being happier and more productive being paired up with anybody… Well, anyone except—

She squeezed her hands into fists and closed her eyes as she squashed the little quiver that chased through her. She thought of a particular pair of dark brown eyes. Broad, muscled shoulders. A dimple in a stubble-dusted cheek. Her skin flashed hot, and her pulse scampered. Oh, Lord love a duck!

She shoved aside the mental image of her highly inappropriate crush…only to open her eyes and find those same muscled shoulders, sexy dimple and brown eyes staring at her from the doorway.

"You asked to see me, Colton?" said Detective Carmine DiRico.

Eva's heart slammed against her ribs. *No! Oh, no, no, no… Please don't say—*

But Sean did say it. "Carmine, Eva, you'll be partnering for the next few weeks until Mallard gets back."

Chapter Two

"Excuse me?" Carmine scrunched his face, uncertain he'd heard Detective Sean Colton correctly.

"Did I stutter?" Sean replied. He wagged a finger from his little sister, Eva, to Carmine and back. "You two. Partners. Until I say otherwise. Mallard's out sick."

Carmine scratched his cheek, which was rough with a short beard since he'd not had time to shave this morning. And hadn't bothered over the weekend. "I already have a partner. I don't—"

"Hayes can finish up the paperwork on the vape-shop robbery and Garrison mugging without you. I want you frying bigger fish."

Carmine arched an eyebrow. Sean had done his homework. And, yeah, he wasn't deeply involved in a major case at the moment. But partnering with a rookie? Especially one as distractingly hot as Eva? Who was Sean's *sister*, for the love of—

Even now, without looking at her, Carmine could feel his body humming, heating, tightening just from feeling her eyes on him. And smelling the so-sweet aroma of some flower, which was probably her shampoo, because her thick hair still had damp streaks from her morning shower... And he had to cut that picture off now before—

"What bigger fish?" Carmine asked, redirecting his thoughts to his new assignment.

"The Lana Brinkley murder and Humphrey Kelly's disappearance." Detective Colton's desk chair creaked as he leaned back and stacked his hands behind his head. "We got some puzzling DNA results back in the Kelly case, and it raises a whole new set of questions regarding our lead suspect in the Brinkley murder."

"I thought the Kelly case happened in Manhattan. How did you catch it?" Carmine hazarded a glance at Eva, who was being unusually quiet. Typically, her dulcet laughter and jovial teasing could be heard throughout the precinct. But she sat staring at her brother with a look that wavered between a thirst for vengeance, desperate pleading and sheer panic. Her fingers were curled into the arms of her chair, her knuckles nearly white from her grip.

"Back in January when Kelly disappeared at the courthouse where he'd been prepared to give expert testimony, his wife asked me to aid the investigators in Manhattan."

"Why you?" Carmine asked.

Sean cracked the knuckles on one hand with his other. "Because Humphrey is a close family friend, and she knew we'd give it the attention it deserved. The Manhattan precinct that caught the case was all too happy to have our assistance. The point is, Humphrey's DNA was found in a utility closet at the courthouse. The report we got back just last week says that among the other DNA in the closet—the janitors and other personnel that can legitimately be excluded—was trace evidence that someone related to Wes Westmore was also in that closet recently. Specifically, someone female."

"Hang on." Carmine raised a hand, then folded his arms over his chest as he processed this tidbit. "Isn't Wes Westmore the guy sitting at Rikers as we speak for killing Lana Brinkley?"

Beside him, Eva finally stirred, glancing at him and touching her finger to her nose. As in, *Bingo. You nailed it.*

He turned back to Sean. "So the cases are connected?"

Sean shook his head. "We can't say that yet with any authority. But I've already had Eva—" He stopped and, with a flip of one hand, gave his sister an apologetic look. "Sorry, *Officer Colton* helping me with the Brinkley and Kelly cases, but I want the two of you to devote yourselves to it full-time. I promised Lana's parents we'd find her killer. While my gut says Wes is guilty, we need more proof. We also need to learn why Wes's relative left DNA in the courtroom closet and if the cases have any links."

Carmine rubbed the back of his neck where fresh tension coiled. Landing a place on the team working a high-profile murder like the Brinkley case was the kind of thing cops jonesed for. He should be grateful for the opportunity. But...

He stole another glance at his new partner, whose back was ramrod straight, her lips pursed in what he assumed was disdain. Not only was Eva a rookie, still learning the ropes, but—

She raised her gaze to him, and her green eyes widened, then narrowed dubiously. Damn, had he been staring at her puckered and pouty lips? He jerked his attention away, pinching the bridge of his nose and growling in his throat.

"We need to head to Rikers," he mumbled, thinking aloud.

"Exactly," Detective Colton said, righting his chair and shoving to his feet. "I'm going up there now to have a word with Wes Westmore. I want you two to study the case file and follow up on any tips that came in on the hotline over the weekend." Sean rounded his desk, pulling on a jacket and snapping his gun holster at his waist.

Carmine had just stepped aside to let Sean pass when Eva said, "Sean, wait a sec."

Detective Colton stopped, and Carmine shifted his focus to his new partner.

After clearing her throat, Eva said, "Give me a crack at him. At Westmore."

"What?" Sean said, stunned and echoing the surprise zinging through Carmine. "No. Not a chance."

Eva gritted her teeth and glared at her brother. "Why not?"

The older Colton rolled his eyes, as if the answer should be obvious. "Wes Westmore is—"

"A scuzzball," she finished for him. "I know."

Her brother's face hardened. "And you want me to send you up to the lion's den to get mauled?"

Eva's jaw worked, and she sent Sean the kind of glare that only a younger sister could get away with. Anyone else in the department would be ripped a new one for showing that kind of dissension and animosity toward a superior so openly. "I've warned you before, Sean. Don't coddle me. I can do this job. I'm a member of this precinct now, and I deserve a chance," she argued, her eyes bright with passion and anger. "I'm going to be dealing with guys like Westmore all the time now. Besides, he knows you, knows you're working to send him away for life. He hasn't talked before now because he has his guard up. Maybe sending in someone new—especially a woman—will rattle him just enough to catch him out somehow."

"Eva—" Sean sighed, then, squaring his shoulders, started again. "*Officer Colton*, you just don't have the experience needed to interview—"

"But—" she interrupted, then visibly bit back her objection when her brother shot her a quelling look.

In the intervening silence, Carmine said quietly, "She has a point."

Both Sean and Eva angled startled glances toward him. Carmine shrugged. "She wouldn't be going in alone. I'll go with her. And you could always go and watch from one of the observation rooms. She could be wired, wear a discreet earpiece so that you could be in her ear, feeding her questions. Pulling her back."

Detective Colton folded his arms, his expression wary, but he was clearly listening and considering.

"How am I supposed to learn and get experience if I'm not allowed to do the hard stuff? It's a prison, for pity's sake. There are armed guards everywhere. There'll be a sheet of plexiglass between me and Westmore." She hesitated and seemed to swallow her pride before adding, "Detective DiRico will be with me." She inhaled deeply and flexed her hand at her side, before saying under her breath, "Geez, Sean. C'mon. I'll be fine. Let me do this!"

Her brother squeezed his eyes shut and groaned. "Okay. But I'm going with you, will be watching from an observation room—"

"No wire!" Eva inserted before her brother could stipulate it. "He'll know, and he'll clam up."

Carmine gave the senior detective a look that said, *She's not wrong.*

Sean gritted his teeth so hard his jaw cracked. "Fine. I'm driving. And I reserve the right to intervene and stop the interview if it goes sideways." He strode away with brisk steps, calling to a desk sergeant, "Call Wes Westmore's attorney. Let him know we're on our way to Rikers to have a chat with his client."

Eva and Carmine looked at each other. Her expression seemed as stunned by the rapidly changing situation as he felt. "Um, thanks…for sticking up for me," she said.

He motioned that she'd better hustle toward the exit. Her brother was leaving them in the dust. They walked out of the squad room together, and without looking at her, he said, "That's what partners do. They look out for each other. Right?"

"Well, yeah. I—"

"And I believe in chances. In trying things outside the box. And, honestly, I wanted a chance to look the guy accused of killing his girlfriend in the eye and tell him with a cool glare what I think of turds like him who hurt women."

"Allegedly," Eva corrected, holding up a finger. "He hasn't been convicted."

Carmine grunted, telling her what he thought of that technical distinction. She was such a noob… "Hey, rookie, you better take the factory-protective film off those rose-colored glasses," he said as they hurried down the corridor. "Lesson one…police work is no place for tunnel vision or idealistic blind spots." He shoved through the door to the parking area, pulling a pair of sunglasses from his jacket pocket as he trotted down the steps. "It's a hard, cynical world out there, and you better have eyes in the back of your head, or you'll be shot in the ass before you can pull out your Miranda cheat sheet."

He slowed long enough to slide his shades on, and she jogged past him with a snarling side glance and a haughty sniff. "Save the pedantic sermon for someone who needs it, *partner.* I may be a rookie, but I am not stupid. I know what I'm doing. Okay?"

Carmine watched Eva cross the asphalt to the vehicle where Detective Colton was waiting. Her uniform did nothing to hide her trim body and toned limbs. As she approached her waiting brother, she twisted her long auburn hair into a knot at her slim nape and tucked in the ponytail's thick end. When a kick of lust punched him between the eyes, Carmine exhaled harshly. *She's your partner. And Sean Colton's sister. She may be sexy as hell and a sassy piece of work, but she can be nothing else. Remember that, DiRico.*

CARMINE DIRICO.

Eva stared at the back of her new partner's head, studying the way his dark brown hair curled slightly around his ears and the collar of his shirt. She chewed the inside of her cheek, replaying his warning not to be too starry-eyed, and tried to fit it with the composite she was drawing of the man she'd be working with. She knew he was a rule bender and a risk taker. She'd seen him called into Captain ColleenColleen Reeves' office for his unorthodox methods more than once. That could be a problem for her. As a rookie, with the entire precinct looking over her shoulder, and a rule follower from birth, she could easily see her and Carmine clashing over procedure.

But more than that, Carmine DiRico was the only man in years to tempt her to break her own rule about getting involved with anyone her brothers knew. The rule was for the man's sake. Her brothers were impossibly overprotective—case in point, Sean's reluctance over letting her interview Westmore at Rikers Island. Sean, Cormac and Liam would hassle and try to intimidate anyone she dated. All the more so if they knew the guy. Which they did in Carmine's case since he, too, was cop. Which really made him off limits anyway. She simply would not—*could* not—get involved with anyone at the precinct. Besides, word in the department was that Carmine had a dating history as long as a drugstore receipt. She didn't want to be a check mark on anyone's tally sheet.

But Carmine was oh-so-nice to admire from afar. Her thing for Carmine was her secret, and she was disciplined enough to keep it that way.

Sean drove the squad car to Rikers Island, and Carmine rode in the front passenger seat because of his long legs— which left Eva to ride in the cramped back seat. She didn't mind so much, other than the odd smells and seat stains for which she would *not* think about the source. Instead, she focused on what to ask Westmore when they were with him. She'd convinced her brother she could contribute something fresh and unique that would get answers out of Westmore, so she felt an onus to deliver.

She mentally reviewed what she knew about the murder suspect. Wall Street hedge fund millionaire before he left college. Witnesses claimed they'd seen Westmore strike the murder victim, Lana Brinkley, in the past. So a history of violence...

And the guy was disturbingly handsome. Not that good-looking men couldn't be guilty of atrocities—look at Ted Bundy. But if Wes went to trial—no, *when* he went to trial—the district attorney's office would have a harder time convincing the jury that the man was the monster they claimed. Human nature being what it was, people found it difficult to believe beautiful things could be evil. And by all accounts, Wes Westmore was...well, *evil* might be too strong of a word. But he was accused of murder. Accused, she reminded herself. Not convicted.

A change in tire tone made Eva look up from the file in her lap. They were crossing the East River and would be at the prison soon. The complex of buildings that comprised Rikers Island Correctional Facility was already visible through the windshield.

"'Home of New York's Boldest,'" Carmine said, quoting the famous sign at the entrance to the prison, even before they reached the gates festooned with razor wire.

A little shudder raced through Eva. As hard as the job was for patrol officers and detectives in the city, the correctional officers who worked daily with the criminals in lockup at Rikers had an even harder job. They did, indeed, have to be *the boldest* to deal with the toughest criminals New York had to offer.

Even with their credentials, the process of checking into the facility, completing security screening, and waiting for Wes and his attorney to be brought out to the interview room took close to ninety minutes. Plenty of time for Eva to get antsy.

As prearranged, Sean watched the interview via video feed from another room. Even though Carmine was sitting beside her, and an acrylic window shielded her from direct contact with Wes and his shark of a lawyer, Ed Morelli, she still experienced a chill as the prisoner was led into the room. If the evidence bore truth, this man had callously strangled a woman he claimed to care for. The Wes Westmore who strode toward the table with a cocky stride looked little like the polished Italian-suit-wearing Wall Street genius who had been taken into custody. Without his hair products and private barber, Wes was rumpled and unshaven. His face was slightly creased and shadowed, evidence of poor sleep and the stress of living on the cell block.

Wes's strut faltered for a moment when he spotted Eva sitting next to Carmine. Rather than hide his surprise, he arched a black eyebrow and curled his mouth in a leering grin. "Well, well. You're a nice upgrade from the previous clown parade of cops and lawyers." His gaze slowly raked over her, and Eva's gut twisted with revulsion. "Very nice."

Beside her, Carmine stiffened and grated, "Watch it, Westmore."

"Oh, I am watching," he said, his tone oily. He took a seat smoothly, despite his hands being cuffed in front of him, and continued to stare boldly at Eva.

She met his dark eyes without flinching. She'd be damned if she'd show any weakness or agitation in front of Wes. If she wanted to keep the upper hand in the interview, she couldn't let Wes know he'd rattled her. Calmly gathering her composure, her eyes still locked on Wes's, she introduced herself and Carmine for the official record.

"Colton?" Wes said and snorted. "Any relation to Sean?"

She started to acknowledge the family connection but stopped herself. Her relationship to Sean was irrelevant and, frankly, none of Wes's business. "We have a few questions for you?"

Another snort. "Obviously. I didn't think this was social. But I've told you cops everything I have to say. You've wasted a trip." Wes cocked his head and leered again. "Although Mr. Morelli here could arrange a conjugal visit if you wanted to come back later, sweetheart."

"Hey, show some respect!" Carmine said hotly, and Eva broke eye contact with Wes to send her partner a quelling glance that said, *I've got this.*

"Our questions aren't about Lana's murder. They pertain to another case we're helping with, and if you're cooperative, it could prove valuable to you in negotiations with the DA's office later."

At this point, Morelli leaned close to confer with Wes, and Wes shrugged.

"You can ask me anything, sugar. No promises whether I have answers."

When Carmine shifted in his chair, growling under his breath, Eva touched his leg discreetly, out of Westmore's line of sight.

Her partner leaned close enough to whisper, "I can take over anytime if you—"

"No. I'm good," she cut him off, irritation thick in her voice. Then, channeling that irritation toward Wes, she stated flatly, "Mr. Westmore, you will address me as Officer Colton. Not sugar or sweetheart or any other cutesy moniker you've got in your repertoire. Am I clear?"

Wes chuckled and folded his arms on his chest to the extent the handcuffs would allow. "Crystal, *Officer Colton*."

The exaggerated emphasis he put on her name still felt smarmy, and Eva suppressed the shiver that formed at the base of her neck. "Good. We're interested in tracking down members of your family. Specifically, female relatives."

Wes played it cool, but she could tell by the twitch of a muscle in his jaw that she'd touched a nerve. He grunted and said, "Good luck with that. I don't have any family, female or otherwise."

"Public records say otherwise," Carmine said.

"Your paternal uncle, for example, lives in Manhattan," Eva said.

"Orrin?" Wes laughed and shook his head. "That invertebrate doesn't deserve the name Westmore. He and his love-guru-schtick wife haven't been my family for years. And I'm sure if you ask him, he'll disavow me too."

"Why don't you count him as family?" she asked.

"Let's just say they weren't there when it mattered, so they can kiss my ass. Okay?"

"When weren't they there?" Carmine asked before she could.

Wes sent Carmine a glare. "You're the cop. You figure it out."

"All right. Let's put a pin in your uncle," Eva said, leaning forward. "It's your female relatives we're more interested in."

"Why?" Wes asked and mirrored her by leaning forward…and raising an eyebrow as he tried to look down her shirt.

It took all of Eva's strength not to react and clap a hand over her cleavage. Let him look. He wouldn't see anything she didn't have on display when she wore her favorite bikini to the Jersey Shore. Instead, she narrowed her eyes and asked, "Excuse me?"

"Why do you want the dirt on my female relatives?"

"We're asking the questions," Carmine said. "Tell us about your mother. Any aunts or female cousins. Who are they? Where are they?"

"Again…you're the cop. Why should I do your job for you?"

"We're giving you the opportunity to score points with the DA's office," Carmine said, his disdain for Wes clear in his tone. "You help us with these questions, and we'll let the prosecution know you were a good boy today."

Wes shook his head. "I don't need points with the DA or you or the freaking governor. I didn't kill Lana."

Morelli cleared his throat, effectively shutting Wes up.

"Your father died when you were a boy. Is that right?" Eva asked, and Wes's attention snapped back to her.

"Well, someone did her homework. Bravo, *Officer Colton.*"

Again the smug emphasis on her name. She gritted her teeth and curled her fingers into the pockets of her uniform pants.

"Do you miss him?" Carmine asked, and for just a split second, Eva thought she saw Wes's composure crack.

"No. Why should I?"

"What about your mother?" Eva asked.

Wes shook his head. "Can't say I miss her either."

"When's the last time you saw your mother?" Carmine asked.

"I don't have a mother," Wes said, his expression blank.

Eva drew a breath and exhaled slowly without being obvious. No need tipping Wes off that he was trying her patience. "Everyone has a mother, Mr. Westmore. You weren't hatched in a laboratory. Your birth certificate lists Maeve O'Leary Westmore as your mother."

"That is a fact."

"So…" Eva pressed. "Tell us about her. Where does she live? How can we reach her?"

Wes's face blanked. "You can't."

"Can't what?"

"Reach her. Were you not listening when I said I don't have any family?"

"She died?" That would explain why all trace of Maeve O'Leary Westmore had disappeared just after her husband's death.

"This conversation is getting tedious," Wes said.

"Did your mother have sisters? Nieces? Cousins?" she pushed.

"You can search those ancestor websites same as I can." Wes turned to his lawyer with a hard look, then back to her. "Are we done here?"

Eva frowned as she glanced at Carmine and squelched the urge to look up at the camera through which Sean was viewing the exchange. If Maeve O'Leary Westmore was dead, then who had left the DNA in the courthouse closet where Humphrey's DNA was also found? Ellie Mathers, Liam's girlfriend and an analyst from the precinct's CSI department, had explained to Eva just last week that DNA analysis had shown a close connection to Wes Westmore, whose DNA was already in the system. The sample from the courthouse belonged specifically to a female whose DNA was not in the system. Eva still needed something that would point them toward the specific relative who had been in that courtroom closet, but she didn't want to show Wes her cards.

"How did DNA from a female relative of yours get in the courthouse closet where Humphrey Kelly was last located?" Carmine asked.

Eva barely caught the gasp that rose in her throat. She whipped her head around to gape at her new partner. Forget showing her cards—DiRico just gave Wes the whole deck!

"That's what this is about?" Wes asked, pulling a bemused expression. "We could've saved a lot of time here if you'd just led with that question."

Eva faced Wes again, her heart in her throat. "And?"

Wes's brow furrowed, and he shifted in his chair. With his eyes serious and penetrating, he divided a stern look between Eva and Carmine and leaned forward.

Eva's pulse accelerated with anticipation as she canted forward as well.

After drawing a deep breath and giving his lawyer a quick, silencing glance, Westmore said, "I. Don't. Know."

Wes leaned back in his chair again with a gloating laugh for having baited them.

Disappointment twined with disgust in Eva's gut for having been duped. Without reviewing the video feed of this interview, she could guess how eager and gullible she must have looked, leaning in when Wes had.

"Right. I think we're done," Carmine said, shoving to his feet. His body vibrated with frustration and tension that Eva could feel rolling off him in waves.

Or maybe that was her own sense of futility and annoyance. Damn, but she'd wanted to score big in this interrogation and impress Sean, get something useful to move the case forward, prove that even as a rookie she had skills and finesse. With a huff, Eva stood.

"I'm sorry, Officer Colton," Westmore said, his tone dripping false sympathy. "I can see I've let you down. If you come in here, so that plastic wall's not between us, I can comfort you."

Wes's smile twitched with sarcasm and skankiness, and the leer was back in his eyes. He blew her a kiss then and licked his lips seductively, and Eva tasted bile at the back of her throat. She would have reeled back from the plexiglass had Carmine's solid body not been behind her. Carmine put a steadying hand on her upper arm, and the heat of it was like a brand. She flinched away from his grip.

"You okay, Colton?" he asked in a low voice.

She lifted her chin and jerked a nod. "Fine," she lied.

A queasy feeling roiled in her belly. If she'd had time to eat anything this morning, she probably would have chucked it on Carmine's shoes about then. As it was, she struggled to compose herself as she watched the guard lead Wes away.

They met up with Sean in the corridor outside the interview room, and her brother hurried toward her.

"Eva, are you all right?" Her brother's tone matched his creased brow and worried eyes.

She nodded, not trusting her voice yet.

Sean's concern burrowed deep inside her, a balm and also an irritant. She didn't want to be treated like the overprotected little sister on the job. It was bad enough she endured her brother's smothering protectiveness outside the precinct. But when her brother drew her forcibly into an embrace, a lump of emotion welled in her throat. She allowed herself just a moment, just a couple of seconds to savor the comfort her brother offered.

"Oh God, Eva. If I'd been in the same room with him just now, I'd have—"

Sean wisely didn't finish his sentence, given there were ears all around them.

"You and me both," Carmine said darkly. "If not for that wall between us, I'd have happily put a fist in his haughty face."

Steeling herself, she wrenched free of her brother's embrace and squared her shoulders. "I said I'm fine. If I dissolved every time a jerk gave me a lecherous look or made a crude comment, I'd be a puddle of goo most of the time, every day. I'm used to ignoring or dealing with rude men."

She exhaled and firmed her mouth. "I'm sorry I didn't get more from him. I really thought I could—"

"You did fine. It was a crapshoot. Westmore hasn't been forthcoming about anything, and with that shark lawyer of his sitting beside him, I'm surprised he said as much as he did."

"Which was a lot of nothing," she said, not hiding her despondency.

Carmine was pacing the hallway restlessly, patting his security-emptied pockets and adjusting his jacket sleeves. "Back to the station?"

Sean gave her one more hard, considering look, scratched his chin and said, "The warden is supposed to be getting us a list of Wes's visitors with photos, a log of calls and mail. I'll go pick that up and get a copy of the video feed of your interview with him for our files. I'll meet you at the car."

Eva turned and headed back to the security station to retrieve her personal belongings. She couldn't wait to put Rikers Island and the botched interview in the rearview mirror.

CARMINE STUDIED EVA via the mirrors in the squad car that allowed the officers in the front seat to keep an eye on suspects in the back seat. He kept replaying Westmore's slimy come-ons toward his new partner, and every time the overtly lewd behavior flashed in his mind's eye, the indignation and protective urges flooded him again. But was his reaction because Wes had disrespected his partner? Because Eva was so young and new to the job? Or...something else?

He wanted to think he'd have the same reaction if he'd been with Captain ReevesReeves. ColleenColleen Reeves-Reeves was also an attractive woman, though probably twenty years older than Carmine's thirty-eight years, but had years of experience with criminal behavior. Yes, he decided, he'd be irked at witnessing contemptible behavior directed toward the captain—toward any woman—but some-how, with Eva…

He flexed and balled his fist, trying to ease the tension still humming through him. Eva said she dealt with inap-propriate men every day. His jaw clenched involuntarily. He would be sure to have his partner's back and put any scum who crossed the line back in their place. His private vow made him feel marginally better. But an uneasy feeling still rattled inside him, making him jittery.

Eva Colton.

Oh, Judas Priest! It wasn't even noon on their first day, and he was already conflicted about how to approach being partnered with the fiery young rookie. Truth was, he might not have said any of the crude things he'd heard spoken about the Colton rookie, but he'd thought some similar things. She was beautiful. And smart. And tough. And… Sean Colton's sister.

Carmine groaned and rubbed the bridge of his nose.

"What was that?" Sean asked from the driver's seat.

He blinked and shook his head. "Nothing."

Eva knocked on the partition between the front and back seats, calling out, "Can we stop somewhere and get food? I never had breakfast, and I'm famished! Preferably some-where with coffee. I'm getting a caffeine-deprivation head-ache."

"Why didn't you eat or have coffee?" Sean asked, his expression saying his sister's oversight was some kind of rookie mistake.

"I didn't have time," she said. "You called me into your office before I could even get a bagel, and then we were off to visit the murderous Wizard of Wall Street."

"So you're saying it's my fault?" Sean asked with a teas-ing light in his eyes.

Eva scoffed. "Well…"

"Allegedly," Carmine said.

"Huh?" Eva angled a look at him through the divider.

"Allegedly murderous. Remember, he hasn't been convicted," he said, throwing her words back at her with a grin.

She snorted. "Yeah, right. Although we all know he's guilty. We just haven't found the proof that will stick yet."

"Don't do that," her brother said, raising a warning glance to meet hers in the rearview mirror.

"Do what? Oh, there! A deli. I want a Reuben and fries!"

"Don't fall into the trap of making conclusions without hard facts to support you." Sean checked the traffic and eased into the next lane. "We have to follow the evidence, no matter what we think we know."

Eva sighed. "I know. I know! That was just low blood sugar talking. Feed me quick, before I toss the procedure manual and follow a hunch!"

Sean stopped the car, horns blasting behind him, so that Eva could hop out at the deli. "Get me a turkey and Swiss on wheat. Extra mustard."

"Uh, sure. And how am I supposed to get out?" She motioned to the handleless door designed to keep arrested individuals from escaping.

"DiRico?"

Carmine shouldered the passenger door open, climbed out with a wave to the cars behind them, then let Eva out of the back seat. He followed her into the deli, and while they waited in line, he said, "Procedure is fine and all that, but don't dismiss the value of instinct. Experience. A gut feeling."

She gave him a side-glance and a frown. "Oh, that's right. I've been partnered with Detective Rogue. Mr. Bend the Rules." She narrowed her eyes. "I hope that won't become a problem. I have no intention of getting written up because you went off script."

He arched an eyebrow. "Detective Rogue?"

She faced him with hands on her hips. "'How did DNA from a female relative of yours get in the courthouse closet where Humphrey Kelly was last located?'" she mimicked in a deep voice. Her eyes widened in a manner that said, *Explain that.*

He gave her a mild shrug. "We weren't getting anywhere, and I wanted to see how he'd react."

"And still we got nothing."

"It was worth a shot." He hitched his head, motioning her toward the order counter. "You're up."

After they received their to-go orders, they went out to the street to wait for Sean to circle the block. Eva opened her bag and ate her fries, two at a time, while she watched the passing traffic.

"Do you always eat like that?" he asked.

"Like what? On the go?"

"Like three days' worth of fat and cholesterol in one meal."

She gave him the side-eye. "What's it to you?"

"Just wondering if I should be on alert to my partner dropping suddenly from a heart attack. Seems the answer is yes." He spotted the cruiser down the block and moved closer to the curb.

"I figure I can splurge now and then, considering how many meals I skip, my workout routine and how many salads I eat at night."

He grunted in response and waved for her to precede him between the parked cars and out to where Sean had stopped. More horns honked as they climbed in, and Carmine grinned and shook his head. *New Yorkers... Who else would be ballsy enough to honk at a police car?*

Back at the precinct, Carmine moved a few of his personal items—his signed Yankees baseball, his favorite pen, a stress ball in the shape of a patrol car—to Mitch Mallard's desk so he could confer as needed with Eva, whose desk sat at a right angle to Mitch's. Eva was just finishing her Reuben, the sauce and melted cheese leaking from the rye bread. She sucked the drippings from her fingers one at a time and gave a satisfied moan.

A quiver of something forbidden shook Carmine at his core, and he had to clamp down on the impulse to imagine Eva making such pleasurable noises in bed. Or pressed up against a wall. Or in the back seat of his father's old Chevy. *Judas Priest!*

Noticing the curious—and intrigued—looks from the other male officers near them, he dug a stack of napkins out of his own lunch bag and tossed them to her. "For God's sake, Eva. Seriously?"

"Is it a crime to enjoy your food?" she said, wiping her mouth with the napkin.

"No, but you're making a scene." He couldn't say why the looks from the other men bothered him so much. He wasn't embarrassed, for himself or for Eva. He was…irked. Maybe because Wes Westmore's slimeball comments were still fresh in his head. With a sigh, Carmine snatched his grilled chicken sandwich—hold the mayo—from the bag and balled up the empty sack with more force than needed. She wasn't his little sister. Why was he so prickly and concerned about the attention Eva got from men? She seemed perfectly competent at handling men's advances. But…

He Reevesed on his laptop and unwrapped his sandwich. But what?

"I've been thinking about what Westmore said this morning," Eva said as she cleaned up her lunch detritus.

"And?" He navigated to a search bar where he could begin researching…what? "As far as I can tell he didn't give us anything useful." He waved a hand at his screen. "What's our next move with the Lana Brinkley case? Or Mr. Kelly's disappearance, for that matter?"

"I'm still thinking about the DNA from Wes's female relative…" Eva tugged at her earring and stared into near space.

"He claims he has no family. Does that mean his mother is dead?" he said.

Eva shrugged. "That would explain why we've had such a hard time tracking Maeve O'Leary down. She's the first relative we looked for in the system when we got the DNA profile back, but there's almost no information about her after her husband, Joseph Westmore, died."

"The hotel big shot?"

"The same," she said with a nod. "He died a good while back, while Wes was still a kid."

"But despite what Wes said today, he does have family. He said something about his 'invertebrate' uncle. So even though he considers the man spineless for some reason, the man is still around."

Eva nodded and pulled a sheet of paper from a file to hand him. "Orrin. Sean talked to him earlier this year but didn't get much out of him."

"Another tight-lipped Westmore. Must be a family trait." Carmine scanned the report Sean had filed.

"But why won't they answer questions?" Eva asked, then tapped the tip of her pen against her teeth. "What are they worried we'll learn?"

Carmine bit into his sandwich and mulled over that question as he chewed.

After opening her laptop, Eva started pecking at her keyboard and twisting her lips as she studied the results of her search. "Thing is, while he didn't give us much, Wes did say more about his uncle and his wife than just dismissing them. He was bitter. And derogatory. What was it Wes called them?"

Carmine thought back, pulled the small notepad from his breast pocket and checked the comments he'd made. "They hadn't been there when he needed them. I'm thinking that means when his parents died. Didn't he leave home for college at an early age?" He flipped through his notes. "Where did I read that?"

"Love guru schtick," Eva said, her gaze focused on the ceiling. She snapped her fingers. "That's it. He referred to Orrin's wife as his 'love-guru-schtick wife.'" She wrinkled her nose, and Carmine was struck by how adorable she looked with her face scrunched that way. Not that he'd ever dare to call Eva *adorable* to her face, even if he meant it as a compliment.

Eva thumbed through the paper file on her desk. "Here. Orrin and Kitty Westmore live in Manhattan—wow, swanky address by Central Park—and are both licensed therapists."

Carmine took another bite of sandwich and leaned back in his seat, fascinated with watching Eva work. Her face was an open book, and he could read every question and emotion as her expressions shifted. She'd need to train herself to be more stoic. Especially when working with suspects.

"Hang on, they have a website," she said, rolling her wireless mouse and clicking.

She'd been controlled and authoritative when they interviewed Westmore this morning, however. He had been impressed with her command of the situation, even when Wes had been taunting and leering. Only after they'd left the interview room did she show her revulsion for the inmate's crude overtures. Carmine gave Eva silent kudos for that.

"Huh."

He set his sandwich aside and sat forward, drawn by the intrigue in her grunt. "What?"

"The Westmores' specialty is marriage counseling. They offer private counseling in their office and group sessions…

Oh, and for the uber-wealthy couple in crisis, they are offering a marriage retreat on a three-day cruise around the city."

"A cruise around the city? Why would locals pay to cruise around the city?"

"It doesn't say it's just for locals. Maybe they draw out-of-towners. Celebrities? Besides, if you're drowning in cash and your marriage needs help, why not a cruise? And then there's this…" She turned her laptop to show him the screen. "Get a load of the superyacht where the retreat takes place."

He studied the pictures of a huge multi-deck craft that would likely be insulted at being called a *superyacht*. It was nearly a ship. And a well-appointed one, at that. He whistled appreciatively. "That'll do."

Eva turned her laptop back around and shook her head. "It's not fair. Why couldn't I have been born into money? I'd give my right arm for the chance to…"

Carmine, his mouth full of sandwich, cut a look to his partner when she fell silent. "What?" he said around his lunch.

She held up a finger, signaling him to wait a moment, but the speculative gleam in her eyes told him she'd had an inspiration or made a connection of some sort. Then she snorted and shook her head. "Never mind."

Carmine swallowed his food and wiped his hands on a napkin. "What? You looked like you were onto something." He waved a hand, indicating she should continue, as he raised a mug of cold coffee to his mouth. "Share."

She pulled a wry face. "It's…" She rolled her eyes and tugged a lopsided grin. "I was just thinking… What if you and I posed as a married couple to go undercover on this marriage retreat cruise thing?"

Coffee went down his throat the wrong way, and he coughed and spluttered. "What!" he rasped, still strangling from his inhaled drink.

She shrugged. "We'd have three days and four nights of close contact with the Westmores in order to ask them questions and learn about Wes and the rest of the Westmore extended family without them throwing up walls when they see a police uniform." She chuckled dismissively. "But obviously that's not—"

"I like it."

Hearing the clear female voice behind him, Carmine swiveled in his chair to find Captain Reeves behind him, her arms folded, her head cocked to one side. A look of intrigue and razor-sharp intelligence filled the gaze she narrowed on Eva.

Eva bolted to her feet and straightened her shoulders. "Captain."

Colleen Reeves flapped a hand, motioning for Eva to sit. "Tell me more about this undercover idea."

Chapter Three

Eva swallowed hard and sent a brief panicked look to Carmine. "I wasn't serious, Captain. I was, um...just kidding around about this luxury retreat cruise the Westmores offer." Eva pointed to her laptop screen. "But it costs—"

Captain Reeves waved away the concern. "Forget the cost for a minute. I didn't make captain without learning how to find funds for special operations. Let's talk strategy. If you were to go on this cruise with the Westmores, do you think you could question them about Wes and his parents and his other female relatives without raising suspicion?"

Across her desk, Eva met Carmine's dark eyes, which burrowed into her with a look that asked, *What have you done?*

Eva cleared her throat. "Well, it is a marriage retreat for—" she glanced at the description on the laptop "—couples in relationship crisis."

Raising her eyebrows, Captain Reeves nodded. "Easy enough. DiRico and Colton, I hereby pronounce you married and in crisis." She folded her hands as if in prayer and bowed her head toward Eva, then Carmine. "What else does it say?"

Eva gaped, heart thumping like a bass speaker turned up full blast. "Uh... 'A couple in crisis is a family in crisis,'" she read. "'We promote the value of family in society, heal broken marriages and teach skills to last a lifetime.'"

Colleen nodded. "Mmm-hmm. I like that *family in society* bit." She snapped her fingers and aimed one at Eva. "That's your opening—how the Westmore family fits in New York City culture and current events. Book it. When does it sail?"

Coughing into his fist, Carmine rolled his shoulders and pushed to his feet. "With all due respect, Captain, this idea is—"

"Brilliant?" Captain Reeves suggested.

Despite the niggle of dread in her gut over what seemed to be brewing, Eva experienced a flicker of joy at having her idea praised so highly. By the captain. In the middle of the squad room. With most of the precinct within earshot. She bit the inside of her cheek to keep from smiling too broadly.

"This sort of creativity is right up your alley, Detective DiRico. It's inventive. Outside the norm. A work-around solution with high potential to get critical information—not just on the Brinkley murder case, but regarding the odd DNA results in the Humphrey Kelly disappearance."

Eva blinked. She'd been kidding around, but now, having given it more thought in light of the captain's insight, Eva goggled at the possibilities open to them with ready access to the senior Westmores. If she and Carmine solved not one but *two* cases while undercover...

Her pulse tripped with excitement.

"Don't you agree, Detective DiRico?" Captain Reeves said, and Eva cast an expectant look at her partner.

He frowned. Scratched his chin. Stretched the muscles in his jaw. Sighed, and jerked a tight nod. "It's ingenious. And could work." He folded his arms over his chest and regarded Eva with admiration in his eyes. "Good thinking, Officer Colton. It's a very out-of-the-box plan for someone who's typically by the book."

Eva narrowed a suspicious gaze on Carmine, trying to decide if he was masking condescension or sarcasm behind his words. But his tone, his expression, his body language were all sincere. She gulped and twitched a smile at him. "Thanks."

"All right, then," Captain Reeves said, clapping her hands together in the universal signal that something was a done deal.

Wait...a done deal?

Eva's brain, which had been spinning and running to keep up with the sudden shifts of events and attitude, took a stutter step. *I'm going to be undercover for three days and four nights as Carmine's* wife?

"Don't worry about the billing," the captain said, although her voice suddenly sounded as if it were coming from under water. "I'll have the department accountant cut a check to cover the expense before the end of the day. Obviously, you can't use your real names, so come up with an alias, a background and case history." Carmine was nodding, his expression rather stunned as the captain continued. "Let me know if you need anything arranged by the department to complete your cover. Take your service weapons, obviously. And...hmm, what else?"

Captain Reeves turned to Eva. "Oh, right. The reason I came over to begin with. I heard you interviewed Wes Westmore at Rikers this morning and that he was...well, not polite." She pulled a scowl to let Eva know the harassment bothered her. "I'm no stranger to that kind of crap. I just wanted to check on you and make sure you're okay. If you want to talk to someone about it, my door's always open."

Eva's head was spinning. Suddenly, Wes's crude remarks seemed a lifetime ago. The captain was staring at her in a way that said she was waiting for a response, so Eva blinked, wet her lips and croaked, "Yes. I'm...f-fine. Thank you."

Her boss smiled. "All right. I'll let you get back to it. Good work, rookie."

As the captain returned to her office, the buzz of voices rose around her. She glanced from Captain Reeves' retreating back to the other officers who were chortling and whispering around her.

Yacht cruise. Undercover. Married to Carmine.

She glanced at her partner, whose face was slightly red and his expression stricken. He met her eyes and mumbled, "Judas Priest."

"I WAS KIDDING, CARMINE!"

Eva trailed after Carmine as he stalked toward the men's room, but he didn't slow his pace or respond to her appeals for...what? Forgiveness? Understanding?

His temples throbbed. He needed to splash cold water on his face and get his head together. *Undercover as Eva Colton's husband?*

"I didn't know Reeves was in earshot. And I especially didn't know she'd think the cockamamie idea was a good one! That she'd make us *do it*!"

He turned when he reached the door of the men's room and braced a hand against Eva's shoulder. "Stop."

"I'm just saying, I'm as shocked by this farce as—"

"Stop."

"But, Carmine, I—"

"It's a good idea. A *great* idea. Wish I'd thought of it." He wasn't lying. But then, he'd known Eva was smart. Creative. He shouldn't be surprised she'd thought of the ruse to get them on the Westmores' cruise.

"But you still hate it," she said, her sculpted auburn brows knitting together. "I can tell. Good idea or not, you're mad about something. What?"

He raised both palms toward her. "Let's just say I'm getting in character. We're supposed to be a couple in crisis, right?"

Her forehead dented further. "Yeah."

"Go with that." He arched one eyebrow at her. "Now, were you planning to follow me in here—" he hiked a thumb toward the bathroom door "—or what?"

As if just realizing where they were, Eva blushed and clamped her mouth in a tight moue. "We're not finished with this conversation. Not by a mile."

Fisting her hands at her sides, she pivoted on her toes and marched back toward their desks. Carmine watched her go—back ramrod straight, chin high, hips swaying like a model in high heels... *Whew!*

Even when she was buttoned up and in full professional mode, Eva Colton couldn't mask her sensuality.

When he returned to his desk, through the maze of other workstations and fellow officers' comments and looks—ranging from jealous to hostile to humored—he discovered Eva waiting for him impatiently.

"I wasn't serious," she said as he took his seat. "This is...a disaster."

"Captain doesn't see it that way, so get used to it...*honey.*"

She scowled. "Don't call me that."

"No? Clearly, sweetheart is out. You were quite clear with Wes about that—but as a married couple, we'd have pet names and endearments. So...pick one."

"This is ridiculous," she grumbled.

"We have our orders. Suck it up, rookie."

She shot him a hot look and snarled. "Honey, then."

At the next desk, Officer Jalenski hooted and made exaggerated kissing noises. "Oh, honey! I want to rip your clothes off and...frisk you!"

Carmine gave him a quelling look that did no good. He closed his laptop andbegan stacking paper files.

"What are you doing?" Eva asked and huffed. "You can't be leaving for the day. It's only two o'clock."

"Watch me. We have things to discuss, and this isn't the place to do it."

She opened her mouth as if to argue that the squad room was the perfect place to hash out their strategy, but the smirks around her quickly dissuaded her of that notion. Her shoulders dropped, and she sighed. "Fine."

She packed her laptop as well, and as they were leaving the station, he said, "I can't believe I'm saying this, but… your place or mine?"

A PRICKLE THAT she could only call *awareness* flowed through Eva from head to toe. A physical tingle spread to her core any time Carmine's elbow accidentally bumped her on the subway or his shoulder brushed hers as they wove through pedestrian traffic at Union Park. To distract herself, she mental catalogued every aspect of this odd day, starting with being partnered with her crush right through to their unorthodox assignment. And now she was taking Carmine DiRico back to her apartment. Holy mother of pearl!

Every time he cleared his throat, or rubbed his chin, or touched her back to guide her around an obstacle in the sidewalk, her nerves sizzled, and she could imagine her brain sparking and popping like an overtaxed computer shorting out.

When she stopped in front of her building and pointed to the nondescript door that led to the stairs to her apartment, he paused and stared at the wide picture window of Franco's Pizzeria. He took a step back and took a more encompassing view of the front of the building. Frowned. "I know this place."

"Um. Okay. It's not so different from a hundred other pizzerias in the city but…whatever."

He twisted his mouth in thought. "No. This one…" He left

his words hanging and marched inside the restaurant, releasing the rich aroma of oregano, garlic and yeast into the street.

Eva followed. When Mrs. DeLuca gave her a puzzled frown, Eva returned an embarrassed wave and grin. "Hello, Maria."

Calling to someone in the kitchen, the restaurant owner hurried from the back and around the counter to greet Eva and gave Carmine an appraising scrutiny. "Ah, Eva. Are you all right? Why are you home so early?"

"Um. Carmine and I needed some privacy to hash out some…stuff." She rolled her eyes, and when the speculation in Maria's eyes sharpened, Eva added quickly, "Work stuff. This is my new partner. Carmine DiRico, Maria DeLuca."

Maria gave Carmine a warm smile and sent Eva a secret wink. "Did you eat? I can fix your favorite pie, *presto!*"

"No, thank you. *We have work to do.*" She said the last while glaring at Carmine and trying to catch his attention.

His gaze wandered over the decor and furnishings, his eyes narrowed and his expression thoughtful. "Ms. DeLuca, how long has this restaurant been here?"

Maria raised her chin to meet Carmine's eyes. "Long time. My Franco's father, Franco Senior, opened here in 1956!"

Eva hadn't known that and lifted her eyebrows in awe. "Wow! That's fantastic. *Bravissimo!*"

Carmine's cheek twitched with an odd smile, and he nodded. "Yeah. This is the place. I'm sure." He divided a glowing look between her and Maria. "My grandparents used to bring us here on Sunday evenings when I was a kid. Me and my sister, Rosa. Not every Sunday. But pretty faithfully."

"Oh! How nice!" Maria cooed.

"Sunday night was date night for our parents, so Gran and Pops would take us for the night and see us to school on Monday morning." He inhaled, and a wistful smile touched his lips as he shook his head. "We always had the Sunday family special. A large pepperoni pizza with drinks, and for dessert—"

"Cannoli with chocolate sauce!" Maria said cheerfully, interrupting him.

Carmine snapped his fingers, his eyes brightening. "Yes!"

Eva checked her watch while Maria and Carmine chattered, then cleared her throat. "Um, I hate to cut this walk down memory lane short, but Carmine and I have a boat to catch."

Literally.

Well, not until Wednesday night, but still…

Nodding to Eva, Carmine wrapped up the conversation smoothly and was headed for the door when Maria shouted, "Mr. DiRico, wait, *carissimo!*"

The pizzeria owner hurried to the pastry display and placed two large sugar-dusted chocolate chip cannoli into a to-go box. "Take these. For old time's sake."

He demurred politely; then, when the woman insisted he take the treats, he offered to pay for them. Maria refused both gestures. "Go. Enjoy. Share with Eva, yes? And come back Sunday night for the family special!" She laughed as she squeezed Carmine's arm.

"Nice lady," he said when they were finally trudging up the four flights of stairs to her walk-up apartment.

"Very nice. And you made her happy, letting her feed you." She dug her key out of her backpack and unlocked her door, calling, "Carnegie? I'm home, baby! Where are you?"

"Carnegie?" Carmine asked, setting the cannoli on her two-person dining table while he slipped off his jacket.

Her yellow cat came trotting out of the next room with a yawn and stretched his back legs as he meowed a greeting. She waved a hand toward the feline. "This is Carnegie. Say anything about his weight, and I'll hit you. He was skin and bones when I found him two years ago, and I don't blame him a bit for eating all he can, whenever he can. The poor boy had a rough start." She scooped the cat into her arms, and a grunt of exertion slipped out. She scratched Carnie's head and muttered, "Although, really, buddy. You could stand to lose a few."

Carmine stepped closer, hand out, and when Carnegie saw the stranger coming, he jumped down and scuttled to the other side of the room.

Carmine snorted. "Fine. No cannoli for you, Carnegie."

"You're home early. What's—" Her roommate, Kara, wearing her work scrubs, hesitated as she entered the front room from her bedroom. "Oh, sorry. Didn't know you had company."

"Carmine's not company. He's my new partner. We're working on a case and needed to get away from eavesdroppers in the squad room." She introduced the two, and Kara backed toward her room with a little finger wave.

"I'll be out of your way in just a minute. I'm leaving for my shift as soon as I get my purse."

"No problem," Carmine said with a gracious smile.

"Oh, Kara, hang on. I need a favor. It seems Carmine and I will be working a case undercover for several days that will keep me away from the apartment. Will you feed Carnegie for me? I should be back Sunday night."

Kara blinked. "Undercover? Wow. Uh, sure. Carnie and I will be fine. Right, fuzzface?"

Eva hung her backpack and jacket on hooks by the front door and turned in time to see Carmine toss his jacket over the back of a chair. Irritation niggled at her core. "Um…" She motioned from the discarded jacket to the empty coat hook next to the one she'd used. "As my mom used to say, 'A place for everything and everything in its place.'"

He arched an eyebrow, one hand on his hip, before sighing and moving the jacket. "Are you this an—" he stopped himself and restarted "—*fussy* in all areas of your life?"

"Are you a slob? Because if we're going to be sharing quarters on this yacht, that will not be—" She froze, realizing what she'd said. "Oh my God. Are we supposed to share a room on this assignment?"

"Married couples generally do."

"But…" She dropped onto the edge of her love seat and let that fact really sink in. "Do you know how small staterooms are on yachts? I mean, they call them staterooms, like they are so luxurious, but I've seen pictures. I doubt the precinct is springing for anything more than a janitor's closet for us."

He picked up the cannoli and strolled over to a chair across from her. "This wasn't my idea. The question is, are you up to the task? 'Cause if you can't handle—"

She bristled and sat straight. "I'm up to the task, thank you!"

Lifting the lid on the dessert box, he took a deep breath, inhaling the scent of the cannoli. She thought she saw a shadow cross his expression, but then his jaw tightened. He gave his head a tiny shake, and he schooled his face.

Remembering his grandparents? Certain scents could still conjure memories of her mother and father, both of whom had died, years apart, from cancer.

Carmine nodded to the box. "Want one?"

Normally, she'd pounce on one of Franco's cannoli, but the thought of their upcoming undercover adventure had her stomach in knots. She shook her head, and he lifted one tube and bit into it. His eyes closed, and he hummed with pleasure. "Oh, yeah. That's good."

Eva flexed the fingers of one hand with her other and looked away from the bliss on Carmine's face. Picturing that face during other pleasurable activity was far too easy and—

"Rules!" she said, quickly shaking herself from that dangerous line of thought. "We need rules for this…disaster."

Carmine pressed his free hand to his chest and contorted

his face to look wounded. "Disaster? Would being married to me really be so bad? I'm hurt, Colton."

She scoffed. "If the marriage was anything like your past—what, four, five?—relationships, then we should be divorced by the end of the month."

He blinked as he shoved the last bite of cannoli into his mouth. Around the dessert, he said, "Ouch. Catty."

Compunction stung her. "You're right. Sorry. But…are you honestly looking forward to this assignment?"

He shrugged. "Sailing around the city in a monstrous yacht, eating primo meals by a top chef—"

"Really?"

"You read the website description of the retreat, didn't you?"

"Well…"

"So yeah. It sounds pretty good. And if I have to pretend I'm married to a pretty woman for a few days in trade?" He raised a hand in dismissal, then licked the cream filling from his fingers. "Sounds good to me."

Pretty? He thought she was pretty? Eva worked to hide the thrill his casual compliment stirred in her. She didn't consider herself vain, but growing up with brothers, her attractiveness—or lack thereof—had been generally dismissed with teasing comments thrown around in jest.

Stinkyface!

Well, you're a toad head!

Carrot top!

"Anyway… Rules. One, no matter how small the cabin we get, we do *not* share the bed. You can have the floor or a chair."

Carmine paused with the second cannoli inches from his mouth and glowered at her. "Why do I have to sleep on the floor? Your rule, you take the floor."

"Well, that's not very chivalrous of you!"

"You want chivalry, find a knight. I'm your partner, and

on the job, we're equal players." Tossing a smug look her way, he took a big bite of cannoli...and cream oozed out the back and plopped on his shirt.

Eva did grin then, reveling in the instant karma. "Rule two, no unnecessary touching or kissing."

Carmine sputtered and coughed as he choked on his food. "What?"

"We're supposed to be married. One would assume that means we'll have to, I don't know...act married!"

"A couple *in crisis*," he corrected. "It should be easy enough for you to keep your hands to yourself." He raised an eyebrow. "Although I know how tempting it might be to get a piece of this." He waved a hand, indicating his well-muscled body.

Did he have suspicions about her crush? A cold horror pooled in her gut until he twitched a teasing grin and rolled his eyes. She threw a decorative pillow at him. "Be serious!"

"No! Serious is boring. You loosen up. We don't need rules, Eva. I'll be respectful of you and vice versa. But you have to be open to whatever acting needs to happen for the sake of the assignment. If that means a touch or a hug in public—" he turned up a palm "—so be it."

Eva bit her bottom lip, unable to hide the worry that assailed her as she contemplated the days ahead. When would she learn to keep her mouth shut! If she hadn't glibly teased about going undercover on this cruise...

Carmine nudged her foot with the toe of his shoe. "Hey, come on, Colton. It'll be fine." He clapped a hand over his heart and said, "I promise not to fall madly in love with you or ravish your young body while on this assignment. Okay?"

She exhaled a slow breath, trying to cleanse the stress from her core. With a half smile at her partner, she muttered, "Yeah. You'd better not."

Chapter Four

The evening the marriage retreat set sail from a public marina in Manhattan on the Hudson River, Carmine escorted Eva up the gangway and onto a yacht even bigger than what he'd imagined. The *Westmores' Folly*, as the superyacht was named, had four decks, including one below where the crew and staff bunked. Guests' quarters were the top two decks, with the main deck reserved for the large dining room where the retreat meetings would be held, a bar and lounge, a patio with numerous lounge chairs for sunning, a swimming pool and hot tub, and the Westmores' private quarters.

In the tiny top-deck cabin they were assigned, they found a large welcome pack on the side table that included an itinerary, a workbook with questions to answer before the various group and private counseling sessions, a dietary sheet to list any special health concerns for the chef, and a pair of name badges that would be their ticket to side trips made into the city.

Dina and Daniel Eggers. He snorted a laugh as he handed Eva her badge. "Here you go, Dina."

She clipped her tag on the provided lanyard, then narrowed her eyes to read his tag. "Thanks, Daniel. Wonder where the captain came up with these names. Why not Joe and Jane Smith or something simple like that?"

"Really? You don't think Jane Smith doesn't reek of trite alias?" He moved his duffel bag onto the luggage shelf built into the wall.

"Not for someone named Jane Smith, of which I'm sure there are many." She reached for the handle of her small suitcase at the same time he did. "I've got it, thanks." She stowed her bag in the matching built-in space on the other side of their tiny sink. "I want to know where Captain Reeves came up with *these*." She waved her left hand, flashing the multistone diamond ring and gold band she'd been issued as part of her cover. "It's kinda showy, don't you think?"

"I'm sure it goes back to the evidence room or something when we're done here. So don't get attached."

"Nah. I personally go for a simple cut. Maybe an oval or marquise?"

"I'm wondering how I, as a simple accountant, I could afford that thing." He put his hands on his hips. "Do you think I come from money? Did I inherit that from Granny Eggers?"

"Hmm. Probably so. Although I've heard the best way to lie is to stick as close to the truth as possible. I think we should just use our real information regarding our past, our family, our likes and dislikes—other than the scripted stuff in our alibi profiles, I mean."

"I agree. Kiss."

She gave him a startled look. "What?"

He grinned. "K. I. S. S. It's the acronym for 'Keep It Simple, Stupid.'"

"Oh. Right." Eva turned, slowly taking in the confining quarters with a wrinkle at the bridge of her nose. "I guess that's the bed?" She pointed to a wall with a fabric loop that could be used to pull down the Murphy bed.

He tugged on the loop and found the mattress and flat pillows. "Yep."

She pulled a wry grin. "Wow. So much luxury for the low,

low price per night of just... How much did the website say this cruise cost?"

"More than my monthly rent." He scrubbed a hand in his hair and blew out a breath with a buzz of his lips. "Captain Reeves really wanted us on this boat, if she scrounged up that much funding." He sent Eva a level look. "Let's make it count. We need to go back to work Monday with something useful."

"Of course. I don't intend to squander this chance to make a real contribution, prove I'm up to the task."

Hanging his lanyard around his neck, he tapped the top sheet in the welcome pack. "Well, Mrs. Eggers, we have a get-to-know-you reception to attend. Shall we?"

Eva flexed her fingers, drew a deep breath and waved a hand to the door. "Lead on, Daniel."

ALL BUT ONE of the other couples from the retreat were already gathered in a circle of chairs, and champagne was freely flowing to toast the event. Around the perimeter of the dining room, tables were overflowing with a wide variety of savory hors d'oeuvres, from shrimp cocktail and salmon pâté to stuffed mushrooms and marinated veggies. Eva fixed herself a plate, her stomach growling when her attention snagged on the dessert table. Holy cheesecake, Batman! The variety and decadence of the pastries and sweet treats boggled the mind.

Okay! Let's do this, Dina*!*

"Welcome! Welcome, friends!" Kitty Westmore gushed as she entered the dining room and motioned for everyone to take their seats in the circle. "We're ready to start. We are still missing the Boones, but like a ferry, we wait for no one. Punctuality is expected as a courtesy to others. So..." She smiled broadly to the group and looked to her right, patting Orrin on the knee. "We're your hosts for the cruise and leaders of this marriage retreat, Orrin and Kitty Westmore. We are confident we can help you and your spouse or life partner overcome any conflict you are having, but—" She paused dramatically and held up a finger.

"You must be honest," Orrin finished for her, as if scripted. "With the group, with your counselors—" he waved a hand indicating himself and Kitty "—with your spouse and most important...with *yourself.*" He smiled at the gathered couples like a patient father. "No problem in a marriage is ever the sole fault of one person. You have to be able to take a hard look in the mirror and admit your own failings and biases if you want to heal your marriage."

"And you wouldn't be here if you didn't want to find peace, healing and unity again with your spouse. Right?" Kitty said, her blue eyes bright with enthusiasm.

Eva leaned close to Carmine's ear and whispered, "Wanna bet?"

His mouth twitched in a muted grin.

Kitty told the group about how she'd met Orrin twenty-six years earlier, how they'd found a mutual passion for helping other couples and how, together, they'd grown their therapy office to the thriving practice it was today.

"His family's money didn't hurt either," Carmine whispered to Eva, and she clamped down on a grin.

"Any questions before we start?" Orrin asked.

Eva shot her hand in the air. "You're Wes Westmore's uncle, right? The guy accused of killing his girlfriend over in Brooklyn in January?"

Kitty's smile slipped, and Orrin stiffened.

Carmine snapped his head toward Eva and frowned. "Subtle," he said in a low, sarcastic tone.

A nervous twitter of laughter rose among the other couples, and Eva shrugged. "I think it's the elephant in the room for anyone who follows the local news."

"Well..." Orrin cleared his throat and glanced at Kitty. "Yes. I am."

"But we are not here to discuss the news or estranged relatives. Tonight is about *you*." Pasting her beauty pageant smile back in place, Kitty motioned to the couple to her left and said, "Why don't you start Jim? Sarah? Then we'll go around the circle. Introduce yourself—tell us a bit about who you are, what you do for a living—and finish by giving us a one-sentence summary of the issue you are here to resolve with your spouse."

Disappointment plucked at Eva, but she pushed it aside. What did she think? That she could mention Wes once, and Orrin would spill a litany of facts and figures that would solve Lana Brinkley's murder and locate Humphrey? *Yeah right.*

"I'm Sarah McKinney, and this is Jim. We have two children, two dogs...and one mistress." Sarah pursed her lips and was obviously fighting back tears.

A muted mumble stirred among the couples, and Kitty said, "Welcome, both of you. Let me also repeat that everything said, both in private sessions or in group, is to be held in complete confidence. It was in the contract you signed when registering. Now, who is next?"

Eva tried to pay attention to the other couples introducing themselves but was preoccupied with figuring out how to raise the subject of Wes again, having been shut down so quickly just now.

"Dina?"

Carmine elbowed her, rousing her from her private deliberations. "Pay attention, honey."

She discovered the whole group was staring at her. "Um..."

"We're Dina and Daniel Eggers," Carmine said when Eva hesitated a moment too long. "I'm an accountant in a small office in the Financial District, and Dina teaches first grade. We've been married for five years, and we're here because we're having trouble communicating."

Around the circle, heads bobbed in sympathy…or understanding.

"More like, he doesn't listen," Eva improvised, sending Carmine a frown.

He blinked, clearly startled by her ad lib, then arched a dark eyebrow. "Maybe because you tend to talk all the time and *say things you shouldn't*." He widened his eyes meaningfully.

Kitty laughed awkwardly. "Now, Dina, Daniel, there'll be time for airing our grievances later. This is just the welcome session. Who's next?"

The door to the dining room opened, and a blonde woman crept in with a chagrined smile. "Sorry I'm late. I was waiting on Bill, but he's got a terrible headache and decided to skip tonight."

Orrin directed the woman to a seat, and she introduced herself as Molly Boone.

Thirty minutes, several introductions and a fat slice of what had to be Junior's cheesecake later, Eva returned to the tiny stateroom with Carmine—no, *Daniel*. She needed to practice thinking of him that way, or she might slip in public.

"What was that bit you tossed out about me saying things I shouldn't?" she asked as soon as he closed the door behind them. "Were you referring to my question for Orrin about Wes?"

"I was."

"What's your beef? Aren't we here to find out what we can from Orrin and Kitty about Wes and his family connections? His potential as a murderer?"

"We are. But there is a certain finesse to undercover work and extracting information from people. Drilling our host about his notorious nephew five minutes into session one does not earn us trust and confidence points with Orrin and Kitty."

"Maybe I was hoping that catching them off guard would give us their truest reaction, something revealing," she defended.

Carmine scrubbed his chin. "Eva, we have three days. Pace yourself. Ease into it. *Capisce*?"

Eva's cheeks heated in frustration. She wanted to pace, but in the tiny room, what was the point? Instead, she patted her hands restlessly on her hips. "You're probably right. I just…really want to get something useful for Sean…and to prove to Captain Reeves that her trust in us and this plush assignment—" she waved her hands to encompass the room "—was not a waste of department money."

"I get that. But Rome wasn't built in a day. Patience is a virtue on assignments like this."

"Okay, Mr. Cliché. You made your case."

Carmine stretched his shoulders, then swept a gaze around their cabin. "So I've been thinking about your rules. Once that bed gets pulled down, there won't be room for anyone to sleep on the floor. You'll have to crawl off the bottom end just to go to the bathroom as it is."

"The head. On a boat, it's called *the head*," she said, not really wanting to think about the necessity of sharing a bed with Car—Daniel.

"Touché," he said, pulling his shirt off over his head and tossing it on the floor.

Eva was torn between scolding him for being sloppy with his shirt and staring at the shockingly arresting sight of his bare chest. Her cheesecake did a somersault, and she gaped at the defined muscles and sprinkling of crisp dark hair. *Oh my!*

"My point is, we'll be sharing," he continued as he started unbuttoning the fly of his jeans. "But I promise you're safe."

He toed off his shoes and left them in a tumble on the floor. "I got a very clearly worded text from your brother Liam earlier today regarding your chastity and my responsibility to protect it."

"What?" This piece of news was enough to distract her from the peek of his underwear where he'd left his fly gaping at the waist.

"I think he mentioned that he still has contacts with some seedy characters, if I do anything ungentlemanly on this cruise." He flashed her a crooked smile full of charm and sex appeal.

The room seemed to lose all its oxygen, and her head felt light. She inhaled slowly and cut her gaze toward the floor.

"I value my privates and don't want my legs broken so... you're safe."

"Liam is not—" She stopped. If threats from Liam kept things between her and Carmine on platonic footing, then...

"I'll give you first turn in the head if you want," he said, stretching up to grab the bed loop and tug it down into place.

She scuttled back a few steps to make room for the bed. "Um...no. I'm having a sugar rush from that cheesecake, so... I'm going to walk out on the deck and get some air."

He sent her a concerned frown. "You want me to come with you?"

She waved him off. "I'm fine. And, uh..." She paused, patted the small of her back, where she'd stashed her service weapon earlier. "I have Betty with me."

"Betty?"

She flipped up the hem of her pocketed sweatshirt and showed him her back. "Betty."

"You named your weapon?" Then, without waiting for an answer, he mumbled quietly, "She named her weapon. Geez."

"Back in a few." She exited quickly and sucked in a few deep breaths as she stepped out of the cabin and pulled the door firmly closed behind her. The narrow walkway outside their cabin was dark and quiet, other than the lapping of the waves against the yacht's hull and the distant city noises that drifted across Upper New York Bay. The air had turned cool, and she stuck both hands in the front pocket of her too-big sweatshirt, one she'd inherited from one of her brothers years ago. Eva strolled around the aft end of the upper deck to gaze at Lady Liberty, who was lit up from her base, her torch shining like a beacon in the spring night. Eva smiled to herself, savoring the beautiful view. She'd forgotten how lovely the iconic statue looked at night, a glowing sentinel and—

She heard a door slam and the scuffling of feet on a deck below, and she sighed. So much for her private time.

"Y're a h'rrible bastard!" a woman said, her words slurred as if drunk.

"Shut up!" a man snarled back in a semi-hushed voice.

Eva shrank back into the shadows, not wanting the couple to know she could hear them, and winced at the harsh tones.

"How could y—I g'v you ev'rythin'!" the woman slurred.

"No. You have slowly drained the life from me, you miserable bitch! And now I return the favor."

Well! It seemed some of the retreat couples had more work to do than others. Curiosity bit her hard. She was dying to take a peek over the railing to see which of the couples she'd met tonight was having this row, but she didn't want to risk being spotted and interrupting the personal moment. She decided to sneak around the far side of the yacht to return to her cabin so the quarreling couple had some privacy. As she tiptoed away, more sounds of shuffling feet wafted up, along with a whimper, a slap. And another sound she recognized. She hesitated a second as the noise registered in her brain. A muzzled gunshot. Contrary to popular belief, a suppressor didn't douse all sound from a gunshot, and now the taut popping noise sent a chill slithering through Eva.

She rushed to the railing and leaned as far forward as she dared, craning her neck to search for the couple she'd heard.

Two decks below, she spotted a tall man in a dark hooded jacket, struggling at the railing with the inert form of a blond-haired woman.

"Hey!" she shouted to him, just as he hefted the woman over the rail, and Eva heard the ominous splash of a body hitting the water.

The man, hearing her, jerked his head up and raised a gun with a long, narrow suppressor. Instantly, Eva reached for her own weapon and shouted, "Stop! Drop the weapon!"

Instead of dropping the pistol, he took off at a run.

Muttering an epithet under her breath, Eva gave chase. "Stop!"

She almost shouted, *Police!* But she swallowed the warning, not ready to blow her cover on the first night of the assignment. Her feet slid a bit as she scuttled to the steep stairs of the lower deck. Rather than navigate the cumbersome steps one at a time, she leaped down five at a time—one flight…two—then landed in a crouch at the bottom main deck. She used the stair railing as an anchor to hoist herself up and to propel her to running speed again. She darted in the direction she'd seen the man escape and scanned the deck, searching the narrow corridors without luck. He'd vanished.

She nearly collided with a door that opened, and as she skidded to a halt, bumping her elbow on the open door, she took stock of the pudgy waiter who'd bustled out in his white serving uniform. Shoving Betty in her sweatshirt pocket and panting for breath, she asked, "Did you see a man in a black jacket come through this way?"

The waiter looked her up and down slowly. "No. I've been in my cabin. Just came out for a smoke."

She grabbed him by the arms. "Call the police. Hurry! I've just witnessed a murder!"

Chapter Five

Both the Coast Guard and officers from a Lower Manhattan precinct arrived within minutes, and Eva repeated her story to the officers. She'd already told both Carmine and the Westmores what she'd witnessed. As the officers scoured the lower deck for evidence and members of the Coast Guard searched the water for a body, a crowd of curious passengers had gathered to watch the drama unfold. By agreement, to maintain their cover, Eva and Carmine did not disclose their true identities to the responding officers. If trouble arose later because of this omission, they knew Captain Reeves could sort things out with the other precinct.

Eva paced the Westmores' much larger stateroom, where they'd been directed to wait while the police officers conducted a cabin-by-cabin search of the yacht. Gut twisting, she replayed the scene she'd happened across in her mind. Where had the man in the hooded jacket gone? Whom had he killed? She'd assumed it was his wife or lover, based on the snippets of the argument she'd heard.

I g'v you ev'rythin'! She'd assumed that meant *everything* as in heart and soul. But could it have been a business relationship gone sour?

No, you have slowly drained the life from me, you miserable bitch! The man's reply indicated something more personal than a business transaction…bringing her back to her first assumption of an intimate relationship.

Don't assume anything, she told herself. *A good cop deals in facts. Evidence. Proof.*

"Dina, are you sure you heard a gunshot?" Kitty asked with a furrowed brow. "Out here on the water, without impediments like buildings or trees, sounds travel a long way. Maybe you heard a car on shore backfire."

"I'm sure it was a gun. I saw it when he pointed it at me!" She glanced at Carmine for backup, and he shrugged. She gave him a disgusted *thanks for nothing* look and faced the Westmores again. "It all happened just as I described. He tussled with a woman, threw her overboard before—" *Before I pulled my weapon on him.* Could she have saved the woman's life if she'd intervened sooner? Guilt poked her. She'd thought it was just an argument. This was a cruise for couples "in crisis," after all. "Before he ran off. I tried to follow him but he'd—"

"Why?" Orrin asked.

"Excuse me?"

"Why in the world would you follow an armed man you claim had just killed someone?" Orrin asked.

"Well, b-because…" Eva fumbled. *Because a cop runs toward danger, while citizens run away.* But she couldn't say that, couldn't break cover. "I just, uh…"

She was spared from answering when the lead responding officer knocked on the door and stepped into the room. "Mr. and Mrs. Westmore, I think we're nearly through."

Eva stiffened. "Nearly through?" She glanced at the wall clock, then back at the stout officer who filled the doorway. "It's only been ninety minutes! How could you have interviewed everyone on board in less than ninety minutes?"

"Because interviewing everyone was not necessary. We've found no evidence a crime took place."

"Come again?" Carmine asked.

The officer directed a hard look toward Carmine. "No evidence. No body, no blood, no bullet casing, no weapon. No one else we've spoken to saw or heard anything."

"What?" she cried, her pulse spiking. "That's impossible!"

"But E—my wife saw *something*. How do you explain the struggle she saw and the man that ran from her?"

The officer shrugged. "A vivid imagination, maybe? I'm thinking she's probably watched a few too many episodes of *Law & Order*."

Eva's jaw dropped, too stunned by the condescension and dismissal to speak.

"Maybe she's just looking for attention?" the smug officer continued. "This is a marriage retreat, I understand. Could your wife be looking for something you're not giving her?"

Carmine tensed up and narrowed his eyes, and through gritted teeth, he said, "No. If Dina says she saw something, I believe her. And so should you."

Carmine's defense of her, his support, stirred a warmth in her core she needed at that moment more than she'd realized. The night's events had rattled her. The officer's dismissiveness angered her. She sent Carmine a look that said, *Thank you.*

"You need to talk to *everyone* on board. Not just those who've come out of their cabins to watch the show. I couldn't have been the only one who—"

"Are you saying I don't know how to do my job, ma'am?" the officer asked sourly.

Fisting her hands at her sides, Eva countered, "If you haven't taken a comprehensive statement from everyone on board, then yes!"

The officer—Lou Richie, she made a point to note from his name tag—glared at Eva. "If we'd seen anything that indicated your story had merit, we'd have done just that. But with no sign of anything amiss, interviews are a waste of time." He adjusted his belt. "Be glad I'm not filing charges against you for making a false report, ma'am."

"False re—" Eva glanced to Carmine for help. This couldn't be happening!

"Mrs. Eggers," Kitty said in a sickeningly sweet voice, "maybe things will look better in the morning."

Whirling toward her hostess, she pointed an accusing finger. "Don't you care that someone has been murdered on your yacht? Don't you feel any responsibility toward your passengers? Your retreat clients? Your crew?"

"Of course we do! But the officer said nothing was—"

Eva spun back toward Officer Richie, not letting Kitty finish. "Did you go over the manifest? Is everyone on the crew, all of the staff and passengers, accounted for?"

Richie folded his arms over his barrel chest. "We did. Everyone is accounted for." Then, turning to Orrin, he bobbed a nod. "Good night, folks. Thank you for your cooperation."

"Good night, Officer," Orrin said.

"But…wait!" Eva shook with frustration and confusion. She knew what she'd seen! A woman had been thrown overboard, regardless of what the cursory search Richie and his team had found…or not found.

"Good night, Mrs. Eggers. And lay off the late-night crime shows, okay?"

Eva lunged toward the officer, but Carmine, in a swift, deft move, blocked her with his body, catching her in a hug to mask Eva's intent. "Don't," he whispered as he held her firmly. "Let it go. We'll talk in the cabin."

"I'M NOT LYING or making anything up! A couple was fighting, and the man threw the woman overboard. I swear!" Eva was near tears as she paced and ranted.

Carmine wanted to hug her again, to calm her and reinforce his support of her. He knew she was telling the truth, but his restless partner clearly needed to burn off some steam. "I believe you."

"The man had a pistol with a suppressor. I saw it. I heard it. I know what a gunshot with a suppressor sounds like. I didn't imagine it." She patted her jittery hands against her thighs as she paced and talked…apparently to herself. "Because of the hood on his jacket and the dark, I didn't get a good look at his face, but I know he was Caucasian."

"I believe you."

They'd both donned nightclothes, taking turns in the head to change, and Carmine was more than ready to get some sleep.

"He was tall. Lean. He threw her overboard. I watched him do it."

"I believe you," he repeated patiently.

"She was slurring, so I assumed she was drunk. But later she was limp. She didn't struggle like she had earlier. I assumed she was dead—and yes, I know assumptions make an ass of 'u' and me, or whatever the saying is. I just—"

He caught her arm as she stalked past him for the umpteenth time. "Hey! I. Believe. You."

She turned eyes bright with agitation and anger on him and blinked. "You do?"

"Haven't I said so from the minute you burst in here in a fluster three hours ago?"

Her expression melted, and the tears in her eyes welled again. She drew a deep breath, clearly regaining her composure, and said quietly, "Thank you. That means…a lot." Then the bridge of her nose wrinkled, and she added, "And I wasn't flustered. I was…urgent. Emphatic. I'd just seen a woman murdered, for crying out loud!"

"So you've said. Multiple times. But…" He released her arm and crossed the room to pull down the Murphy bed he'd stowed earlier to give her room to walk and stew. "We have a full day of undercover work and our own investigation to do in about three hours." He punched his pillow and crawled under the sheets. "I need my sleep. If you want to stay up and brood, be my guest. But hit the light, huh? And keep it quiet."

"Carmine! A woman was murdered!"

"Shh," he said with a stern look and a finger to his mouth. "Hold it down. And it's Daniel. Until this assignment is over, I'm Dan—"

"I know! I know…" She dropped heavily onto her end of the bed and frowned. "That Richie guy was so…"

"He was an ass toward you. Yes. And I plan to call Captain Reeves tomorrow and report everything that happened tonight, including Richie's bad attitude. This isn't our precinct. It isn't our case. We're not going to solve it tonight, so…" He patted her pillow.

With a groan, she snapped off the overhead light and crawled across the thin mattress. After slipping her bare feet under the covers, Eva… Dina…lay on her back, staring at the ceiling.

Carmine folded one arm under his head and rolled to his side to face her. "You did everything right tonight, Eva. I can't explain why the responding team didn't find anything, but I don't doubt you. Something will turn up. Someone will speak up. Something will come to light that wasn't evident tonight. At some point, the killer will make a mistake, show his hand. They always do."

She rolled to face him, and in the darkness, the confined quarters and heightened tension of the moment, he felt a ripple of something wash through him. Compassion for Eva's frustration, maybe. Defensiveness for Richie's demeaning treatment of his partner. Protectiveness for the woman with big green eyes that stared at him from mere inches away.

The feisty redhead was definitely the most attractive woman he'd had in his bed in…well, ever. Eva Colton was a stunner. And off-limits. Carmine clenched his back teeth and shoved down the sensual hum that vibrated through him and warmed his blood. "Tomorrow is a new day. A fresh start. We'll get him, partner."

She sighed. Nodded. And rolled away. "Good night, Daniel."

"Good night, Dina."

But he didn't sleep. How could he? There was a murderer on the cruise with them. A forbidden beauty snoring softly beside him. A day of fake marriage counseling ahead of him. And an accused killer sitting on Rikers Island whose female relative might have contributed to the disappearance of a prominent citizen. It was a lot to process.

EVERYONE KEPT LOOKING at her. No, not just looking. Staring. Some even glaring. Clearly, word had spread quickly that she'd been the one to call for the police last night, claiming she'd seen a murder, and disturbed their beauty rest for no reason. Eva swore she'd heard a woman whisper, "Attention seeker," and another man mumble to his wife, "Troublemaker, maybe even delusional."

She wanted to stand on her chair—which, after a sumptuous breakfast she couldn't eat, thanks to the nerves knotting her gut, had been moved into a circle like last night—and shout, "I'm not crazy! One of you is a murderer!" But she didn't, because clearly yelling from her chair would only confirm the theories about her mental state and probably get her and Carmine tossed from the cruise. She settled for using what she did know about the man whom she'd seen dump a body to study her fellow retreatants. He was Caucasian, tall and lean. She passed her gaze over the husbands on the cruise and narrowed down the suspects. Jamal Miller, who was African American, could be eliminated. And Mr. Gupta, who was short and South Asian.

She swigged her coffee from the too-small china cup—three sips, and her morning brew was gone—and strolled among the other retreatants. She missed her massive Central Perk mug Liam had found at a souvenir shop and given to her as a gag gift four years ago. That thing held almost a quart of coffee, and she loved it.

Orrin and Kitty arrived, smiling in greeting to the other couples, and Eva did a double take. Orrin was tall and lean and pale as the moon. Could Orrin have been the man she saw on deck last night? Her focus sharpened on her host as he spoke to Bill Boone, also tall and lean, then moved on to wish Aanan Gupta and his wife, Zara, a good morning. Her gaze tracked to Jim McKinney. Too short. Then Samuel Leech. Too heavy. Greg Harvey? Maybe.

"Did you try the scones? They have real clotted cream and fig jam. I'm in heaven!" Allison Leech said as she sidled up next to Eva.

Eva blinked and shook herself from police-mode. "Oh, uh. No. I haven't eaten this morning. Real clotted cream, you say?"

"Best I've had since Samuel and I were in London last spring," the older woman said and took a big bite of scone. She rolled her eyes in pleasure and hummed. "So good!"

Carmine arrived beside her and gave Allison a nod of greeting. "G'morning."

Allison's eyes lit up and raked over Carmine appreciatively. "Good morning."

He leaned close to Eva. "A word?"

Eva let her partner tug her aside, eyeing the coffeepot the server was about to clear away.

"I know what you're doing," Carmine said in a low tone.

"Jonesing for more coffee before that guy absconds with

it?" She pointed toward the silver urn and flagged the waiter. He brought her a fresh cup, along with sugar packets and a delicate cream pitcher. "Thank you!" she told the man, whom she sized up as he left. Tall enough, but the shoulders were too narrow maybe?

"Captain Reeves has promised to look into what happened on the yacht last night and keep us informed."

"I know."

"So let the local precinct do their job, and you do yours. Stay focused on the Westmores."

"But if I can identify—"

"Have you considered that the man you saw could have left the yacht and be anywhere today? Would you stick around if you'd killed someone? Been seen doing it?"

Her shoulders drooped. "Good point."

Carmine hitched his head toward the other side of the room, where the chairs were being moved into a circle for a group session. Eva took a deep breath, centered herself, focused on the job at hand.

"Good morning, friends!" Kitty chirped as she took her seat, and the group quieted. "We have a busy day ahead, so let's get started!"

Only when Carmine pressed his hand to her knee did Eva realize she'd been bouncing her leg restlessly. As he leaned over to set his empty coffee cup on the floor by his feet, he whispered, "Pull it together, partner."

Squeezing the edges of her seat, Eva forced a neutral expression to her face and gave Kitty her attention. *The Westmores. Marriage counseling. Focus, Colton.*

"Today, we are making an excursion to the Statue of Liberty and Ellis Island!" Kitty clasped her hands as she beamed joyfully at the couples. Beside her, Orrin grinned and nodded his approval.

Her news was greeted with far less enthusiasm by the group.

One of the men—his name badge read, Todd Johnson—spoke up, voicing what was clearly the pervasive thought among the couples. "Why? This is a marriage retreat, not a fifth-grade field trip. We can go to the Statue of Liberty any time we want. Seems like a waste of our time."

"Yes, you can," Orrin said. "But do you?"

Eva glanced at Carm—Daniel. She didn't. Life kept her too busy, and what spare time she did have was spent tucked away in her apartment with relaxing pursuits...reading, Netflix, baking.

"Most of you live in or near one of the greatest cities in the world," Orrin continued, waving a hand toward the large windows of the dining room, through which the New York skyline reflected the morning sun. "Home to priceless art exhibits, historical monuments and important American icons, sporting venues, four-star restaurants, top tourist destinations... But when do you visit any of these treasures? Do you take the resources and majesty of the city for granted?"

The husbands and wives around the circle exchanged glances and nodded.

"Exactly." Kitty punctuated her comment by stabbing the air with a finger. "And if you take your city's treasures for granted, what does that mean for your marriage? Your spouse is your personal treasure, someone you promised to cherish all the days of your life. But do you? Or do you take the treasure right in front of you for granted, day after day, instead of enjoying the things that made you fall in love all those years ago?"

"Right!" Orrin cleared his throat. "We'll talk more about why we picked Lady Liberty and Ellis Island at tonight's session, but right now we want you to tell us what made you fall in love with your spouse? Todd, why don't you start?"

Eva's heart pounded against her ribs like a prisoner demanding to be released from detention. What made her fall in love with Carmine? *No, Dina. Daniel. Pretend. It's basic acting.*

"...and he picked me up in a convertible Bimmer. We had the best day, laughing and drinking champagne, dining on filet and caviar and truffles," Todd's wife, Carol, was saying. "And he arranged the most romantic proposal. How could I say no to one hundred roses, a three-carat diamond and a Vermont sunset?"

Eva cringed internally, wanting to tell Carol to be less materialistic and more attentive to Todd's character, his morals, his personality, his—

"Dina? Why did you fall for Daniel?" Kitty asked, pulling her from her thoughts.

Eva swallowed hard, her mouth suddenly dry. "Well, um..." She sensed more than saw the judgmental stares of her retreat mates land on her. Eva's attention was on her partner. Her crush. She couldn't say she loved him, but she sure had been drooling over him for the past several months. But if Carol shouldn't be materialistic, then she shouldn't be superficial. But *damn!* Carmine DiRico was easy on the eyes. Now she held his dark brown gaze, studied his strong jawline and watched his cheek dimple when he smiled self-consciously at her. The prisoner banging his fists on her ribs now stutter-stepped back from the cell door and gaped in awe. She held her breath, tongue-tied for a moment, as if she were about to reveal her most carefully guarded secret. *You see, Detective DiRico, it's like this. I have fantasies about stripping you naked and—*

"Dina?" Kitty prompted again.

Eva shook herself from her daze and blurted, "Well, obviously he's gorgeous. That doesn't hurt."

The circled couples chuckled, and Eva cleared her throat

and regrouped. *The best way to lie is to stick as close to the truth as you can.*

"Right, um… He's kind. And, um, smart." Eva imagined she could hear the others groan at her trite answers. And the spark that had lit Carmine's eyes moments earlier had dimmed. A fist of disappointment grabbed her by the throat. She didn't want to disappoint Carmine. They had a job to do, and if that job included praising her partner for his attributes, who better to let the world know the man Detective Carmine DiRico was?

"Daniel is brave and strong—and I don't mean physically strong, although clearly he's that, too, but he carries a lot on his shoulders without breaking. He's, uh…wise and compassionate and good. Deep-at-his-core good, you know? He's got integrity."

Carmine raised one eyebrow, clearly intrigued by the list she was rattling off. He reached over to tuck a wisp of her hair behind her ear and quietly said, "Thanks."

His touch startled her and sent a ripple of sweet sensation through her. *He's just playing the part*, she told herself and, taking a beat to find her voice, continued, "Yeah, um, he cares about people. And in doing what's right. He's…" She flipped up a palm and gave Carmine a half smile and a shrug. "One of the good guys in a world of bad guys."

Her partner dropped his gaze to the floor, his cheeks flushing a little, and she chuckled. "And he's easily embarrassed by praise."

The group laughed again, and Orrin cut in. "Daniel, why don't you tell us about Dina now?"

Eva cast an awkward glance to the faces watching her. The retreatants seemed to collectively lean forward, as if eager to hear what Daniel would say about his attention-seeking and delusional wife. She felt a hand on hers and jerked her attention to Carmine. He'd wrapped her hand in his bigger one and laced their fingers. He kissed her knuckles and began in a low voice, "Dina is...special."

She gave him a skeptical frown. *Special* made it sound like she was a head case or...well, exactly the presuppositions the group had made about her.

"I know you all have formed opinions about my wife based on what happened last night."

Eva arched an eyebrow, silently asking him, *What are you doing?*

"But one event is not enough to judge a person," he continued, shifting his dark gaze to the people circled around them. "One night is not enough to know the heart and character of a woman like Dina." His mahogany eyes returned to her, and Eva felt his warm stare to her core. "My wife is honest. Blunt at times but never cruel. She's a hard worker, a champion of the underdog and passionate about the ideals she holds dear."

Eva heard conviction in her partner's tone, as if he truly meant the things he was saying, and her breath snagged in her lungs. Her pulse slowed. The prisoner in her chest sat down to listen, intrigued. Touched.

"Family is important to her, and she is loyal to her family. She's true to her word and dependable." His brow beetled, and a fiery intensity filled his face. "Which is why I know," he said, turning his head to look at the other couples, "a woman was killed last night."

The others gasped. Murmured. Exchanged glances and shifted in their chairs.

Orrin coughed and raised a hand. "Uh, Daniel, that's not—"

"I can't explain why the police didn't find any evidence to support Dina's claim," Carmine continued, talking over Orrin with an authority in his voice that brooked no resistance. Assertive and confident. Intentional and authentic.

"But I believe my wife. If she said something happened, it happened."

Eva sat taller in her seat, stunned by Carmine's bold defense of her. Her throat tightened, and a flutter of gratitude beat in her chest. She squeezed his hand, which was still wrapped around hers, and curled up the corner of her mouth.

He gave a subtle nod as he said, "She is as intelligent as she is beautiful. And stubborn. She's all redhead in that department." He grinned before growing serious again. "When someone says, 'You can't,' she has the guts to say, 'Watch me.' And she has the skill and determination to make it happen." His jaw flexed as he narrowed a fiery gaze on her, and something in her belly quivered with delight. "She is energy and truth and courage, all wrapped up in a damn-fine package."

Eva could only blink slowly at Carmine, her mind buzzing with endorphins and shock. Where had all those compliments and kindness come from? She was used to being the butt of rookie jokes at the precinct, lovingly harassed by her brothers, goaded by criminals and having her competence doubted by Mitch Mallard. And Carmine was looking at her like…he *meant* it.

"Wow," Jim McKinney said, scoffing. "Get a room."

The others laughed awkwardly, and the man beside her, added, "Seriously! You know this is a marriage retreat, right? For couples with problems. Why are *you* here?"

Eva swiveled in her chair to face the man who'd spoken. Harrison Nash, his name tag read. The thirtysomething guy with poindexter glasses, a wrinkled broadcloth shirt and wavy brown hair emanated negativity from his pores. He sneered and folded his arms as he slumped in his chair. His wife, clearly unhappy with more than just her husband, elbowed him and said meekly, "They said last night they were having trouble with communication."

Kitty clapped her hands. "Remember, friends, this is a no-judgment zone. And no one should be made to feel they can't share openly. Honestly. Who's next? Bill, we're glad to see you're feeling better. Will you go next?"

The man who'd missed the welcome reception last night sat taller in his chair and turned a bright smile on his wife. For her part, Molly Boone beamed at her husband and looped her arm through his in a show of solidarity.

"Well, my honeybunches is special too. She's beautiful and fit and, uh…"

When he hesitated, Molly's eyes widened expectantly, clearly lapping up the praise like a thirsty puppy. Bill's gaze cut to Carmine. As if meeting a nonverbal challenge, Bill squared his shoulders and said, "My wife has the prettiest eyes I ever saw, and great legs, and a sexy smile… And she's, um, great in bed!"

Molly play swatted Bill and giggled. "Oh, honey!"

Oh, gag. Eva glanced at Carmine, then back at Bill. Mr. Boone clearly thought this was a he-man best-husband competition, and that he had to gush about his wife, truth or not, to beat Carmine and save face. She bit the inside of her cheek, telling herself not to let anything show on her sometimes too-expressive face.

"Bill," Kitty interrupted. "What was the first *nonphysical* attribute of Molly's that caught your attention? Think about when you two fell in love. What was it that made her special?"

Molly turned wide eyes to her husband, and Bill frowned, fumbled. "Well, uh… She's real sweet. And she paid attention to me. What I mean is…she listened. She made me feel like I was important and what I had to say mattered."

"Very good," Orrin said with a soft clap. "Very insightful. We'll come back to that later. Molly? Your turn."

And so it went, one couple after another, sharing compliments, grudging respect and happy memories until Kitty announced they had to hurry to catch the ferry to Ellis Island. During the morning session, the *Westmores' Folly* had sailed to the mouth of the Hudson River at the Upper New York Bay and had docked at a public marina in Liberty Harbor.

Later, as they disembarked the ferry at Ellis Island, Eva's cell phone buzzed. *Sean.* She dismissed the call and pulled Carmine aside. "That was Sean. I'm going to call him back, see what he wanted, update him. Cover for me?"

Carmine glanced in the direction the rest of the group had filed, toward the redbrick main building, its cupola-topped towers rising into the blue spring sky. When he looked back to her, he jerked a nod. "Don't be long. I'll miss you."

He stroked her cheek and winked, and she blinked her surprise and stared somewhat slack-jawed as he followed the others into the domed three-story registration room.

She swallowed hard and told herself he was acting. He was putting on a show for the other retreat participants, for the Westmores. Of course. As a faux-married couple they were supposed to have an intimate connection, communication issues or not. Their relationship was supposed to be one worth saving. *So...get with the program, Colton. Show your "husband" more affection. More...whatever it is married people do.*

She thought about the warmth in her brothers' eyes when they talked about their lady loves; the way Sean, Liam and Cormac responded to the women who'd turned their lives around in recent months. She had to admit she felt a tug of envy for the happiness they radiated. The fulfillment.

Happiness...right. She needed to remember to act happy around Carmine... Daniel. Happy and in love and fulfilled. Check.

Drawing a deep breath, Eva looked for a building nook or natural privacy screen—tree, hedge row?—where she could call her brother back with at least a little seclusion. She settled for walking a fair distance from the rest of the crowd and turning her back to the bustle of tourists.

"Detective Colton," Sean said by way of greeting when he answered.

"Rookie Colton checking in, sir," she said, her tone somewhat flippant. Perhaps too flippant, she thought belatedly. Sean might be her brother, her childhood tormenter and teasing opponent, but he was also her superior now. Due her respect, if she wanted to be taken seriously in the precinct. "I, um…saw that you called, sir. Is there news?"

Sean made a noise somewhere between a grunt and a short laugh. Clearly, her calling him *sir* still gave him pause too. *Don't gloat, buddy.*

"Yeah, um. I heard about your drama last night. You okay?" His tone held brotherly concern.

"Unharmed. Just…frustrated that I didn't catch the guy."

"Well, Captain Reeves wanted me to make sure you knew that your priority, your assignment is not catching whoever may or may not have dumped a woman overboard last night. Leave that to the responding officers."

"They wrote me off, Sean. They didn't believe me!" she said, the tension from the night before returning. She fisted her free hand and huffed. "I know what I saw!"

"I'm not doubting you, Officer Colton." His use of her formal title instantly put her in her place, and she stiffened, coming to attention as if he were standing in front of her. "I'm just reminding you that the department has forked out a small fortune for you to be on this cruise with the Westmores. Get us information about Wes Westmore. His relatives. His private life. Did he hurt animals as a child? What insights do they have that could help us build a case against him in Lana Brinkley's murder? In your spare time, go over the list of Wes's visitors at Rikers and see what pops. That is your job. Not chasing other leads outside your jurisdiction. Am I clear?"

She sighed. "You're clear."

"Good. But to satisfy your curiosity… I ran a background check on the other passengers from the yacht's manifest overnight. No one involved with the marriage retreat has a criminal background. Parking tickets and unpaid loans are the extent of it. One of the crew members, a George Fulton, had a scrape with the law twenty years ago. A drunk and disorderly. One of the kitchen staff is here on an expired green card. But that's about it. So…at least you know the people you're sailing with are upstanding citizens for the most part."

Now Eva grunted. "Upstanding and petty."

"Sorry?"

"Never mind."

"So have you made any progress?" Sean pressed. "Any tips yet about who the female is that left her DNA in the courthouse closet?"

She gritted her back teeth, wishing she had something to tell him. "The cruise only started last night, Sean. Sir."

"And it only lasts three days, Officer Colton. Get crackin'."

Chapter Six

Carmine strolled through the cavernous domed room that had once been the main intake and processing center for immigrants entering the United States and drifted from one display to the other. While the information was interesting, half of his attention was on the entrance door, waiting for Eva to return.

"My relatives entered the country through JFK Airport," the man beside him said.

Carmine looked over to find Aanan Gupta standing beside him, grinning.

"My father taught at Columbia for most of his career," Aanan added. "He became a citizen the year before I was born."

"So you were born here?" Carmine said, then wanted to kick himself for stating the obvious.

"Mount Sinai Hospital, class of 1974." Aanan waved a hand toward the museum display. "And you? Do you know when your ancestors arrived?"

Carmine paused, shifting mental gears in order to answer Aanan's question. "Actually, I do. Sort of. One branch of the family, anyway." He glanced around the impressive tiled room and allowed himself to imagine the man he'd heard stories about as a kid filing through stanchioned lines, waiting to be screened and logged with the hundreds of other immigrants packed in the room, fresh off the ship.

"Oh?" his companion said.

"Yeah, um…a great-great-grandfather. Came over from Italy with his pregnant second wife and my great-grandfather." Carmine turned, seeing the building in a new light. Curiosity tugged at him.

"He came through here?" Aanan raised his eyebrows. "Have you ever looked up his records? You can do that here, you know."

Carmine swiped a hand down his cheek and nodded. "Yeah. I should do that while we're here. Thanks." With a nod to the other man, Carmine went in search of a docent for directions on researching his relative. Within minutes, he was working with one of the park's researchers, and he sent Eva a quick text to let her know where to find him.

A few minutes after that, he was staring at an entry in the massive data bank of immigrant arrivals that named his two times great grandfather, his second wife and his great-grandfather at two years old. An unexpected poignancy blindsided him, left him feeling raw and vulnerable. At the same time, he wanted to share this moment, this discovery with someone. It felt…momentous somehow. As if the universe had read his mind, Eva arrived at that moment. She furrowed her brow when she met his eyes. "What's wrong?"

"I found him. I found Giuseppe."

EVA HAD SPENT a few minutes glancing over the exhibits in the main hall before locating Carmine where he was doing personal family research. He looked up from the computer he and the docent had been studying, and her steps faltered. Carmine had an odd look on his face. Her heart tripped, immediately assuming something terrible had happened. "What's wrong?"

His answer about finding someone confused her, and she shook her head a little. "Who's Giuseppe?"

He tapped the screen. "My great-great-grandfather from Italy." He turned to the museum employee. "Can I get a copy of this? Hard copy or digital. Doesn't matter."

"Sure." The docent pulled the keyboard in front of himself and typed something. Then, scooting his chair back, he nodded to Carmine. "I'll be right back."

Carmine took a deep breath. Exhaled. Scrubbed a hand over his face...and the awe-struck look in his eyes was gone. Eva couldn't help but think she'd just glimpsed a hint of something rare and real about her partner, and disappointment plucked at her that he'd shoved it aside so quickly, before she could delve into his truth more fully. But the moment was gone.

He rose from his chair and tugged Eva closer to the door. "What did Sean have to say?"

She briefed him on the conversation, and once the museum employee returned from the back room, she gave Carmine a moment to finish his business before they returned to the large main hall of the museum.

Tucking a folded sheet into his back pocket, Carmine thanked the man for his help. As they emerged into the main exhibit hall, he tipped his head back to gaze at the cream-and-beige-tiled dome over their heads. "Wow. Impressive, huh?"

"All the more so having a personal link, a confirmation of a relative that passed through these halls more than a century ago, I bet."

He scratched his chin and shrugged. "I guess."

"You guess? How can you be so blasé about finding a personal link to this beautiful building and its historic importance to our country?"

He rubbed his eyes with the pads of his fingers before

cutting an even look toward her. "Because my story is no different from thousands of others. No point getting worked up over it. It is what it is."

"Bull. It's your family's story, and that makes it special."

He glanced away, took a breath, rolled his shoulders. She thought maybe—*maybe*—she'd gotten through to him, but when he lowered his gaze to meet hers, he was her same stoic, controlled partner. "Looks like the group is headed for the ferry. Let's go."

If she hadn't seen the ghosts in his eyes, the wonderment in his face when she'd first found him, she might have believed that he could disregard the significance of his find, of his family's history. But that hint, that tiny flicker she'd seen gave her pause. And while he could downplay what had happened, she knew what she'd seen on his face, knew in her core that it meant more to him than he was admitting. Heck, *she* was moved by his discovery in the immigration records. Eva could only imagine how she'd feel if she'd found records on the Coltons' migration from Ireland. If Carmine wanted to pretend it didn't matter, she wouldn't try to convince him otherwise. But she knew the truth.

THE STATUE OF Liberty was much as Eva remembered from field trips in elementary school. Lady Liberty still loomed proudly over the tourists meandering the walkway at her base. The view of the New York City skyline from her island still inspired awe. And while the Statue of Liberty Museum was new, reading "The New Colossus" from a replica of the bronze plaque on her pedestal still brought a lump to Eva's throat. So… Carmine wasn't the only sentimental one. She smiled at Carol Johnson, who stood beside her in the museum, dabbing her eyes. "Gets me too."

Carol gave her a sidelong look, a tight smile, and moved off to join her husband across the room. Eva tried not to be offended by the woman's dismissal, but she couldn't deny the other retreat participants all seemed cool toward her. She was the group's pariah because she'd alerted everyone to a homicide last night. She'd put their hosts on the spot with her questions about Wes Westmore the first night. To the group, she was an attention seeker. Maybe even mentally unstable. Eva swore she could *feel* the eyes of the other retreatants watching her as she moved through the museum. *Paranoid much, Colton?*

She buzzed her lips as she blew out a cleansing breath. Didn't matter. Her job was not to win friends. Her job was to get information from the Westmores. To that end, she searched the crowd for Kitty and Orrin.

She jolted when Carmine moved up from behind and squeezed her shoulder. "There's a group going back to the yacht early. Kitty and Orrin want to start one-on-one couple sessions this afternoon. We can go now or take the next ferry. What do you think?"

She faced him and chewed her bottom lip. "I know what I should say." She twisted her lips in regret. "We should go back to our cabin and work on the case, but…"

"But?"

"Well, look at this day!" She waved toward the large glass windows that faced Lady Liberty. Puffy white clouds blew across the cerulean sky, and a gentle breeze made the budding trees and flowers dance and sway. "Let's get some lunch and enjoy this weather. This is our reward for enduring New York winters." She arched an eyebrow. "And if we happen to observe the other couples that stayed behind from the cruise for suspicious behavior…"

He appeared ready to argue, but, placing a hand at the base of her spine, he guided her outside and angled a glance at the sky. "You're right. Let's grab something from the snack bar and have a picnic. That's what a married couple would do, right?"

A tingle raced down her neck when he grinned at her. "Right."

His agreement to her plan, in the face of direct orders to leave last night's shooting on the yacht alone, surprised her. Heartened her. His backing meant the world to her. But then, Carmine was known for being a bit of a rogue cop, bending the rules and following his hunches. What did it say about her that so soon after starting as his partner, she was willing to disobey orders and follow her gut instincts?

Nothing, she told herself. *This is just a one-off situation.*

But it was nice to have a partner who believed her, who believed *in* her. For the first time since joining the 98th Precinct, she felt validated.

AFTER PURCHASING A junk food lunch, Carmine and Eva found a sunny spot in the grass to settle in for their picnic.

"I feel kinda guilty, sitting out here, enjoying this weather while our cohorts are cooped up in that stinky squad room," Eva said as she crunched her way through a bag of potato chips.

"Are you kidding?" Carmine unwrapped his hot dog and took a bite.

"I'm not. The squad room stinks! Body odor from arrestees, the garlic-and-onion lunches you men insist on bringing in, stale cologne, burnt coffee. It reeks." She popped another chip into her mouth and gave him a mischievous glance, indicating she knew his question was not concerning the smell of their precinct workspace.

"On a day like this," he said, jerking his chin toward the blue sky, "I promise you that our coworkers will find any excuse to patrol local parks, direct traffic, walk their beat. If a case can be worked outdoors, they'll find a way." He took another bite of hot dog with relish. "And I agree the squad room could use better ventilation."

She waved a chip toward him enthusiastically. "Right? That's all I'm saying. Air the place out somehow."

He spotted Harrison and Gail Nash walking toward them, scowling at each other and bickering in low tones. In case he and Eva were seen, Carmine sidled closer to her and draped an arm around her shoulders.

She stiffened in surprise, and he directed her attention to the other couple with his eyes.

"Oh." Playing along, she put her hand on his knee.

He leaned in. "Feed me a chip."

She did, adding, "Okay, but if you're going to eat my lunch, you have to buy me an ice cream bar for dessert."

"You drive a hard bargain," he said, casting another glance toward the Nashes…in time to see Harrison lift a hand in an exasperated gesture. And Gail flinch.

A prickle raced down his spine. "Did you see that?"

"See what?"

He worked to keep his expression and his body language neutral as the couple continued walking and drew closer. "I think there's a history of violence in the Nash home."

Eva sat taller and cut a glance toward the couple, who were now nearly within earshot. The Nashes noticed them and dropped their scowls in favor of tight smiles.

"So you two stayed behind to enjoy this pretty day too?" Eva called out cheerfully.

"More like, someone couldn't be bothered to leave the gift shop in time to catch the ferry," Harrison Nash grumbled.

Gail shot him a dirty look, then said brightly, "It is a lovely day, isn't it? Harrison, we should have a picnic too. I mean, as long as we're here for the next hour."

"You could join us," Eva said, waving a hand to the grass beside her.

"Oh, no. Thank you." Harrison jammed his hands into his pockets and gazed off across the bay. "I need to make a business call."

"Harry!" Gail said, her tone close to a whine. "We're on vacation."

Harrison's mouth firmed. "Just because I'm away from the office doesn't mean the company shut down. I have to check in with Greg."

With her shoulders sagging, Gail gave a little wave as the couple strolled away. When they'd moved far enough down the sidewalk, Carmine said, "Sean told you he'd run a background on the other passengers, right?"

"Mmm-hmm. Nothing significant came up." She glanced toward the retreating couple and narrowed her eyes. "But we can dig deeper when we get back on board. You thinking Harrison might be the guy I saw?"

"Does he fit the profile?"

Eva studied Harrison's retreating back. He was tall enough. Similar body type, but...

"Close," she said. "It's worth looking into."

Carmine bent his legs and rested his arms on his knees. "No arrest record doesn't always mean someone is completely clean. Friends in power can see that police reports aren't filed or that compromising incidents get buried."

"Or that neighbors didn't report what they knew, afraid to get involved," Eva added and turned her gaze to lock with his. "The one person who reported seeing Wes display violence toward Lana later recanted. But if there was a history of arguing—of battery—surely the neighbors heard them, saw something before the night she was killed. If only someone would talk." Eva grimaced.

He shared her frustration. The neighbors in the swanky high-rise where Wes lived were defiantly tight-lipped.

"Yeah. If only." He squinted against the sun as he glanced

up at Lady Liberty's torch, marveling again at the sight. "We need to be on the same page today when we talk to Orrin and Kitty in our private counseling session."

"Really? I thought poor communication was our vice." She lifted a corner of her mouth to let him know she was teasing.

Sunshine sparkled in her green eyes and made her auburn hair flame with red highlights.

Carmine experienced a kick in his ribs that stole his breath. When he reached for her this time, brushing a flyaway wisp of her hair behind her ear, it had nothing to do with playing the part of her husband and everything to do with his desire to touch her. *Damn, she is beautiful.*

And too young for me. And she's my colleague. And my boss's sister.

He snatched his hand back and needed a beat to find his voice again. "I'm just saying that blurting out questions about Wes without context got us nothing but wariness from the room last night. They'll be all the more cautious around us today, so—"

Eva sighed heavily. "I messed up! I said I was sorry."

"My point is, having some idea *how* we'll weave Wes or female relatives into the conversation can help us steer the ship in that direction. You know?"

She was staring at him, her eyes soft, her lips slightly parted—and clearly distracted by...something. Then, as if shaken from a stupor, she blinked hard and pressed her lips in a taut line. She swallowed hard enough to make her long, graceful throat convulse. "Well, the theme of the day seems to be family history. Ancestry and immigration. Can't we use your story of finding your great-great-grandfather's name in the immigration records to... I don't know, ask about their family history?"

"You're in the right neighborhood, but they're good at deflecting direct questions. We need something more organic to a conversation."

"Inherited traits? Height and hair color and that sort of thing could lead to mention of DNA." She scrunched her nose at her own idea. "Yeah. *That's* organic to most discussions," she said under her breath. "Try again, Colton." She chewed her bottom lip, drawing Carmine's attention to the full pink bow void of makeup. He wanted to taste her for himself. Wanted to lick the tiny grains of potato chip salt at the corner of her mouth and suck gently on her—

"Carmine? Daniel!" she said and snapped her fingers in front of his nose.

"Huh?"

"I said, what about pets? People love to talk about their pets. Could we use an animal as a bridge topic to talk about the animal's owners?"

Refocusing his thoughts, he nodded. "Maybe. Assuming the Westmores have pets. But that's the kind of planning I mean. Good work, Officer Colton."

She beamed at his praise, and he felt her grin all the way to his marrow. Such a simple thing, a compliment for a good idea, but he had a suspicion Eva had not received nearly enough encouragement from her previous partner. A yearning filled Carmine, unlike anything he'd known before. He wanted to make Eva happy, if only to earn more warm smiles from her. But also to make her feel appreciated, to give her the credit she deserved when she made valuable contributions to a case. He'd been a rookie once, and he knew how difficult it could be to find your place in the precinct, to earn the respect of the other officers. And he wasn't living in his brother's shadow. Or a woman in a traditionally male role.

A ferry horn tooted, and Eva, crumpling her chip bag, glanced in the direction of the pier. "Shall we go get lined up for the ride back? I'd like to do some research of my own regarding our fellow passengers before dinner. And we still need to see what we can find out about Wes's visitors at Rikers."

"Yep. And I got information from the docent about more effectively searching ancestry data banks for records on specific people, how to weed down the responses."

She dusted grass and dirt from her jeans as she rose, and Carmine made a concerted effort not to stare at the way the denim hugged her perfect tush.

"Are you wanting more details about Giuseppe?"

He took her lunch trash from her. "Maybe one day. But I thought I'd look for better information of when—or if— Maeve O'Leary Westmore died and if she had sisters or nieces. We still don't know who the female DNA at the courthouse belonged to, and I find it highly suspicious that Wes implies his mother is dead and the trail of records for Maeve O'Leary Westmore goes cold shortly after her husband's death, yet there's not a death certificate on file." He stuffed their trash into a receptacle and fell in step with Eva.

"Could Maeve have been killed?" Eva speculated, her gaze fixed on some undefined point in the distance and her nose doing that cute wrinkling thing that said she was lost in thought. "Could she be a Jane Doe from an unsolved murder? If Wes could kill Lana—" she turned to him with an aside "—*allegedly*, then who's to say he didn't kill his mother? Maybe his father, too, for that matter? Could he have hidden shrimp in his dad's food? Didn't Joseph Westmore die from an anaphylactic reaction to shrimp?"

"All good points," he said and, spotting another couple from the retreat, he took Eva's hand and laced their fingers.

She gave him a slightly startled look, then noticed the McKinneys, and the tension in her body relaxed. And what did it say about him that he was that in tune with Eva's body language?

Shoving that notion aside, Carmine kept a close eye on the McKinneys. If Jim, in fact, had a mistress, as Sarah had said last night, could he have been the man Eva saw on deck last night?

"I know this," Eva said, sighing. "Sean was right about us needing to get better answers pronto. We have approximately sixty-eight hours left on this marriage retreat to learn something useful from the Westmores. Let's not waste a minute of it. My uncle Humphrey is out there somewhere. We need to find him before it's too late."

Chapter Seven

On the ferry ride back to Liberty Harbor and the Westmores' waiting yacht, Eva silently mulled over all the questions and angles of Humphrey's disappearance, Lana's murder, the cold trail to find Maeve O'Leary. Too many people were within hearing range on the ferry for her and Carmine to discuss the cases openly. Besides, it fit the profile of a couple with communication issues for her and *Daniel* to not be talking after a pleasant and moving day at the historic landmarks.

Unfortunately, the silence between them also gave her too much time to contemplate the arm he had draped around her shoulders as the ferry chugged across the bay. Carmine's proximity was hard enough to keep in perspective without his snuggling close and putting that muscled arm around her. Pulling her closer to the spicy-bodywash scent of him. Allowing her to feel the steady rise and fall of his chest as he breathed. The strong rhythmic thump of his heartbeat…

Think about the case. Think about the case. Thinkabout-thecase!

"Dina, Daniel?" She turned toward the woman who spoke, shaking herself from her reverie and distraction. Sarah McKinney smiled from the row of seats across from her. "When is your session with the Westmores? We're scheduled to see them in thirty minutes and, honestly, I'm kind of nervous."

Eva returned the smile. "Um, five o'clock, I think."

Carmine nodded in confirmation.

"Just tell the truth and speak from the heart," Eva said. "Isn't that why we're all here?"

Jim McKinney grunted, and Sarah gave her husband a frown.

Over the speakers, the ferry's arrival at Liberty Harbor was announced, and the passengers began filing toward the exits. Carmine placed a warm hand at the small of her back, ushering her toward the gangway, and ripples of pleasure washed over her. She liked being the focus of his attention, having that physical connection to him, even if it was all for show. Sometimes she got so caught up in proving her competence and independence to her overprotective brothers that she forgot how much she enjoyed having a personal connection with someone.

They walked toward the marina where the *Westmores' Folly* was docked with the other couples who had stayed behind for the later ferry. At the yacht, she preceded Carmine up the narrow ramp that took them on board and was crossing the main deck when a woman screamed.

"Look out!" Carmine shouted as he tackled Eva, shoving her forward as he did so. A loud crash reverberated behind her, the deck shaking. The crowd gasped as she and Carmine tumbled together onto the deck. His muscled weight landed on top of her, knocking the breath from her. Yet his arms had encircled her, and his hand cushioned her head from the hard planks of the deck. Adrenaline pumped through her belatedly, and a dull buzzing filled her ears.

What had happened?

"Judas Priest! Are you all right?" Carmine asked. He shoved himself off her, and as he rolled to a squat beside her, his hands roamed her body as if searching for injuries. She needed a moment for her stunned lungs to loosen and allow her to inhale properly, but she nodded. She couldn't detect any obvious injury, although her hip hurt where she'd landed on it.

Angling her head, she scanned the deck behind her. An extra-large cooler, far bigger than any she'd ever seen in common use for tailgating or picnics, lay on its side with a huge ice sculpture tumbled out, broken in pieces and scattered across the deck. She stared, not really comprehending what she was looking at or how—

"That fell from one of the upper levels," Carmine supplied, turning to look at the mess.

"And…it nearly hit me?" she rasped, the picture of the events crystalizing. She bent her head back to gaze at the upper decks, expecting to see one of the cruise chefs or waiters peering down in horror at their mistake. But the upper decks were empty, were private lodgings. So why…? "But…"

Word of the accident had clearly reached the Westmores, because Orrin rushed out and surveyed the detritus of the ice sculpture before approaching Eva. "Dear God! Dina, are you hurt? Should we call an ambulance?"

Eva rolled her shoulders and shifted to get her feet under her. "I don't think…" When she winced, Carmine and Orrin propped her under each arm, helping her stand. "I'm okay."

Orrin frowned at the shattered ice. "Well, the mystery of the missing ice sculpture has been solved," he said, his frown darkening, "however tragically."

Eva could feel Carmine stiffen. "It was missing earlier?"

"Well, yes. The delivery from the caterer came this afternoon, but the sculpture couldn't be accounted for…until now." Orrin regarded Eva with a hand clasped over his heart. "I'm so very sorry. Can I get you anything, Dina? A drink from the bar, perhaps?"

She shook her head, her mind clearing from the muddle

of adrenaline and shock. "I…just want to go to our cabin and…lie down for a moment."

"Right." Orrin took a step back and dragged a hand down his haggard face, clearly worried she planned to sue.

She attempted a smile. "I'm fine. Lucky and fine."

As her nerves settled, her brain cranked up, processing what she was learning. An ice sculpture had gone missing. Then fell. From an upper deck?

But…the galley was below deck. The bar was on the main level. As was the dining room. Why would the sculpture have been taken to an upper deck? And how? She nudged a chunk of ice, the body of one of two swans, and estimated that hunk alone had to weigh sixty pounds. The whole sculpture, plus the dry ice in the cooler and the thick-walled cooler itself had to have weighed somewhere north of two hundred pounds combined. Maybe more.

Eva shuddered. If the cooler had landed on her, she'd be on her way to the hospital now…if not dead. Her grip tightened on Carmine's arm, and she gave him a sidelong glance, whispering, "Can we go now?"

He pulled his attention from the upper deck where he'd been staring, frowning. Jerking a nod, he helped her to the stairs and up toward their cabin. At the end of the upper walkway leading to the cabins, a mop lay haphazardly across their path. Carmine stepped over to study the position of the mop, peered over the railing and sent Eva a dark look. Even without his speaking, she knew what he'd concluded. The mop was directly over where the cooler had fallen. Had the mop been used to push the massive ice sculpture off the upper deck? The cooler could have been shoved under the bottom bars of the railing…

Carmine bit out a curse word and strode back to her. "Let's get back to the cabin. We need to talk."

CARMINE CHEWED THE inside of his cheek, stewing, fuming. The evidence would imply that the ice chest had been pushed off the upper deck on purpose. At the exact moment the second group of retreat couples was returning from the ferry. When *Eva* was returning to the yacht. As in, the only witness to whatever crime had happened on the main deck the night before. As in, Eva had been targeted.

One look at his partner's wan complexion told him she'd reached the same conclusion. She raised her haunted green eyes to his, and he was assailed by the overwhelming urge to wrap her in his arms and shield her from any threat.

"I know how it looks, but…" She drew a tremulous breath. "We don't have any real *proof* the cooler was pushed off, that someone did this on purpose."

Carmine grunted. "Yeah, well, I don't have to be mauled by a lion to know it would hurt. Some things are just…understood." He braced his hands on his hips and gritted his teeth. "My gut is telling me it was intentional. It's the logical conclusion. The cooler was stolen from the delivery, hauled upstairs, and an industrial mop was used to help tip it over the edge while the person responsible stayed out of the line of sight. And…" He paused, his gut roiling. "It's pretty obvious you were singled out. You were meant to be hurt…or killed."

She looked away, flexing the fingers of one hand with her other and biting her bottom lip. She looked uncharacteristically frazzled. Even when Wes Westmore had bombarded her with crude insinuations and filthy comments, she kept it together. But now…

"We have witnesses," she said quietly. "The McKinneys were right behind us. And the Nashes…" She met his gaze, her expression eager. "Maybe they saw what happened or… who was up there when the cooler fell."

He considered that, remembered someone screaming. "It's possible. We can ask them." He dropped in the chair across from her and scrubbed his face. "At dinner tonight, I can question the group, see what people know."

Eva groaned. "And I'll look like the attention-seeking drama queen again." She twisted her mouth in frustration and lifted one shoulder. "Maybe we should let it go and just... stay alert to any other attempts?"

He narrowed a stunned look on her. "What?"

She sighed. "If we ask too many questions, we could tip off the perp, and he'll cover his tracks. Or we'll blow our cover. Or we'll lose important time and opportunities to work the case we're here to investigate."

He slapped a hand on the tiny table between them in frustration. "Judas Priest, Eva! Someone tried to kill you, and you want to sweep it under the rug? Pretend it didn't happen? What kind of cop are you?"

She bristled. "The kind that can look out for herself!"

"Oh, really? And if I hadn't shoved you out of the way this afternoon, would you have avoided getting crushed on your own?"

She blanched, and he immediately wished he could reel the words back in. Shoving to his feet, he muttered, "I'm sorry."

"No." She blinked at him, her face reflecting the riot of emotions that had to be churning inside her...as they were in him. "You're right. You...saved my life. I—thank you."

He rubbed his temple and took a slow breath. "I wasn't looking for... I didn't mean..." He sat down again and reached for her hand. "No thanks needed. That's what partners do, huh? Watch each other's back?"

She twitched a half smile at him. "Well, yeah. And it seems we'll need to be vigilant in that until we figure out what I witnessed last night and who's responsible."

Carmine held her gaze and nodded, losing himself in the tumble of thoughts that vied for supremacy in his brain.

The Westmores. The attempt on Eva. Their assignment on this cruise.

The sexy trail of freckles that decorated Eva's nose and cheeks. Her lips. Her spring green eyes...

He followed the direction of her gaze as it dipped to his hand on hers. How long had he been stroking her wrist with his thumb? He snatched his hand back and jammed it into his hair. Tore his gaze away.

Wow, DiRico. Subtle. He cleared his throat. "We, um... are supposed to meet with the Westmores in a few minutes. Are you up to it?"

Predictably, Eva squared her shoulders, and a fire of purpose lit her eyes. The woman was nothing if not driven and resilient. "I am. We have a job to do. Let's do it."

THE ONE-ON-ONE COUNSELING sessions with the Westmores were held in their hosts' private office. Carmine took in the small but well-appointed space and thought about the money the department had spent to send him and Eva on this assignment. The rich get richer...

He sat in one of the chairs in the conversational grouping, renewing his determination to learn something valuable, something that would move one of the investigations forward. Or solve it. That would be a significant win, not just for himself and the precinct but also for Eva. Solving a major case as a rookie? Big points in the department. Promotion-worthy. And why did he want that so much for her? He wasn't typically so invested in his coworkers' careers.

"Dina, I heard what happened...with the ice sculpture," Kitty said to Eva as she took her seat. "I'm so glad you weren't hurt!" She pressed a hand to her chest and smiled.

Carmine didn't think the sentiment reached Kitty's eyes. Her wishes sounded flat to his ear, but...he might be overly cynical. He cut his eyes toward Eva, who returned a grim smile.

"I'm glad too. I hope your investigation into what happened will ensure nothing like this happens again," Eva said pointedly.

"Investigation..." Kitty consulted her husband with a side-glance.

"We absolutely will look into the matter." Orrin divided his attention between Eva and Carmine and gave a quick nod. "The unfortunate incident aside... I trust you had a good day? Enjoyed yourselves at the historic landmarks?"

Carmine nodded. "It was moving. More than I'd expected."

"Oh." Kitty shifted her focus to Carmine. "How so, Daniel?"

"Well, I don't know much about my mother's family, but I have heard stories my whole life from my father, his parents, my aunts and uncles about my great-great-grandfather Giuseppe D—" He paused and cleared his throat. "De Santis."

"What stories?" Kitty asked, her expression bright with enthusiasm.

"How he immigrated to the U.S. with only a few lire and a harmonica in his pocket and a dream of making a fresh start for his family."

"The American dream," Kitty said, nodding and smiling.

"Yeah, but...today's trip gave the stories context, um... color, as it were." Carmine divided a look between the Westmores. The couple seemed genuinely interested, and he made quick calculations. Could he milk this topic as a lead-in to a discussion of the Westmore family line?

"I, uh...found my relatives on one of the ship-arrival manifests as well as the official immigration in-take records. And I read the accounts of other Italian immigrants from the

1880s and 1890s who left Southern Italy after the Franco-Prussian War."

Orrin was nodding, his expression intrigued, so Carmine continued. "Poverty was rampant in Southern Italy at that time, as was cholera and malaria. I had heard Giuseppe's first wife died the year before he immigrated, and now I can see it might have been from one of these epidemics. He wasn't just looking for a fresh start—he was desperate for work, eager to take care of his family and to escape bad conditions at home." Carmine shook his head slowly as he digested these facts again for himself. "This was my two times great-grandfather. My dad still has that harmonica. It's one of the most precious things we own."

Kitty dabbed at her eyes. "Oh my! How touching. That's tremendous, Daniel. I'm so glad you were able to make that connection. Family history is so important. Roots are important."

"My family has an heirloom like that," Orrin said, his forehead wrinkled in thought. "One worth far more in sentiment than its dollar value."

"Oh, yes! The Victoria vanity set!" Kitty said, nodding to her husband.

Eva sent Carmine a knowing look; then, eyes full of wonder, she prompted, "Can you tell us about it?"

Orrin opened his mouth, then closed it. "No. I—this is your time. We're here to talk about your family, your issues in your marriage. We couldn't waste your time with—"

"Oh, please! I want to know." Eva turned to Kitty and asked, "When you say Victoria...do you mean the set is from the Victorian era?"

Kitty cut a glance to Orrin and, as if unable to hold in her secret, said, "Better than that. The set—a gold filigree comb, hairbrush and hand mirror—was a gift from Queen Victoria to Orrin's great-great-grandmother."

Eva's eyes widened. "Queen Victoria!"

Kitty beamed, clearly proud of the family link to royalty. "Yes. His two times great-grandmother served briefly as a royal dresser in one of Her Majesty's vacation homes. Not palace staff, but…"

"Still! Wow!" Eva gushed, and Carmine swore the enthusiasm was real. "And you still have the set?"

"Thank God, yes. But we almost lost it to Orrin's awful sister-in-law!"

"What? How?" Eva canted forward, her expression distressed and fully engaged. *Bravo, Eva…*

Kitty gave a haughty sniff. "I hate to even speak of her. The family is well rid of her." She pursed her lips and seemed to consider whether to continue.

"What… What did she do?" Eva pushed, her brow furrowing in concern. Real or acting? Carmine couldn't say.

"Well, for one thing, she *used* the comb and brush!" Kitty leaned toward Eva as if conspiring with an ally. "Delicate antiques! When we got the set back after Joseph's death, the brush had broken bristles, and Maeve's slut-red hair was all twined in the comb." She seemed to realize she could have insulted Eva then and added, "No offense meant, dear. Your hair is a beautiful auburn. Maeve's red was straight from a bottle. She was always changing her natural blond. God knows why."

"Oh, uh… No offense taken." Eva glanced at Orrin. "Your brother Joseph died?"

Orrin sighed. "Yes."

"I'm so sorry. Was this recent?"

Orrin shifted in his chair, scowling. "No. Almost twenty years ago."

Eva's expression grew more sad and sympathetic. "Oh dear. He must have been young. May I… May I ask how he died?"

Carmine bit the inside of his cheek to hide a grin. Eva was a natural. He sat back and followed the conversation with interest but didn't interrupt his partner's flow.

"Well, the official coroner's report said allergic anaphylaxis, but I..." Orrin frowned. "I'm sorry. I've never bought the official story surrounding Joseph's death. He had a known, lifelong allergy to shellfish, but he ate shrimp the night he died? I doubt that. And why didn't Maeve seek medical help before he'd passed out from a closed windpipe?" He gritted his teeth and growled under his breath. "Pardon the French, but that's a crock of bull!"

Kitty patted Orrin's leg. "Let's get back on track, shall we, dear?"

He nodded at his wife and mumbled, "I'm sorry. Obviously still a sore spot, but that's not why we're here. Um, Dina, tell us about your family tree."

"Did Joseph and Maeve have any children? I mean, for him to die so young..."

When Orrin shot Eva an irritated look, she added quickly, "I only ask because... Well, see, I lost my parents at an early age myself. To cancer. I was raised by my oldest brother, so I sympathize with other kids who lose parents..."

"Oh, don't feel bad for Wes. The boy made out like gangbusters," Kitty groused. "He was never close to his father, but he and his mother inherited a small fortune. She disappeared, and he entered college with the world at his feet."

"Wes?" Eva prompted.

Orrin grimaced and nodded. "Yes, *that* Wes Westmore," he said grudgingly. "As you pointed out last night. But kindly don't make this a point of discussion with the rest of the retreatants. We don't like to talk about him, because we haven't had anything to do with him in years. He wrote us off when he was young, and we were happy to do the same when we saw him following in the questionable footsteps of his mother."

"Questionable how?" Carmine asked.

"Well," Kitty scoffed a humorless laugh. "I don't for a minute believe all of his Wall Street wheeling and dealing is legitimate."

"Really?" Eva cut a side-glance to Carmine, then back to Kitty. "Do you think he's capable of murder? I think it was his girlfriend… Laura, was it?" Eva wrinkled her nose as if confused, and Carmine wanted to laugh at the clever question meant to imply ignorance of the situation.

"Lana," Orrin corrected, clearly suspicious of the continued questions. "And we have no knowledge of the crime, and our lawyers have asked us not to speculate or make comments that could be misconstrued or used against us somehow."

"Used against you how?" Eva asked.

Kitty narrowed her eyes on Eva. "I think we've said enough. Too much." She checked her watch and grimaced. "We've used up most of your time and still haven't covered what we were supposed to. *Your* family history. The impact of that legacy on your lives, your marriage. You know, we often repeat the patterns and behaviors we see modeled by our parents. Understanding your family history can often shed light on why our parents raised us the way they did, and where some of the fears and beliefs we bring into a marriage came from."

A knock sounded on the office door, and Samuel Leech peeked in the door. "Are you ready for us?"

"Almost," Orrin called. "We'll be right with you."

Eva clapped her hands together once. "Right. My family history in a nutshell. We're Irish on my father's side. I never really learned much about our mother's family before she died. I have three older brothers, all still living in the city. Our father died when I was eight, leaving my oldest brother in charge of raising me. I'm named for a medieval Irish noblewoman—no relation that I'm aware of. My family means everything to me, and I appreciate everything my older brothers did for me growing up. Boom." She made a mic-drop hand gesture.

Kitty and Orrin exchanged a look, and after a moment, Orrin said, "Okay. Well…until next time…" He paused, consulting a paper file with "Eggers" printed on the tab. "Work on your communication skills by sharing more stories and memories of your family with each other, and we'll see you at the evening group session."

Carmine rose from his chair and, placing a hand at Eva's back, nudged her toward the door. "Thank you. We will."

Once they were in the corridor again and away from the Westmores' stateroom, Carmine grinned at Eva as he tugged her into a hug. "That was inspired! I could kiss you!"

She levered back from him and gaped like a landed fish.

"Don't look at me like that. I'm not *going* to kiss you." *More's the pity*, he thought as his attention flicked briefly to her perfect mouth.

"I… I know! I'm not—" She backed out of his embrace and tugged him farther away from the corridor and out onto the main deck, where engine noise and seagulls and space gave them more conversational privacy. "This is huge!"

He frowned. "Come again?"

Her eyes lit up with excitement. "Think about what we just learned!"

"You mean the fact that Orrin clearly believes foul play was involved in his brother's death? And more specifically questions Maeve's role in Joseph's death?"

Eva blinked and shook her head. "No. But now that you mention it…the shrimp story does sound fishy. Um, no pun intended."

"So…we should look at Joseph's death certificate again, maybe check to see if any investigation was done. Huh?"

"Um, sure." She nodded, her mind clearly elsewhere as she gazed across the water toward the city.

"Eva," he asked, snapping his fingers to get her attention. "What are you thinking?"

She met his gaze again, and her body language, her expression hummed with exhilaration. "Somewhere—like at the Westmores' residence or in a lockbox at a bank in the city—there is a brush with Maeve's hair in it."

Carmine straightened his back and gave his partner his full attention. "And?"

"We need to call Sean." Even as she said this, she was pulling her cell phone from her back pocket. "We need him to get a warrant for that antique vanity set. If Maeve used it like Kitty said, there's a good chance we can find a hair with an intact root."

A tingle raced through him as he made the connection. "For DNA comparison to the sample found in the courthouse closet!"

"Exactly!" Eva's face glowed with a grin as she lifted her phone to her ear. "Hi, Sean, it's me. Listen, I think we've got something…"

Chapter Eight

That evening after dinner, Eva felt compelled to pull Gail Nash aside after the cringe she and Carmine had witnessed on Liberty Island that afternoon. "Gail," she said, keeping her tone low and private, "if Harrison has ever hurt you, emotionally or physically, there are organizations available to help."

Gail blinked, clearly taken aback by Eva's presumptuousness. "What?"

"You aren't alone," Eva added quickly, seeing Harrison headed their way. "Incidents of violence should be reported to the police so that—"

"Ladies, why so serious?" Harrison asked, putting a possessive hand at Gail's nape.

"Nothing," Gail said, her voice bitter and offended. "Dina was just being overly dramatic and nosy. Again." She faced Eva and curled her lip in disdain. In a too-loud voice, she added, "Do you have some weird police fetish? Honestly, I'm surprised you didn't call the police this afternoon when that cooler fell close to you."

Eva narrowed her eyes. "Maybe I should have. Do you know anything about that?"

"I know it was an accident," Gail said.

Carmine moved up beside Eva. "Do you? You're sure of that?"

"Oh God! Don't tell me you buy into your wife's attention-grabbing schemes," Gail said, casting a look of disgust and disappointment toward Carmine.

Kitty called the group together at that moment, saving Carmine from making a rebuttal, but Eva was grateful for his backing just the same. The Nashes whispered to several other retreat participants as they made their way to the circle of chairs. Heads turned, and stares followed Eva to her seat.

Bill Boone, who occupied the seat next to her once they were all gathered, gave Eva a withering glance and muttered, "You really should learn to stay out of other people's business."

She hiked up her chin. "Not happening. If I have reason to believe someone could be in danger, it's my job to—" She stopped, realizing what she'd almost said. She'd almost let on she was a cop, sworn to protect and serve. "It's *everyone's* job to look out for each other. The world would be a better place if people were more willing to get involved, to take care of each other."

"Dina, a good point!" Kitty said.

She turned toward her hostess and felt heat rise in her cheeks. She hadn't realized anyone else was listening. But it seemed the whole group had heard her reply to Bill. Carmine's expression asked, *What are you doing? We need to blend in, not call more attention to ourselves.*

"And caring for others should start at home," Kitty said, making a smooth segue into the topic of the evening. "Let's talk about how we can support our spouses and strengthen our connection to each other. Today, we focused on family histories. Where we came from, traditions and family roots. Understanding each other's pasts, hurts and cherished memories can help you build a blended future that appreciates both sides of your union." Kitty laced her fingers together and sent a smile around the circle.

The discussion moved on, giving each couple the opportunity to share a new insight into their partner or a family tradition they wished to incorporate going forward.

Eva tried to pay attention, to play her role as Dina as best she could, but found herself dwelling on recent events, especially the lead concerning the vanity set she'd passed onto Sean before dinner. As she scrutinized the other couples, it became clear they all bought into the "Dina is an attention seeker and busybody" theory. The other participants took turns sending her dirty looks. Jim McKinney seemed wary of her. Linda Miller gave her a disappointed headshake. Samuel Leech met her gaze and rolled his eyes as he turned away.

"Dina..." Orrin's voice pulled her from her distraction, and she snapped her attention to her host. "What new insights do you have from today that you think you can build on to strengthen your bond with Daniel?"

"Erm..." Eva glanced at Carmine. She scrambled mentally for something, a truth or fiction, that would satisfy Orrin's direct query. "He, uh…has his two times great-grandfather's harmonica."

Around the circle, there were chuckles and groans.

Carmine leaned close to her, mumbling, "I just told that story."

She gave an awkward laugh. "Oh. Oops."

"Maybe if you paid more attention to your husband and less to other people's marriages, you wouldn't be here," Harrison Nash groused.

Kitty gave Harrison a weak scowl and waved to Bill Boone. "Let's move on. Bill, how about you?"

Bill gave a bland answer about learning his wife's family had come to the United States in the early eighteenth century, and an ancestor had fought in the American Revolutionary War. Without further comment, he gave the floor to his wife, and Molly simpered on about how she cherished Bill's family and the sacrifices he made for those he loved.

Eva worked hard not to snort her amusement at the saccharine answer.

As the discussion moved on, Bill slanted a dark glare at Eva that sent a skittering sensation down her back. She sensed a venom and malice from him that chilled her to her bone.

Crud, had she snorted aloud? She didn't need to do anything else to encourage animosity from the group.

"All right, let's move on to our closing exercises," Kitty called, her tone rife with enthusiasm. "I want you to hold your spouse's hands and look into their eyes, hold their gaze." Kitty paused. Waited. When the couples in the circle only glanced at each other awkwardly, she waved a hand. "Go on. Do it now. We spend far too much time with our eyes on our phones, on the television, in a book..." She cast a not-so-subtle look at the McKinneys before adding, "...on other people. But when was the last time you really *looked* at your spouse?" Kitty strolled slowly around the circle, observing each couple.

Eva faced Carmine, and he her. She raised her eyebrows in a silent *Oh well. Here goes nothing.*

His throat worked as he swallowed hard and locked gazes with her.

"Not just a fleeting glance," Kitty said, "but a long, meaningful look. A deep dive. Look into their soul. Hold their gaze and see their hopes, their fears. Eye contact is one of the most intimate ways we connect without touching. Good, Linda, Jamal. That's it!"

Carmine squinted as he stared at her, his expression comically focused, and Eva had to muffle a laugh. She swatted at his knee, whispering, "Be serious!"

Now his face hardened to a stone-cold neutrality.

She rolled her eyes and gave a little snort.

"Is there a problem, Dina?" Kitty asked as she strolled by.

"No. I just…" She exhaled, worked to school her face. If Carmine could play the fake-marriage game, so could she. Fixing her attention on Carmine, she stared straight into his dark brown eyes and…noticed a fleck of green on his left iris. *Huh.* She focused on that fleck, grateful to have something specific to hold her attention…until she noticed his pupils dilating. His breathing grew shallower, more obvious. His nostrils flared slightly.

Was he…getting turned on?

She dented her brow and tipped her head slightly in silent inquiry.

Carmine's jaw muscles flexed, and he blinked hard. Blew out a sharp breath. And returned his stare to hers, his countenance more rigid, more controlled.

"Okay," Kitty chirped from across the circle. "Great job, everyone. Now, let's move on to the next step. It's an exercise we've borrowed from other successful family counselors. It's called the Ten-Second Kiss."

Chapter Nine

Carmine's face blanched, and he whipped his head around to face the Westmores. "The what?"

"The Ten-Second Kiss," Kitty repeated, a smug look on her face.

Eva felt a little dizzy. Kiss Carmine? Her heart thudded, and her nerves jangled. While part of her—the secret part that had had a crush on Carmine for months—was high-fiving and doing a little dance, a bigger part of her was looking for a bed to hide under. Kissing was so—

"Kissing is one of the best ways we can establish intimacy with our partner," Orrin said as if completing her thought for her. "But most kisses—to say goodbye or hello, maybe congratulations or thank you—are so quick. A second, if that. A mere peck."

"Unless the kiss is part of foreplay leading up to sex," Kitty added. "But intimacy needs to be part of every day of your marriage. Not just during sex, but in ordinary moments to make your spouse feel seen. Valued. Appreciated. To keep the special connection you had at the beginning of your relationship alive and strong."

Eva cast her gaze to the other couples. The rest of the group also looked uncomfortable with the suggested PDA. Well, except for Bill and Molly Boone, who leaned close, nuzzling and giggling to each other. As if feeling Eva's gaze on them, Bill shifted his attention to Eva again and glared. A chill raced down her nape from the open hostility in his glower. Okay, she got the point. The man didn't like her. And maybe she had been staring at the Boones, and she deserved his mind-your-own-business scowl, but...come on! They were acting like newlyweds at a marriages-in-crisis therapy cruise. Did they think anyone in the room was buying their act?

Carmine squeezed her hands, pulling her gaze back to his. He had a strange look of his own on his face, as if he were steeling himself for a difficult task.

"Daniel," she said softly, "You good?"

He squared his shoulders. "Of course."

She would have laughed at Carmine's matter-of-fact demeanor, except Kitty called out, "Ready? And begin!"

And then things got real. Really real. Carmine drew her close, jamming his hand through her hair to capture the back of her head, and pressed his mouth against hers so fast and hard that their teeth clicked. Eva sucked in a startled breath through her nose and grabbed Carmine's shoulders to keep from toppling backward. Her brain caught up a second later, awareness crackling like static in her head. She was kissing Carmine.

Kissing. Carmine.

Kissing!

Carmine!

No. *Daniel.* Better if she thought of this exercise in the framework of her undercover assignment. And kissing was a rather generous term for what she and Carmine were doing. He'd pressed his mouth to hers, tightly, but there was no movement. No caress of lips or gentle suction or tangle of tongues or...or...passion. It was cold and stiff and completely uninspired.

And as the seconds ticked by, the kiss became increasingly awkward. Not that she was contributing anything to the act. She took her cues from her partner. *No way* would she risk revealing her true feelings with some ardent display of tenderness or a lusty sweep of her tongue against his taut lips. Beneath her hands, Carmine's shoulders were rock solid. Not just firm muscle and plenty of it—which she'd expected, given his obvious attention to his fitness—but tense. His body strung as tight as a guy-wire.

Eva cut her gaze sideways to the other couples. Some were clearly awkward with the kiss, while a few others had taken the assignment to heart and were locked in tender or passionate embraces.

"And *ten*. Very good," Kitty called out and faced Orrin. "What do you think, dear? Should we give it another try? I'm not sure everyone was in the spirit of the exercise."

"Let's do it again!" Aanan Gupta called out, waggling his eyebrows at Zara.

"Good man!" Orrin boomed and aimed a finger at Aanan. "Again, everyone! Ready…"

Eva's gut clenched. *Note to self*, she thought. *Kill Aanan.*

She faced Carmine again, who looked equally distressed by the thought of another kiss. Eva frowned. Hang on. Was it really so distasteful to him to kiss her? Irritation tickled her belly, and a rebellious pride reared its head. Her brothers would attribute her competitive, prideful streak to her red hair, but Eva knew better. It came from being raised by her brothers. She just hated to be dismissed without cause.

Challenge accepted.

"Begin!" Orrin called, and Eva leaned in to catch Carmine's lips with hers.

She slanted her mouth and applied a gentle suction at first, then plowed her fingers into his hair and deepened the kiss. She felt the jolt that shook him, the brief tensing of his muscles before he took charge and tugged her closer, assumed command of the kiss.

Instantly, sensations flooded her that made her head spin. She clutched Carmine tighter when she seemed to tip over drunkenly...except she hadn't consumed a drop of alcohol. No, she was intoxicated from just the urgency and skill of Carmine's kiss. Because, although she'd initiated the kiss and set their course, he had well and truly taken the helm. Her pulse raced hard enough to make her ears buzz and her body hum all the way to her core. She'd foolishly waded into this kiss, but the riptide that was Carmine had carried her out to sea.

"And ten! Well done," Orrin said.

But Carmine didn't release her. His lips lingered for a count of eleven, twelve...

As much as Eva wanted to stay lost in that moment, an odd panic washed over her. She was in over her head. Drowning. If she yielded to Carmine's magnetism and prowess, how would she save herself from falling for him? From the sure heartbreak and humility of forming a real romantic attachment on her first undercover assignment?

His firm embrace and erotic kiss were for show, an act to convince Kitty and Orrin that he was taking the marriage counseling seriously. The truth of that pinged painfully inside Eva, evidence that she'd already grown too attached to her faux husband. Wedging her hand up between them, she pushed against Carmine's chest and tore her mouth from his. She took a beat to catch her breath, her heart thumping wildly, before raising a dazed look to her partner. Carmine seemed shaken as well. His pupils were large black pools of need, and his expression was a cross between confusion and fervor. Then, as if snapping from a trance, he gave his head a shake and inhaled deeply. He twisted in his chair, away from her, and scrubbed a hand over his face.

Still tingling in her most intimate places, Eva faced the circle, trying not to appear as overwhelmed and befuddled by what had just transpired as she felt. *Just go with it. You are Dina. Who just kissed her husband. Nothing new. Nothing earthshaking. Right?*

Then why did her whole world seem to have shifted? Why was she quaking to her bones?

"Now here's the catch," Kitty was saying. "The point of the exercise is to create intimacy independent of the bedroom. So when you leave here tonight…no sex, friends! We want you to learn to experience closeness with your spouse in everyday moments, not as foreplay. Sex brings a whole new set of emotions and issues to bear. For these few days you're on the retreat, we want you to focus only on the emotional issues that have complicated your marriage."

Orrin dismissed the group, and for long seconds, Carmine sat, staring at the carpet and taking long, slow breaths. Finally, Eva nudged him with her shoulder. "Daniel? You, uh…ready to go back to our—"

He shot to his feet and jammed a hand through his hair. "Sure."

Eva rose and trailed after him as he strode out of the dining room and up the outer stairs to the top deck. "Hey!" she called after him. She only caught up to him when he stopped at their stateroom door and keyed the lock open. "Are you okay?"

"Yeah," he chuffed unconvincingly.

She followed him inside the room, and once she'd closed the door behind her, she leaned against it. The small cabin seemed all the tinier with the energy pulsing palpably from Carmine. Eva swallowed hard. "I'm sorry. I shouldn't have—"

"No." He raised a hand and gave her a quick guilty glance. "I'm sorry. I…" He exhaled harshly then, after dropping heavily into one of the flimsy chairs, slapped his hands on the arms and barked a curse word. "What the hell was that?"

"I just thought if we were—"

"Kiss for ten seconds—twice!—then, hey, friends...no sex!" he ranted, his hands fisted.

Eva furrowed her brow, moved a couple of steps into the room. "What specifically is it you have a problem with? Did I mess up?"

He glanced up at her, his eyes bright, his face tense. "I—no. The rest of it."

"Um...this is a marriage retreat. Married people kiss."

The muscles in his jaw bunched and flexed. She could hear his teeth grinding. "I know that!"

His mood truly had her baffled. "Then...were you hoping the kiss meant we'd have sex?"

He scowled at her. "God, no!"

She scoffed. "Okay...easy, Sparky. You're gonna hurt my feelings." She wiped her moist palms on her jeans and tried again. "Then... I don't get it. Why are you...?" She waved a hand toward him, indicating his snarly mood.

He buried his face in both hands, saying nothing for a long time. When he spoke, his voice was quiet, muffled in his palms. "I'm mad at myself. I didn't... I shouldn't..."

Eva moved to sit in the chair beside him. His slumped shoulders and bowed head were heartbreaking. What was he beating himself up over? They were playing a role. Working undercover. Pretending...

"You didn't what?" she prompted.

He raised a penetrating dark gaze to hers and sighed. "I didn't want to...like kissing you so much."

CARMINE HAD ENJOYED their kiss.

A giddy thrill spun through Eva, breaking her concentration for about the hundredth time since they'd returned to the cabin. By mutual assent, they'd both *theoretically* set the kiss aside as something they'd had to do to maintain their cover, not to be mentioned again. Right.

But there was an undeniable mood in their compact stateroom as they both set to work on their laptops, reading emails, searching databases and filing written reports of the day's progress to Captain Reeves. They hadn't been working for more than ten minutes before Carmine packed up his laptop and headed for the door. "I, uh…need some air. I'm going to work out on the deck."

Eva blinked. "But it's—"

He didn't wait to hear her argument. The stateroom door closed firmly, and he didn't return for three hours.

His abrupt departure stung. He might have truly needed air—the cabin *was* a bit stuffy—but she felt rejected. Alone. Maybe he liked their kiss, but clearly he didn't like liking their kiss.

To distract herself from the hollow ache in her chest, Eva started reviewing the visitors' log from Rikers Island, as Sean had directed. She researched each person on the list to see if anything stood out among the visitors who'd come to see Wes over the months he'd been held pending trial. Before long, she'd decided Wes's visits could be categorized into two lists. List one: his lawyer, Ed Morelli. List two: a variety of young women, all of whom seemed to throw themselves at the inmate like groupies clamoring for a rock star. After the sixth such fangirl became evident, Eva muttered, "Pathetic."

"What's that?"

She glanced up, her heart skipping as Carmine entered the room, his laptop tucked under his arm and his cheeks and nose red from the evening's chill. Eva shifted awkwardly in her narrow chair and pointed at her computer screen. "These women fawning over Wes Westmore. Sure, he's handsome.

Sure, he's wealthy. But there's a strong case that he also killed his girlfriend."

Shaking her head, she clicked through to another woman's social media page, where several posts were rants regarding Wes's arrest or gushing homages to the sleazeball. "Like this lady…" She flicked her hand toward her computer. "She's created a group called *Justice for Wes*. And…geez, she's asked him to marry her!"

Carmine grunted and rubbed a hand over his already-mussed hair. "Any chance any of the ladies could have been involved with him before he killed Lana? If he was in a relationship with one of them, we could have a stronger motive or an accomplice we missed."

"*Allegedly* killed Lana. And not that I've found yet. The fascination seems to have started soon after his very public arrest."

She clicked back to the list of visitors and the corresponding security photos. She pulled up the next on the list and scoffed. "Cripes. This one looks old enough to be his mother."

Carmine shrugged and settled in the second chair. "Cougars need love too."

"Ugh." She gave him a withering glance; then, as he opened his laptop and resumed working, she refocused her attention. She ran an internet search for Myra Smith, the name of the older woman, but found nothing that matched the woman's description—not on social media or in police records or in local court documents…

Eva put a question mark next to Myra Smith's name on the list and angled a glance at Carmine. He was, by all appearances, absorbed in whatever he was scrolling through on his laptop.

She returned her attention to her own work and moved on to the next woman in the log. The thin brunette—Virginia

Wolverton—was a repeat visitor, and even Wes seemed disturbed by her presence. Eva watched a short snippet of the security-camera feed that had been included with the visitors' log and still shots. The brunette seemed to be arguing with Wes. And he walked out on her. Interesting.

"Hmm," Eva hummed as she placed a star next to Virginia Wolverton's name. She'd do more extensive background research on this woman tomorrow.

She reached the end of the list of names just after midnight and stood with a back-arching stretch. "I'm ready for bed. You nearly at a stopping place?"

Carmine cut a quick glance at her, pinched the bridge of his nose and slapped the lid of his laptop down. "Sure. I'm not getting anywhere, so..."

"What were you doing?"

He toed off his shoes and heaved a sigh. "It bugs me that there's no trace of Maeve O'Leary in the last several years. Her husband dies, and within a few months, she just kind of goes *poof* into the ether. No death certificate. No sightings. Her bank account was closed, and there's been no activity on her credit card or Social Security number."

"Wes did imply she was dead." Eva pushed the chairs out of the way and pulled down the Murphy bed.

"Implied," Carmine said, and his mouth twisted as if he were ruminating on that word. "What he said was he had no mother. He also said he had no family, but we know that's not true because his uncle Orrin is still alive. So..."

"But to deny he had a mother is different somehow. To me that says his mother is dead."

"Maybe," Carmine countered. "Or maybe he's just estranged from her. Or—here's a thought—he's *lying*."

Eva growled her frustration as she dropped onto the end of the bed to remove her shoes.

"My gut is telling me there's a hell of a lot more to that

story. I want to know what it is," Carmine said, pulling his arms out of his sleeves.

Eva averted her gaze just before Carmine whipped his shirt off over his head. Wasn't it enough that she had memories of that kiss zinging through her every five minutes? If she added an imprint of Carmine's bare chest and gym-worthy arms to the mix, she'd never accomplish anything ever again. Training her focus on her suitcase, she pulled out the flannel pants and the oversize T-shirt she slept in and hustled into the phone booth–sized bathroom to change clothes and brush her teeth.

When she finished with her nightly ablutions and returned to the bedroom, Carmine was waiting, clad only in his sleep pants, for his turn. Dear God, he looked delicious—all rumpled hair and warm skin and those dark eyes that met hers and clung. An electric energy crackled in the short distance between them.

Carmine had enjoyed kissing her.

The thought tripped through her brain again, and her mouth seemed to tingle in response. She sucked her bottom lip between her teeth, only meaning to quell the irksome reminder of their kiss. But Carmine's gaze locked on her mouth. He inhaled a breath in a hiss. His hand balled on his lap, and he squeezed his eyes shut.

Finally, in a hoarse tone, he said, "I'll be back in a minute. Don't wait up."

He brushed past her and left their cabin. Again.

Eva blinked. Took a breath. Then another.

What had just happened?

Carmine lay next to Eva, listening to her indelicate snoring, trying to think about the Brinkley murder, the Humphrey disappearance, his Italian immigrant relatives…anything other than that mind-numbingly sexy kiss he'd shared tonight with Eva. How had things escalated so quickly? The first kiss, chaste and controlled as it was, had been hard enough. Her feminine scent had filled his nose, and her silky hair tickled his skin...but he'd survived. He'd kept himself in check. Damn Aanan Gupta for encouraging a second kiss!

He'd thought he could get himself back in line by avoiding her most of the evening, sitting out on the cold deck in the even colder wind. But when he'd returned to the room, nothing had changed. As they'd worked in awkward silence before bed, he'd found himself watching her all too many times. Her little unconscious habits—twirling her auburn hair around her finger, tugging her earrings in her earlobes, drumming her fingers against her lips—were so simple and ordinary...and yet so enticing to him. He wanted to run his own fingers through her hair, nibble her earlobes, kiss that rosy mouth until she gasped for breath.

He fisted his hands in the sheets, and his mouth dried as he remembered the sizzle that had snaked through him the instant Eva's lips had touched his...the second time. Like pouring water on a grease fire, he'd flashed hot, lost control, feasted on her lips like a starving man. Hellfire! He hadn't been able to stop himself. All thoughts of their age difference, their working relationship, Liam's promise of bodily harm evaporated when he'd tasted her. Just...poof! Every practical reason to maintain a level head and rein in his attraction to Eva had simply vanished.

And when she'd stepped out of the bathroom in ratty flannel pants and a loose T-shirt... He shouldn't have been turned on, but the impression of her nipples against her shirt, the way she'd bit her bottom lip, the thick swaths of her hair framing her freshly scrubbed cheeks...

He'd needed several more minutes of the cold harbor air to cool the heat that had surged in his blood. Now he lay in the dark, unable to sleep, acutely aware of her breathing, the jiggle of the bed when she rolled over, the scent of her shampoo. Was he going to have to sleep in a deck chair in order to—

Eva shifted to her side, facing him, and her hand flopped onto his chest. He tensed as if her touch scalded him. As the spike in his pulse settled, Carmine squeezed his eyes shut and rolled away from Eva. What was wrong with him? It was a kiss. One damn kiss!

He'd kissed plenty of women and enjoyed the hell out of it. Why was *this* kiss bothering him so much? He dared to replay the kiss in his mind, telling himself it was purely for analysis. To ferret out the small thing, the nuance that had triggered this sense of confusion and panic inside him.

And as he allowed his brain to review the taste, the feel, the heat of the kiss, an undeniable truth filtered to the surface. A terrifying truth. The kiss meant something to him. He hadn't been acting. He couldn't dismiss his struck-by-lightning reaction to kissing Eva…because he had feelings for her. That was when the image of Rosa's bullet-riddled body flashed in his brain, and he sucked in a breath. His body went cold, and a pain he'd thought he'd shoved far-enough down that he'd never have to confront it again seeped out of hiding.

Carmine lay still in the darkness, battling his old demon. He was in big trouble.

THE NEXT MORNING, Carmine sat bleary-eyed at breakfast, having lain awake much of the night. Beside him, Eva tucked into a huge breakfast of eggs, croissants, fresh fruit, yogurt parfait and an enviable pile of bacon.

"You sure I can't get you some waffles to go with that?" he asked his partner with a teasing side-eye.

She paused, a buttery croissant at her mouth, and her gaze

darted to the waffle iron, where a chef was creating custom waffles of various flavors and toppings.

"You're considering it," he said, amazed. He chuckled and took another bite of his own cheese omelet. "Geez, E—Dina. I don't know where you put it."

Across the table, Carol Johnson poked at her fruit and cottage cheese and frowned. "I, for one, hate you."

Eva gave the woman a hurt look. "Ouch."

Molly Boone, sitting next to Carol, grinned smugly.

Carol waved her fork with the cube of pineapple and sighed. "I'm just saying… Most women would kill to be able to eat that much of whatever they wanted and keep their figure. Just you wait, though. Middle age is coming. Childbirth. Menopause. It's all downhill from here, honey."

Eva blinked in disbelief at the woman's rudeness. Then, holding Carol's gaze, she stabbed her knife into the jelly on her plate, smeared a big blob on her croissant and took a big bite. "I'll enjoy it for the both of us. Okay?"

Carmine muffled a laugh behind his napkin and directed his attention to the front of the room, where Orrin was organizing the group to leave on their next field trip.

"Today we will be visiting the September 11 Memorial & Museum before lunch." Orrin swept the room with a somber gaze before perking up to continue, "We'll then enjoy lunch at a favorite restaurant of mine and Kitty's. Please gather your personal items for the trip and meet us on deck in ten minutes."

Carmine gulped the rest of his coffee and helped Eva with her chair as she pushed back from the table.

His partner watched the other women whisper as they headed out of the dining room, and she frowned. "Geez, it's like I'm in first grade again, getting teased for having red hair. Pure unprovoked malice."

Zara Gupta touched Eva's arm. "Ignore them, Dina. Some

people are not happy unless they have someone to target and feel superior to."

Eva smiled at Zara. "True enough."

"You became an easy and obvious target of their disdain when you woke everyone with your story about seeing a murder the first night," Zara said with a shrug as she peeled away to head to her cabin.

"But I—" Eva started, and Carmine made a sound in his throat to cut her off.

He gave her shoulders a squeeze and shook his head. "Let it go. Let's stay focused on our task, huh?"

Eva gave a reluctant nod. "Speaking of… I'm going back to our room to make a call, check in with Captain—" She quickly fell silent as Bill Boone bustled past, clearly eavesdropping as he did.

"I'm sure the sitter is feeding Captain," Carmine said as cover, "but if it makes you feel better to check on your pooch, go ahead."

Boone moved on, and Eva exhaled heavily. "Thanks. A dog named Captain? Quick thinking!"

He shrugged off the save, and she turned for the cabin. "Back in a minute."

Eva returned just as the group was leaving the yacht, and he asked quietly, "How was our pup this morning?"

"Nothing new to report." She pitched her voice even quieter, whispering, "Waiting on the judge to issue the warrant to search the Westmores' house. Eager for us to kick our investigation up a notch. I told her we were working on it while trying to maintain our cover."

With that, he led her to the waiting van that would drive the group to the first stop of the day. On the drive through the Financial District, Carmine did his own eavesdropping on the Boones and Leeches. The Leeches, it seemed, had had a small breakthrough in their private session and were quietly discussing a possible extension of their counseling arrangement with the Westmores. The Boones' chitchat was ordinary and dull, sprinkled with sappy endearments and giggles from Molly. He had to agree with Eva's assessment that the Boones were a bit of a mystery. They hardly fit the bill of a troubled marriage. But if you had money to burn, the cruise was a nice trip. And he'd heard that some couples attended counseling as a preventative measure. Maybe that was the Boones' story.

After unloading from the van near the soaring Freedom Tower, Carmine fell in step next to Eva and tipped his head back to take in the 1,776-foot structure, whose height was a nod to the signing of the Declaration of Independence.

Ahead of him, the Millers held hands as the group made their way to the large reflecting pools built in the footprint of the twin towers. Carmine saw Kitty nudge Orrin and direct his attention to the Millers, clearly pleased with the couple's progress in reconnecting. He glanced back at the couple's linked hands. The gesture was so natural, so easy. Simple yet…significant.

A tug of conscience reminded him he needed to play his part in their undercover charade. Act married. Appear to be making an effort to heal some imaginary rift with Eva. With a quick side glance at his partner, he caught her hand in his and laced their fingers. She shot him a startled look, then seemed to catch on and relaxed.

If he were honest, touching Eva today—or ever again—was at the bottom of his list of ways to keep his unwise desire for her under control. He hated how he'd lost his battle last night with his emotions, with his libido. His growing attraction to Eva was not only unwise on a professional level, but his affection for her bothered him as well. He'd avoided personal attachments for years because… Because ofwhat happened to his sister. And now that failure with Rosa, that nightmare, was rearing its head again.

He had to do better distancing himself from Eva. Typically, he could suppress his emotions and maintain a rigid command of himself. Given the volatile situations and heartbreaking things he saw on the job, he'd learned that a cop didn't have the luxury of feelings. And last night proved that point. He'd let his guard down with Eva and nearly made a colossal mistake with his partner, his boss's sister.

He rolled his shoulders, loosening the kink of tension that knotted there. With Eva, he approached the edge of one of the massive concrete pits, a manmade waterfall framed by a bank of names engraved in the border. He stared at the rushing water, avoiding the inscribed names at his fingertips. What hope did he have of keeping a stiff upper lip if he let the ghosts of that tragic day seep in? Those ghosts would invite more tragic memories of his own to haunt him.

"It's really a lovely memorial, isn't it?" Eva said quietly, respecting the sanctity of the spot and in deference to the other visitors' private reflections. She gently fingered a rose that had been left on the ledge of the reflecting pool.

He gave her a nod, working to quiet the memories that flashed in his head. High school. A sunny autumn day. His teacher arriving to math class whey faced and visibly shaken.

And the next summer, a new loss, one that struck closer to home.

Carmine pinched the bridge of his nose and inhaled sharply to clear his mind. *Geez, don't go there. Don't let it in. Control it...*

Eva moved on, and as she walked from one end of the memorial to the other, she moved through a patch of sunshine that lit her hair like burnished copper. His fingers twitched at his side, remembering the silky feel of those auburn strands against his skin when they'd kissed. With a grunt, he choked back that dangerous reminiscence as well. *Think of something else...*

Baseball. The Yankees were off to a pretty good start this year.

The last grisly crime scene he'd attended. So much blood...

Franco's pizza and cannoli. He couldn't believe Eva lived upstairs from Franco's. He grunted. Don't go there! Franco's reminded him of Rosa again, pizza sauce smeared on her young face. Oh, man...

He watched a pigeon cross the pavement, its head bobbing. Gazed up at the new green growth on one of the swamp white oak trees that had been planted around the memorial site. Anything to keep his mind off where he was and the hand he held.

"Daniel, you ready to go inside the museum?"

He met Eva's gaze and, taking a deep breath to steel himself, gave a nod. "Sure, Dina. Let's do it."

She tipped her head as they strolled toward the museum entrance. "You all right? You seem...distracted."

"Thinking about the case," he lied in a whisper.

His answer seemed to satisfy her, and he released her hand, allowing her to precede him through the security checkpoint and into the exhibits. They milled from one somber exhibit to the next, hearing the occasional sniffle or heavy sigh from fellow tourists. He moved through the museum, staying close to Eva and dutifully holding her hand or draping an arm around her shoulders or guiding her with a hand at the base of her spine. He watched the people in the museum more than he looked at the gut-wrenching exhibits, anything to get through this uncomfortable field trip. When his cell phone vibrated in his pocket—thank God he'd silenced it before coming inside these hallowed halls—he checked the caller ID.

Sean.

He showed Eva his screen and mouthed, "I'll be right back. I'm going outside."

She nodded.

"Hang on," he said as he answered the call. Once he'd exited the museum and found a relatively private spot, he said, "Okay. What's up?"

"I could ask the same," Sean said.

A stab of guilt slashed through Carmine. "Um…"

Had Sean somehow heard about the kiss exercise last night? Or… No. He shook his head. Nothing happened. He'd been playing his part as Daniel…

"I'll take that to mean you don't have anything new?" Sean said. "You gotta work faster, man. Get me *something*."

Carmine frowned. "We're trying, but we can't blow our cover either. Besides, we got you a fat lead last night. Have they executed a warrant yet for that antique hairbrush yet?"

"That's actually why I called. They did. Just in the last hour. The vanity set in question was recovered. An analysis of the hair in the brush is in process. Good work."

"Great." Knowing something had gone right was a relief. He blew out a cleansing breath. "Do me a favor. Tell your sister what you just told me."

"You can't pass on a simple progress report—"

"The 'good work' part. She needs to hear your praise. Being a rookie is tough. Expectations are high, and the stress of trying to prove herself is weighing on her. An 'atta girl' would go a long way toward encouraging her."

Through the phone line, he heard Sean sigh. "Yeah. You're probably right. Thanks, DiRico."

Carmine disconnected the call, tucked his phone in his pocket and headed back to the front door to go through security again. He found Eva standing at the base of a giant steel column, spray-painted with police and fire departments' precinct and station numbers.

Eva gave him a quick glance as he stopped beside her before returning her attention to the steel column. "Those numbers with each department are how many people each of them lost," she said gravely.

Carmine inhaled deeply to fight the twisting ache that fact caused. "Yeah." He heard a sniff and gave Eva another side glance. Tears were on her cheeks, her nose red from crying.

The ache inside him wrenched harder, and he put a hand on her back. "Hey, you okay?"

She pointed to the steel tower. "That…" Her voice broke, and she swallowed before continuing. "If something like that happened today, it would be Sean and Mitch and Hernandez and—" She faced him with raw emotion in her eyes. "Our precinct! Our friends and…and—" She hiccupped. "Us. You…"

Next to them, Jim McKinney angled a curious glance at Eva. "I thought you said you were a teacher and an accountant." He waved a hand toward the graffiti. "Those men were first responders. Heroes."

"Men *and women*," Eva replied.

Carmine gave Jim a tight smile. "Her brother is a first responder, so it's difficult for her." He put an arm around Eva to tug her away from the exhibit.

Jim frowned, calling, "Yeah. Same for all of us."

When they were a safe distance from the others, Carmine pulled Eva into his arms and held her. She was trembling, and he wished he could absorb her grief and anguish. "I know," he murmured, his lips pressed against her hair. "I know. It's still as hard to wrap your head around as the day it happened."

She sniffled. "That's the thing. I don't have any memory of that day. I was only a toddler."

Carmine jolted at the reminder of their age difference. Eva had no firsthand memories of one of the darkest days of his life, in their nation's history.

"I guess seeing all this for the first time since joining the precinct just sharpened the truth for me."

"You knew when you signed up to be a cop that dangerous circumstances were part of the job," he said gently.

She levered back and met his gaze with fierce eyes. "I did. And I willingly accept that danger for myself. But Sean is my brother! It's different knowing..." Her voice cracked, and she paused, gulped. "I can't imagine losing so many friends, so many brothers and sisters in uniform..." She exhaled and bit her bottom lip, giving him a hesitant look. "Partners."

A tremor rolled through him at the notion of losing Eva in some tragic way. Losing a partner would be hard enough, but somehow the idea of losing Eva shook something elemental at his core. He told himself it was basic male protectiveness toward a woman but couldn't quite make himself believe it. The something he'd started to feel for her, the something that had woken his memories of Rosa, went deeper than normal and touched something raw inside him.

A lump swelled in his throat, and he swallowed hard several times before he felt he could speak. "I know. It's one of the harder aspects of the job, but one we accept in order to keep our city safe."

"Protect and serve," she muttered on a sigh. "I can do that. I *can*. But losing Sean...or Cormac or Liam...would kill me."

He could understand that sentiment. Better than most. A well-guarded image of a laughing teenage girl with shiny black hair flashed in his mind's eye before he could stop it. Pain lanced his heart.

Damn it. He needed to get out of this place, where memories and grief were laid bare. "Let's head outside, huh? Get some air?"

She wiped her cheeks, nodded and leaned into him as they walked through the rest of the museum quickly and headed out into the warm spring day.

"Tell me what Sean said." Eva found a bench to sit on and tipped her face to soak in the sunshine.

"The warrant was executed. The vanity set recovered, and—"

"Dina! Daniel!"

As one, he and Eva turned toward the angry-sounding shout. Kitty and Orrin were storming toward them, their faces matching masks of fury.

Chapter Ten

"Oh no," Eva groaned and rose from the bench to face the Westmores with her shoulders set. Already on edge after the museum woke her deepest fears of loss, Eva held her breath, her gut swirling. "Look who got word from home that police had stopped by."

Kitty reached them first and poked a manicured finger in Carmine's chest. "Who are you? Why are you on our cruise?"

"Daniel Eggers," he spouted dutifully with a straight face. "We're here to learn better communicat—"

"Bullcrap!" Orrin barked. "You've been asking prying questions from the moment you got on board. Yesterday, we made the mistake of telling you about our heirloom vanity set from Queen Victoria—and suddenly today, cops are at our door with a warrant for that set?" His eyes narrowed dangerously. "That's no coincidence."

The angry expression on Orrin's face nudged Eva's memories of another angry face. A tingle raced down her spine. Orrin was the right height and general body shape. Was it possible he was the man in the hooded jacket she'd seen the first night, struggling with a woman?

Her mouth dried as he stopped inches from her face,

scowling darkly. "You passed information about that vanity set to the cops. Why?"

"Hey, take it easy," Carmine said, his tone even and reasonable.

"You lied to us! You broke your promise of confidentiality!" Kitty said, her voice getting higher pitched as she worked herself into a tizzy. "You betrayed us!"

"We can explain," Carmine said, casting a glance to Eva that asked, *Now what?*

"Why are you so damned determined to involve the police in our lives at every turn?" Kitty wailed, turning to Eva.

"We're not—" Eva started.

But Orrin puffed up and cut her off with a sharp "Don't you dare lie to us again. Why did you call the police about that vanity set?"

Carmine exhaled and ran a hand through his hair.

"We didn't call the police," Eva said quietly. "We *are* the police."

Her partner made a low choking sound and gave her an incredulous look.

Kitty and Orrin gaped at her, then each other, then at Carmine. Kitty recovered from her surprise first, bristling. "You're *what?*"

Eva raised a conciliatory hand and continued calmly, "We mean no disrespect or offense. We came on your cruise, undercover, because we need information from you to solve two major open cases."

Kitty's eyes flared with heat. "Police! Are you even married? Is everything you've said a lie?"

"I—not everything." Eva glanced at Carmine for help. His face was pinched in a frown of disapproval and resignation. "But when my brother, Detective Sean Colton, tried to interview you earlier this year about Wes Westmore's case, you were most uncooperative."

"Because we have nothing to say about our nephew's arrest!" Kitty said, her teeth clenched.

"Maybe not, but you do have answers to questions that could steer us in the right direction on two high profile cases we are working," Carmine said. He swiped a hand over his jaw and shot Orrin a querying glance. "For instance, your lingering suspicions about your brother's death could have bearing on what we're working on."

Orrin jerked his chin higher. "What does Joseph have to do with—do you think Wes killed my brother too?"

Eva caught a glimpse of Bill and Molly Boone standing at a window of the museum, watching them. The last thing they needed for this discussion was an audience. She placed a hand on Orrin's arm. "Could we continue this conversation back on the yacht? We have a lot to discuss, and a more private location would be better for everyone."

Kitty twisted her mouth in a moue of discontent. "How are we supposed to trust you after the way you've deceived us?"

Eva let her shoulders drop. "We're sorry about that. Truly. But our need to get what information you weren't sharing was the exigent concern for the investigation."

Orrin continued staring at her through narrowed eyes. Kitty huffed and tapped a foot in irritation. "We should kick you out of the retreat for breaking the rules."

"Please don't. We still need your time and assistance with our investigation." She thought of what she'd witnessed the first night of the retreat and added, "*All* of our open investigations." Three sets of eyes focused on her. "So…for now, we really need you to protect our cover just a little while longer."

Even Carmine gave her a curious look when she said this.

"Now that we know you're cops, why maintain some charade?" Orrin asked.

Carmine arched a dark eyebrow at her as if to ask the same question. Eva rubbed her palms on her jeans and met Orrin's eyes. "There's still the matter of the scene I witnessed the first night of the cruise."

Kitty grunted and flapped a hand. "Honestly! The police came. They found nothing! Why are you still—"

"Because I'm a cop, too!" Eva clapped a hand to her chest, barely maintaining her composure. "I saw a man and woman struggling, saw him dump her overboard. I heard a suppressed gunshot. This same man aimed a pistol at me! I can't just walk away from that!"

The older couple exchanged a dubious look.

"Don't you care who that man was, where that woman is now?" She watched Orrin's reaction closely. If he were guilty, would she see it in his face, in his body language? To his credit, he did seem concerned by her allegation and lifted a frustrated grimace to the sky with a sigh.

Carmine stepped closer, speaking through gritted teeth. "Not our case, rookie. Let it go."

She gave her partner a fleeting disappointed glance before returning her attention to the Westmores. "The department did pay for the cruise in full. We can use our counseling time to go over police matters with you and the group time to continue observing the other couples in case the responding officers missed something."

Orrin exhaled in a huff. "Fine."

"What?" Kitty sent her husband a look of dismay.

"I don't know what further information you think we have, but if it will get you out of our lives and stop this harassment, then…" He pressed his mouth into a grim line. "We'll answer your questions."

"But, Orrin—"

"It'll be fine, honey. And if they are willing to listen to our theories concerning Joseph's death, then all the better. Maybe my brother will get justice." He gave Eva a stony glare. "You can finish the cruise, keep your cover, and we'll answer your questions. But don't ever lie to us again. Understood?"

Eva dropped her chin in agreement. "You need to be forthcoming and honest with us as well."

"Deal." Orrin checked his wristwatch. "For now, we have to go. The group has reservations for lunch in Brooklyn."

BILL BOONE SIDLED up to Carmine as the group gathered beside the van waiting for instructions. "I saw you in a huddle with the Westmores a little while ago. Looked acrimonious. What was that about?"

Carmine gave the other man a flat look. "None of your business."

Bill grunted in offense. "No need to get testy. It just seemed like there was a problem, and if—"

"Still none of your business." He punctuated his comment with a hard look. Bill tucked his hands in his pockets and, with a returned glare, walked back to join his wife.

Eva inched closer to Carmine. "What was that about?"

"Tell you later," he muttered as Orrin called for the group's attention.

"All right, I hope you are hungry, because you are in for a treat! We are heading over to Brooklyn now to have lunch at Café Mogador. They have wonderful Moroccan cuisine and are a favorite brunch spot for me and Kitty. You'll love it!"

Carmine grimaced. Yeah, the group would love Café Mogador. But so did a lot of the cops from the 98th Precinct. If one of their coworkers spotted him or Eva and blew their cover...

Clearly, Eva was thinking the same thing, because she looked at him with wide eyes and mouthed, "Oh no."

He gave her a side hug, leaning in to whisper, "I'll handle it." He peeled away from the group and caught up to Kitty, who was taking a call a few yards away.

When Kitty disconnected her call, she spotted Carmine and gave him a disgruntled frown. "I hope you're happy. Our housekeeper is quite upset following that visit from the police. She says they rifled through everything and left a big mess."

"I'm sorry, but that set may crack our case wide open."

"How?" Kitty arched an eyebrow, clearly intrigued.

"Now's not the time for that conversation." He rolled his shoulders. "Look, Gina and I aren't going to lunch with the group. Café Mogador is too close to our precinct and is frequented by our officers. Very few people know about our undercover assignment, and if someone from the department sees us—"

"Fine, fine," she said, flapping her hand in a shooing motion. "Do what you must. I guess this means you won't be walking the Brooklyn Bridge with us either?"

He shook his head.

Kitty rolled her eyes. "Okay. I'll...tell the others Dina felt ill or something." She buzzed her lips as her face twisted in disgust. "Great. Now I'm the one who'll be lying to the group."

"Thanks. We'll take a cab back to the yacht and see you at four for our session."

Kitty's response was an unhappy grunt.

When he and Eva got back to the *Westmores' Folly*, Carmine opened his laptop and dug into some research that had been left undone for too long. He ran an internet search for articles that might have run at the time of Joseph Westmore's death. Joseph, being a well-known and successful hotelier, would have warranted mention in the local papers if not national news. The fact that Orrin was so suspicious of the circumstances surrounding his brother's death and Kitty held Maeve in such low esteem gave Carmine pause.

"I'm going in search of some lunch. Can I bring you anything?" Eva asked.

He gave her a quick glance as he scrolled through the search results. "A sandwich or something would be good. Thanks." As she turned for the door, he noticed the lump at the small of her back. "Is that Betty under your shirt?"

Eva raised her chin. "Yeah. Why?"

"You really think you need to be armed? It's not well concealed at the moment, and if you don't want to raise suspicions, then…"

She inhaled deeply and flexed and balled up her hands at her sides. "I prefer to be ready if there's trouble. Like the other night. Besides, while I'm in the galley rustling up our lunch, I thought I'd ask the crew what they know about that massive cooler and ice sculpture that nearly crushed me yesterday. There was no reason for that thing to have been on the top deck if the galley and dining room are below deck and on the main level." She shook her head. "The only thing that makes sense is that someone wanted to push it off with that mop handle to hurt someone below." She twisted her lips into a pout that reminded him all too well of the kiss they'd shared in the group session. "And I have the distinct feeling I was the intended target, based on the hate I've been getting from the rest of the group."

Carmine cleared the sudden thickness from his throat. "Want me to come with you?"

She shook her head. "I'll be careful. I'm capable of getting lunch and asking my questions by myself. You finish whatever it is you're doing." With a wiggle of fingers toward his laptop, she hustled out of the cabin.

He sat staring at the closed door for several minutes after she left, stewing. Partners were supposed to work together. Her independent streak and determination to prove her mettle could prove counterproductive at some point. Perhaps he should go join her despite her argument to the contrary.

Or was he manufacturing reasons to follow her because he was also concerned about her safety after the rather odd circumstances surrounding the falling cooler and events of the first night? If he believed Eva, someone on the cruise had killed a woman. If he believed Eva…

Did he have some reservations about her story? He knew she saw something but…what?

His gut roiled. The killer also saw Eva, and since she kept talking about what she'd seen, the killer might be trying to shut her up. By scaring her or by more permanent means?

A ripple of disquiet chased down Carmine's spine. He slapped the lid of his computer closed and stalked toward the door to find Eva. She was his partner. He was supposed to have her back. Never mind the other niggling hollowness that had plagued him since that damned kiss last night, the one that said he wanted more from Eva than a professional partnership. The one that screamed about his failure to protect Rosa. He pinched the bridge of his nose, trying to shove *that* quandary aside until he could look at it more dispassionately later. Right now, he needed to find Eva and guard her six.

"THANK YOU!" EVA took the sack with the fruit, cheeses, crackers and cookies the assistant chef had gathered for her. "This looks wonderful. All of the meals have been so good! And so artistically arranged!"

The woman nodded her appreciation. "So glad you are enjoying our creations."

Eva frowned now. "A real pity that the ice sculpture got ruined yesterday."

The assistant chef's eyes grew large, and she glanced over her shoulder with a wince at the chef, who was busy at the stove, prepping for the evening meal. "Not so loud.

Emilio was incensed about that. You'll just send him into another rant."

"Oh?" Eva lowered her voice. "Any idea how it happened? I mean, why on earth was the ice sculpture delivered to the top deck to begin with?"

"Not delivered!" Emilio, a short man with graying black hair and a bald spot on the crown of his head, shouted in heavily accented English, waving the spatula in his hand. "Stolen!"

The assistant chef's shoulders drooped, clearly dreading the coming rant. Eva gave the woman an apologetic grin.

"The ice was with the order when we took inventory of delivery that morning, then…gone after lunch. Someone stole the sculpture! Five hundred dollars, I pay for it. Then poof! Gone! Ruined!"

"Why would someone want to steal the ice sculpture? It doesn't make sense to me." *Unless it was intentionally positioned to be used as a weapon.*

"It not make sense!" Emilio shouted, his hands waving. "Senseless!" He aimed the spatula at Eva like a knife. "When I find thief—" He made a slashing motion with the spatula as he shouted something in a foreign language Eva didn't catch.

Speaking of catching people… Eva chewed her bottom lip, then asked, "Did either of you hear the ruckus on deck the first night? A couple fighting?"

The assistant glanced toward Emilio expectantly, and he returned a wary glare. Eva's pulse kicked. They knew something.

"Because I'm sure I heard something," she continued, "but no one else in the marriage retreat did."

"Huh. They wouldn't. Guests' rooms are on upper decks," Emilio said.

Eva stepped closer to the chef. "Are you saying you did hear something?"

He stared at her hard and long before shrugging. "You're not wrong."

"Emilio…sir, if you heard something, why didn't you tell the police when they came? They think I made it up. No other evidence or witnesses corroborated what I told them."

He stirred the sautéing onions and fell silent.

She moved closer, touching the chef on his arm. "Emilio?"

He lifted the pan from the burner and moved to a prep table, where he dumped the grilled onions into a cheesy-looking mixture. The dish looked and smelled delicious, and Eva's stomach growled, but she worked to stay focused on the reluctant chef. "Please—"

"You should not be in my kitchen. Go!" He waved a hand, shooing her.

Rather than leave, Eva squared her feet and slid the bowl with the cheese concoction out of Emilio's reach. "Does it not bother you that a woman may have been murdered?"

The chef faced her, his face growing florid and his dark eyes flaming. Clearly he was unhappy that she was inter- fering with his food prep and pressing him on a matter he didn't wish to discuss. "I cannot get involved! I tell police nothing, and they leave me alone."

"But—"

He reached past her, snagging the bowl. "I want you out of my kitchen!"

Eva studied the chef, and a recollection of her call with Sean while she was at Ellis Island replayed in her mind. He'd said the background search revealed one of the yacht's kitchen staff had an expired green card.

She trailed after Emilio as he moved to take a tray of tiny pastry shells from the oven. "The police already know about your green card."

Emilio's head jerked up, and his eyes widened as he gaped at her.

"If you tell the cops what you saw, what you heard, I promise to help you get your green card–renewal paperwork filed."

He took a few deep breaths but shook his head.

Eva huffed her frustration. "You can be charged with withholding evidence if you don't."

Now the older man narrowed a look of suspicion on her. "You are cop?"

Not willing to give up her cover to the yacht's crew, she hedged. "I have connections with the police. My brother is a detective in Brooklyn, so…"

Emilio made a low rumbling sound in his throat.

"If I could guarantee you won't get in trouble over your green card, will you speak to the police?"

Emilio wiped his hands on his apron, his dark eyes locked on Eva's. "You are very stubborn woman. Yes?"

"Oh, yes. I get that a lot." She smiled. "Emilio, I have many connections with people who can help you renew your green card. I'll see that you get all the assistance you need to stay here legally. You'll be fine."

The man's nostrils flared as he inhaled deeply. "I heard scream," he said so softly she almost missed it.

Her heartbeat accelerated to the point she could barely hear the chef over the thumping in her ears.

"When I go out to look, I see man running. He throw something in water."

The gun? Eva wondered. "Please, Emilio. Tell this to the police. Go on your own. Volunteer the information. It will go much better for you if you cooperate and talk to them without being subpoenaed."

His face paled. "Subpoenaed?"

She nodded. "You can be compelled to give your statement. Don't let it come to that."

Emilio sighed. He looked truly frightened at the prospect

of getting involved with the investigation, but he gave her a small nod. "Soon. I must work now. I have job to finish with the cruise."

"Today," Eva countered.

"Not today. But soon."

She gritted her teeth, wishing she could drag him down to the police station right then and prove to her naysayers that she hadn't fabricated anything. She should. If she was following the letter of the law, she should take Emilio into custody and force him to tell the investigating officers what he'd just shared with her. But...

But she wanted to give Emilio a chance to do the right thing on his own. It struck her that such bending of the rules was the sort of thing Carmine might do. Was her partner rubbing off on her in so few days as a team? Or had the Italian chef simply found a soft spot in her Irish heart?

She aimed a finger at him. "The cruise ends Sunday morning. I'll give you until five p.m. Sunday night to go to any precinct in town and give your statement. Not a minute later." She let the *or else* go unspoken. She could see from his expression that he understood what would happen if he didn't meet her deadline. "All right?"

Emilio bobbed a short nod. *"Sì."*

As Eva made her way back to the cabin, her cell phone chimed with her roommate's unique ringtone. A flutter of ill ease stirred inside her. *Carnegie!*

"Is my boy okay?" she said, bypassing a greeting.

"He's fine," Kara said. "He misses you. He spent hours last night in your room, meowing and looking for you."

"Aw, I miss him too." A small, hollow ache tugged at her heart as she thought of her feline companion. "Hug him for me."

"I will. I have. How's the swanky cruise with that hot partner of yours going?"

"It's been…crazy." Eva stopped at a deck chair and filled Kara in on the events of the last few days that weren't considered confidential to the ongoing investigations. When she mentioned the retreat-exercise kiss she'd shared with Carmine, Kara whooped with laughter. "Oh my God! And? Is he a good kisser?"

Eva buried her face in her hand, admitting softly, "Fantastic, actually."

Kara gave another excited whoop. "What a dream come true for you! A ready-made, work-sanctioned excuse to lock lips with the guy you've been into for months… Lucky girl!"

"Hardly! It's a nightmare!"

"What? How is it a nightmare?"

Eva raised her head and gazed out across the harbor where the yacht had docked for the day. A lone seagull swooped and dove toward the water. "Because now I know exactly what I'm missing. And…well, the exercise was for troubled couples, right? It was supposed to create intimacy and closeness. And… I think it has. For me. All his staged touches and our constant proximity is making me…fall for him. Really fall for him. Not just crushing from afar but…feelings."

"And that's a problem?"

"It is if he doesn't feel the same way." She sighed. "Besides, we work together. A precinct romance would be… wrong somehow. I don't think we could do it. Or that it would be allowed."

"Hey! The NYPD can't tell you who you can or can't have a relationship with!" Kara said hotly.

"They kind of can. There are policies in place." If only she weren't such a stickler for rules… "I mean, maybe if one of us moved to another precinct or department…" The wind blew her hair in her face, and she combed it out of her face with her fingers. "Moot point. It takes two to tango, and Carmine…" She thought of the way he'd bolted from their room the night before. "I don't think we are on the same page. He was kind of distant last night after the kiss happened. As in, he left the room for a long time so he didn't have to face me."

"Well, I don't know what that was about," Kara said, "but I think you have an opportunity here if you don't blow it."

"An opportunity for what? Humiliating myself?"

"Winning him over," Kara said, her tone enthused. "Use what nature gave you, Eva. You've got the looks, the brain, the good heart… You're the whole package."

Eva smiled. "Thanks. Any chance you want to marry me?"

"I'm serious, E. Granted, I only met him once, but he seemed like the real deal. If you want him, go for it. Fight for him. Show him what you two could have together."

"I don't know. It's risky…putting it out there when we work together and—"

"I've never known you to shy away from a challenge. You became a New York City cop, for Pete's sake! You don't do scared."

"Yeah, well, I'm scared now. If I let him know how I feel and he pushes me away—" Just thinking of the hurt and embarrassment made her heart contract.

"Oh, hon. I know. I've been there. But think of how you'll kick yourself if you let this chance—this *man*—slip away because you didn't try."

Eva groaned. Kara made a good point. "And if it all blows up in my face?"

"I promise to stock the freezer with Ben & Jerry's and help you drown your sorrows."

"Phish Food?"

"Absolutely. But you won't need ice cream. You have your Colton looks, determination and brains. The guy is toast."

Carmine appeared on deck at that moment, and Eva sat straighter in the deck chair. "Speaking of… He's coming over. I've gotta go." She gave Carmine a little wave of acknowledgment, then said, "Thanks, Kara. I appreciate the pep talk. Kiss Carnegie for me."

As she disconnected, Carmine took the chair next to hers. "My stomach was growling waiting for that sandwich you promised. Have you been talking to your roommate this whole time?"

"No. I got this from the kitchen." She handed him the sack with the food she'd retrieved from the kitchen, including the sandwiches Emilio had made for her before she left. "And…" She paused, waiting for Carmine to look up. He did, and she rocked her shoulders smugly, "I found another witness to the argument I saw the first night." She twisted her mouth. "Sort of."

Carmine paused in the act of unwrapping his sandwich and heaved a sigh. "You are like a dog with a bone. What part of 'That's not our assignment, leave it alone' is unclear to you?"

"But I found someone to corroborate what I reported!" She related what Emilio had told her, the chef's excuse for not coming forward earlier and the promise he'd made to make a statement.

Carmine plowed fingers through his thick hair and looked across the water. "All right, listen. I'll help you gather information about what you saw for the next couple days, until the cruise is over…"

A smile bloomed on her face. Her spirits were heartened to have his faith and support.

"But—" he held up a finger "—only in our spare time— what little we have—because the Brinkley murder and Kelly disappearance *have* to be our focus. We're making some progress on those cases. I feel it in my gut. And we can't lose the little bit of momentum we've got going."

Eva nodded enthusiastically. "Agreed!" Without thinking about it, she leaned forward and dropped a quick kiss on his cheek. "Thank you!"

When she sat back and saw the heat in his eyes, her stomach somersaulted. Kara's voice whispered in her mind, *Don't blow it.*

Chapter Eleven

Back in their stateroom, Eva pulled up the work she'd been doing the night before, reviewing the list of Wes's visitors at Rikers Island. She studied the chart she'd made that analyzed where the women visitors lived, tidbits from their social media profiles, and points where their lives might have intersected with Wes's and the outliers'. His lawyer was the only male to have visited Wes. Myra Smith was the only one over age thirty. Virginia Wolverton was the only repeat visitor. One—Helena Upshaw—had driven in from Canada, apparently. Eva tapped her pen on her notepad and chewed her bottom lip. What was she missing? Was anything here hiding information that was vital to their case? She rolled her aching shoulders and groaned.

"Problem?" Carmine asked, looking up from his phone.

"I don't know. I'm just not getting anywhere with the visitor's log from Rikers. You got anything new on…whatever it is you're doing?"

"Looking for possible aliases for Wes's mother, Maeve. If she were dead, there would be a death certificate…somewhere. So she has to be using an alias. But…what?"

"So you're stuck on the idea that Maeve is alive, despite lack of evidence to that fact and Wes implying she was not."

"Call it a hunch."

"Hmm. Fine. Let's pursue that for the moment." She stood and paced across the floor to the door—all six steps—and back to her chair. Maeve... Aliases... Wes... "Wait a minute," she said as a prickle chased up her neck. She went back to the still photo of the older woman who'd visited Wes. Was it possible? "Try Myra Smith."

"Why?" he asked.

"Just...try it." She pulled out her phone and hit the speed dial for Sean. "See what comes up." When her brother picked up, she said, "Sean, do something for me, will you?"

"Good evening to you too. I'm fine, thank you. Things are great with Orla. Oh, of course I'll tell her you said hi."

Eva rolled her eyes. "You done? I have business to discuss."

"Business? Ooh, I thought this must be a social call considering you addressed me as *Sean* instead of *Detective Colton* or *sir* or *boss* or some other honorific a rookie such as yourself would use to address a higher-ranking officer—"

"Fine! I need someone to check something out for me, *sir*." She all but growled the last in concession. "Excuse me if I get enthusiastic about a lead, and I forget, in private, that you're more than my brother at the precinct."

"Just...try to remember when you're around the office, huh?" he replied. "So this lead... What can I do?"

"Remember back in February when that former patient of Humphrey's came forward saying he thought he'd seen Humphrey near Columbia University with a woman? Rob something... Witcomb? Whittle?"

"Hang on," Sean said, and she could hear papers shuffling in the background, "Widdecombe. Right. What about him?"

"Has anyone showed him the photo of the older woman that visited Wes Westmore at Rikers? She signed in as Myra Smith."

Carmine lifted his gaze from his screen and pinned her

with a curious and intrigued stare. One eyebrow rose in query, and he cocked his head. She smiled, pleased to have piqued his interest.

"Um… I don't think so. Why?" Sean said. "What's the connection?"

"Maybe nothing but…if this Myra woman—who has no local address or social media profile that I can find, by the way—is visiting Wes, she could be a relative. And the DNA results we got back last week from the closet at the court-house showed—"

"A female relative of Wes's had been in that closet," Sean said, finishing her sentence even as Carmine's face lit with realization. Carmine grinned at her and tapped the tip of his nose as he mouthed, "Good idea."

She heard the telltale creak of Sean's office chair, and she could picture him with his clothes rumpled from a long day, his hair untidy from restless fingers plowing through it as he worked, and files spread in front of him for his perusal. Her heart gave a little tug. She was proud of her big brother and so happy for his newfound joy with Orla Roberts.

"Way to connect the dots, rookie," Sean said. "I'll have someone get in touch with Rob Widdecombe right away and see if he recognizes Myra Smith."

That *someone*, she knew, would most likely be Sean himself. He had trouble delegating, an issue she hoped Orla would help convince him to change before he overworked himself into an early grave. "You'll let me know what Rob says?"

"Of course. Would've even had you do the interview with him if you weren't off on your honeymoon with your partner."

"My h—" she sputtered, then scowled when Sean chuckled. "Ha ha." She shot a quick glance at Carmine, praying he hadn't overheard her brother's teasing.

"And how is your undercover assignment going?" Sean asked.

"Okay, I guess. Baby steps, but... I feel like we're on the verge of something big that's just out of sight, like a word at the tip of your tongue you can't quite conjure. It's...frustrating."

"Welcome to police work, dear sister. A life of forever chasing threads until one pays off." He cleared his throat. "Is, uh... DiRico behaving himself? No inappropriate *under covers* work, if you catch my drift?"

"Oh, I catch it." She stepped into the tiny cabin bathroom and closed the door, adding in a hushed tone, "But I also reject your overreach. *That* is none of your business, big brother. *Sir.* And don't you dare make any more threats to Carmine. His love life is none of your business either."

"Threats? I didn't—"

"Liam did. And he seems to have gotten a warning vibe from you, whether spoken or just implied."

"Moi?" Sean said, all false innocence.

"Yes. So knock it off, whatever you did or said."

"Eva," her brother said, his tone more serious now, "is there something going on between you and Detective DiRico?"

Carmine knocked on the door of the closet-sized head. "Five minutes until our one-on-one appointment, Dina dear."

"Coming," she called.

"'Dina dear'?" Sean said with a chuckle.

"Hey, Sean, it's Friday. Don't work late. Take Orla to dinner and a movie, huh?"

"Way ahead of you, Eva."

A COUPLE MINUTES LATER, Carmine and Eva checked in at their private counseling session and took their seats across from Kitty and Orrin as they had before. By Carmine's calculation, the mood was decidedly awkward and more tense, but now the tension radiated from the Westmores rather than from him and Eva. He waited a moment in the pregnant silence for one of their hosts to say something and start the conversation. When they didn't, Carmine drilled Orrin with a steady gaze and asked, "When was the last time you saw or spoke to your nephew Wes?"

Orrin exhaled with a guttural sound rumbling from his throat. His mouth firmed, and his hands fisted on his knees. "We've told you, we don't know anything about Lana's death."

Kitty folded her arms across her chest in a classic defensive I'm-shutting-you-out gesture. She turned her face away to stare at the bookcase beside her rather than her interviewers.

"I didn't ask about Lana's murder. I asked when you'd last seen Wes," Carmine said calmly.

"Should I call our lawyer to join us for this discussion?" Kitty asked.

Eva shrugged. "You are certainly at liberty to do so, if you feel the need, but you are not under arrest or suspicion. This is just a fact-gathering conversation for us. Strictly voluntary on your part."

Carmine waited, looking from Kitty to Orrin and back again. "Are we good?"

Orrin scratched his chin. Bobbed a nod.

Carmine repeated his question about Wes.

For a long moment, Orrin said nothingFinally, he tore his gaze away, staring at the floor in a manner that said he was thinking, remembering. "I can't say exactly. Years ago."

"How many years?" Eva asked. "Two? Ten?"

"He was a teenager." Orrin glanced at Kitty as if to consult her. "A school event we attended with our neighbor. Their daughter was being recognized for some scholastic award."

She nodded. "Yes. That's right. She was in Wes's high school class." She pursed her mouth and leveled a resentful glare on Eva. "Although…" Kitty huffed. "I did see him about four years ago as well."

Orrin sent his wife a startled look, and Eva said, "Oh? Tell us about that."

"He was at Tiffany's when I went to have the clasp on a necklace repaired. He gave me a haughty look and a snide salute and left the store with his purchase."

"You never told me this," Orrin said.

Kitty shook her head. "I didn't see the point. Nothing happened. We didn't speak, and it would only stir up sore memories for you. So I blew it off."

"And Maeve? When was the last time you saw her?" Carmine asked.

Orrin's face tensed again, and his mouth puckered as if he'd eaten something sour. "The reading of Joseph's will after his funeral. She only wanted to know how soon she could cash out all of Joseph's investments and spend the fortune he left her. Once we recovered the vanity set, I wanted nothing else to do with that greedy witch." He divided a look between Eva and Kitty.

Eva pulled a lopsided smile. "Trust me, I hear far worse daily in our line of work."

"Have you heard anything from Maeve recently, even if just through the grapevine?"

Kitty shook her head. "Haven't cared to."

"Just the same," Eva said. "Have you received any indication or confirmation that she's still alive?"

Orrin blinked. "You have reason to believe she's not?"

"Well, Wes was rather cagey in his answers on the subject, but…" Eva glanced at Carmine as if asking permission to divulge what they knew…or didn't know. He jerked a nod. "Our search for her through traditional sources has not yielded much. She seems to have dropped off the face of the earth."

Kitty snorted. "Well, we can hope, can't we?"

Carmine mused for a moment over the level of animosity Orrin and Kitty held toward both Wes and Maeve. If Maeve was missing—or dead—could Kitty and Orrin be involved? "Did you ever know Maeve to use an alias?"

Orrin shook his head, and Kitty shrugged. "Not that I knew of, but that doesn't mean she didn't. I keep telling you…we wanted as little as possible to do with that woman. She was…insufferable. Grating to be in the same room with. It was so obvious to us she was a gold digger."

Carmine opened his mouth to ask his next question, but Eva's phone buzzed, and he paused as she took her phone out.

She gave the Westmores an apologetic wince as she checked the screen. "Sorry. I'll just—" Eva stilled, her eyes widening, and Carmine's pulse bumped expectantly.

EVA HAD INTENDED to dismiss the call, but when she saw it was from Ellie Mathers, the 98th Precinct's CSI analyst and her brother Liam's girlfriend, she knew she had to take it. Either Ellie had significant news about one of their cases… or something had happened to Liam.

"I, uh, have to take this." She gave Carmine a meaningful glance as she excused herself to the adjoining restroom. She swiped to answer the call, her heart in her throat. "Ellie? Is everything okay? Is Liam—"

"Liam's fine. Liam is…" Her coworker and friend gave a contented sigh. "So fine."

Eva grinned as relief washed through her. Her older brother had, at one time, attracted trouble like a magnet.

The newly reformed Liam worked to keep at-risk teens from making the same mistakes he had made, but Ellie and Liam had recently been entangled in some nefarious and dangerous happenings that had revived Eva's concerns for her brother's safety.

"Okay, then, if not Liam, does this call mean you were able to get useful DNA samples from the vanity set?"

"Got good samples and already have preliminary results. A full analysis will take a couple days but…" She heard papers shuffling and then Ellie's muffled voice as she said something to someone with her.

"Ellie! What?"

"Hang on to your hat, Eva."

Eva squeezed her phone tighter. "What?"

"We're almost certain the female DNA found in the courthouse closet belongs to Maeve O'Leary, Wes Westmore's mother."

Eva sat down heavily on the closed commode in the tiny bathroom. "But…"

"I'm making copies of the preliminary report for Sean and Captain Reeves, which I'm sure they'll share with you. But I know the tip about the vanity set came from you, so I wanted you to be one of the first to hear."

"So… Carmine's hunch was right."

"Well," Ellie said with an ironic chuckle, "does that really surprise you? Detective DiRico has a pretty impressive arrest record."

The shock of the news was fading quickly, replaced by a thrill of discovery, of the case sharpening and shifting and—

"This is big. This means…"

"This means looking at everything again in a new light," Ellie said.

"Yeah," Eva said distractedly, her mind spinning off in a hundred directions.

"So what's it like being partnered up with Carmine DiRico?" Ellie's singsong tone brought Eva back to the moment.

Eva glanced at the closed bathroom door, knowing Carmine was on the other side. A tingle raced through her as she remembered the Ten-Second Kiss, holding hands on the side trips, his possessive hand at her back when they walked together. Every touch tested her ability to play it cool. The kiss had stirred feelings at her core that she hadn't been able to shake all day. Worse, all this up-close-and-personal time with Carmine was giving her insight to the character of the man beneath the muscles, the heart behind the bedroom eyes and the soul hiding behind his rigid control. And she was falling a little harder for him by the minute. Should she follow Kara's advice to grab this opportunity with Carmine, or should she play it safe and avoid the potential blowback from a misstep with her partner? She realized Ellie was waiting for an answer, so she croaked, "It's…fine."

"Well, I'm going to need a full account when you get back."

"Um…"

"Geez, why can't I get undercover assignments on a yacht? And, no, I'm not bitter," she quipped with a laugh.

Eva thanked Ellie for the call and sent her regards to Liam before disconnecting. She took a moment to gather her thoughts and composure before returning to the next room. The DNA at the courthouse was Maeve's. Maeve was *alive*. Or at least, she had been on that fateful day in January when Humphrey disappeared. What was the connection? How did Wes figure into this puzzle? And if Maeve was alive, where had she been all these years? Why hadn't she and Carmine been able to find her? An alias, of course. Disguises? Maybe. If not, she would have been spotted by someone who'd known her as Maeve O'Leary Westmore.

And Humphrey…

Her heart gave a twist, knowing the man who'd meant so much to her family through the years was proving to have had secrets—perhaps even fatally dire secrets. She set that disturbing notion aside, squared her shoulders and returned to the room where Carmine and the Westmores sat in an awkward silence. Waiting for her? Had they overheard her conversation?

Carmine met her eyes with a lift of his eyebrows that asked, *Well?*

"Right, so…that was the tech from the satellite CSI lab for our precinct." She took her seat and gave Orrin and Kitty a hard look. "Just to confirm… The Victorian vanity set—did anyone use it besides Maeve? Maybe a great-grandmother or—"

Orrin shook his head. "No. Absolutely not. The set was treasured and respected by my grandmother and her family. It was kept in a sealed shadow box until Maeve got her hands on it."

"And would you be willing to testify to that under oath?"

"I—why? What did the DNA analysis show?" Orrin asked, his cheeks growing pale.

She cut a glance to Carmine, who waved a hand as if to say, *Go ahead. Share with us.*

"The preliminary results of the DNA analysis run on the hair sample from the brush are back. Maeve's DNA from the hair root matched the sample found in the downtown courthouse closet where Humphrey Kelly disappeared in January."

Carmine gave a low whistle and leaned back in his chair, rubbing his face as he processed this news.

"Are you saying Maeve killed Humphrey Kelly?" Kitty asked, her eyes wide with shock.

Eva shook her head. "No. I'm not. Yet. I mean, we have no conclusive evidence that Humphrey—I mean, Mr. Kelly—

is dead. At this point, he's only been identified as missing. But the presence of Maeve's DNA at the last-known location of Mr. Kelly before he went missing is…significant to our investigation."

Eva took a beat to let the Westmores, and Carmine, digest the news. Then, leaning forward in her chair and working to contain the excitement that pulsed through her, she asked, "Can you tell us anything that might help us locate Maeve O'Leary? We really need to talk to her. Obviously."

Orrin seemed to be recovering his faculties more quickly than Kitty, so Eva held his gaze, waited for him to respond.

Her host shook his head, turned up a hand in a wordless gesture of resignation. His gaze shifted to a spot on the wall as if searching his memory for anything that might help. "We cut off all communication with her and Wes soon after Joseph died. I couldn't shake the idea she was responsible for Joseph's death in some way, even if only that she didn't get him help soon enough when the allergy attack started. Heated words were exchanged at the reading of the will, and our already-sour relationship was severed. We've never looked back."

"Until January, when we heard about Wes's arrest for murder," Kitty added. "Naturally, we worried about how Wes's legal trouble could negatively affect our business, our privacy. We knew nothing and didn't want anything to do with the investigation." She raised her gaze to Eva's. "That's why we were so…well, *short* with your brother."

"What about Humphrey Kelly? Being in similar professions, I'd think you would have had opportunities to meet him. Am I right?"

"Certainly," Kitty said. "We've met him on occasion. He seems like a nice man."

"And when did you last speak to Mr. Kelly?" Eva asked.

"I, uh…a few months ago at a Christmas party in the

Rainbow Room that a mutual friend hosted," Kitty said. "We only spoke briefly, in the most mundane terms. *How are you? Merry Christmas. You look well.* Yada yada…"

"Did anyone at the party seem to have a beef with Mr. Kelly?" Carmine asked.

Orrin frowned. "Wait, so now you think we have some knowledge of Humphrey Kelly's disappearance?"

"Do you?" Carmine asked.

Kitty's expression grew angry. "How many times do we have to say we don't know anything about Maeve or Wes or…any of these recent events? We want nothing—*nothing*—to do with any of this horrible business! We have a successful counseling practice to protect and our good reputations to think of." Her tone grew more shrill and hysterical as she continued. "We cannot let any of this…this…disaster ruin everything we have worked years to build!"

When Kitty fell silent, her breathing agitated, no one spoke or moved for several taut seconds. Finally, Eva cast a glance at Carmine, and her partner, deadpan, said, "So that's a no?"

Kitty's eyes flared hot, and Orrin reached over to touch her hand. "Kitty, honey, take a breath." Then to Carmine: "We're done here. We have another couple coming in five minutes, and I think my wife needs a moment before we talk to the Leeches."

"Oookay," Eva said, pushing to her feet. "Then we'll see you at dinner and the group session later."

Kitty seemed to shake from her fit and pulled her eyebrows into a frown. "Group session? You're still going to pursue the idea that someone on the cruise is a murderer? Even after the police confirmed everyone on board had been accounted for and no signs of a crime were found?" She appealed to Carmine. "Even you told her to let it go."

"Let's just say new information has come to light, and…

I consider the matter still open," Carmine said, and Kitty's face blanched. "Meanwhile, please remember, everything we've discussed with you today is part of an ongoing investigation. Not a word of this conversation to anyone. Got it?"

The Westmores exchanged worried, defeated glances but nodded their agreement.

AT DINNER THAT NIGHT, Eva was surprised to find that only half of the marriage-retreat group ate with them in the yacht's dining room. The other half of the group had gone into Manhattan to dine at Tavern on the Green for a special date night.

"The rest of you will get your turn tomorrow evening. It promises to be a most special evening for you and your loved one," Kitty assured them as the evening session began. "Tonight, with this smaller group, we hope you'll also feel more comfortable sharing some of what you've been discovering about your spouse, about yourself and any helpful insights you wish to share. Who wants to start?" When no one volunteered to go first, Kitty turned her gaze toward Eva and said, "Dina? How about you?"

Eva blinked, her heart tripping at being put in the spotlight. What was Kitty doing? She knew she wasn't really Dina...

Then again, Kitty could be helping, playing up her and Carmine's fake personas.

"Okay," Eva said and rubbed the moisture from her palms on her jeans. She could enter a building where an armed suspect lay in wait without breaking a sweat, but public speaking, sharing her thoughts with this group that already gave her the side-eye, felt monumental. "Well... I did realize some things today that were meaningful."

Carmine glanced at her, his eyes warm and supportive. That simple look gave her the courage to continue, to be Dina or Eva or Officer Colton or whomever she wanted to be and share whatever truths or fabrications she chose. Did she want to be honest with this group or play her role?

Honesty, she decided, reaching to take Carmine's hand. "At the September 11th Memorial today, I was moved by so many aspects of what happened that day. The courage and sacrifice of the first responders, the fragility of life and the importance of not wasting a minute we have with our loved ones. You can't take anything for granted." She turned to Carmine, held his gaze. "That includes you."

His eyes widened, surprise flickering across his features, but he quickly modified his expression as if remembering his role as Daniel. He gave her a tender smile.

Kara's encouragement from that afternoon echoed in Eva's memory as she added, "You mean more to me than I expected. I don't want to ruin this by saying or doing the wrong thing, but I also don't want to miss this chance we have to make our relationship…more."

Carmine furrowed his brow as he stared at her, as if trying to solve a puzzle, as if trying to decide who was speaking to him—Dina or Eva?

"Very good, Dina," Kitty said quietly. "Group, do you see how she looked into his eyes as she spoke? As we've been discussing, that eye contact is so important for communication and understanding. To show respect, to let your partner know they have your full attention. Now… Daniel, how would you like to respond to what Dina has just said to you?"

Carmine cut an alarmed-looking side glance to Kitty, and he shifted awkwardly in his seat before meeting her eyes again.

Eva held her breath, her pulse throbbing in her ears. Would Carmine's reply be equally honest? Would she be able to recognize his real reaction versus a staged reply for their audience?

He swallowed hard, and the muscles in his square jaw

flexed as he gritted his teeth. "I, um…" He squeezed her hand in his and used his free hand to scratch his chin. "I don't know. I'm not good with this kind of thing." He shrugged. "I mean, that's why we're here, right? Because I'm not good at communicating?"

He gave a stiff chuckle, and Eva's heart sank. He was playing Daniel, probably hadn't detected her sincerity at all and missed her profession of her feelings for him. An ache grew in her chest that she worked to squelch. She lowered her eyes to her lap, hoping he wouldn't see her disappointment reflected in her expression. It was probably better that he had missed her point. Did she really think that after being partners for a few short days that Carmine DiRico would suddenly notice her in *that* way and decide he had feelings for her?

Carmine scooped her other hand into his then, and squeezed them both, hard. "But that doesn't mean I don't feel anything."

Eva's pulse kicked. She heard a fervor and passion in his tone now that she hadn't before, and she angled a curious look toward her partner.

"I've spent most of my life—my whole career, really— shoving down my real feelings, because to acknowledge them would be…too much. I've seen too much. Done too much." He took a breath and dropped his gaze to their hands. "Lost too much. In order to face the bleakness I see on the job and stay in control of myself and of every situation, I have to keep what I feel in check. I—"

"What a load of crap!" Jim McKinney said.

Several of the women in the circle gasped at Jim's blunt interruption, and a rush of stinging anger swamped Eva. She shot the other man a hot glare.

"Jim," Orrin said firmly, "you'll get your turn to speak.

Please don't interrupt. And I remind you all that we must show respect for each other and encourage openness and truth."

"Well, that's the thing. I don't think you're getting truth from these two." Jim waved a hand toward Eva and Carmine. "He's going on about shoving down his emotions in his career and controlling his emotions because of what he sees every day? He told us he's a frigging accountant. How is that emotional or hard to handle?"

"Jim," Orrin said, "if you would please—"

"No!" Jim sat taller in his chair, warming to his wrath. "And I'm not convinced she's a teacher either. Today at the museum, she was talking about the cops and firemen that died, saying, 'That's us.' So which is it? Is she a teacher or a first responder?"

Eva couldn't say whether she was more upset because Jim had interrupted Carmine's possibly real explanation of his feelings or because his rude outburst was close to exposing them to the group. Either reason was enough to stoke her redhead temper. Taking a beat to calm herself, she squared her shoulders, hoping to do some damage control. "I *am* a teacher. What I meant at the museum was—"

"Liar!" Jim snarled.

"Jim, stop," his wife said under her breath, shooting daggers with her eyes. "Haven't you done enough damage?"

"And what about her delusions about a murder the first night?" Jim continued, blatantly ignoring his wife. "I passed the galley today on the way to the gym, and she was in there with the staff, talking about the supposed murder two nights ago. Why is she still asking questions?"

"Mr. McKinney," Kitty said, rising to her feet, "if you can't be respectful, I will have to ask you to leave."

"I don't know who they *are*, but I can tell you they're frauds!" Jim said hotly.

Sarah McKinney shoved to her feet, tears in her eyes. "I've had it with you! And I am done!" Sarah stormed out of the room, and Kitty gave Orrin a look of horror before rising to follow Sarah.

Wow. Eva cast a glance at Carmine, wondering if his thoughts were following the same track. The rift between Jim and Sarah went deeper than she'd first thought. Could Jim have been the man she saw that first night? She'd dismissed him earlier as being too short, but her perspective from the upper deck could have skewed her notion of how tall the man below was. And if the woman he was with had also been short…

Eva bit her lip. Sarah wasn't short. And she was here and in apparent good health. Jim's mistress? Could the woman Sarah had indicated at the first session that Jim had had an affair with have come aboard at some point and confronted him? Perhaps, but…

She eyed Jim now, and he returned a dark glare before standing and stalking out of the meeting himself.

"Okay, friends, let's, uh…regroup a bit," Orrin said with a strained smile. "How about a positive-reinforcement exercise? I'd like you to face your spouse and tell them three things you admire about them."

The couples turned their chairs as directed, and a collective murmur rose as the exercise moved forward. Eva looked at Carmine with an expression that said, *What do you make of all that?*

He grunted and returned an expression of bemusement. "Look at us, making friends wherever we go."

She snorted her amusement, then sobered a bit. "What was it you were saying before he interrupted?"

Carmine pulled a face and waved her off. "Nothing. Forget it."

When Kitty returned, sans the McKinneys, she redirected

the session. "I think it would be a good idea tonight to repeat the exercises we did last night. I want you to hold each
other's hands and gazes for a full minute, then share a Ten-
Second Kiss. No! Make it twenty seconds. You're all making good progress in your counseling. Why not?"

"Yeah, baby!" Aanan said with a grin for his wife.

Eva's stomach swooped. She pivoted toward Carmine, her
mouth drying. Did Kitty really expect them to kiss again,
knowing that they weren't actually a couple? Not that kissing Carmine would be a hardship. She'd certainly enjoyed
it last time…as had he, he'd said. If they were to maintain
their cover, one Jim McKinney had just questioned, they
had to go all in on their roles as Dina and Daniel. Right…

Carmine's nostrils flared as he took a fortifying breath,
and the rigidity of his jaw indicated he was steeling himself
for a task he dreaded. Eva curled her fingers into her palms
and raised her chin as she met his eyes, hoping to hide the
hurt that pricked her. If he'd enjoyed their kiss, as he'd admitted, why was he so clearly disturbed by the idea of kissing her again?

He met her eyes, and she whispered, "What?"

"Silently," Kitty said. "We're learning to communicate
with our eyes, our touch."

Carmine took her hands as instructed, his grip strong and
assured, and she prayed he didn't notice the dampness of her
palms, the tremble she couldn't quell.

His eyes. Just focus on his eyes. Don't think, just…do.
But, damn it, the rich coffee color and warmth of his gaze
had the same effect as a shot of caffeine. Her pulse scampered, and her mind raced. *Don't waste this opportunity*, she
could hear Kara urging in her head.

As the seconds of the imposed minute of eye contact
passed, Carmine's grip on her hands eased. His thumb
moved across her wrist in a gentle caress. The tension in

his body seemed to leak out of him as if in defeat. She'd just furrowed her brow to question him silently about his obvious mood change when Kitty called, "Good! Now kiss your wife, gentlemen!"

Her breath snagged in her lungs as Carmine cradled the back of her head and drew her close. Without hesitation, he slanted his mouth over hers and parted her lips with a gently probing tongue. Eva raised her hands to his broad shoulders, holding on for dear life as his lips seared hers, shaping and demanding a response. The surge of heat in her veins and the heady buzz of pleasure that swept through her made it easy to comply with the urgency in his kiss.

As she canted toward him, wrapping her arms around his neck, the dining room and other couples fell away. Her world narrowed to two people. One incredible kiss. And a world of possibility.

Carmine stroked his fingers from her nape, down her spine and then back up to fist her hair in his hand. She leaned even closer, wishing she could find the means, through their kiss, to tell him all the secret feelings she'd harbored for him since she saw him across the squad room her first day at the precinct. She raised a hand to stroke his cheek and reveled in the roughness of his end-of-day stubble against her fingers.

"And time," Kitty called.

The sudden intrusion of the world outside her bubble of bliss was jarring and unwelcome.

But Carmine didn't pull away—his kiss continued, his grip on her hair, her nape, tightening as if he were fighting to hold on to the moment by holding on to her.

Kitty cleared her throat, and there was a rumble of chuckles around them.

"That's right. Get it, man," someone said. Aanan, she thought, although her head was spinning and her brain was so scrambled at the moment, she couldn't be sure of anything. Except…she wanted to go on kissing Carmine all night. Longer.

"Well, the rest of you are dismissed. Have a good evening, and we'll see you in the morning," Orrin said.

Finally, Carmine backed away, his eyes bright, as if he had a fever. His eyes stayed locked on her for a moment before he cut his glance toward Kitty and Orrin, as if just remembering they weren't alone.

Kitty gave them a crooked smile. "Well, well, well. That was quite the…convincing kiss. If I didn't know better, I'd say—"

Before Kitty could finish her sentence, Carmine shot to his feet and, raking fingers through his hair, left the dining room in quick, long strides.

Eva watched him go, at a loss for words or explanation or any real sense of what had just happened. She gave Kitty a stunned look and sputtered, "I… I d-don't know wh—"

Kitty crossed the now-empty circle of chairs and sat in the chair Carmine had just vacated. "You may not always understand it when it happens, or why, but in my experience, the heart is usually right…" She shrugged. "If you can get your head out of the way. My advice—not that you asked for it—is to listen to your heart. Follow your instincts."

Eva glanced at Orrin, who merely shrugged and smiled. "The rule of the exercise is no sex after the kiss. It's supposed to be about recreating intimacy… But I think we can waive that rule for you two."

Eva lurched to her feet, shaking her head. "I—we're not—"

Her hosts rose and left the room together, smirking to each other. Good grief! Did they just give her permission to have sex with Carmine? A tremor coursed through her.

So…what are you going to do about it?

Chapter Twelve

When Eva entered their stateroom, she found Carmine pacing restlessly around the small space. He was a caged panther, exuding raw strength, wild energy and feral magnetism. His gaze snapped to hers when she closed the door, rousing him from his brooding.

"Carmine," she said carefully, stepping deeper into the room.

His hand shot up to cut her off. "I know." He inhaled deeply, closed his eyes. "I know. I'm sorry."

Eva tried to swallow, but her mouth and throat were dry. "I'm not."

His dark eyes found hers then, hot and penetrating. "Eva," he growled. A warning.

She took a beat, looking for the right words. "If we—"

"No." He huffed a sigh of frustration and stormed toward the door.

She sidestepped, impeding his path. "Wait…"

"Eva, don't." His hands gripped her arms, trying to move her aside, but she backed up until she was against the door, blocking his escape.

"Don't walk away from this." Her heart was thundering, and she could barely hear her own voice over the whoosh of adrenaline-spiked blood in her ears. She dug deep for the courage to show her cards, lay her heart on the line. "Please."

He released her, and with both palms up and facing her, he eased backward. "Sean—"

"Screw Sean!" she blurted, her tone full of frustration.

Carmine's eyes grew even darker as his pupils expanded. "I'd rather screw you."

Her breath left her in a gush, and she surged forward, wrapping herself around him. "Good. Same here."

She seized his mouth with hers, capturing the back of his head so that he couldn't pull away. His arms snaked around her waist, and he steadied her with strong arms as she rose to her toes to kiss him harder, deeper. His palm slid down her back to cup her bottom, squeeze her buttocks. When she raised a leg, wanting to envelop him with her body, every limb, he lifted her, his embrace tightening, their kiss clinging and frantic.

Desire ramped higher and higher in her core, until she was shaking with need. "Now, Carmine. Please..."

"We can't—" he gasped "I won't—"

She ripped her mouth from his and glared at him, her breathing ragged. "Don't you dare go all rules and regulations on me now, DiRico. If I can follow my heart, so can you."

He made a low animal noise in his throat. "I was only going to say that I wouldn't take you against the wall like you were some cheap floozy in an alley." He released her and moved to pull down the Murphy bed. As he turned back to her, he unbuttoned his jeans and toed off his shoes. "I have nothing against spontaneous sex in general, but your brothers would never—"

"Hey!" she said, grabbing the front of his shirt. "Are you trying to kill the mood? Can we please stop mentioning my brothers while we do this?"

She saw the flicker of guilt and doubt that crossed his face, and she quickly yanked off her shirt and bra. "I don't need my brothers' permission or stamp of approval on my love life." She grabbed his wrist and placed his hand over her bare breast. "I want you, Carmine. I can't be any plainer than that."

With a lusty growl, he kissed her hard and tumbled with her onto the bed.

EVA ARCHED HER NECK, providing Carmine better access as he nibbled and teased his way from her jaw to the throbbing pulse at the base of her throat. Her sigh of pleasure rippled through him, creating his own tingle of satisfaction. Eva was easy to please. Every touch and kiss and nip elicited new gasps and moans and set him on fire. When he held her and slid his naked body against hers, shutting out the voice of recrimination and doubt was easy. Making love to Eva felt good, felt right. He'd deal with the repercussions later, he knew. But when she'd stepped in front of the door, lifted those big emerald eyes to his and asked him not to walk away, he'd crumbled. What man could be offered an opportunity to share a night of reckless passion with a woman of Eva's beauty and fire and confidence, and walk away?

You should have.

Carmine determinedly shoved the nagging whisper of conscience aside. He'd given in to the desire that had clawed at him for days—working, living, *sleeping* at Eva's side— and wouldn't look back. He'd own up to his actions when the time came, but right now... Right now he didn't want to do anything but *be, feel. Savor.*

Her sweet scent surrounded him. Her skin was satin beneath his questing hands. Her lips were hot and arousing as they moved across his belly, then lower...

When he moved on top of her and joined their bodies, all

rational thought fled, and his existence became a bubble of sensation and bright color and experience that shook him to the core.

She panted his name as she climaxed, and he captured her mouth to inhale her pleasured sigh. In the quiet moments of exhaustion and ecstasy that followed, Carmine held the doubt demons at bay, focusing on the contentment on Eva's face, the way her limp arm draped over him and her breath fanned gently against his skin as she nestled close.

"Wow," she whispered. "Well done, you."

He answered with a grunt and a kiss to her temple. "And you."

She shifted to her side suddenly, propping her elbow and resting her cheek on her hand. "Earlier, before Jim interrupted with his tirade—"

"He could be a problem. We need to be careful around him."

Eva placed a finger on Carmine's lips. "You were saying something about keeping your feelings in check."

Carmine sighed. He didn't want to go there. Why had he even brought it up at the group meeting? Other than wanting something to say in response to Eva's heartfelt words about not taking people for granted. Of course he'd thought of Rosa. He'd believed his older sister would always be there, nagging him, teasing him, loving him…until she wasn't.

He gritted his teeth, battling back the stab of pain that always accompanied memories of his sister.

"Care to finish what you started?" Eva asked, drawing a fingertip down his chest.

"No. Not really."

She made a rough sound in her throat. "Carmine?"

He stroked a hand along her long, silky hair, enjoying the way it slipped and twined around his fingers. "Eva, it's late. We should sleep."

"I want to talk."

She slid her toes up and down his calf until he wanted to roll her over and fill her again. If he could stall her, maybe he could put *that* particular talk off long enough that he could avoid it all together.

Avoidance, DiRico? Doesn't Eva deserve better? said a voice in his head that sounded a lot like Sean Colton.

And Cormac Colton. And Liam Colton. And Rosa DiRico. And his last girlfriend, Yvette Storm. And every other woman he'd ever broken up with rather than form a deeper, more meaningful relationship. There were several of those. He wasn't proud.

His hand fisted on the sheet, and he searched for the right words to put Eva off without hurting her feelings. Damn, he hadn't thought his reckoning would come quite so quickly. "Please, Eva. Can we save this conversation for tomorrow?"

She eyed him suspiciously, her eyes glinting in the dark room. "Will we? I know the past couple hours have changed things for us—our relationship and our partnership. I'm not looking for promises or a commitment from you, but... I do want your honesty."

He slowly took a breath. Nodded. "You'll have it."

Chapter Thirteen

Eva and Carmine found themselves the topic of discussion at breakfast the next morning. The couples who were at the group session the night before gossiped to those who had gone into town for dinner about Jim's voiced suspicions and Carmine-Daniel's extended kiss. Eva was used to the eyes following her, the quickly hushed whispers when she approached, and the overheard snipes and guffaws. She ignored the petty gossiping as best she could.

She had other, more pressing concerns. She had one last day to figure out what and who she'd witnessed their first night aboard the *Westmores' Folly* and roughly twenty-four hours left to wheedle any last scrap of useful information from Orrin and Kitty. And just one more night sleeping next to Carmine, hoping it would be as heavenly as last night and that it might be the beginning of something long-term. Last night had been Earth-shifting and fantasy-inspiring. But this morning, Carmine had risen early and said little to her since she found him on deck, staring out over the water as the yacht sailed up the Hudson River.

"Are you all right, C—Daniel?" she asked as he pushed his scrambled eggs around his plate, clearly distracted by his thoughts.

"Hmm? Oh, yeah."

She watched him another minute, then asked, "Are *we* okay?"

Her question earned a side glance, his eyes dark with subtext she couldn't translate, and an unconvincing, "Yeah. Sure."

An uneasy flutter started below her ribs. Maybe he was just focused on the case, feeling the same pressure to come up with something solid that would advance the case today... any of the three cases that had landed in their purview. She knew the feeling of wanting to have something worthwhile to show for their time on the cruise, prove themselves worthy of the investment and risk Captain Reeves had entrusted them with.

"Are you—" she started before Orrin interrupted with a loud clap.

"May I have your attention, friends?" he shouted.

Carmine shifted his gaze and angled his body toward their host, effectively shutting her out. Her disquiet grew. Something was eating at Carmine, and she had a sinking feeling it was their lovemaking. Morning-after regrets? Oh Lordy, she could overthink this and fret herself into a real stew. Clearly, that wouldn't be productive. In order to move past this speed bump and concentrate on the cases that needed solving, she should make a heart-to-heart with Carmine a priority once they got to...

"—the Bronx Zoo," Orrin said just as her attention focused, answering her question of the day's agenda. "After yesterday's rather somber excursion, we wanted to end the cruise with something fun. But today's trip is not trivial."

"Not at all," Kitty picked up, "We want you to spend some time while at the zoo today considering how humans and animals share certain societal and, yes, emotional attributes. Why do lions form prides? What other animals form monogamous-pair bonds? Why do apes groom each other?"

She paused long enough to straighten Orrin's collar and pick a bit of lint from his sleeve, and he brushed a wisp of her hair behind her ear. The group chuckled. "And be sure to visit the penguins, a species known to have same-sex couples that raise chicks together. The lesson there should be self-explanatory." She gave a nod, then waved her hands, dismissing the group. "The vans will leave in ten minutes!"

When Carmine turned back to his plate, dropping his wadded napkin in the middle and pushing back from the table, Eva quipped, "One...for protection and hunting." She held up a finger. "Two...swans, wolves, bald eagles and... I think some foxes." She added a finger. "And three..." She smoothed an errant lock of Carmine's hair and grinned. "Because they get messy?"

He wrinkled his brow. "Huh?"

"The answers to Kitty's questions." She flashed a sheepish grin. "Trivia nerd here. And the real answer to three is, monkeys groom each other to form social bonds and express affection."

She reached toward him to finger comb his hair again, and he surged to his feet, pulling away from her touch. "We need to go. The vans will be leaving soon, and I want to make a quick call to Captain Reeves before we head out."

A sharp prick of rejection needled her, and she sat frozen with humiliation for a moment before pushing her chair back to follow him. She felt chastened by his abrupt withdrawal, his spurning of her intimate gesture. After last night, she'd have thought they could share such moments freely; but with his dismissal, the rumble of dread in her middle ramped higher.

Carmine was already on the phone by the time she reached their stateroom. He didn't acknowledge her when she came in, just kept his eyes on the floor as he sat on the end of the mussed Murphy bed. He pinched the bridge of his nose and sighed as he answered a question from whoever was on the line. "Nothing else? It's just so frustrating! There has to be something that supports—yes. I understand that, but—"

She stepped into the tiny bathroom—right, *head*, since they were on a yacht—and got her toothbrush. She kept one ear on Carmine's conversation as she brushed her teeth and combed her hair into a ponytail for the day and spread a thin layer of sunblock on her nose and cheeks. As a redhead, she burned so easily, and they'd be outside this morning, so—

"Damn it!"

She poked her head into the cabin, where Carmine was evidently finished with his call but not at all happy. "Carmine, what—"

"Reeves hasn't heard boo from the precinct that responded to your 911 call the first night. No progress. No leads. No nothing. A woman was likely murdered, and they can't be bothered to give the case any real attention." He stood and slipped his phone in his back pocket.

Her heart pattered. She was touched that he'd cared enough, believed in her enough, to make inquiries. "Well, we'll see what happens after Emilio, the chef, makes his report. A second witness has to move the needle."

"And you trust that he'll make his statement?"

"I do. Because if he doesn't, I will tell them what he told me. And he has the status of his green card to consider." She collected a jacket to wear, in case it was chilly, and asked, "Did the captain have any other updates?"

"She didn't mention anything. Just reminded me to stay in touch with Sean." He glanced up at her. "I asked her if the alias Myra Smith had turned up any more hits, but nothing has panned out yet. Maeve is clearly operating at a high level, and she's done a good job hiding her tracks."

"Which leads to the question, why? What is she hiding from?"

He twisted his mouth in thought. "Exactly. Her disappearing act and untraceable aliases has all my instincts pinging. When we get back, I want to focus some time on Maeve. Starting with why she was in the closet where Mr. Kelly was found." He stood and stretched his back. "Ready to go?"

She waved a hand toward the door. "After you."

Two hours later, Eva strolled beside Carmine, stopping at each animal exhibit but not really seeing anything—which was unusual because she loved the zoo, the animals, the twitter of excitement from the school groups. Her mind remained preoccupied with their lovemaking the night before. Carmine hadn't yet mentioned it, which was telling in and of itself. Each time she tried to speak of it, she found the words knotted up in her throat.

Last night she'd promised him she wasn't looking for promises or commitment. It had seemed like something she needed to say to put him at ease. He was a known lothario at the precinct, after all. But she wasn't sure she meant it. How could she walk away from a night of the most incredible sex with a man she admired and had crushed on for months? She wanted more. She wanted a chance for a real relationship.

She wanted forever. Heck, if penguins could find their happily-ever-after, why couldn't she? And why hadn't she thought about Carmine's reputation as a no-strings love-'em-and-leave-'em guy before she'd thrown herself at him last night?

She only had herself to blame. She'd let Kara's optimism and romanticism convince her that seducing Carmine—her partner, for cripes sake!—was a good idea.

But she was a Colton, and her family's history had given her practice picking up and carrying on. They'd done so after the death of each of her parents, and she could do it now. If only she didn't have roughly twenty-four hours left in this undercover assignment. Sure, she could quit now and walk away. The Westmores knew who she and Carmine were, and they were grudgingly cooperating with the investigation. Mission accomplished. Sort of.

But a stubborn streak in her refused to leave the cruise prematurely. She knew—just *knew*—that the man whom she'd seen the first night was still on board. There had to be a good explanation for why the police had found no evidence of a crime, and she wanted to figure it out, find that man and get justice for the murdered woman before leaving the cruise tomorrow.

"I've been watching Jim this morning," Carmine said, rousing her from her morose thoughts.

She gave her partner her attention, and he directed her gaze with a hitch of his chin to the next exhibit. Jim and Sarah stood several feet apart, watching the birds of prey. Their body language exuded hostility.

"The more I watch him, the more I think he's nothing more than a bitter man, lashing out at others to redirect attention from his own failings."

Eva grunted. "That's your gut feeling, huh?"

He gave her a flat look. "It is."

"And I'm thinking the retreat hasn't helped solve the issues in their marriage." Even as she said this, she experienced a pang of sympathy for the couple. No matter her feelings toward Jim, she hated to see anyone unhappy or any marriage crumble.

Carmine turned from the snowy owl exhibit and strolled over to the next majestic bird.

"So are you ruling him out as our guy from the first night?" Eva asked, matching his slow, meandering pace. Any time their arms accidentally brushed or their hands bumped, her heart kicked…and Carmine flinched as if burned.

"No. That would be premature. Let's see what Captain Reeves comes up with." Carmine gnawed his bottom lip and stopped to gaze at a bald eagle. "Remember, we saw her flinch the other day. He likely has used violence against her. And everyone remains a suspect until we have hard evidence or a solid alibi to rule them out."

They fell silent again, standing side by side, while a burrowing owl blinked at them.

"Carmine," she said finally, at the same time he blurted, "About last night…"

"Go on," he said with a flick of his hand.

"No, you. You've been withdrawn today, and I want to know why. Do you regret what happened last night?"

He wouldn't look at her, but his mouth pinched tighter. After a moment he muttered, "Yes. And no."

Eva scoffed, trying to swallow her hurt and keep her tone even. "Well, that clears everything up."

He shot her a scowl, adding, "Just…give me a second, okay? This isn't easy for me."

The pain she saw shadowing his face reproached her impatience. Her chest squeezed, and she nodded to him. "Okay."

After another long moment of silence, Carmine said, "When I was fourteen, my older sister Rosa was caught in the cross fire when a couple of rival drug dealers started shooting at each other in our neighborhood. She died in the ambulance on the way to the hospital. I never got to tell her goodbye."

"Oh, Carmine! I'm so sorry!" Whatever Eva had expected him to say, this tragic bit of his family history was not it.

"The creeps responsible were never held to account. No one would admit having seen anything, knowing anything… despite the fact the streets were full of folks headed home from work and school and getting tacos from a food truck on the block."

Eva's heart sank, all too familiar with mute witnesses who feared for their lives and families. "Geez."

"That was when I made up my mind to become a cop, to fight back, to—" He spread his hands as if at a loss for words. "Make a difference."

She placed a hand on his arm. "And you have."

He shook off her touch and snorted harshly. "Have I? Really? Her murderers are still out there! Walking around free, poisoning other kids, ruining other families!"

"Carmine, you can't—"

"No, stop!" He faced her and jammed both hands through his hair. "You promised to give me a chance to tell this in my own time. Just…"

She nodded.

He fell silent, casting an awkward glance at a mother who walked past with a stroller and two young children, frowning at him for his outburst. He cast his gaze about, then caught Eva's elbow. "Come here."

Carmine led her to a bench in the shade, off the beaten path. Once they'd settled, he began again. "The pain of losing Rosa was so crippling for me…"

He took a breath and exhaled it heavily, rubbing his chest in a way that told her he was remembering that pain, experiencing it again. Her heart ached for him, and she reached for his hand. He seemed emboldened by her show of support and gave her a quick, sad smile of gratitude before sobering again.

"I had to find a way to shut it off," he said slowly, carefully, as if he was realizing the truth of his words for the first time as they fell from his lips. "Put my feelings away in order to move forward. I learned to…lock down my emotions, to not form attachments to people that could hurt me if the bond was broken."

Eva sat silently, not knowing what to say. She absorbed

what he was telling her with a twist of grief in her core. For him to have not allowed himself to love or be loved for fear of losing, of hurting… This new understanding of Carmine dug claws into her heart, knowing what it meant for their relationship.

"I've always tried not to mislead women, not let them think I could offer more than casual company and no-strings sex. Some women are okay with that for a few weeks before they get restless and want more. But I can't. I…just can't go back to the way things were after Rosa—" His voice broke and he stopped short to inhale deeply again. His hand tightened around hers.

"So…you've never been in a committed relationship with a woman?" she asked in a stunned voice. She'd known his reputation but hadn't realized how deeply entrenched Carmine's reasons for his bachelor lifestyle were. The pain in her chest swelled, and a strange feeling of cold swept through her. She'd formed deeper feelings for Carmine last night, and already the foolishness of her actions was bearing grievous fruit.

"I, um…had one relationship that lasted a couple years. I started to think maybe I'd found someone I could be with, someone I was willing to risk my heart for…" When his brow furrowed and his jaw tightened, Eva didn't need to ask how that relationship had ended. "She got tired of waiting on me and…cheated on me with one of my friends." He snorted derisively. "I actually miss my ex-friend more than Yvette. Mo and I used to go to Yankees games together and…" He scoffed and waved a hand in dismissal. "Anyway…"

She waited for him to continue, but he only stared at a crack in the sidewalk, his face scrunched in a deep frown of contemplation. Finally, she covered their joined hands with her free on and squeezed harder. "I am truly sorry for the losses you've suffered. I wish I could take away the pain somehow…"

He cut a look to her quickly. "Look, I didn't tell you because I was looking for sympathy or pity or—" He grunted, and his jaw tightened. "I only wanted you to understand why I can't let what happened last night happen again."

"You do regret it," she said, crestfallen. She'd hoped, even if they never built a relationship, that at least he wouldn't remember their lovemaking and cringe.

But then he surprised her with, "Not entirely."

She looked at him, confused.

He sighed, then drew his back upright as if rallying to face a challenge. He turned on the bench to face her and unlinked his hand from hers in order to skim a hand along her cheek and cup her chin. "After last night, it should be obvious that I find you extremely attractive and desirable. I had been fighting that attraction because of our working relationship, and because…"

When he hesitated, she supplied, "Because of my brothers' threats?"

He smiled just a little, and a dimple formed in his cheek that was so appealing her heart wrenched. "I'm not scared of your brothers. I can take 'em." He flashed a teasing grin, adding, "Unless they gang up and come after me as a unit."

She chuckled. "And they would."

Carmine paused before continuing, "I do respect them, though. I count them as friends. Especially Sean—who is, of course, also my boss, so…that gets tricky. I understand their protectiveness toward you. I do have my poor past showing with women to account for. I can't blame them for warning me away from you."

"So your regrets have to do with our work situation and your friendship and respect for my brothers?" she asked, trying to make sense of his explanation.

He opened his mouth. Closed it. Gave her a hum of frustration. "I'm making a mess of this." He scrubbed his cheek with one hand. "The problem is, I don't regret last night as much as I should."

Eva twitched back from him, wrinkling her nose in confusion. "Um... Huh?"

His face contorted with what she could only call a battle. He was clearly struggling to find words, or else fighting to keep words contained. Or maybe both. All tangled in what she now recognized as emotions he didn't know how to cope with, feelings he'd shunned most of his life.

Her breath jammed her throat, and she searched his face while her heart banged out a tattoo of reluctance, of expectation, of dread. Digging deep, she found the courage to rasp, "Please, just...say what you're thinking. Don't edit it."

When he pinned his dark gaze on her again, the heartache she saw there raked her soul. "I can't give you what you deserve. I felt more for you last night than just...casual sex. But for so many reasons—our work, your family, Rosa, Yvette—I can't let myself fall in love with you."

Chapter Fourteen

The wounded look that darkened Eva's face sliced through Carmine with hot, sharp tines. He knew he'd feel the pain of those internal gashes for the rest of his life. He'd never wanted this, had tried hard to avoid hurting her. But in a moment of weakness, he'd given in to his consuming desire for her. And ruined everything. His greatest and most potent regret was hurting Eva.

After her initial reaction, in which her pain was an LED spotlight glaring at him, Eva schooled her face, mustered a tight smile and drew her body into a stiff and erect posture. Pure forced control, clearly tenuous and fragile, but Eva wielded the act bravely as she rose from the zoo bench and smoothed her hands over the seat of her jeans as if straightening wrinkles. "Well, not that I ever asked for anything from you, but...okay. Good to know where we stand."

"Eva..."

"Shall we go? If we want to see the penguins before we have to meet the rest of the group, we should probably hurry." She strode away—her back rigid, her stride clipped—and Carmine shoved to his feet to go after her. His own legs felt leaden, as if he were having to drag heavy sacks of guilt behind him, on his back, in his heart. When he caught up to her, he grabbed her arm and she flinched, shook his hand loose.

Whirling toward him with a fake smile, she said, "Don't... It's okay. I'm fine. It was just...sex." She tried to brighten her smile, and the effort was...heartbreaking. "No harm, no foul."

But the faint quiver in her voice said otherwise.

"I'm sorry, Eva."

Her gaze cut to something behind him, and she replied, "No problem, Daniel. Can we go see the penguins now?"

With a glance behind him, he spotted Jamal and Linda Miller approaching. Even if one of the retreat couples hadn't been nearby, Eva's tone and body language both signaled she was finished discussing the matter. Carmine wished he could count the subject closed, but he knew he had to do more to help ease Eva's pain—pain he'd caused. He couldn't undo the events of last night, but he prayed he could mitigate some of the damage.

WHEN THEY REACHED the penguin exhibit, they found most of the marriage-retreat group there, watching the Little and Magellanic penguins swim and waddle and flap their flipper-like wings. A docent was standing before the group, relating the story of how a sister zoo in Syracuse had recently allowed two pair-bonded male Humboldt penguins to hatch and successfully foster a chick.

As they joined the group, a strange prickling sensation nipped Eva's spine, and she shook off her distracted thoughts about Carmine to focus her attention on her environment. Something subliminal had triggered the learned vigilance every police officer honed. Despite the relaxed and jovial scene around the penguin exhibit, something was amiss.

She scanned the scene, then looked to her partner to gauge whether he'd sensed whatever had rung warning bells for her. He seemed calm, if brooding, but as if sensing her gaze, he glanced at her, and his brow furrowed in query. She pulled a face, letting him know she was on alert but hadn't yet pinpointed…

And then she met the hard glare of Bill Boone standing across from her. He and Molly stood heads together with the McKinneys, whispering. Jim was no doubt filling Bill and Molly in on his suspicions. Eva sighed. As if Bill Boone needed another reason to glare at her. No wonder her lizard brain was firing. Bill really creeped her out, and now Jim was clearly filling Bill's head with more poison about her.

The sting of isolation filled her core. She would be so glad when this assignment was over. She was tired of being the pariah in a group she didn't belong to. Her previous days' consolation—sharing time and tight quarters with Carmine—was now a source of heartache. Carmine couldn't, wouldn't, let himself feel anything for her. His old hurts and disappointments had so scarred him that he'd shut himself off from having a meaningful intimate relationship. His determination not to allow himself to be vulnerable to love saddened her—not just for her own lost opportunity with him but for what it meant for Carmine. She hated to think of him alone for the rest of his life, holding people at arm's length.

One more day—less than that, really—and then she could go back to her apartment, to Carnegie, to the routine of the 98th Precinct…

"Dina?"

She startled when Kitty touched her shoulder, having moved up behind her while she was lost in thought. She gave her hostess a shaky grin. "Oh, hi. I was woolgathering…"

"I could tell. About something…sad or difficult. Am I right?"

"I—" Eva cut a gaze toward Carmine, whose eyes seemed wary. Did he think she would spill his secret heartache, betray his trust to Kitty? That lack of faith poured acid in her already-open wounds. Returning her attention to Kitty, she nodded. "I got some bad news. But... I'll be all right."

Kitty's expression was sympathetic. "I'm so sorry. Anything I can help with?"

Eva shook her head. "No. But thanks."

Kitty pursed her lips, pensive. "Since you and Daniel are in the group that will be going to Tavern on the Green for dinner tonight, I'd like to move your private counseling session with Orrin and myself to early afternoon. Say, two o'clock?"

Carmine angled his body closer to Eva and Kitty. "You know that's not necessary. You can give our spot to someone who really needs it. A couple with real issues."

Kitty divided a glance between them and shrugged. "True, but..." She pitched her voice low. "I've thought of something concerning Wes and his mother that we should discuss."

Eva perked up. "What?"

"Two o'clock?"

"Um..." Eva consulted Carmine with a glance. He nodded his agreement. "Two o'clock."

As Kitty strolled away, Eva wondered aloud, "What do you suppose that's about?"

"No idea." He crossed his arms as he stared straight ahead at the docent, who was still lecturing on conservation efforts and interesting facts about penguins in general. Carmine's body posture alone was enough to tell her he wasn't ready to talk, even about the case.

When Orrin signaled that it was time to head back to the vans, Eva excused herself to use the restroom. She wound her way through the milling zoo guests to the closest facility and, after finishing her business, studied her reflection in the mirror over the sink as she washed her hands. Even to own eyes, her expression looked bleak.

I can't let myself fall in love with you. She exhaled, and her shoulders sagged. Hadn't she known going into this undercover assignment that letting herself grow more attached to Carmine was a bad idea? Yet she'd let Kara's encouragement influence her judgment. And she'd pushed too hard, too far. She had only herself to blame for her heartache. Eva paused just outside the ladies' room door to gather her composure before returning to the group. Regardless of her personal situation, she had a job to do. She had to get her head together before returning to—

"Ow! Stop it!" She heard a woman hiss from somewhere nearby. "That hurts."

Instantly, Eva's senses went on full alert.

"Stop whining," a familiar male voice replied. "All you do is complain."

"Because all you do is disappoint and embarrass me!" The woman's reply was followed by a sharp slapping sound and a gasp.

Quietly, Eva stepped farther down the sidewalk, listening carefully to determine which direction the voices were coming from.

"I'm done. Stick-a-fork-in-me done," the man said.

"What?" the woman asked. "Wh-what does that mean?"

Eva moved off the sidewalk and around some tall bushes and spotted Jim and Sarah McKinney in a hidden recess at the back of the building. Jim's hostile body language sounded alarms in her mind. She clicked quickly into police mode. "Is there a problem here? Sarah?"

Jim swung around to glare at her. "Well, if it isn't little Miss Busybody. No, there is no problem, and I'll thank you to stay the hell out of matters that don't concern you!"

"Oh, but I am concerned anytime I hear a woman say they're being hurt. Sarah, if he's hurt you, you can press charges—"

Jim took a long step toward Eva and stuck a finger in her

face. "Butt out, Dina!" Then he whirled back toward his wife and seized her arm. "Come on," he grumbled as he dragged Sarah away. "I'm done with this charade. We're leaving this touchy-feely, pseudo-psychology retreat. I can't believe you wasted our money on this crap."

Sarah glanced over her shoulder as Jim hauled her away, her expression pleading, even as she shook her head and mouthed, "It's fine."

Eva muttered an unladylike word that was frequently bantered about in the squad room and fell in step behind the troubled couple. Her gut twisted, because she knew Sarah McKinney was not fine—and Jim's anger issues had just raised him to suspect number one in whatever violent scene had played out on the first night of the marriage cruise.

EVA AND CARMINE skipped the restaurant lunch that the rest of the group, minus the McKinneys, went to after the zoo. She'd reported to Carmine what she'd witnessed as soon as she found him by the vans, but by the time she'd related her concerns to him, the McKinneys had already left the zoo grounds and hailed a cab. When Carmine and Eva reached the yacht and inquired about the arguing couple, no one from the crew knew anything about the McKinneys' whereabouts. They didn't answer a knock on their cabin door, and no one on the yacht crew could remember seeing them since that morning at breakfast.

"Do we send a squad car around to have someone check their residence?" she asked Carmine, fretting over Sarah's welfare.

"If she doesn't want to press charges..." he replied, spreading his hands, leaving the rest unsaid.

"You're right. And I didn't actually *see* him do more than grab her arm. For all I know, she slapped him. But it just…" She fumbled for words, her frustration making her hands shake.

"I know," Carmine said. "Me too. As a cop, you're going to see a lot of stuff that you want to fix and…can't."

She saw a shadow skirt across his eyes before he clenched his teeth and apparently willed the dark emotion away.

And there it is, she thought. *A perfect example of what he tried to explain to me earlier.* In a job full of things that were ugly and heartbreaking and frustrating, Carmine had trained himself not to feel. To care, but not to feel. A tightrope that took all his energy and focus to walk. This was the legacy of Rosa's murder and his inability to bring his sister justice.

Eva opened her laptop and waited for it to start up. "Maybe so, but I'm still going to dig into Jim's past a bit more. He may have a clean record, but something else may pop that might be useful. For instance, did she mention the first night that Jim had had an affair? Where's that woman now?"

"Are you thinking what you saw the other night was Jim arguing with his mistress?" Carmine suggested.

"Anything is possible. But he's clearly got anger issues, violent tendencies. It's worth looking into."

Carmine nodded and sat down across from her, opening his own laptop. "We have about an hour until we meet with the Westmores. Let's have a look."

WHILE THEY WORKED, Eva received a text from her brother Cormac, a private detective who frequently assisted the DA and police with gathering information on high profile cases.

I'm outside your love boat on the marina. Can you meet me?

He was outside? What could he need to see her about that couldn't be done over the phone?

Be right there, she texted back.

"Cormac is outside," she told Carmine. "He wants to meet. Want to come?"

Carmine leaned back in his chair and stretched his back, rolled his shoulders. "He's here?"

When she nodded, he said, "I'll give you two privacy. If he's here in person, I figure it must be family business, not the case."

She shrugged. "Guess I'll see."

She spotted Cormac easily on the marina, his strikingly handsome face turned up to soak in the sun as he waited for her. He was smiling—a good sign since he'd been through more than his share of difficult times in recent years.

"Well, if it isn't the father-to-be," she said brightly as she approached him. "Does that grin mean you were thinking about Emily and the baby?" Warmth spread from her heart thinking of Cormac's impending nuptials to Emily Hernandez, the bright, beautiful and pregnant Assistant District Attorney involved in prosecuting Wes's murder case.

Cormac spun to face her, his expression shifting as he greeted his sister but still cheerful. "Oh, she's never far from my thoughts and a reason to smile, but in this case, I was remembering that time we went sailing with Humphrey and you made the boat capsize."

"Me? You and Sean did that!"

He clucked his tongue. "Oh boy. Senile and forgetting your history at twenty-six. How sad."

She opened her mouth to argue the point but stopped herself, choosing to dismiss her brother's teasing. "So what's up? What could you not discuss over the phone?"

"Can I not stop by to see my baby sister without my motives being questioned?" he asked with a false look of hurt.

"I know you, Cormac. You're checking up on me because I'm on this assignment with Carmine, a known womanizer. You're worried about my *virtue* or some bull like that, aren't you?"

She schooled her face, praying the truth of what *had* happened between her and Carmine last night didn't show. What she and Carmine had shared was private, none of her brother's business.

"Well, there's that…" Cormac arched one dark eyebrow before continuing, "But I actually wanted to pass on some news I got through my sources that you might find interesting." He twisted his mouth before adding, "And I wanted to lay eyes on you. I heard about the close call you had with some ice sculpture the other day. Carmine implied he thinks the 'accident' was no accident." Her brother studied her closely. "Are you okay?"

"A little sore from the spill when Carmine pushed me out of the way and landed on me, but nothing more than the bumps and bruises you guys inflicted on me as kids with your rough-and-tumble. So what's the news? Did Sean show the picture of Myra Smith to Mr. Widdecombe? Did he recognize her?"

"That, you'll have to ask Sean about. But there might have been a break in the case of the woman you saw dumped overboard the other night. A Jane Doe washed up near where your cruise set sail. No ID yet, but preliminary reports show a needle mark on her neck and hair samples had traces of ketamine."

Eva stiffened, and her pulse accelerated expectantly. "Ketamine? So…she could have just been a drug user? An OD?"

Cormac shrugged. "Possible. But she was wearing some high-end designer clothes. Not that wealthy women can't be drug users. Some are, but…"

Eva grabbed her brother's arm. "Any sign of a gunshot wound? If she is the woman I saw tossed overboard, there should be a bullet wound."

He twisted his mouth in dismissal. "Bruising on her wrists and the needle mark on her neck, but no GSW. She had water in her lungs, Eva. Coroner says she died from drowning, not from whatever happened to her before she went in the bay."

Eva chewed her bottom lip. "Still could be the woman I saw. If the shot I heard missed her, that would explain why there was no blood found on the railing or deck." She pinned a hard look on her brother. "Any word on how long it will take to make an ID?"

"Probably not long." He poked his hands in his pockets. "The responding precinct is working to cross-reference known missing person reports to see if anyone can make a positive ID. Checking dental records, blood types. A DNA confirmation will, of course, take longer, but there could be news soon."

Eva pressed a hand to her mouth, considering what this development could mean. If the Jane Doe proved to be someone connected to a member of the marriage retreat or the yacht's crew… "Wow."

As if reading her mind, Cormac added, "And just a heads up… You'll be asked to come view the body to see if she matches the description of the woman you saw dumped overboard."

She met her brother's gaze. "I…didn't get a good look at the woman. I heard more than I saw. But…of course I'll go. I can go now, if—"

He put a hand up to stop her. "Wait for the precinct to call you. Captain Reeves is getting that set up."

"Thank you, Cormac. I—keep me posted?"

He drew her into a hug. "Of course. And you'll look out for yourself? If that ice sculpture accident wasn't accidental, the culprit could make another move on you, especially if he senses authorities closing in on him."

Eva felt a prickle on her neck. "I'll be careful."

"Good. Okay, Stinky Feet, I love you." He gave her a quick embrace and kissed the top of her head. "I gotta run."

"Tell Emily hello for me," she said.

He gave her a wink and thumbs-up as he sauntered down the marina. Eva watched her brother go, happy for his new family while wondering if she'd ever find the same level of bliss and fulfillment that her three brothers had all found in recent months. As she often had growing up, she experienced a tug of melancholy, a sense she was running to catch up, loved but also left out of her brothers' tight circle, odd woman out and struggling for recognition by her big brothers. That she'd found something she thought she could be happy with in Carmine, only to be rejected by him, only made her longing sting all the more.

She mentally clamped down on the personal pity party before it swelled fully. Carmine had his reasons for his choice, and she could respect them…even if it hurt her in the process.

Chapter Fifteen

Carmine was waiting for Eva when she got back from her meeting with her brother. His and Eva's research into Jim McKinney hadn't yielded much in the hour they'd had to look into the man's business connections, police records and social media. But Carmine sensed, as Eva clearly did, that something significant about the crime she'd witnessed the first night was hovering just beyond their grasp. With a little more searching and mulling, they might find the lead they needed before they left the cruise tomorrow morning.

And damn it, he needed a win. The 98th Precinct needed a win. The Humphrey Kelly disappearance and the Lana Brinkley murder cases seemed hopelessly stalled. Even clues like Maeve O'Leary's DNA at the courthouse closet raised more questions than they answered. Knowing the Westmores had something of importance to share made him edgy and impatient.

"We're due for our session with the Westmores. I hope whatever Cormac had to say was worth it," he said when she returned to their cabin.

"Wow," she replied, giving him the stink eye. "Someone needs his nap."

He hitched his head toward the door. "Let's walk and talk."

Her hand shot past him and blocked the door, shoving it

closed again. "Let's not. I don't want eavesdroppers hearing this."

That got his attention. "Really? What did he say?"

"A woman's body washed up today, and there are signs she met with foul play. It could be the lady I saw dumped the first night of the cruise."

He gave a low whistle. "How soon until they ID her?"

"It's in the works. I'm supposed to view her soon to see if I recognize her." She opened the door now. "Stay tuned for further developments," she intoned, mimicking a newscaster's resonance.

"Anything else?" he asked.

"Wow. Greedy. I thought that was pretty big on its own."

He rubbed his forehead. "It is. And we'll talk more about it later, but the Westmores are waiting, and they could have the piece that makes this puzzle fit together. Can we go?"

She waved a hand and fell in step with him as they hurried to the Westmores' office.

Orrin and Kitty were ready for them and ushered them to their chairs with nervous smiles.

"Okay. What did you have to discuss? You remembered something about Wes? Maeve?" Carmine asked before he'd even settled in his chair.

Kitty inhaled deeply, her expression a mask of guilt. "Well, in truth… I have nothing more on Maeve or Wes."

Eva frowned. "But this morning at the zoo, you said—"

"I know." She spread her hands and kicked up her chin. "You're not the only one who can lie when it suits you."

Eva's mouth opened, and her eyes widened. "Ouch."

A spike of heat gnawed inside Carmine. He was already tense after the gutting conversation he'd had with Eva that morning and the ticking clock to find more evidence and resolve three crimes.

"You lied?" His tone was clipped and unforgiving. Clenching his back teeth, he slapped his hands on the arms of his chair and surged to his feet. "Then there's nothing to discuss? Because if not, we have important work to do."

"Please, sit." Orrin motioned to Carmine's chair, his tone calm and maddeningly reasonable. "There is something we wanted to talk with you two about. Just…not Wes and Maeve."

"I lied to be sure you came today," Kitty admitted.

Fisting his hands, Carmine sat. "Then what?"

The Westmores exchanged a look, and Kitty took a deep breath, squared her shoulders. "We want to talk about the two of you."

"Pardon?" Eva said, her complexion growing wan.

"Orrin and I have been marriage counselors for a long time. We've learned what a couple in crisis looks like. And what a relationship that can be saved looks like…if the partners are willing to do the work."

"That's all well and good," Eva said with a nervous smile, "but we're not married, remember?"

"I know you were pretending to be married as a cover story, but…we've been watching the way you two interact. There's more between you two than a working relationship. Am I right?" Kitty divided an insightful gaze between them.

Carmine slouched in his chair, glowering. "That's not your business."

"But…it is our *business*," Orrin said, lending emphasis to the word. "And since you did pay for the retreat, you are entitled to our professional services like the other couples, if—"

Carmine snorted and stood again. "No."

"Daniel, please." Kitty stood as well, catching his arm. "We want to help. No one who saw how you two kissed last night and how you look at each other in unguarded moments could miss the very *real* affection you have for each other."

He huffed, hating how close to the truth Kitty was.

"Maybe we're just that good at acting." He nudged Eva's shoulder. "Come on. Let's go."

Sirens blared in his head, and he wanted out of that room, fast. *Now.*

He moved toward the door, but Eva didn't follow. He paused, hand on the knob, and glanced back at his partner, his scowl impatient. "Eva?"

When she raised her eyes, tears were pooled in their green depths. "Maybe..." She released a shuddering sigh. "Maybe if you told them what you told me earlier today..."

His jaw tightened so hard he could have cracked a tooth. His glare hardened as he stared at her, warning her not to say more. Angry she'd even hinted at his confession to her. Didn't she understand how much it had cost him to tell her the painful facts of his past? Share the deep scars he carried? That she would even hint at exposing his secret hurts to the Westmores filled him with a bitter fury of betrayal.

And yet...he hesitated. The grief in her eyes, the conflict that played out on her face, the longing in her voice ripped through him. His head told him to leave, to retreat. He wanted no part of some tell-all gabfest. But a tender spot that had grown in his soul for Eva in the last week throbbed with a need to vanquish the pain he saw in her face. A pain that mirrored his own.

"I understand that there is no...*us*," Eva continued, her voice thin and trembling. "I heard what you said today and... I accept it."

Razor-like claws raked his heart. Sure, he'd told her as much just hours ago, had sworn he couldn't give her the relationship she seemed to want, but...hearing her say she'd accepted as much and moved on... Hell! This was exactly why he didn't do relationships!

"But..." she was saying, and he closed his eyes, unable to continue holding her teary gaze.

"If they can help you find some peace with your…past—"

"Daniel, we only—"

"Carmine," he interrupted grimly. "Carmine DiRico." He exhaled a harsh breath and jammed his hands in his pockets. "If we're going to do a deep dive into my life and most personal experiences, then…shouldn't we get rid of the whole Daniel pretense?"

Kitty offered a gentle smile. "Carmine." She tipped her head and patted the back of his chair. "Will you please give us a chance to help?"

"We don't have time for this. It's the last day of the cruise, and we still haven't found the man who—"

"Carmine," Eva said. "Please. You have an opportunity to lay down some of the burden you've been carrying and find some happiness. Do you really think Rosa would want you living like this? Depriving yourself of love and connection because of what happened to her? Haven't you hurt long enough?"

He gave her a silencing glare. "So glad to know I could trust you with my private pain, *Eva*," he growled.

When a tear broke free of her lashes and dripped onto her cheek, Carmine bit out a curse and turned his back to her. He grabbed the doorknob again, squeezing it for all he was worth. But, somehow, he was unable to walk out. Something anchored him where he stood, kept him frozen in his tracks.

Behind him, no one spoke. The only sound he could hear was the thrashing of his own heart. He inhaled. Exhaled. Released the doorknob. He glanced over his shoulder at Eva and met her tender, pleading emerald gaze. A pure and poignant longing blind-sided him—a yearning so deep and organic that it knotted his throat.

As he held Eva's gaze, Orrin spoke quietly. "Carmine, are you content with the path you're on, the way your life is going? Or…do you want something different for your future, something more, something better?"

I want Eva, a voice from his soul whispered.

"In order to get a different result, you have to employ a different approach." Orrin stood slowly and spread his hands. "That starts with releasing the past and living for today."

Carmine turned slightly to cast a dubious look at the older man. "How?"

Orrin motioned to the chair. "One step at a time. Shall we talk?"

When Carmine returned to his seat, Eva felt a rush of warmth and hope rise in her chest.

"I'll go and give you privacy." Placing her hands on the arms of her chair, she started to rise, but Carmine reached over and covered her hand with his.

"Stay. I—" Shadows and turmoil filled his dark eyes. He was scared, she realized. Opening himself to the pain he'd kept bottled up for years had to be difficult. A simple unspoken request for her silent support and strength through her presence was written in his penetrating gaze.

She sat back down, nodding and turning her hand over to lace their fingers.

Carmine took a moment to gather his thoughts and then recounted the tragic story of his sister's death and his grief that he'd told her about earlier. He touched on his trouble with relationships, which led the Westmores to ask a few related questions to draw him out, make him dig deeper. The further the Westmores pushed, the more Carmine seemed to withdraw. After several minutes of discussion, he even pulled his hand away from Eva's and tucked his hands under his armpits. She glanced at Kitty, who signaled with her eyes for Eva to be patient with Carmine, that the self-protective body language was not uncommon.

Eva hadn't expected anything between her and Carmine to change after one conversation with the counseling power couple, so she gave Carmine all the space and understanding he needed. Her heart swelled with respect for him. Opening up couldn't be easy after years of nursing his private pain. Once or twice, she thought he might leave the session. He'd scoot to the edge of his chair, leaning forward and bouncing his heel in agitation. But then Kitty or Orrin would say something that calmed or validated Carmine, and he'd slide back in his seat for the moment, take a deep breath and continue to answer the questions the Westmores had.

A surreptitious glance at the wall clock told Eva they'd gone over their allotted time for the session, but neither Kitty nor Orrin seemed to care. She gave them points for that, for not cutting Carmine off and rushing him along, slave to a clock rather than their client's breakthrough. Carmine was the one who ended things, twenty minutes past the scheduled time for the next couple to come in. Swiping a hand down his face, he exhaled harshly and said, "Look, you two aren't going to fix me in one meeting. I'm gonna need time to digest all this. I—"

Now he did rise to his feet and plow fingers through his short-cropped hair.

Taking her cue, Eva rose, too, rubbed his arm and flashed a comforting smile, one she prayed he didn't read as condescending or patronizing.

"Carmine," Orrin said, stopping him as he made his way toward the door and holding out a business card. "If you want to continue talking after the cruise, in our office—"

Carmine grunted, a negative sound, but took the card and looked at it long and hard.

Eva eased past him, putting her hand on the doorknob, then turned back toward the Westmores. "Oh, and… I know we've run over our scheduled time, but…there's one last thing I think you should know before we go."

"Yes?" Kitty said.

"I spoke to my brother this afternoon. He has numerous contacts within law enforcement and the DA's office and… he let me know a woman's body was pulled from the water this morning. No ID has been made, but there are signs she met with foul play. It could be the woman I saw shoved overboard a couple days ago."

Orrin seemed to bristle.

Holding up a hand to forestall his arguments, Eva added, "I just wanted you to know the police could have more questions for you if a connection between the woman and this cruise can be made. I've already been asked to view the body and see if I can identify the woman as the one I saw that night."

Orrin repeated their willingness to work with the police as well as his skepticism about any crime having taken place. "No one is missing from our manifest. All of our crew and guests are accounted for."

"I know. And this woman could be anyone, but… I thought you should know." Eva shrugged. "A gesture of good will? Reciprocity?"

"Thank you," Kitty said after a moment of staring at Eva with a frown denting her brow.

Eva opened the door to the adjoining room and practically ran into Bill and Molly Boone, who were waiting rather impatiently on the other side.

"Finally," Molly said, overtly checking her watch.

Bill only met Eva's gaze with one of his usual dark glares.

As she made her way back to their cabin, Eva snorted and muttered, "I will not miss *you* when this retreat is over. Creep."

"What?" Carmine asked, as if being shaken from deep thoughts.

"Nothing. You okay?" she asked him, seeing the haunted look still shadowing his eyes.

He scrubbed a hand over his face and paused on the deck to gaze out over the water. "I will be." His hands squeezed the railing, and he took a few long, slow breaths. "I just want a few minutes alone, if..."

"Of course." She touched his shoulder. "I'll meet you back in the cabin."

He twitched a melancholy half grin, and she retreated, leaving him with his thoughts. Eva was deep in a search for information on the McKinneys when Carmine returned to their stateroom. Whatever thinking he'd done on deck seemed to have helped calm his mind, and he joined her at the tiny table with his laptop without any mention of what had transpired in the counseling session.

"What have you got going on there?" He nodded to her laptop, his manner and expression peaceful.

Had he found some reconciliation with his past, or had he simply stuffed it all back down again? She wouldn't ask. For the sake of finishing this assignment with some semblance of harmony between them, Eva squashed the myriad questions pinging in her brain.

"I found the McKinneys' home address, then did a search in police records for calls to that address."

He raised his eyebrows with interest. "And?"

"Seems the neighbors *have* called the police regarding disturbances there in the past, but no charges have ever been filed, thus no arrest record for either of them."

Carmine's cheeks puffed as he blew out a sigh of exasperation. "An all-too familiar pattern."

Eva twisted her mouth, mirroring his frustration, and closed her laptop. "Do you want to skip the dinner out? We can eat in the dining room or bring something back here to the cabin if you'd rather," she said.

He paused, regarding her with a searching scrutiny. "Do you want to skip it?" She opened her mouth to decline, but he pinned her with a hard stare. "Be honest."

"Honestly, I want to go. I haven't been to Tavern on the Green since my sixteenth birthday." She smiled and bit her bottom lip as the memory of the boisterous celebration and fine food rushed back. "My brothers saved up for weeks to take me there, wanting to do something special for my sweet sixteen." She paused, calling up more details. "I think Humphrey had a little something to do with us getting a private dining room and the massive chocolate cake decorated with real pink roses that was brought in after the meal." A bittersweet pang plucked her heart as the reminiscence of Humphrey played in her mind. "Oh, Carmine... We have to find him. I can't bear to think he could be in trouble."

Carmine nodded brusquely. "All right, then. We're going. I'll change."

She cocked her head to one side and studied him. "Are you sure you're okay with this? If you're not in the mood or you'd rather take some time tonight to chill—"

"No. I'm fine. It's fine." The smile he gave her didn't reach his eyes, clearly indicating he was *not* fine. She wanted to challenge him on the point, but she'd forced his hand in the counseling session. Hadn't she pushed enough for one day? Conceding the point, she swore to herself she would not challenge him on this point or any other tonight. He needed time and space to process things in his own way.

"Okay," she said, pulling her dress out of the shallow cabinet that passed as a closet. She pulled the dry cleaner bag off the dress and took the gown into the head to change. Fortunately, the dress was made of a light, flowy material that didn't wrinkle, so the past couple days scrunched in the tiny closet hadn't done much damage. She dabbed a little extra color on her face and swept her hair up in an easy chignon. The tiny mirror over the sink was entirely unhelpful in getting a full-effect view of herself or knowing whether she'd applied her makeup with too heavy a hand. But...whatever.

After putting on dangling gold earrings, she stepped out of the bathroom, smoothing her hands over her skirt and wishing Kara was there to give her honest opinion. Instead, she turned awkwardly toward Carmine, asking, "Is this okay? Is the makeup too much? Too dark?"

Her partner raised his gaze from tying his shoes, and his expression stiffened. He swallowed hard and muttered, "Judas Priest, I'm screwed."

CARMINE GAWKED AT EVA, his throat growing dry and his body humming with desire. His partner looked, in a word, stunning. Breathtaking. Unbelievable. Okay, that was three words but... Have mercy! *That's* what had been hiding under the police department's clunky and unflattering patrol uniform?

Her formfitting forest green dress brought out the emerald color of her eyes and flared out into a swingy style that danced around her shapely legs. She'd arranged her hair in a sexy way that showed off her slim throat and left tendrils of her fiery auburn hair framing her face. A shiny application of a bronze-toned lipstick beckoned with promises of cinnamon and sugar so vivid he could practically taste her kiss now.

This was not good. How was he supposed to share an intimate gourmet dinner at one of the city's most atmospheric restaurants and not lose his mind for wanting to take her back to bed? He'd sworn to himself that, despite the incredible experience they'd shared last night, he could keep himself in check and maintain a gentlemanly distance and detachment from his partner until this undercover assignment ended tomorrow morning. But with Eva looking so gorgeous, so tempting, he would be hard-pressed to keep his promise.

Orrin's question from that afternoon echoed in his brain… *Are you content with the path you're on, the way your life is going? Or…do you want something different for your future, something more, something better?*

Opening up to the Westmores about Rosa's death, his frustration and pain over her murder case going unsolved, and his ongoing difficulty with relationships as a result had been cathartic. True. Not a magical elixir, for sure. Picking off that scab had left him raw and more conscious of how much his life lacked, how much more he wanted but kept at bay.

Orrin had called it fear. Carmine recoiled from the word. He was a cop, damn it. He didn't do scared. Maybe *pain-avoidant* was a better descriptor, because who the hell wanted to go through life constantly dragged down by all the baggage and wounds from your past every day? When he thought about Rosa's death, he couldn't breathe. Why would he want to keep that front and center?

"Is something wrong with the dress? Do I have too much makeup on?" Eva asked, ducking into the bathroom to check her image again in the mirror.

"No," he rasped.

She stepped back out and frowned at him. "Then what's with the grimace? You look…repulsed or something."

He rubbed a hand over his face and stood. He took a fortifying breath and said quietly, "Quite the opposite. I'm just deciding how to get through this evening without ravishing you, when you look so..." He grinned in spite of himself. "Ravishing."

Color stained her cheeks, and she bit her bottom lip as if to subdue her own grin. "Oh. Um, thanks. You look very nice too."

He rubbed his hands together, jitters dancing through him as if he were a teenager on his first date. "Well, shall we go?"

She retrieved a sweater, which she draped around her shoulders, tucked a compact beaded purse under her arm and gave a nod. "Ready."

With a guiding hand at the small of her back, he guided her off the yacht to the waiting limousines. Conversation in the limo started as a praise-fest of compliments for the women about their attire and the perfect spring weather for the outing but moved on to gossip about the McKinneys soon after.

"They've left the retreat, gone home!" Gail Nash said, her tone dismayed. "I heard he's filing for divorce!"

"Humph, should be the other way around," Carol Johnson replied. "If my man had that kind of temper and cheated on me... I'd be gone, gone, goodbye gone!"

Carmine glanced at Eva, who was clearly biting her tongue, determined not to be dragged into the discussion. It occurred to him that in such a short time, he'd learned to read Eva's expressions and know where her mind was. While not unusual for partners in the department to share the same wavelength, for them to have reached that level of understanding and accord so quickly was...telling to him. They clicked.

And he sensed something else with her—an intimacy beyond the physical that they'd shared last night. The best he could describe it was a personal safety. An odd choice of words for a cop, he knew, but he was new to this business of analyzing his emotions. He just knew that he hadn't wanted Eva to leave the meeting with the Westmores that afternoon, despite the fact she'd thrown him under the proverbial bus. He'd liked having her beside him, having her support, knowing that, despite her revealing his secret, she had his best interests at heart. And purging his soul, at least in part, to the Westmores had been both excruciating and liberating. He was still grappling with that paradox, but tonight he seemed to breathe easier.

That is, until Eva had stepped out of the bathroom looking like ten kinds of temptation. Now every time he glanced at her, oxygen backed up in his lungs all over again. Having vowed to her and to himself that he wouldn't—couldn't—have any sort of relationship with her, he was stuck juggling a bone-deep lust for her and a stubborn determination not to mislead or hurt her. Or tie himself into more knots of confusion and emotional entanglement. If he could just get through tonight, survive this test of his willpower, the undercover assignment would be over tomorrow. Once they were back on home turf, surrounded by the sights and sounds and cops of the 98th Precinct, his relationship with Eva would settle back into proper balance and perspective.

"Don't you think so, Daniel?" Eva said to him, and it took him a beat to drag himself from his wandering thoughts.

"Um, sorry. What?"

"We were saying that while we hate to see a marriage end, sometimes it's better not to prolong the inevitable," Carol Johnson said.

Eva leaned closer. "You all right? You looked a million miles away."

He caught a whiff of her herbal shampoo, the aroma promptly reviving memories of being surrounded by her sexy scent last night while wrapped in her limbs and—

Carmine swallowed hard. "I'm good."

As they arrived at Tavern on the Green, a jangling tune

sounded from the small clutch Eva had tucked under her arm. She rapidly dug out her cell phone and checked the caller ID. Her mouth twisted in consternation, and she shot him a look of regret. "Go on in and claim our table. I should take this."

He arched an eyebrow, silently asking, *Who is it?*

"Sean," she mouthed.

He glanced at the backs of the other retreatants as they disappeared inside the restaurant, reluctant to leave Eva standing outside alone. If Sean had an update on the case, he wanted to hear it. But knowing he could have called on private family matters, he blew out a breath and nodded. "See you inside."

Eva would, of course, fill him in on any development concerning the case. However, if the information was too sensitive to share in public where they could be overheard, he'd have to wait until later in their cabin. He growled to himself as he caught up to the group. He hated waiting.

Orrin, with the maître d', showed the couples to the small tables where each couple could have the illusion of privacy for their dinner. Carmine assured Orrin with a nod that all was well when his host frowned at the empty seat across from him.

Eva joined him a moment later, and as she took her seat, he said, "I ordered you a dry white wine. Was that right?"

She blinked and smiled. "Good guess."

He shrugged. "Naw. Just remembered from the other night when you ordered the same with dinner on the yacht."

"In that case, good attention to detail." She put her napkin in her lap and opened her menu.

"Goes with the job," he replied. He watched her over the top of his own menu and tried to gauge her expression for some clue to the content of Sean's call. "Good news from your brother?"

She folded the menu and met his gaze. "Maybe. Kind of."

She glanced around them as if weighing the chances of being overheard, then said in a quiet tone, "The guy who claimed to see…" She paused. "*H. K.* with a woman in February—" she gave him a meaningful look, and he nodded to let her know he understood H. K. was Humphrey Kelly "—said the picture of the older woman that visited *W.* was a match."

Carmine took a beat to process the news. The woman who'd signed in as Myra Smith to visit Wes at Rikers had been seen in February on the street with Humphrey Kelly. He sat taller in his chair, his interest piqued. "He's sure?"

"Mostly. The guy said the eyes were different. Same big doe eyes but wrong color. And the woman in the photo looked older."

"So it likely was Ma—" He caught himself. "*M.*, but in a disguise, as we assumed."

"Mmm-hmm." Eva started to say something, then closed her mouth and smiled formally as a waiter arrived with their drinks. After giving their order—the organic Scottish salmon for Eva and the chardonnay-braised short rib of beef for him, with the wild mushroom–toast appetizer to share—she continued. "So that raises the question, what was M. doing with H. K. in February? What's the nature of their relationship? Professional or…" She hesitated, frowning before saying, "Romantic?" Her tone clearly expressed disbelief, even dismay, for that notion.

"Well, we already had her DNA in the courthouse closet, so this February sighting confirms a link," he mused, staring into the highball glass of whiskey he'd ordered. "What's your issue with the romantic angle?"

Her eyes widened. "Seriously? He's married! I know that it's just a marriage of convenience, but still. If he wanted out, why wouldn't he just ask for a quiet, equitable divorce?"

Carmine bit the inside of his cheek for a moment, debating whether to share his honest opinion with Eva, knowing how it would disappoint her. Finally, knowing their professional partnership required they be straight with each other, he said gently, "Maybe he's not the same man you remember from your youth any longer. Or he never was, and you saw the man you wanted him to be."

The expected flicker of pain ghosted across her face before she sobered and squared her shoulders. "I guess that's a possibility I have to consider. It doesn't sit right with me. My gut says—"

"Your gut?" he interrupted with a startled laugh. "Ms. By the Book, listening to her gut?"

Eva hiked up one sculpted eyebrow. "Fine, laugh if you want. Maybe I'm learning there's room for both regulations and instincts in solving a case. Isn't that what my rookie season is supposed to be about? Learning all the ropes?"

He lifted his glass to her. "It is. Well done."

The glow that filled her cheeks and her smile when he praised her tugged hard in his chest. She worked hard to earn recognition, he'd noticed. Did her brothers, the department, not give her the credit she deserved, or was that just her perception? He'd heard women say they felt underrated, underappreciated, undervalued in traditionally male roles. Carmine cocked his head as he considered her and reviewed his interactions with her. "Have I treated you fairly?"

Eva's wineglass stopped halfway to her mouth. "What?"

"You're talented, hardworking, intelligent... I just want to be sure I don't... That I haven't diminished that by anything I've said or done."

She smiled shyly. "I, uh... Wow. Thank you." She sipped her wine; then, as she set it back on the table, she said, "Nothing too overt, that I recall. I'll tell you if you do. Don't worry."

"And the rest of the 98th? Your brothers?"

"A few guys at the 98th, yes. Mitch can be a jerk. But I am a rookie, and so some hassle is expected. My brothers… Hmm, they mean well, I know. But they tend to be overprotective. I want them to see me as the fully competent, fully self-sufficient adult I am and not as their kid sister." She rubbed her fingertip around the rim of her wineglass, her brow furrowed. "I want them to trust me, believe in me."

"They do."

She angled a skeptical look up at him and snorted.

"Sean sent you out on this assignment, didn't he?"

"Reeves did."

"He could have argued the point and put someone else in once Reeves latched on to the idea. But he trusted you to handle a delicate part of the investigation with the Westmores that he hadn't cracked. And you've delivered in spades. The DNA from the vanity set? All you." She held his gaze, her expression surprisingly dubious. A new thought occurred to him that plucked at his heart. "How much do you trust yourself? Believe in yourself? Could you be trying to prove yourself *to yourself*?"

His question clearly stunned her. She leaned back in her chair, and her mouth opened and shut like a landed fish. Her gaze fixed on the table as she considered his point until their dinner arrived, and she rallied enough to smile for the waiter. When they were alone again, he touched her hand where it rested on the table beside her wineglass. "Just think about it. I only mention it because…"

Her eyes met his, so bright and earnest and vulnerable that his chest gave a painful squeeze. "I just want you to know your worth and…be happy." The ache inside him gripped tighter. He'd give anything if he thought he could be the one to make her happy.

Her eyes misted as she flipped her hand over to hold his and whispered, "And I want the same for you."

AN ODD, TANTALIZING mood had crept into their dinner, and Eva found herself fighting to keep her emotions at bay. Carmine's kind words were just that. Kindness. The atmosphere of the swanky restaurant was intended to be romantic for the retreat couples...which she and Carmine were only pretending to be. She needed to keep that perspective. This was all an illusion. Carmine had stated plainly just that morning that he wasn't looking for a relationship with her, that his past precluded him giving his heart to her. So she needed to check herself. If she got hurt, it would be her own fault.

She took a deep breath and determinedly steered the conversation to safer ground. The cases. The exquisite food. Her cat.

"I found him behind Carnegie Hall on a cold night and took him home, not really intending to keep him but... Well, he snuggled up to me and purred as he slept, and I caved."

Carmine smiled politely as he stabbed a bite of beef, and Eva cringed internally. *Oh God. I've become a cliché. The lonely single woman talking about her cat.* She laughed awkwardly and waved a dismissive hand. "Sorry, I'm boring you."

"Not at all. Your story just proves again that you are compassionate and softhearted."

"You lie. I could see your eyes glaze over when I mentioned Carnie. But thanks for cutting me slack."

Carmine shrugged. "So I'm not a pet owner. Doesn't mean I'm bored."

The ting of a spoon tapping a glass caught their attention, and Orrin stood to announce, "As you all are finishing your meal, you are welcome to move into the bar area for a drink. The limo doesn't leave for the *Westmores' Folly* until nine thirty. So relax, enjoy yourselves. And as a reminder, we will have one final wrap-up group session after breakfast tomorrow morning before we dock and send you forth." He raised his glass. "Cheers."

A murmur rose from the other couples as one by one, they moved to the bar. Eva, who'd never been a big drinker, sent Carmine as small head shake along with a glance that demurred.

He leaned in to ask, "Not interested in a nightcap?"

"Well, I'll go to the bar with you if you want one."

He arched an eyebrow. "Answer the question. Do *you* want to go?"

She considered trying to read his eyes, guess at what he wanted, but finally just told him the truth. "No. I'd much rather get some air. We can go for a walk in the park? We can stretch our legs and meet the group back here in thirty or forty minutes."

The corner of his mouth kicked up in a satisfied grin. "Sounds perfect."

Before leaving the restaurant, they let Kitty know they'd be back soon, then headed into the quiet paths through Central Park. They headed north, past Sheep Meadow, where, come summer, people would flock to sunbathe and picnic. As they walked, she got the itchy sensation of being watched. Or…followed? She glanced behind them. A few other pedestrians meandered the paths, but the night was still, mostly quiet, especially as they reached the Imagine Mosaic and Strawberry Fields, designated quiet zones in memory of John Lennon.

By mutual unspoken accord, they paused to view the black-and-white mosaic on the path.At Strawberry Fields, Eva peered through the darkness, catching glimpses of blooming plants from around the world. As they moved on down the walkway, the sense of having a tail continued, even as they turned east and ended up at the Bow Bridge. She spotted another couple, walking hand in hand, and a guy on a bike whizzed past. Nothing out-right suspicious. She grunted softly and tried to shove aside the prickly feeling to focus on her time with Carmine.

Reaching the bridge, they stopped in the middle to savor the view of the stars reflected in the lake.

Carmine draped his arm loosely around her shoulders and sighed. "Funny. Now that we truly have some privacy to discuss the case, talking is the last thing I want to do."

"Aha," she teased quietly. "I knew I'd prattled at dinner. I wore you down, didn't I?"

He glanced down with a smile and shook his head. "Naw. It's just so nice here. Calm. I hate to waste this moment. Life will be frantic and stressful enough tomorrow when we get back to the precinct."

"Mmm. True enough." She leaned against the bridge railing and savored the warmth of his arm around her, knowing, in his eyes, it meant nothing but wanting to store up memories of these quiet moments while she could.

"Thank you," he murmured after several moments of sharing the tranquility.

"For what?"

"Getting me to open up to the Westmores today."

She turned to face him, flashing him a crooked smile. "So I'm forgiven for forcing your hand? For making you walk the plank with a gun at your head?"

He chuckled and touched her cheek. "I was pissed at the time. But… I know why you did it. And…" He let his wrist rest on her shoulder and bumped his forehead against hers. "Opening the wound has bled out a lot of poison. I can see that now."

Her spirits lifted. "So…what does that mean for…" *Us?* she wanted to say but opted for "Your future? Will you continue with counseling?"

He lifted a shoulder. "I don't know. It's all so…new. So much." His gaze dropped.

Framing his face with her hands, she tipped her chin up to meet his eyes. "Don't go backward now that you have taken the first step. At dinner you said you believed in me. Well, I believe in *you*."

Something powerful and poignant ghosted across his face, and he canted toward her.

Her heart swelling, Eva firmed her grip on his cheeks and rose on her toes to capture his lips with hers. She felt the shock that rippled through him, the sweet pleasure that swept to her core.

But then he planted a hand on her chest, and he levered away, shaking his head and rasping, "Eva, wait…"

And just like that, her heart crashed to her toes, and she realized how stupid she'd been. Just hours ago, he'd told her he didn't want what she wanted. At dinner, she'd warned herself to curb her feelings and manage her expectations. Then one staged romantic meal, one atmospheric stroll, one tender look from him, and boom! She'd let her unreasonable hopes lead her down a false path. She'd kissed him and made a fool of herself.

Carmine furrowed his brow and, with pity in his eyes, whispered, "Eva, I just—"

She didn't hang around to listen to his awkward apologies. She didn't want him to feel compelled to open his painful past again as he untangled himself from her. Again.

Tears of shame and embarrassment stung her eyes as she shook her head and stepped back from him. "No. You don't have to say it. I get it. I—"

Like a deer spooked from a meadow, she turned and fled. She didn't think about where she was going, as long as it was away from the soulful, hurting gaze of the man she'd fallen in love with despite her better judgment. She ran, following the path before her, zigging and zagging until the heel of her dress shoe snapped, and her ankle twisted as she stumbled.

She stopped to snatch off the broken shoe, muttering invectives. Glancing up, she gathered her focus enough to realize she'd wound up in the Ramble. The spiderweb of paths through the wooded section of the park was dark with shadows, and she took a moment to wipe her eyes and orient herself. She could hear the gurgle of the man-made stream that flowed through the nature preserve, but she'd lost track of which path she was on or which direction to go to get back to the restaurant. She wasn't panicked. Retracing her steps would be easy enough, but she didn't want to pass Carmine before she'd had sufficient time to regain her composure.

As she bent at the waist, hands on her knees to catch her breath, she heard footsteps. She raised her head, expecting to find that Carmine had followed her. A blur of movement in the trees to her left drew her attention. A small figure— clad in black, face obscured by a ski mask—darted out from behind a shrub…and lunged for her.

Chapter Sixteen

"Eva!" Carmine shouted as his partner darted away and disappeared into the dark wooded area just north of Bow Bridge. He muttered a curse under his breath. He'd handled that badly, given her the impression he didn't want to kiss her when, in truth, he had wanted her lips on his more than he'd wanted his next breath. But…

Damn. He didn't even know what the *but* was anymore. How could he want her so fiercely when his head was telling him it would be a mistake, that he'd hurt her? And he couldn't risk the pain of losing her the way—

Carmine slammed his hand on the bridge railing and cursed again as he realized where his track of thought had gone. Disgust pooled like acid in his gut. He was a coward. Had he backed away from Eva for her sake or for his? While he stewed and castigated himself, a shout came from up the path, in the direction Eva had run. And a fresh wave of dismay washed through him, leaving him chilled to the bone.

Eva had gone into one of the darkest, most secluded parts of the park. Alone. At night. Though capable and strong, as a woman, she was still a target of predators. And he hadn't gone after her.

EVA CRIED OUT in surprise as the black-clad assailant attacked her. Without more than a split-second warning, Eva didn't meet the attack with the defensive moves she'd learned at the police academy. She gasped as her assailant swung a switchblade toward her in an awkward arc. Eva twisted instinctively, dodging the thrust, but the tip of the blade caught her side at her ribs. The sound of tearing fabric told Eva the assailant had slashed her dress. Anger piled on top of the shock and adrenaline already coursing through her veins. When her attacker raised the knife to attempt another strike, Eva blocked the arc of the thug's arm. She shoved the blade up and delivered a knee to the assailant's gut.

Her attacker gave a feminine-sounding "oof" and quickly backpedaled. Eva blinked as an over-processed floral scent hit her nose, and she mentally recalculated. Her attacker was a woman?

"Eva!" Carmine's shout sent her attacker racing up the pedestrian walk, deeper into the dark wooded area.

Eva took a few stumbling steps in pursuit, then stopped long enough to kick off her other high-heeled shoe, which gave Carmine time to catch up.

"Eva!" He seized her by the arms and sized her up with a sweeping glance. "What happened?" he panted. "Are you okay?"

She wriggled in his grasp, pointing toward the shadowy woods. "She went that way!"

"Who?"

"Hurry! She'll get away!"

Carmine cursed and dropped to a crouch. "You're bleeding!"

"What?" She bent her head to look, and in the murky darkness, she could just see a dark stain spreading at the tear in her dress. She'd been so caught up in defending herself, adrenaline had apparently muted the sting that now blazed at her seeping wound.

"It's not deep." She tested the wound with her fingers and winced when she met the ripped flesh.

Carmine batted her hand away. "Don't touch it with dirty hands. Think about infection."

Agitated, Eva pointed toward the woods again. "Meantime, the woman who did this is getting away!"

Her partner gave the dark path a brief glance as he pulled the tail of his shirt from his dress pants and ripped off a strip. He folded the scrap of fabric and pressed it to her bleeding side. "Little chance we'll find her now. I'm more interested in getting you to an ER for stitches. Here. Hold this in place."

She did, arguing, "I'm fi—"

"This is Carmine DiRico of the 98th," Carmine said, his phone at his ear. "I need backup. A woman has been stabbed in the Ramble. Have an ambulance meet us at 77th and CPW."

Eva gasped as Carmine scooped her into his arms, cradling her against his chest. "What are you doing?"

"You can't walk back to the street with bare feet. Just pipe down, and let me do this for you, okay? I feel bad enough that I let this happen."

She growled, shoving down the urge to fight with him about blame and responsibility.

"You're sure it was a woman?" he said as he carried her back to the Bow Bridge.

"Pretty danged sure. She smelled like cheap perfume and had a high-pitched gasp when I kneed her."

Carmine paused long enough to collect his jacket and her clutch, which had both been left on the bridge railing. "You kneed her?"

Eva grimaced in frustration. "I'd have done more than that if I hadn't been caught off guard and dressed in this girlie getup. I could claw her eyes out just for ruining this dress. It cost a fortune, and I'd planned to wear it to my brother's wedding."

"Sean's?" Carmine asked as he shifted her in his arms, tucking her closer to his warmth and brawn.

Eva's breath hitched, and her thoughts scattered briefly. She hated to admit how good it felt to be held. To lay aside her need to prove herself and allow him to take care of her. To feel protected. To rest her head on his chest and just…be.

She swallowed hard and searched her brain for the answer he was waiting for. Brothers…weddings…

"Um, all three of them, it would seem." She gritted her teeth as the insult of losing her dress sank deeper. "Do you… suppose that could have been Maeve? Could she possibly have caught wind that we're on her trail?"

"You're the one who saw her. What did she look like?"

"Petite. That's about all I could see. It was dark, and she had a ski mask. Dang it! I had a feeling we were being followed!"

"So a planned attack, then, if she was protecting her identity."

"Mmm-hmm." She hummed, feeling a bit lightheaded now that the adrenaline in her blood was fading.

He jostled her. "Hey, no passing out. We're almost to the street. Hopefully, the ambulance is already there."

"I'm fine. I promise you, the cut's not deep. I bet I don't even need stitches." When he said nothing, she punched his shoulder. "Put me down! I don't need to go to the ER." She clung to Carmine's muscled shoulders as he hustled out of the park, and when he set her feet on the sidewalk along Central Park West, she swallowed a hiss of pain.

"Stubborn," he grumbled, keeping a shoulder under her arm to support her.

Knowing this could be her best chance to explain herself, she started, "I want to explain why—"

At the same moment, he said, "About the kiss—"

Before either of them could finish, a patrol officer jogged up to them, out of breath. "Are you DiRico?"

The wail of a siren signaled the ambulance's approach, and the matter of their kiss was stoved to a back burner.

DESPITE HIS BEST arguments to the contrary, Eva rejected Carmine's pleas that she go to the ER. The EMTs that arrived at Central Park West after his 911 call cleaned her cut and applied a butterfly bandage, which Eva deemed sufficient. Carmine knew the wound wasn't as serious as the blood had led him to believe. But when he considered how much worse things could have been if the knife had stabbed a couple of inches to the right or a little deeper...

Carmine shuddered. The attacker had clearly been going for her heart, but a punctured lung could have been devastating as well.

As he watched the EMTs treat Eva, the sights, sounds and smells of that day twenty-four years ago, when the medics had been unable to revive Rosa, paraded through his mind in macabre replay.

He stood back, scowling and his heart thundering anxiously as Eva signed the papers saying she'd declined transport to the hospital. She promised the EMT to visit a doctor to get an antibiotic to stave off infection.

The rest of the marriage-retreat group had returned to the yacht in the limo already. Carmine had contacted Orrin to let him know what had happened, and Orrin had just arrived. Now Eva approached them both, wearing Carmine's jacket around her shoulders. She clutched the lapels closed at her throat.

"Now do you believe us about the ice sculpture being set

up to fall on me? That maybe I really saw something nefarious on deck the first night of the cruise?" she asked Orrin.

Orrin pinched the bridge of his nose. "I don't know what to believe anymore. This is all so…unprecedented. Disturbing." He divided a look between the partners and, with troubled eyes, asked, "Do you have any reason to believe any of this is directed at me and Kitty? That someone is trying to destroy our reputation, taint the good name of our marriage retreat and scare away customers?"

"That someone being Maeve or an associate of Wes's?" Eva asked.

Orrin's frown deepened. "Yes."

She shook her head. "No. Not at this time. There's no evidence the incident on your yacht is related to our other investigations."

Orrin exhaled, clearly relieved by that news. "Well, if you're ready to return to the retreat—" He waved a hand toward the taxi queue.

Carmine hesitated, catching Eva by the arm. "Let me take you home. If you won't go to the hospital, I can at least take you to your apartment, where you can rest."

But, as he'd predicted, Eva shook her head, her expression firming with purpose and fire. "No chance. I'm sticking with this assignment until the end."

"Eva—" Carmine pinned her with a dark look.

Squaring her shoulders, she pulled Carmine a few steps away from Orrin and said, "I refuse to be scared off by this. This attack is related to what I saw that first night. I know it."

"Eva—"

"I've been targeted again, which smacks of someone trying to silence me. Somehow the guilty parties—plural, because clearly a woman is also involved with this—have learned we're getting close, and they're getting desperate. Maybe they got a tip about the Jane Doe that was found or that Emilio plans to give a statement. Or they learned our real identities or...*something*. But they're spooked. I want to go back to the yacht and look the rest of the retreat group in the eye and see who flinches."

"This is the second attempt on your life in two days. What if the third time's the charm?" A shard of ice speared Carmine's heart even as he asked the question.

"You're my partner. You have my back, right?"

He scowled. "Of course."

More than that, he'd step in front of a bullet to keep her safe. But an even better way to protect her would be to convince her to go home. Keep her tucked away, removed from the proximity of the threat.

"Then we're done here. I'm finishing this." Her jaw was set and her expression unyielding.

He could make one call to Sean or Captain Reeves and get her pulled from this undercover assignment. Hell, he outranked her. He could even make the call and send her home himself. But he also knew forcing that option on her would crush her spirit. Such high-handedness would be tantamount to betrayal to her. A full-fledged statement of no confidence in her abilities as a police officer. He'd be playing into the very hurdles that she'd obviously struggled to overcome her whole life. And she'd hate him for it.

Or maybe that was the solution to his conundrum, his unwise and growing attraction to her. He gritted his back teeth and glanced away from her penetrating gaze. *Attraction...* What an inadequate word to describe the roil of emotions and passions his fiery partner stirred in him. He sighed, relenting. "All right." He drilled her with a no-discussion look. "But no more heroics tonight. When we get back to the yacht, you rest. You can *look people in the eye and watch them flinch* in the morning."

She gave him a satisfied—almost smug—smile. "Deal."

Chapter Seventeen

Eva slept fitfully, her dreams haunted by images of black figures chasing her in dark mazes, of Carmine reaching for her then disintegrating into dust, of an ever-changing woman's face taunting her, only to vanish when she got close. When Carmine nudged her at seven o'clock the next morning, she groaned and draped an arm over her eyes. The movement tugged her wound, and she hissed in pain.

Sitting up carefully, she rubbed her eyes and met the worried knit in Carmine's brow. "I'm fine," she swore before he could ask—again.

She declined his offer to help her get dressed. Moving with care, she donned a fresh blouse and jeans, slicked her hair into a ponytail and headed out, sans makeup, to their last breakfast and group session. Once she fueled herself with coffee, she would be ready to confront whatever the day brought.

And she prayed that *whatever* would be closure. For the retreat murder case, for her information-gathering assignment. For her feelings toward Carmine.

Okay, she knew the latter would take more time, but she wanted to find some off-ramp that would take her in the right direction. If all the signs he'd put up weren't enough, last night's debacle on the Bow Bridge was a flashing streetlight, a clear signal he didn't want her the way she needed him to. Casual and temporary weren't enough for her, but that was all Carmine could do. She cared enough about him not to push him, not to torture him with regrets or consternation over his choice. She would hold her head high, smile at him and let him go with dignity...no matter how much it hurt.

Her stomach knotted as she and Carmine arrived at the breakfast buffet. Where she'd taken full advantage of the tempting spread the past mornings, she could barely stand to look at or smell the breakfast this morning. After selecting a plain bagel and pouring herself coffee, Eva took a seat next to Carmine and started her survey of the other couples.

Several heads had turned to stare at her as she took her place at the table. Carol Johnson gave her a quick smile, which Eva returned. Samuel and Allison Leech gave her furtive looks, then bent their heads close to whisper to each other. Bill and Molly Boone glanced her way, then continued eating, Molly simpering for her husband while feeding him a bite of her toast. Jamal and Linda Miller held her gaze, and Linda's was particularly dark with concern.

Zara Gupta left her seat to come over to Eva's. "Dina, oh my goodness! I heard you were attacked in the park last night! Are you all right?" Her gaze scanned up and down. "I mean, you're here, so...there's that. And I'm so glad, but... Gosh!"

Eva nodded and smiled at Zara. "I'll live. Thanks for asking." She cast a glance to the other faces gathered at the long table. "Once again, I am the center of gossip for the retreat, huh?"

Zara twisted her mouth into a teasing grin. "Well, since the McKinneys left yesterday, someone had to fill the gap, huh?"

Eva made a wry noise in her throat. "Lucky me."

"Glad you're okay. I'll let you eat now." Zara touched her arm and nodded to Carmine before she returned to her seat.

The McKinneys left yesterday, Eva mused. Could the troubled couple be the ones responsible for her attack? They'd had ample opportunity since they were no longer following the retreat schedule.

Carmine leaned close, asking in a low voice, "Anyone giving you a bad vibe?"

"Nothing that especially stands out. You?"

"Nothing new." He frowned at her bagel. "That all you're eating?"

"Yeah. Not feeling it today."

His expression reflected concern, but he said nothing. She could imagine he was blaming himself for her mood, so she said, "I ate so much last night at dinner. I'm still full, you know?"

Kitty clapped her hands and called for the group to gather for the last morning session, the "graduation."

Eva abandoned her bagel but carried her coffee to the circle of chairs, where, with a growing sense of urgency, she watched the others gather. She rubbed her sweaty hands on her jeans and chewed her bottom lip as Kitty welcomed the couples to the session with her usual warmth and energy.

"As we wrap up the retreat," Kitty said, "we'd like each couple to tell us the most valuable tip they learned, what changes they plan to incorporate in their marriages going forward. Okay?"

The couples murmured their assent, and Kitty turned to her right, where the Johnsons sat. "Todd and Carol, would you like to go first?"

"Wait," Eva blurted, even before she fully realized what she was doing. "Can I say something to the group first?"

Kitty gave her a startled look. When she sent a consulting glance to Orrin, he gave a reluctant nod, then sighed and waved a hand in permission.

Carmine's jaw tensed, and he cocked his head to the side, appraising her curiously, warily.

Heart thumping loud enough that she could barely think straight, Eva stood and met every face before saying, "I know I've been rather notorious this trip for many reasons. But here are the facts. I heard a couple arguing the first night. I heard a gun fired. I saw a man throw a woman overboard, and I told the authorities all of this. No one believed me then, and no forensic evidence was found to support my story." She paused. "At that time." She took a deep breath, carefully watching the couples' reactions to her speech. "But since then, another witness has been found."

The husbands and wives around the circle exchanged looks and whispered to each other.

"As you've all apparently heard already, I was attacked last night. Someone in Central Park tried to stab me. I don't believe this was random, and I don't intend to stop searching for my attacker until she is found and put behind bars for her crime."

A gasp rose around the circle.

"Yes. *She*. I'm almost certain the assailant was a woman. And I am coming for you. You can hide behind your ski mask and run off into the night like a coward, but you will not stay hidden for long. That, I promise you."

Again, she moved her stare from one face to the next around the circle. Kitty was pale and clearly flabbergasted. Orrin seemed irritated. She could understand that. She'd hijacked the final session and cast a pall over the meeting that was clearly supposed to be cheerful and celebratory.

Her fellow retreatants showed a mix of wide-eyed shock, dubious frowns and shared whispers.

When Kitty took the floor again, her voice trembled

slightly before she found her composure again. "Well, Dina... I hope...you do find some closure. But now...let's get back to the business of celebrating the great strides and tremendous achievements we've all experienced these past few days. You've all done so much great work with your partners, and we applaud you all!" She clapped and encouraged the group to join in.

Carmine leaned toward Eva. "Chumming the water?"

She met his keen gaze. "I had to do something. I thought if I rattled the cage a bit, someone would bite."

At Kitty's direction, the Johnsons rose to their feet and shared their favorite tip about how to forgive.

Eva heard the quiet buzz of a phone vibrating, and Carmine discreetly checked his screen. His brow beetled, and he sighed. "I should take this. Be right back," he whispered to Eva.

She opened her mouth to protest. She really wanted Carmine's eyes on the group, backing her up, catching things she might miss. But he slipped out of the room before she could stop him.

Orrin frowned, watching Carmine leave, and Eva gave a small shrug.

"Good work, Carol and Todd!" Kitty said. "Congratulations on graduating from the Westmore Marriage-Recovery Retreat! You are free to go and start your happily-ever-after!"

The group applauded, and the Johnsons gathered their belongings and left the circle, smiling and waving to the other couples.

Kitty took a deep breath, smiled. "Who's next?"

CARMINE WALKED OUT to the deck and answered the call from Captain Reeves. "DiRico. What can I do for you, Captain?"

"I have an interesting report sitting on my desk this morning. More than one, actually. I understand Eva Colton was injured last night by an assailant in the Ramble?"

"Yes. Afraid so. Not grievously, and she refused to go to the hospital. But—"

"And where were you when the attack happened? You are supposed to be working as a team, pretending to be married. Why was she alone?" Captain Reeves' tone was more curious than accusing, but Carmine felt a heavy responsibility and guilt that pierced to the bone.

"I *should* have been with her, and I regret my inattention. We had a…disagreement, and I was giving her time to clear her head."

"What sort of disagreement, Detective? We have policies and procedures in place for a reason. You two should have been on the same page."

"I, uh… Yes, ma'am."

"I'd intended for you and Officer Colton to continue partnering until Officer Mallard makes a full recovery from his mono. Will that be a problem?"

Carmine squeezed his eyes shut and dragged a hand over his face. "I don't know. Maybe. I—"

"Well, I'd like to see you both in my office first thing Monday morning to discuss it. Understood?"

"Yes, Captain."

"Which brings me to my second reason for calling. I am looking at the coroner's report on a Jane Doe that was pulled from the water day before yesterday. I think it might interest you."

Carmine perked up, his hand falling to the deck railing. He swallowed hard. "Did they make an ID?"

"They did. They matched her dental records and blood type."

He squeezed the railing, his pulse kicking. "So who is she?"

"I'VE LEARNED WHAT a lucky man I am to have this beautiful woman at my side," Bill Boone gushed, and Molly blushed.

Gag, Eva thought. She had nothing against happy couples or even PDAs, but for the entire cruise, Molly and Bill had been so sickeningly sweet on each other that she had to wonder why the heck they'd come on the cruise to start with. Preventive maintenance?

"And I'm a lucky woman," Molly said.

The group applauded, and Kitty extended her hands toward the Boones, smiling. "Bravo, friends. You graduate with honors and are excused to start your happily-ever-after!"

Eva glanced over her shoulder toward the dining room door. Carmine's call was taking a while. Or maybe she was just impatient to have him back, seeing as how the session was wrapping up quickly. Three couples had already left the circle.

As she turned back to the group, she caught one of Bill Boone's trademark scowls. How could a guy so ridiculously gushy with his wife be so flat-out surly, for no good reason, toward a virtual stranger? Molly and Bill stood and swept out of the room together, holding hands, heads bent close in quiet conversation.

Eva heaved a deep sigh, relieved to be rid of the little black cloud that was Bill Boone. As she turned her attention to the other couples, though, a chill swept down her spine. She gripped the edge of her chair, taking a beat to figure out what had triggered her sense that something was wrong.

She scanned the remaining couples again, taking another deep breath to find her composure, to concentrate…and it hit her. The lingering scent of cheap perfume. The same scent that had clung to her attacker last night. A tingle rushed over her skin, and the hair on her nape stood up. The smell had come from Molly Boone as she brushed past, leaving the room.

"OhmyGod," she whispered under her breath, jerking her gaze toward the door where the Boones had just exited. They'd been dismissed, were leaving the cruise, disembarking. She needed to stop them, question them before they could get away...

Where was Carmine? He needed to be with her for this. Eva shoved out of her seat and hurried to the door, checking both directions of the corridor. She caught a glimpse of Bill and Molly disappearing around a corner to the right. But no Carmine. *Damn!*

She trailed after the couple, walking quickly to catch up. "Molly?"

Knowing the couple's room was on the top deck, not too far from hers and Carmine's, Eva headed in that direction, up the first flight of stairs. Again, she glimpsed the Boones turning from the stairs to the third deck just as she reached the bottom of the flight. "Molly? Bill?" she called out louder. "May I have a word?"

Molly stopped, turned to glance behind her, her expression perturbed. Bill squared his stance and growled, "We have nothing to say to you."

"Well, I have questions for you," Eva said, mounting the steps two at a time. "I just need a minute."

Molly rolled her eyes but squeezed Bill's arm as if needing his support to keep her upright. "What?"

"Where were you two last night at ten p.m.?" Eva asked, a bit winded as she drew even with the couple.

She kept her gaze on Molly, guessing she would be the easiest to read.

"None of your damn business!" Bill said, his face a mask of disgust. "You really are the nosiest woman I ever met!"

Eva bristled and straightened her back. "The nosiest *cop*,

thank you very much." She reached in her back pocket and pulled out her badge. She'd taken it to breakfast knowing that, with the retreat ending, if she got a sniff of anything irregular, she no longer needed to hide her true identity. She flashed it at the Boones, and Molly's eyes widened. Bill tensed and growled a curse word.

"That's right. Jim McKinney was an ass, but his suspicions were right about us. My name's not Dina. It's Officer Eva Colton, New York City PD." She drilled Molly with her gaze. "Now let's try again. Where were you last night at ten?"

"We—here on the yacht, of course." She hiked up her chin and cut a side glance to Bill. "We had our turn at Tavern on the Green the night before."

"Can any of the other couples vouch for you?"

"I, uh…don't—" Molly stammered.

"Shut up, Nancy," Bill snapped, directing his glare at his wife now. "Don't say anything." He returned his dark eyes to Eva. "We don't have to answer anything."

Eva sighed. He was right of course. Legally, she couldn't compel him to explain anything, especially without reading him his rights, formally arresting him and providing him an opportunity to have a lawyer present. Then Bill's words replayed in her head. *Shut up, Nancy.*

She jerked her attention back to Molly. "Who are you? He called you Nancy."

The woman's face blanched, and Bill snarled a vile word as he seized Eva's arm. He jammed his nose close to hers as he grated, "You just couldn't leave well enough alone, could you?"

Eva blinked and tried to free her arm. "Let go of me!"

Instead, Bill's grip tightened.

With her free arm, Eva reach to the small of her back, under her shirt, where she'd tucked Betty. But before she could draw Betty out, Bill saw what she was doing and snatched the gun from her.

"Help me get her inside!" he barked, and Molly/Nancy flew into action. As he dragged her toward their cabin, he pressed Betty's muzzle to Eva's nape and hissed, "You shouldn't have pried!"

Chapter Eighteen

"The woman at the morgue is Molly Garner Boone, wife of William Boone," the captain said, and Carmine stilled.

"As in, the Bill and Molly on the couples' cruise with us?" he asked, a chill washing through him.

"The same. Except that whoever is with Bill is not his wife, because she is lying in a cooler downtown," Captain Reeves said. "Which begs the question, who is the woman with Bill Boone?"

"And how did Molly end up in the river?" Carmine asked before instantly realizing the answer. "Oh, hell. Eva saw Bill murder his wife, didn't she? She was right." The cold that had penetrated his bones upon learning the Jane Doe's identity was replaced with a burning sense of urgency. He had to find Bill Boone and his accomplice ASAP.

"Can you get an arrest warrant—" he started, and Captain Reeves cut him off.

"An officer from the local precinct is already on the way, as well as Detective Colton. Not his jurisdiction, but he insisted on providing you and Officer Colton backup."

WITH MOLLY/NANCY'S HELP, Bill muscled Eva into their stateroom, and they slammed the door shut. Eva worked to keep her head. Her stomach churned sourly with self-reproach for allowing Bill to disarm her. A cardinal sin for a cop. A rookie mistake that could cost her her life. Squelching the distracting, guilty self-dialogue, she focused on remedying the situation. She could employ some of the techniques she'd learned to subdue a suspect, sure. But if she did, she risked Bill opening fire. Perhaps as long as Bill thought he had the upper hand, he'd be more willing to talk. Perhaps even to gloat?

"What are you going to do with her?" Molly/Nancy asked, her body twitching and clearly agitated.

"Well, we can't let her talk. Obviously. She knows too much." He made a growling sound deep in his throat.

Molly/Nancy bobbed her head in grim agreement.

"And yet, if you shoot me, there'll be forensic evidence everywhere. You'll be in custody for murdering a cop by lunchtime," Eva said. She angled her head toward Bill, presenting a casual, curious tone. "I've been meaning to ask, how *did* you manage to murder your wife—I'm assuming it was your wife, right?—without leaving any evidence behind? That was a master play. Quite impressive, I must say."

"Planning," Nancy said, her expression morphing into a smug smile. "We injected Molly with ketamine that I stole from work, so she couldn't effectively fight back. She was basically a large rag doll by the time Bill rolled her overboard."

"Nancy! Shut. Up!" Bill grated. "Are you crazy?"

Nancy shrugged and sneered. "If we're going to kill her, it's not like she's going to tell anyone. And our plan really was quite brilliant. I'm proud of our genius. It was foolproof." She leaned close to snarl in Eva's face, "Until *she* interfered!"

"Take this," Bill said, shoving the gun into Nancy's hand. "Like she said, we can't shoot her here, but if she gives a hint of trouble, cold cock her." He pulled a duffel bag from the tiny closet and dug around in it. "I'll inject her like I did

Mol. But we gotta hurry. Someone will come looking for her soon, and we need to be cleared out of here by then."

"Plane to catch?" Eva said, raising a defiant eyebrow.

Nancy held the gun against Eva's temple and backed her against the wall. "As a matter of fact, yes. Now that we've convinced everyone at the retreat that we are Molly and Bill Boone, happy couple, we've bought ourselves alibis and time to get to Bolivia, where we will be safe from extradition."

Eva considered telling Nancy that the authorities had found a body—one she was now more sure was Molly—but decided to keep that ace up her sleeve. As long as Nancy thought they might still get away with their crime and silencing Eva, she seemed eager to brag on her 'genius.'

Eva's mind spun, estimating the best way to glean more information from her abductors, when to use her skills to disarm Nancy, how long it would take Carmine to figure out where she was and come looking for her...

Her pulse was ragged, and she battled to process all her options and the information she was gaining without losing all control of the situation.

"So you drugged her and threw her overboard. No blood that way. That was...clever." She scrunched her nose as if confused. "But I'm sure I heard a muzzled gunshot."

Even as she said this, she considered what might have happened to the weapon. Did Bill have a gun stashed somewhere he could pull after she disarmed Nancy of Betty?

"The gun was supposed to just scare Molly into compliance. It went off by accident when they were struggling at the railing."

Emilio had said he saw the dark-clad person throw something into the harbor. The gun? "And the cops didn't find the pistol or silencer because you tossed them both overboard too. Right?"

Bill jerked his head up, clearly startled she knew this. "Good guess."

"Logical guess. Like I said earlier to the group, there's another witness who's coming forward today."

Bill pulled a small vial from the duffel bag and took a syringe from a paper sack. His jaw hardened as he uncapped the syringe with his teeth and spit it out onto the floor. "No matter. We'll be on that flight south in a couple hours." He jabbed the needle into the vial and drew up a large amount of the liquid.

Eva's heart leaped. Info-gathering time had passed. Time to regain possession of Betty and claim control of this situation.

Keeping her eyes on the approaching needle, as not to give away her intent, Eva dropped to a crouch, then slammed her full weight against Nancy's knees. As Nancy toppled off-balance, an ear-shattering blast ricocheted through the cabin.

CARMINE'S HEART JOLTED when he heard the gunshot reverberate from somewhere nearby. He raced back to the dining room, his pulse galloping. When he stormed into the meeting space, he scanned the chairs, looking for the Boones. For Eva. But all three were missing.

The faces of the other retreatants said they'd clearly heard the gunshot as well.

"Where's Eva? Where are the Boones?" he shouted to Kitty and Orrin.

"They left. Several minutes ago." Orrin frowned. "Carmine, what's h—"

Carmine didn't hang around to answer questions. He charged out of the dining room and down the corridor, opposite the direction he'd just come. Two attempts had already been made on his partner's life because of what she'd seen. He could only pray he wasn't already too late to save her from the Boones' third try.

EVA USED THE precious seconds after the gun fired—while Nancy and Bill were stunned and reassessing—to pin Nancy to the floor. She easily overwhelmed the startled woman and disarmed her. With Betty back in her possession, she aimed the weapon first at Nancy, warning her, "Stay down! Don't move!"

Nancy held up her hands in compliance and gaped at Eva. The telltale shift of Nancy's gaze gave Bill's approach away and, re-aiming Betty, Eva spun around to face the man. "Freeze!"

He had the syringe ready and, ignoring her warning, he lunged.

At the same time, Nancy surged up from the floor, grabbing Eva from behind, and in the next instant, she felt the prick and sting of a needle, a cool liquid injected under her skin.

No! Eva's heartbeat tripped, realizing she'd been drugged. Already she could feel her head spinning, her muscles growing weak. She only had seconds before she'd collapse and be at the mercy of this murderous couple.

With her last moments of clarity, she sorted her priorities. She couldn't fight them both, but she could summon help. She aimed for the ceiling and fired. Once. Twice. Three times before Bill wrested Betty from her.

Eva's knees buckled, and as she wilted against Bill, images flickered in her mind. The ones she loved. Her brothers. Her friends. Carnegie.

Carmine.

Her eyes grew unfocused, and she battled to stay conscious, muttering, "Carmine…"

MORE GUNFIRE RENT the morning and, taking his sidearm from the shoulder holster hidden under his windbreaker, Carmine hastened his pace, mounting the stairs to the second floor in great bounds. "Colton!" He did a cursory check of the second-deck corridor before sprinting to the stairs again. "Eva!"

Where was she? Where had the gunfire come from?

The idea of losing Eva because he'd been inattentive—had left her side when he *knew* someone on this damn yacht had tried twice to kill her—sickened him.

Rosa's pale face as she bled out on the street flickered in his mind's eye. *Not again! Not again! Not freaking again!*

"Eva!"

The woman in the morgue was Molly Boone. So Bill Boone... Damn! Why hadn't he seen it?

He topped the stairs and raced to their cabin. Some part of his brain was praying, negotiating, even as he fought to stem his panic. If he could just save this woman he loved, he'd do anything—*anything*—not to lose her...

He flung open their stateroom door. Empty.

Carmine barked a curse word in frustration and rising desperation. Then, somewhere nearby, angry voices cut into his recriminations. He hurried back out to the corridor. Empty.

He followed the sound of the bickering voices, his pace quick and silent. His weapon ready. As he stepped around the corner, he spotted a couple at the railing across the deck. "Police! Get on the ground!"

Bill Boone glanced over his shoulder, but not before he shoved a limp body over the railing. Carmine heard the splash, and the truth hit him as if he'd been dunked in ice water.

Eva!

He was too late.

Chapter Nineteen

The New York harbor closed over Eva's head, dark and cold. And terrifying. Because while she knew she needed to kick, to swim, she couldn't get her limbs to respond.

Weak. Helpless. Sinking.

She'd had just enough wherewithal as she was hoisted over the railing to take a breath. Hold it. But not enough. Already her lungs burned. She needed air.

Don't panic... But fear clawed at her.

Don't give up... But the need to inhale was a throbbing, clamoring, desperate animal inside her.

Don't die... But the drug in her veins, the water sucking her down, the darkness closing in were stronger...

CARMINE RACED TO the railing, his lungs frozen with horror. Eva's russet hair and white shirt quickly faded from view as she sank.

"You're next, man," Bill said, producing a gun. Eva's sidearm, Carmine realized, recognizing the NYPD standard-issue Glock 19 pistol Boone aimed at him.

Rage flooded Carmine's blood as he pointed his own weapon at Boone's center mass. He didn't have time to muck around with Bill Boone or his accomplice, whoever the hell she was. Eva hadn't resurfaced, was drowning…if she wasn't already dead.

His mind flinched away from that thought, unwilling to entertain that possibility.

"Drop the weapon, damn you! Right now!" Carmine growled.

The woman who wasn't Molly scuttled behind Bill. "Just shoot him, Bill, and let's get out of here! We can still make our flight!"

But Carmine could hear the ticking of the clock that was Eva's time in the water. He couldn't wait through a standoff with this jerk until his backup arrived. Eva needed help *now*.

Gritting his teeth, he charged Bill. He shoved the pistol Bill clutched up as the other man squeezed the trigger. The shot flew wild, and Carmine tackled his opponent. He had a weight, strength and hand-to-hand skill advantage that made disarming Boone no real challenge. Once he had the pistol, he tossed it overboard, where Bill couldn't regain it. Then he clambered quickly to his feet.

As he ripped off his shoes and jeans, he glared at Bill and the woman. "You better pray Eva's not dead. 'Cause if she is, I won't wait for the courts to get justice for her."

Swinging his legs over the railing, he dove into the frigid harbor. The cold hit him like a freight train. Shocking. Numbing. But for Eva, he closed his mind to his own discomfort.

Carmine could see little beneath the murky water. Though the sun provided some light near the surface, the deeper water was nearly opaque. He kicked and pulled at the water, searching left and right as he swam deeper. A flash of color drew his attention and, his heart squeezing, he headed toward it.

A plastic grocery bag. *Damn it!*

He kicked away from the trash and scanned the depths again, knowing he'd need to take a breath soon but not wanting to take even those few seconds away from looking for Eva. If he needed air, how much worse off was she? Finally, common sense ruled. He couldn't save her if he didn't get another breath, and another—as many as it took until he found her...

On his second deep dive, though, he saw the white of her shirt, like a ghost drifting beneath the sea. He swam toward her, using all his strength to fight the current and reach her before he lost sight of her, before he needed more air.

Once he'd hooked his arms under hers, he executed several scissors kicks to propel them to the surface. He gasped in a lungful of oxygen as they emerged...but Eva did not. She was frighteningly still, disturbingly limp, excruciatingly unresponsive.

Carmine's heart twisted painfully as he fought to keep her head above the waterline.

"Nononono!" The wail was a prayer that he repeated when all other thought and language failed him. Even as he treaded water, struggling to keep them both at the surface, he covered her mouth with his and blew his breath into her. Once. Twice. Again.

"Come on, Eva. Please!"

The sound of shouts behind him called his attention to the yacht. A few people were gathered at the first-deck railing, and Orrin tossed a life preserver ring into the water, a couple of feet from where Carmine was treading.

A few strokes later, Carmine grasped the life preserver and pulled it over Eva's head. He tugged the ring lower so that Eva ended up draped over the foam. He gave Orrin a wave, telling him to start towing the rope in.

Carmine pounded Eva's back as they were hauled through the waves back to the edge of the yacht. Water gushed from her mouth and nose.

By the time they'd been tugged to the side of the *West-*

mores' Folly, a rubber life raft had been dropped, and Aanan Gupta had jumped into the water to assist Carmine in hoisting Eva into the raft. Aanan pressed two fingers to Eva's throat. "She has a pulse. Give her breaths."

Carmine did. He'd give her his oxygen, his blood, his very life if she would just open her beautiful emerald eyes again and show him one of her sassy Colton smiles. Working like an automaton, training kicking in, he bent over her, pinched her nose closed and sealed his mouth over hers. He could not think about the times he'd had his mouth on hers in passion rather than lifesaving mode, or he wouldn't be able to function. Still, his body trembled as he blew air into her lungs. One. Two. Three.

"DiRico!" The shout from above drew Carmine's glance. Sean Colton leaned over the railing of the yacht, pointing out a rescue litter being lowered toward them. Then Sean's face morphed into a mask of horror when he spotted his sister. "Eva!"

Guilt sliced through Carmine. He'd failed to keep Sean's sister safe, just as he'd failed to keep Rosa safe. Bile rose in his throat, but he swallowed hard, forcing down the bitterness, and bent to give Eva more air.

Breathe. Count five. Breathe.

"Please, please, please, God, don't take the woman I love!" he whispered raggedly, then Carmine's whole body stilled when he realized what he'd said, recognized the truth of it. He *loved* Eva Colton. How could he have ever thought he could walk away from that?

Chapter Twenty

Carmine continued giving resuscitating breaths while Aanan caught the rescue-litter basket and lined it up next to Eva on the raft.

"Okay, ready to transfer her," Aanan said. "I'll get her legs."

Carmine's chest contracted. He knew turning Eva over to the emergency crews who'd arrived via the Coast Guard was in Eva's best interest, yet...

He didn't want to let her go. A cold fear deep in his core told him when he let her go, it would be for the last time.

He closed his eyes and saw Rosa being loaded into the back of an ambulance. Heard the slam of the ambulance-bay doors. Tears burned his eyes as, counting five beats in his head, he leaned close to Eva's ear and whispered fiercely, "I need you to fight, sweetheart. Please fight. Forgive me for being so stupid and give me another chance?" He kissed her forehead, gave her another rescue breath, then nodded to Aanan. "Go."

But when he hooked his arms under Eva's to transfer her into the litter, water sputtered from her mouth.

Eva coughed. Expelled more water...and sucked in a rasping breath.

"IF YOU *EVER* scare us like that again," Liam said, frowning at Eva as he hovered over her hospital bed, "I swear on all things holy, I will kill you!"

Eva gave her brother a weak, sarcastic grin. "Well, if that isn't the pot lecturing the kettle." She paused to take a slow, careful breath. "We worried about your shenanigans for years, big bro."

Liam bent to kiss the top of her head and narrowed a softer look on her. "Seriously, Eva. Too close for comfort."

"Agreed," she whispered, her throat raw.

Liam glanced around the room at the other friends and family gathered to visit her. "And where's the man of the hour? I wanted to shake Carmine's hand and thank him personally for rescuing you."

Me too, Eva thought with a sharp pang in her chest that had nothing to do with her struggling lungs.

Emily and Cormac shared a chair, and Kara sat in the next seat over, checking her phone and texting with other friends in their circle.

"Haven't seen him. Last I heard, he was still at the yacht, assisting with the arrest and processing of Bill Boone and his girlfriend," Cormac said. "Same with Sean. But it's only been three hours. I'm sure they'll both be by before long."

The last was said primarily for her benefit, Eva was sure. Was she that transparent? She'd tried to pretend that simply surviving her near drowning and knowing Bill and Nancy had been arrested was enough to ease her mind and give her reason to smile. And she was grateful for both miracles. Immensely. But a foggy memory tortured her, a rasping voice begging her to fight, asking for a second chance. Had that been real or a drugged and near-death delusion? She dared not hope that Carmine had changed his mind. She didn't have the strength to battle heartache on top of the ill effects of having sucked the filthy New York harbor into her lungs.

Her doctors were optimistic she'd have no lasting damage, but she had a date with a hyperbaric chamber later in the day.

"How's the patient?" Sean said, stepping into the room with a vase of flowers in his hand.

"Speak of the devil," Liam said.

Eva cast her gaze to the open doorway, hoping Carmine was with her brother. But Sean was alone.

Sean arched an eyebrow as he divided a look to the room. "Should my ears be burning?"

Emily rose from Cormac's lap to take the flowers from Sean and set them next to the many others that had arrived in the last hour. Like in a small town, news traveled fast through the precinct when real-time reports were broadcast on police radios.

"If you're here, does that mean the Boones have been processed?"

"Boone, singular," Sean said. "The woman with Bill Boone was his lover, Nancy Calhoun. And yes, they've been booked for the night in a holding cell and will be arraigned first thing in the morning on a host of charges, including the murder of Molly Boone, conspiracy to commit murder, and three charges of attempting to murder Eva—the falling ice sculpture, the stabbing in Central Park and today's near drowning." He ticked the crimes off on his fingers as he recounted them. "Plus numerous related charges. They're not going anywhere but Rikers."

"Are they cooperating?" Eva asked.

"A bit. Lawyered up right now, but the evidence we're getting from their stateroom, the Boone home and Nancy's computer is pretty substantial. Molly made the marriage-retreat reservation, and Bill and his lover turned it into a murder plot. It's sick."

"I got a confession and some details before I was drugged."

She paused and took a painful breath. "I'm ready to make a statement whenever—"

"Your statement will keep until you've done a whole lot more healing and resting," Sean said, his finger aimed at her. "Your job right now is to get better. That's an order from your boss, rookie." The words were stern, but his tone was pure brotherly love and concern.

"All right, all right!" She smiled before adding, *"Sir."*

Cormac pulled a face. "Ooh, that's gotta hurt. Baby sister having to concede rank to Sean?"

Eva rolled her eyes and gave a small nod that tugged the oxygen cannula at her nose. "Only at work, though. At home, all bets are off." She gave Sean a grin, then drew her brow into a frown. "Speaking of work, what else have you learned about Maeve's involvement with Humphrey?" She paused to take a breath, cough. "Any other alibis for her panning out?"

Sean rubbed the back of his neck. "We can talk about all of that later. Did you not just hear me say to rest?"

"But—"

"Rest!" her brothers all said at once.

TEN DAYS LATER, Eva woke to a hungry cat in her face and a hollow ache in her heart. In the week and a half since her near drowning, she hadn't seen Carmine once. He'd texted several times, checking on her, and she'd used those opportunities to ask how he was as well...and where he was. Sean had reported to her that Carmine had asked for a few days off, without any explanation other than he'd needed some personal time.

Her phone calls and voice mail to Carmine went unanswered. And so she'd quit calling. She wouldn't badger him. He'd texted he was fine and glad to know she was making a full recovery. Then...radio silence.

Pushing her covers, her cat and her heartache aside, Eva

swung her feet to the floor and enjoyed a full-body stretch before stumbling to the kitchen. She fed Carnegie, took an extra minute scratching his head—dang, she'd missed her little buddy while on assignment and in the hospital—then started coffee brewing and took a shower. Today was her first day back at the precinct, and she didn't want to be late.

When she made it to her desk in the squad room, bagel-and-egg sandwich in hand, her fellow officers stopped what they were doing to applaud. Eva raised her head and blinked her surprise, meeting shouts of "Welcome back, rookie!" and good-natured ribbing about being "thrown in the deep end" or being "in over her head" with her last assignment.

"Hey!" Sean's voice boomed from behind her. "A little sensitivity, people! She nearly died. Have you considered she might still be dealing with that trauma?"

Her colleagues ducked their collective heads, clearly chastened, and got back to work.

Facing her brother, she muttered, "Thanks, Sean. But I'm okay. Really."

He gave her an appraising scrutiny. "You're sure?"

"One hundred percent." She cast a glance to the empty desk next to hers, then spotted a familiar coffee mug. "Has Mitch returned?"

"Yeah. Today is his first day back. Like you."

She gave her brother a weak smile. "Oh. Glad to hear he's feeling better."

"But…" Her brother paused dramatically and raised his eyebrows "He's only here on desk duty and to fulfill his two weeks' notice. Mallard is retiring." She goggled at her brother and was still processing that stunning news when he added, "Carmine is back today too." Sean's tone was gentle, as if he understood the fragile nature of her relationship with Carmine.

"Oh. Okay." She tried to sound blasé, but her voice broke, giving away the quaking that had started at her core.

"He's in the conference room," Sean said, hitching his chin toward the corridor. "I came to get you. A lot has happened in the last few hours, and I want my team up to speed." He flicked a finger to her sandwich. "Bring your breakfast. I'm ready to start the meeting."

Eva's stomach clenched, and she set the bagel on her desk. Somehow the thought of seeing Carmine again stole her appetite. Wiping her hands on her uniform pants, she followed Sean to the conference room, where Captain Reeves, Mitch Mallard, Carmine, Cormac and his fiancée, ADA Emily Hernandez, along with Liam's girlfriend, CSI tech Ellie Mathers, were already gathered.

"I would've been stuck on desk duty for the rest of my career as a precaution, so I just turned in my notice," Mitch was complaining. "But at least I'm out of bed, and my throat no longer feels like it's on fire. I can freelance as a PI or something."

Eva met Carmine's gaze as she took a chair across the conference table from him. He sent her a quick half smile before turning his attention to Sean as he started the meeting.

"So…" Sean cracked his knuckles and swept his gaze around the table. "Interesting developments this morning in the Wes Westmore case, which could have significant ramifications in our search for Humphrey Kelly as well."

Eva tried to ignore the disquieting presence of the man she'd come to love in recent weeks and concentrate on what Sean was saying. In her chest, her heart drummed so loud she was sure the others in the meeting could hear it.

Focus, Eva. This distraction was exactly why a relationship between coworkers was a bad idea. One reason of many why she had to forget Carmine and move on with her life.

"When I came into my office this weekend to do paperwork, I opened Wes Westmore's case file again to review it in light of recent discoveries about his mother and Humphrey Kelly, and…" Sean paused, frowning, then took a stack of stapled pages from the file in front of him and slapped them on the table with a disgruntled sigh. "And I found this."

Emily, who was closest to the stack, took one and slid the extra copies to the rest of the group. Eva picked up her copy and started reading. The heading read, "Psychiatric Evaluation Report: Wes Westmore."

"I find Mr. Westmore to be a man of passions and convictions," she read aloud. "His steadfast determination for success is a key driving factor behind his work ethic and in his personal life. He exhibits a firm grasp of reality and conducts himself in a calm and controlled fashion in all circumstances." Eva frowned, and her stomach turned as the unbelievable report continued, contradicting so many of the conclusions she and the team had drawn. "In our evaluation session, he has demonstrated both a deep compassion for his fellow man and appreciation for the fragility of life."

"What the hell?" Mitch said.

"In my estimation," Cormac read, picking up where Eva left off, his tone incredulous, "it is not in Wes Westmore's nature to exhibit uncontrolled anger, and he does not have the tendency toward violence as has been alleged. In my view, Wes Westmore is not capable of domestic violence, animal cruelty *nor any manner of assault or homicide*?" Her brother's voice rose, reflecting his growing disbelief as he read the shocking paragraph. Cormac slapped the pages onto the table with a snort. "What quack wrote this piece of fiction?"

Sean's eyes were dark, his mouth grim. "Humphrey Kelly. His signature is on the last page."

Paper rustled as everyone at the table flipped to the incriminating signature, an official-looking ink stamp and Humphrey's office address.

Eva's hands shook as she flipped back to the first page, staring at the strange report while her mind churned. "I don't understand. Has Humphrey reappeared? Did he conduct this evaluation of Wes at Rikers?"

Sean was shaking his head. A muscle in her brother's jaw twitched. "Check out the date the report was submitted."

Again, papers rattled as the team flipped to find the information in question.

"February?" Emily said, her timbre as confused as everyone else's.

Captain Reeves leaned forward, her gaze pinned on Sean. "Detective Colton, why are you only now bringing this information to light? Did you not think something of this magnitude was relevant to Westmore's prosecution?"

Sean was, by all appearances, unconcerned about his boss's rebuke. His eyes blazed as he said, "Because this report was not in my file before Sunday afternoon when I found it."

A murmur rose around the table.

"He's right," Mitch said. "This wasn't in the files when I went on leave with my mono. I've never seen this report before."

"So you're saying…?" Carmine said, leaving the rest open for Sean.

"I'm saying this glowing report—stating that our number-one suspect in Lana Brinkley's murder is not capable of murder and allegedly written by our missing man, Humphrey Kelly, who was spotted on the street in February with Wes Westmore's disguised mother—was *not* in my file until I opened it yesterday."

The room fell silent as everyone digested this strange and highly suspicious turn of events.

"You're sure?" Emily asked, her expression dumbstruck.

Sean's granite jaw reflected the gravity of the situation.

"I've been through this file a thousand times in the last few months, as have all of you. I know the information in it backward and forward. It wasn't there."

Eva flopped back in her chair, her mind whirling. "Which raises the question of how it got in your file now. Is it real? Who put it there?"

"All good questions, Officer Colton," Sean said. "Ideas?"

LEANING IN TO prop his elbows on the table, Carmine steepled his fingers as he processed the new information and its implications. He caught Eva watching him, though she averted her eyes as soon as he raised his gaze to hers. Concentrating on this suspicious twist in Wes Westmore's case was difficult knowing the talk he needed to have with Eva later today. So much was at stake, and he honestly had no clue which direction things would break.

"I'll talk to the IT department about reviewing the precinct's online security. If someone hacked into our digital case files, we need to stop that leak ASAP." Captain Reeves turned to Sean. "Detective, you need to let Forensics examine your laptop and office."

"Consider it done," Ellie Mathers said. "He alerted me to the need for a sweep of his office prior to this meeting."

Carmine raised his index finger to catch Sean's attention. "Detective Colton, if I may?"

"Please," Sean said, giving Carmine the floor.

"In the past few days, I've spent a good bit of time talking with Orrin Westmore, Wes's uncle, about…well, a lot of things." He shot a quick look to Eva and took a breath before continuing. She'd learn soon enough what his conversations with Orrin had covered. "Including Orrin's insistence that his brother Joseph's death wasn't an accident. Orrin is convinced Wes's mother, Maeve, intentionally fed him the shrimp that caused his anaphylactic reaction and delayed calling an ambulance until she knew Joseph wouldn't survive."

"Right," Sean said, nodding. "You and Officer Colton reported his suspicions while on your undercover assignment. Do you have something new?"

Carmine rubbed his chin, turning over everything he knew about the Westmores' history, about the mysterious new pysch eval on Wes, the sighting of Humphrey with Maeve...

"I think Maeve is a black widow," Carmine said.

"A what?" Mitch Mallard asked, frowning.

"Female black widow spiders are so named because after they mate, they've been known to kill the male and eat him," Eva explained.

"I know that," Mitch said with a snide look for Eva that raised Carmine's hackles.

"I'm saying," Carmine continued, "that after a lot of thought in the last few weeks and a lot of searching for Maeve under a new alias, I believe she plotted and killed Joseph Westmore, had her escape and a new identity ready and waiting. And if she's done it once, she could have done it again. And again. Maybe we can't find her trail because she's taken pains to hide it. To hide other crimes."

"An interesting theory," Cormac said, "especially if Orrin's instincts about his brother's death are correct."

"And if she *is* that devious and smart and evil," Eva said, her nose scrunched in thought, "Wes could have learned her tricks. *Or...*" Her tone brightened as if she had a better idea. "She could be helping him get away with Lana's murder. She could have found a way to hack the case files to insert this false psych report, or..." She turned her hand up as her voice trailed off, her brow wrinkling as she continued turning ideas over.

"Or she could not only be behind Humphrey Kelly's disappearance," Carmine said, meeting Sean's eyes, knowing how the Coltons hated to hear the possibility that Kelly wasn't the man they remembered, "she could be manipulating Kelly. She could have her fangs sunk into him, planning to use him to win Wes's release, then add him to her list of victims."

Eva sighed heavily, muttered a curse. "She *did* wear a disguise and use an alias to visit Wes in prison. This could be a bigger conspiracy than we had any idea. It could have branches and roots we have yet to uncover."

Sean scrubbed both hands over his face, growling his frustration. Cormac tossed his pen onto the table and spread his hands. "Okay, so what's the next move?"

A silent tension filled the room until Eva said quietly, "Sean, Cormac?"

Her brothers turned their gazes to her, as did the rest of the room.

Eva said tentatively, "What if we brought in…unofficial outside help?"

Sean studied her carefully. "Go on."

"Deirdre and/or Aidan?" she said.

"And these people are…?" Captain Reeves asked, dividing a glance between Eva and Sean.

"Our second cousins. Deirdre is with the FBI and her brother Aidan is with the US Marshals," Eva said.

Mitch snorted a laugh. "Your family does love law enforcement, don't they?"

"You got a problem with that, Mallard?" Cormac asked, and Mitch raised his hands deferentially. Her brother then met her eyes. "I like the idea, for what it's worth. Though I understand the decision has to be made internally." He motioned to Captain Reeves and Sean. "Having feds involved, even unofficially, expands the scope of the investigation in a way that seems prudent."

Sean turned in his chair to face Captain Reeves. "What do you think?"

"I can call Deirdre as soon as right now," Eva said lifting her phone.

Captain Reeves took a deep breath and flipped up a palm. "I'm not going to turn down any help that an outside source is willing to volunteer."

"That sounds like a yes to me," Eva said, thumbing the dial icon to call her cousin. When a sleepy-sounding voice answered the call, she frowned. "Deirdre? Did I wake you?"

"Not a problem. Just sleeping in since I can. What's up?"

"You're on vacation?" Eva asked, feeling a bit guilty for asking her cousin to work during her time off.

"Not exactly. On enforced leave while the higher-ups decide what to do with me after I refused to follow orders."

"Um," Eva fumbled. At one time, she'd have found such disobedience unforgivable. But after working with Carmine and having followed hunches of her own recently, she was beginning to see the shades of gray in law enforcement. Her gaze drifted to Carmine's as if of its own volition and met his dark eyes. Her heart contracted, and she almost missed her cousin's next comment.

"It's all good. The sleazeball was arrested and is off the streets. That's what matters to me. I'll bounce back. So is there a reason for this call?"

"Right. There is." Eva explained the main points of the case and the help they needed finding Maeve and Humphrey. "If you have some time to help—"

"If I have time?" Deirdre laughed. "Eva, I've got nothing but time right now. You're doing me a favor, giving me something productive to do while I'm on leave. Of course I'll help!"

Eva smiled and nodded to the room. "Thanks, Deirdre. I'll call you back with more specifics once this team meeting wraps up." She disconnected and waved a hand. "Voilà. Done deal."

Sean bobbed a nod. "Great job, rookie."

After making specific assignments for the next steps in the case, including Eva liaising with Deirdre, Captain Reeves dismissed the meeting, and everyone scattered to get to work.

Except Carmine. He rounded the conference table and caught Eva by the arm before she could leave. With a glance toward the door, waiting until everyone else had left, he said, "Got a sec?"

Her stomach twirled, and she found it suddenly hard to breathe. "Well, I… I need to call my cousin back."

"I just need a minute, but…maybe not here." He glanced through the open door to the bustling squad room. "Can I buy you lunch? Maybe take something to eat in the park?"

Eva swallowed hard, wavered. She refused to raise her expectations only to have them crushed again. But the plea in Carmine's eyes was so heartfelt and commanding she found herself saying, "Okay. Noon?"

His cheek twitched with a grin. "Noon."

Eva returned to her desk but found it nearly impossible to concentrate. She reviewed information in the system about the string of charges filed against Bill Boone and Nancy Calhoun, reassuring herself that the case against the couple was proceeding without a glitch. It was.

She called the Rikers Island facility to see if Wes had had any new visitors or a repeat visit from Maeve, a.k.a. Myra Smith. No Myra Smith, but one of his groupies had made a return visit. Eva made a note to do a deeper dive on the young woman, just in case.

She started the paperwork detailing her notes from the undercover assignment and what Orrin and Kitty had shared.

And she watched the clock, waiting impatiently—yet anxiously—for noon.

At five minutes before twelve, her cell rang. Seeing Deirdre's number, Eva's pulse leaped as she answered. "Hey, you. Whatcha got?"

"Well, I fed all the details you gave me about Maeve O'Leary and her late husband's death into a search on the dark web, and a few things pinged. Then I cross-referenced that info and ran some facial-recognition software and plied a few other tricks I keep up my sleeve, and boom! I tracked down another alias and dead husband for Maeve O'Leary."

Eva rocked back in her chair. "So she is a black widow."

Carmine had been right.

"Seems so," Deirdre said. "I also have an address of the dead husband's son. Seems he's a rancher in Montana."

"Do you think this rancher could have any information about where Maeve is now, what she's up to?" Eva's mind spun in a hundred directions at once. Finally, they'd caught a whiff of Maeve's trail!

"I intend to find out. I've booked a flight to Montana, and I'm heading out now to buy myself some cowboy boots."

As she disconnected with her cousin, Eva's gaze flew to Carmine's empty desk, then to Sean's closed office door. Wait until they heard this!

A check of her laptop clock told her she was already late to meet Carmine. Tucking her cell phone in her purse, she pushed back from her desk and hurried to the precinct's front steps. Her heart in her throat, she searched the stairs, the sidewalk in front of the precinct, until she spotted Carmine standing beneath a shade tree near the parking lot. She hurried over to him, sending an apologetic smile as she approached. "I got an important call right as I was leaving."

"No apologies needed. Well, except from me..." He sighed. "For not coming to the hospital and..."

Pain raked through her. She didn't want to have this conversation. Especially not at work. She flashed a stiff smile. "It's fine. I—"

He gripped her shoulders and shook his head. "It's not fine for me to have abandoned you like that. My only excuse is that my head was in a bad place, and I needed time to get perspective and—"

"Hey, my nearly drowning was some heady stuff to deal with. I get it. I know that had to have brought up bad memories. So…" She struggled to squelch the tremor in her gut. "Thank you, by the way, for saving my life. That's, um, no small thing."

Someone walked past them on the sidewalk, and Carmine fell silent, his hands in his pockets. Finally, he said quietly, "I've spent a lot of time with Orrin this past week… talking. About Rosa. About my past failed relationships. About…you."

Her chin snapped up. "Me? What did I do?"

He heaved a deep, shaky breath and cracked a smile. "You stole my heart."

For a couple of beats, she could only stare at him, air hovering in her lungs. She replayed the words in her mind, making sure she'd heard him correctly. "I—"

He stroked a hand along her cheek. "Eva, my go-to reaction has always been to squash my emotions and ignore them. So when you made me feel things so strongly…" He paused and swiped a hand over his mouth. "Well, I've never felt the way I do about you before, so…forgive me for taking so long to recognize my feelings for what they were."

You're forgiven, she tried to say, but all that came out of her knotted throat was a squeak.

"Orrin has helped me get past some huge roadblocks and sort through a cargo hold full of baggage. I'm not through talking with him, and it's been…rough." He exhaled through puckered lips before framing her face with his hands and pinning her with a piercing gaze. "But you are worth it. I want to be able to give you all of myself, freely, no reservations."

"Carmine," she rasped, her heart thrashing so hard she thought it might break a rib. "What are you saying?"

"I'm saying I love you, Eva. I want to be with you. I want a future with you. A family. Children...if you want to have them."

Her head spun, and her knees wobbled. Bracing a hand against the trunk of the tree, she struggled for a breath.

Concern washed over Carmine's face. "Eva, honey, are you all right?"

"You love me?" she asked in a rasp.

"Shocking, huh?" He curled up his mouth in a wry grin. "Captain Reeves wants us to stay partners in light of Mallard retiring, but... I don't want to be your partner. I want to be your husband." When she shot him a wide-eyed look, he raised a hand and added, "Eventually. I don't want to rush you. But I wanted you to know I'm serious. Committed. I want a future with you. And if that means changing precincts, I'll do it."

"You're leaving the 98th?"

His brow furrowed. "I—I'll have to if we're going to be together. But That's not the headline here, babe." He swallowed hard. "You still haven't answered me."

Joy burst inside her like rays of sun peeking over the New York skyline to light the day. She pulled an impish grin. "I'm sorry. What question? I don't remember a question."

Carmine eyed her anxiously. "I asked you to marry me."

"Um...no. It was never put into a question. I'm afraid I have to be a stickler on this rule. If you want an answer, you have to ask the question. I will not assume anyth—"

He captured her cheeks between his hands and kissed her into silence. Then, dropping his forehead to hers, he asked, "Eva Colton, will you give me a second chance? Will you be my partner for life? Will you trade a fake marriage to me for a real one?"

Her knees grew weak, and if not for having his broad shoulders to cling to, she might have slumped to the ground. A bubble of laughter tripped from her as she whispered, "Yes, yes and yes!"

* * * * *

COMING SOON!

We really hope you enjoyed reading this book. If you're looking for more romance be sure to head to the shops when new books are available on

Thursday 11th May

To see which titles are coming soon, please visit

millsandboon.co.uk/nextmonth

MILLS & BOON

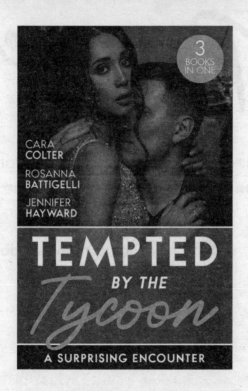

LET'S TALK

Romance

For exclusive extracts, competitions
and special offers, find us online:

facebook.com/millsandboon

@MillsandBoon

@MillsandBoonUK

@MillsandBoonUK

Get in touch on 01413 063 232